WOMEN

of

GOOD

FORTUNE

WOMEN
of
GOOD
FORTUNE

A Novel

Sophie Wan

GRAYDON
HOUSE

GRAYDON
HOUSE®

Recycling programs
for this product may
not exist in your area.

ISBN-13: 978-1-525-80430-4
ISBN-13: 978-1-525-83669-5 (International Edition)

Women of Good Fortune

Graydon House
22 Adelaide St. West, 41st Floor
Toronto, Ontario M5H 4E3, Canada
www.GraydonHouseBooks.com
www.BookClubbish.com

Printed in U.S.A.

To all the women bravely forging paths of their own

From the national lexicon of the Ministry of Education, People's Republic of China:

> *Sheng nu* (Chinese: 剩女; pinyin: *shèngnǚ*; common translation: "leftover women")—unmarried women over the age of twenty-seven. Later adopted by the internet community to refer to often well-educated women who had passed the appropriate age for marriage.

Part 1:

RECRUITMENT

1

10 months to the wedding

LULU

❖ ❖ ❖ ❖ ❖

SOMETIMES, LULU CONSIDERS whether life would be better if she'd been born as a cockroach. Survival would be her only aim in life. She could adapt to anything, even being headless for a week.

And her brain would be tiny. So, so tiny that she wouldn't feel the unease of choosing a wedding dress under her future mother-in-law's watchful gaze. She assumed they'd casually browse racks, not sit so close together on a blush pink velvet couch, ensconced on a private floor as a team of three caters to them with sample booklets and designs and keeps their champagne glasses full.

Only two months ago she'd been blissfully balancing a life of work, friends, and the occasional date to appease her mom, with no intention of getting married. And now she is engaged, pulled from one appointment to another, still barely able to process how she got here.

A well-dressed older woman with a gold measuring tape

around her neck addresses Peng Ayi. "Peng Jie, you said you wanted four dresses?"

She flips through the booklet of beautiful dresses. "Yes, there's the tea ceremony, the Western ceremony, the dance, and the banquet. Let's design a fifth, just in case."

Just in case of what? Lulu wonders. Will there be a secret ceremony where her mother-in-law takes her blood and sends a prayer up to the gods for sons?

Peng Ayi notices her mind wandering. "Lulu, why aren't you giving your opinion? Be more assertive, ah."

Lulu looks down at the booklets of smiling brides strewn on the table. Among the photos of frothy dresses with ballooning skirts, she spots one that looks relatively simple to put on, with a scoop neck and fabric that falls right below the ankle. "I like this one."

Peng Ayi tsks. "That looks cheap. Lulu, you must discard your old mindset. There is no budget, so think bigger! How about this one?" She points at a dress with a train so long that the dimensions of the photo aren't enough to contain it. "Harv told me to get you the dress of your dreams. We can't let him down, ah?"

The tailor giggles. "Wah, your fiancé must love you very much!"

Lulu's not sure *love* describes what they have. Her first date with Harv had been like all the rest, pleasant but unexciting. She usually went out with men once, then never saw them again, returning to her perfectly content single life. When her mom demanded recaps, Lulu would come up with excuses for why someone wasn't a good fit. She'd lied and said Harv had made them split the bill, assuming that was the end.

When Harv asked her out for a second date, it should've been enough for her mom just to know her daughter was *wanted*, especially after all the reminders that she's twenty-seven and officially a *shèngnǚ* by popular definition. But her mom had encouraged her to accept. *What's the harm, Lulu?* she said. *Don't you want to be with someone? Just give him another try. It would make me so happy.* She'd been gentle, pleading.

Besides, Harv was kind, polite, and easy to be around. Harmless. It never occurred to Lulu, a restaurant hostess with nothing to her name, that Shanghai's most eligible bachelor wasn't just having his fun with her. Her mom had been kinder too in the months they dated, calling to check in on her without asking for money, telling her how proud she was. Lulu was more than glad to keep her off her back.

Until six months later, when Harv proposed in grand fashion in front of all their friends and family, and Lulu knew she'd started down a path impossible to turn back from.

Peng Ayi clicks her tongue, bringing Lulu back to the room. "All these dresses are so uninspiring. Perhaps we can revisit the option of getting you something custom-made…"

"I'd be perfectly happy with any of the dresses here," Lulu says quickly.

Peng Ayi sighs. "You're right. If we wanted something haute couture, we should've gotten started over a year ago."

The staff disappear to fetch sample fabrics, and Peng Ayi sets aside her glass of champagne. "Lulu, ah." Her unwrinkled face, which her mother claims must suck up thousands of yuan worth of skin products, is serious. "I want my son to have the best. He is determined to have you as his wife, so I will make sure the entire world knows you're worthy of the title. You wouldn't want us to do anything that makes us lose face, ah?"

Her tone is light, but the warning is clear. Peng Ayi might consider herself worlds apart from Lulu's mom, but on this matter, they sound the exact same. Always whispering warnings in Lulu's ear, like only *her* actions bring embarrassment and disrespect.

"Besides," Peng Ayi continues, "you aren't working anymore. Thinking about this wedding should be your sole priority." She smiles benevolently. "You are going to be my daughter, and that means you will never work again."

She should thank Peng Ayi for freeing her from the drudgery of labor, but she can't bring herself to fake it. Right now, Lulu would give anything to be back at her old hostess job, welcoming guests and secretly smoking cigarettes with the fellow staff. "I'm going to use the restroom."

In the candlelit restroom with lace toilet covers and expensive-smelling soap, she calls her dad. He always has a way of calming her, even from hundreds of miles away.

Instead, her brother's hawkish face appears on the screen. He's chewing on a chicken leg, unkempt hair brushing his shoulders.

"Ge," Lulu greets him in their village dialect, hiding her disappointment. "Where's Ba?"

"He's out." Lulu's about to hang up when he says, "I hear you're getting married. Ma keeps telling everyone it's a rich guy and we're set for life. How'd you manage that?" He looks utterly unimpressed.

"Ah Tang!" His wife chastises him from off-screen. "That's rude. Lulu, don't listen to him. We're all so proud of you. What an achievement!"

Her brother shrugs. "I could help the family too, if there was any good work out here."

"I sent you some job listings in Shanghai," Lulu reminds him. Although she doesn't want to be in the same city as her brother, it would be worth it if he could help with their family's finances.

"Those places just want to use me for my body!" He flexes a scrawny arm. "You think now that you live in the city and hang out with rich people, you know better?"

"Of course not." This is why Lulu avoids going home. Because any time she talks to her brother or her mom, they mock her supposedly lavish city life, even as she sends all her money to them, keeping enough only for rent, her phone bill, and a weekly hotpot dinner with her best friends. Shanghai has shown Lulu a world of luxuries she could never afford. But living here, she's found *her* Shanghai: a place of streetside skewer carts, run-down bookstores, and glittering lights. This city has given her friends, independence, the space to escape her family and breathe—

Her brother scoffs. "Unlike you, I won't settle for any old job, even if I'd get hired in a heartbeat." To punctuate this, he spits out a shard of chicken bone and begins picking at his teeth.

Lulu's heard enough. Even Peng Ayi's demands are preferable to this conversation. "Someone's calling for me," she claims, edging toward the bathroom door.

"You're shriveling up like a shrimp again!" Her brother cackles. "Seriously, what does anyone see in you?"

She hangs up before she has to listen to any more.

Back in the lounge, Peng Ayi gives Lulu's wrist an experimental pinch, her fingers doubling as calipers. "We'll keep track of your weight these next few months. These wedding photos will be the only ones you have, and you want to make sure you're happy with how you look in them."

Yes. Life as a cockroach would be infinitely better.

2

9 months to the wedding

JANE

JANE IS HAGGLING with a woman on WeChat over a Burberry trench when Zihao comes home bearing three giant plastic bags of blue crabs.

"I'm home," he announces, even though Jane has informed him several times that she can always hear his footsteps clomping down the hallway.

Jane grunts in response, focused on the current argument between her and MianHua888. Lulu's wedding updates have made Jane moody. It should be *her* planning a posh wedding, indulged by a fiancé who eats meals with multiple forks.

It's not jealousy, she tells herself. Just indigestion. And this trench coat is the cure.

MianHua888: Xiao Meimei, no offense, but it makes sense for us to split evenly for a purchase like this

Jane sneers. Such blatant disrespect for some random girl with a snotty attitude to call her *little sister.*

WoDeTian: you requested the trench for the first few months, which means October through December. Of course you'll get more value out of it during the winter, so you should pay the amount according to that

MianHua888: if you're going to be such a stickler, why don't you just take your money and go to zara?

Jane gives a squawk of indignation and tosses her phone on the cheap secondhand table Zihao drove across Shanghai to pick up. It skids over the worn wood and stops when it hits the plastic bags he set down. "Wǒ de tiān ah!" she exclaims, staring at the writhing bags. "What is all this?"

"There was a deal. Thirty crabs for a very good price." Zihao beams at her as he loosens his tie and leans his briefcase against the leg of their dining table. His dark hair is ruffled, and despite how early he headed out to work this morning, he's in annoyingly high spirits. To Zihao, a good deal is sweeter than candy.

Jane puts her palms on the table, trying to stay calm. "You realize only two of us live in this apartment?" she asks. "Also, is this the same market that gave us food poisoning last time you fell for one of their deals?"

"That was just once," Zihao says dismissively. "I've bought pork and beef from there before, and we didn't have problems."

"I told you not to buy anything from there anymore! They have no cleanliness standards."

"Just throw them all in the steamer and cook out the poisons. Besides, we should take a break from eating meat. Can you believe the price of beef per pound has gone up three yuan?" He slides her phone back to her. "What are you so absorbed with, anyway?"

"Nothing you'd care about." She grabs the phone, but even thinking about the message from MianHua888 ticks her off. For her sanity, she should leave this WeChat group altogether.

But no. If she leaves, the group moderators won't let her back in when she inevitably sees a post from some beautiful influencer like Cici Xiang and is reminded of everything she doesn't have. This has already happened with two other luxury crowdshare groups. And it's not like Zihao will give her the money to pay full price.

Plus she would have to say goodbye to ever getting her hands on the Chelsea trench. She tried it on at the store in Jing'an and spent a good half hour admiring how the honey color paired with her black sweater. The style totally slimmed her waist, an effect she usually only gets from editing the shit out of herself on Meitu. Unless she splits the cost with these other Burberry zealots, she'll never get the chance to wear one.

"Are you buying clothes again?" It's just Zihao's unique skill to make her feel like shopping is some kind of cardinal sin. She glares at where he leans against the counter. "Do you do anything else?" he asks, exasperated.

At that, she snatches the crabs off the table and marches to the kitchen counter, where she releases them into the sink, their claws clacking against the edges as they scramble.

"I cleaned the house and saved Lulu from the heinous mistake of ordering polyester bridesmaid dresses. I researched footbaths because your mother has been bugging us for one. I watched dramas about rich men who let their wives go on shopping sprees with their credit cards and wished they were about me. So yes, I do." There's no point in playing happy family. Not when Zihao looks down on everything she does.

Jane takes one of the squirming crabs and slams it down on the cutting board before picking up a sharp knife and stabbing it neatly in its ganglia. She imagines the crab with Zihao's face on it.

"Your fictional men might have unlimited money, but I

don't," Zihao says, terse, watching her cautiously as she handles the knife.

"They don't just exist in fiction," Jane mutters as she hacks off a crab claw, thinking of Harv and the giant room he'd booked for Lulu's proposal, where the roast duck came with its own birth certificate.

There's a sigh, then Zihao says, "I'm going to finish up some work." He retreats. Good.

Jane seethes as she hoists the giant wok her mom bought her as a wedding gift. The thing usually requires two people to wield, and every time she cooks with it, she recalls what her mom said when she delivered it. *He's not going to stay for your face, so make sure you keep him with your cooking.*

Getting Zihao to agree to be Jane's husband is probably her mother's greatest accomplishment. The daughter she'd always scorned as ugly and unlovable, finally bargained away. Jane's parents had given her the apartment in Shanghai with the understanding that it would make her a more attractive prospect, and Zihao's parents had been ecstatic their son would acquire joint ownership of an asset otherwise far outside of their modest means. What happened was the best possible outcome for both families, while Jane and Zihao are left acting out the rest of this miserable play.

Once the crabs are steamed and there's a mountain of dishes in the sink for Jane to hand-wash because Zihao insists the dishwasher wastes water, they sit for dinner.

"Looks delicious," Zihao says as she sets down the crab crackers and gingery soy sauce. He's changed out of his suit into a neon running shirt that makes Jane's eyes hurt. She tried to donate it once, but he saw it in the collection pile and lectured her about donating clothes that don't have any visible defects.

She takes her own seat across from him. He's trying to establish a truce, but Jane isn't ready for one. "I should charge you for it."

Zihao chuckles, cracking open a leg and deftly extracting the entire length of meat from inside. "It's not worth *that* much."

Because housework can't possibly compare to the high and mighty work of climbing the corporate ladder.

"Can you believe we've been married for almost half a year?" Zihao asks. "Before we know it, it'll be our anniversary."

"Six months? How?" It already feels like forever.

In between chewing, he asks, "Do you want to plan something? For our anniversary, I mean."

No, she doesn't want to *plan something*, in addition to all the chores she already does. "What I want is access to your bank account."

"Sure." He reaches for more crab.

Jane's eyebrows go up. In their half a year of marriage, she's never asked so directly for money. Is it possible that sort of directness got through his thick head?

"Really?" she asks.

But he's not finished. "If you let me see everything you're spending it on."

Of course. Jane stares stonily at Zihao.

"Isn't it fair? It's money I'm earning. I want to see where it's going. And you would share that information with me, unless there's something you're ashamed of."

"It's not about shame. It's about *privacy*. Although given your line of work, I guess you don't care about that."

Zihao actually looks hurt by this. "I didn't want to work in surveillance. I did it for the money."

"That makes it sound a lot better." Jane pushes away from the table. "You clean up. I feel a stomachache coming on."

"For the last time, there's nothing wrong with that wet market!"

Jane stomps into their room. If she had married someone more generous, someone who felt lucky to be with her and wasn't a total miser, she wouldn't have to waste her days bickering with online strangers.

It's her own fault. A prettier and younger woman would have the power to divorce him. She's thought about it often, but it's not like she can change her appearance with the snap of a finger or turn back time.

Jane flops onto their bed, smashing a pillow over her face. Like they always do when it's dark and quiet, all the cruel things people have said about her resurface.

Mama, she's ugly. Was she born like that? a little boy had asked and pointed at her when she was thirteen. She's avoided playgrounds ever since.

You could be the most successful and intelligent woman in the world, but if you aren't pretty, it doesn't matter. Her mom, when rejections to Jane's matchmaking profile poured in from other families, and Jane was naive enough to go to her for comfort.

I don't really care if she isn't pretty. I just need somewhere to live. She'll do. The words she overheard Zihao say to her parents when they met to finalize the marriage agreement. Her own damn husband.

The insults are lodged in her ribs like tiny daggers, buried too deep to extract.

She can't continue like this, letting one unhappy anniversary roll into the next. If she had more desirable looks, she could divorce Zihao and find someone who appreciates her. They might not understand her love of shopping, the control it gives her, the sense of worth wearing beautiful clothes provides, but they wouldn't judge her for it. Once again, Jane returns to the solution. The one that is clear as day, if only she had the money for it.

Plastic surgery.

3

8 months to the wedding

RINA

THERE ARE PLENTY of hotpot restaurants in Shanghai that offer cleaner surroundings and a more peaceful environment. But Hotpot Palace is singular. Magazine pages of old Chinese idols are pasted over the walls, edges curling or yellowed with unidentifiable stains. The volume is at a constant roar, which makes it impossible to eavesdrop. There are no windows.

It's the perfect hideaway from the world outside.

Toward the back of the restaurant is their self-appointed table. Rina spots Lulu's slender shoulders and Jane's sleek black hair, drawn back to display her glittery chandelier earrings. She's late. Again.

She makes her way over, squeezing between the crowded tables, not apologizing to the patrons who scoot their chairs in; everyone accepts that jostling for space is a byproduct of eating somewhere cheap and tasty. By the time she gets to her seat, she's practically sweating. The lack of ventilation means the air is permanently damp and smells pungently of anise and chili, but nowhere does a better Sichuan spicy broth.

"We already ordered," Jane says authoritatively, pointing at the pot in the center. Like the petals of a flower, red lamb meat is sliced paper thin on platters around it. "I passed on the special."

Tonight's deal scrolls across the foggy TV screens. Pig livers. A basket of them, apparently. Rina doesn't know who orders the specials at Hotpot Palace. On a good day, they're mildly off-putting. On a bad day, the mere description could strip her of her appetite.

"Thanks. Sorry I'm late," she says as she drags her chair in. "How are the dresses coming along?"

Lulu listlessly pokes at a fish ball bobbing in the broth. "We've chosen three of five." Since the engagement, Lulu's been as busy as Rina. When they manage to have dinner together in their apartment, Lulu barely says a word, like all of the wedding activities have been leaching away her energy.

Jane snorts. "Stay strong. With someone like Peng Ayi organizing, this is only the beginning."

Rina leaves her phone next to her bowl, face up. Technically, she's supposed to learn if she's been promoted tomorrow, but it wouldn't be abnormal for her boss to call ahead to share the good news.

Jane grabs her phone and flips it over.

"Hey!"

Jane gives her a droll look. "You're going to become engagement manager, and then you can finally put the deposit down at that fertilization clinic and freeze your future babies. It'll all work out. So stop obsessing and eat."

There hasn't been a single cycle where Rina hasn't been a high performer at her consulting firm. But to be extra certain, she's put in far more than the standard nine-nine-six hours. Instead of nine a.m. to nine p.m. for six days a week, she's been clocking eight to eight for seven. The lost sleep isn't a problem if it secures her promotion, which she needs more than anything. At a recent doctor's appointment, Rina had sat on crinkly exam paper, panicking as a fertility specialist explained she's losing more than a thousand eggs every month. With the bonus from the promotion, she can fly to the US and freeze her eggs. The procedure is banned in China for unmarried women and criminally expensive.

"Before we get chili oil everywhere," Lulu says, just as Rina is about to ignore the communal chopsticks and select her lamb, "I have to give you these. For the wedding."

She reaches for her purse, and Jane blurts out, "Is that the new Hermès? Bitch, that bag sold out before it even got listed!"

"Oh," Lulu says, glancing at her bag. "Harv gave it to me. Is it expensive?"

Jane looks like she's going to explode. "It's from this season."

Lulu blinks. "I guess that's why he seemed so disappointed by my reaction when he gave it to me."

Rina refills their waters. She wouldn't expect Harv to know that Lulu doesn't put much stock in expensive things; she doubts he understands much about her after only eight months.

Jane groans. "Please put that somewhere I don't have to see it. I hate looking at things I'll never have."

"Do you want it?" Lulu appears to be seconds away from removing her things from the bag and handing it over to Jane. "I'm only using it because Harv would notice if I didn't. He keeps hinting that his gifts are getting dusty in my closet."

Rina can almost see Jane straining against her desire to say yes. When Harv proposed, she worried their friendship would crack under the pressure of Lulu marrying someone who, on paper, was exactly what Jane wanted: wealthy, well-bred, from a distinguished family. Jane had been a good sport about it, but moments like these, Rina catches the flash of yearning. Not for the man, but for the access he represents. "No. It was a gift for you."

"Speaking of gifts." Lulu withdraws two small boxes wrapped in gold paper, tied with red ribbon.

Jane immediately perks up, clapping her hands enthusiastically. "Presents!"

Rina unwraps hers carefully while Jane tears into hers, leaving shredded paper everywhere. Inside of each box is a thin gold bracelet and an envelope.

Lulu takes their hands across the table. "Please be my bridesmaids. We've still got eight months of this, and I need you to keep me sane. Maybe you can use me as a case study of what happens to a person who gets dragged into daily conversations about cake flavors and flower colors."

"I'd love to," Rina says. She lifts out the delicate chain and examines the gold-studded bracelet with tiny rubies. It's expensive but understated. Peng Ayi must have chosen it.

"You get to be in the bridal party, but Peng Ayi insisted I make Yaqing the maid of honor." Rina winces. Yaqing is Harv's twenty-year-old, flighty sister who's used to getting everything she wants. Last Rina heard, she was collecting incredibly expensive renderings of instant ramen cups. "But don't feel bad. She didn't want Vic to be the best man either at first."

The mention of Vic has Rina tensing. She can barely handle the infrequent contact they have. Now that Harv and Lulu are getting married, she'll have to see him more often, and be civil toward him for Lulu's sake. The very thought is dreadful.

Jane slurps a noodle before saying, "Are you marrying Harv or his mom?"

"I'm not sure anymore." Lulu hugs her arms. She looks even skinnier than usual.

The meat Rina dunked in the broth turns dark, and she plops it onto Lulu's plate. "Eat more."

"Peng Ayi put me on a diet," Lulu says miserably.

"Oh, come on." In response, Jane ladles a giant heaping of rice cakes next to the meat. "If there's anyone here who needs to be on a diet, it's me."

"Nobody here needs to be on a diet."

Jane waves Rina off, as she always does when either Rina or Lulu try to reassure her about her appearance. "Okay, well, if we're going to make this about me." She shoves the mess of wrapping paper aside and hands Lulu the bracelet. Lulu holds it like she's afraid it'll bite her. "Put this on me while I tell you about my plan for divorcing Zihao."

"This again?" Rina asks. Jane brings up divorce at least once a month.

A tiny furrow forms on Lulu's forehead. "What's wrong with him again? Last time we met him, he was nice. He was so knowledgeable about everything."

"What's *wrong* with him? Everything!" Jane angrily pinches a piece of tofu in half with her chopsticks. "My mom once said to me, 'Only unhappy women are unmarried. It's because their lives haven't begun yet.' Bullshit! My life ended the day I took that ring on my finger."

"Lulu and I could've immediately told you she was wrong," Rina says. The single years—before Lulu met Harv and Jane got married—had been wonderful. Rina and Jane would visit Lulu at Scarlet Beauty, and she'd bring them special dishes from the chef or pour them wine with an extra heavy hand. On Lulu's weekends off, they would pick up cheap, steaming bags of fried crullers and heavy cups of soy milk to consume in one of Shanghai's many green spaces. With their lives moving in different directions, these get-togethers have grown more infrequent.

Jane takes a big gulp of wine. "I know what I need to do. Plastic surgery. Once I'm hot, I can be free. Obviously, I can't be a divorcee on the market looking like this." She gestures to herself. "My face is too square. Look at this flat nose. And these single eyelids." It's a mantra both Lulu and Rina are used to hearing, and sadly, Jane isn't wrong. Chinese people have a very specific standard of beauty: pale skin, small face, double eyelids.

"Jane, don't you remember how the Leftovers started?" Rina asks, referring to the nickname they'd given themselves back when the term *shèngnǚ*, coined to ridicule unmarried women, seemed ludicrous and far-off. Then they got older, and suddenly it was not a joke. It was a label that applied to them, the thing people mocked them for, like being single was the same as being unwanted. Jane surrendered first to marriage, and now

Lulu is next. The engagement may have happened quickly, but Rina knows Lulu wouldn't have been able to support her family on her wages forever, and at least Harv seems like he'll be a reliable partner. He's already treated her like a princess, as he should. She can accept that outcome if Lulu can.

But Rina refuses to give in. She'd tried dating at first, but after meeting far too many men who expected her to quit her job to devote herself fully to their home, she stopped. She doesn't have the time to find a man who's comfortable with her career aspirations right now. She's a Leftover by choice.

Still, that doesn't mean she can't comfort Jane. "This is a matter of attitude, not appearance."

"I know. But you can't deny life is easier when you're pretty."

"Your life isn't bad," Rina says. "You have a house, a husband, and you don't have to work. Isn't that what you wanted?"

"Yeah, but I don't have money! I can't buy a pair of socks without Zihao knowing about it. That's why my new, brilliant plan is to get some outside cash, do something about my face, and find a man who'll really spoil me."

"But Zihao wouldn't have married you if he didn't like you," Lulu says. She still hasn't eaten anything, and she keeps tugging at her engagement ring like it's strangling her finger.

Jane stares down Lulu. "Let me tell you something, Lulu. He settled, just like I settled. It was nothing more than a deal between our families. I just didn't expect him to be such a stingy arse, which shows no man is how he seems. Before you get in too deep, you should ask yourself, do you really want to get married?"

It's like a dam breaks. Lulu's face crumples. Tears streak down her cheeks, little dark rivulets that carry along the sediment of her makeup. Jane's eyes dart to Rina's in alarm as Lulu exclaims, "I don't know!"

4

8 months to the wedding

LULU

AT LEAST LULU kept it together until she was with people she trusted. If she cried like this in front of her mom, she would've been smacked and told to be grateful.

"Wǒ de tiān ah," Jane says, and suddenly there's one hand dabbing at Lulu's eyes while another holds the hair back from her face. "Was it something I said?"

Through her blurred tears, Lulu sees Rina toss a spinach leaf at Jane. It floats uselessly into her teacup. "You've triggered her."

"It was a simple question." Jane cups Lulu's cheek. "Lulu, do you not want to get married?" They're both staring at her with identical worried expressions.

Lulu hesitates. Normally, she's the one listening to their complaints about annoying husbands, horrible coworkers, and various other injustices. As the youngest and least educated, she's always felt a certain deference toward her two friends, and the role reversal is disorienting. Plus it seems silly to be upset about marrying a guy who treats her well...

"Whatever you're feeling, it's valid," Rina adds gently, and Lulu knows that if there's anyone she can spill this awful secret to, it's them.

Slowly, Lulu shakes her head. "It feels like my whole life, my family has pushed me toward this. But this wedding makes me want to run away. To go in any other direction but forward." The thought of donning her many wedding dresses, saying vows, and moving in with Harv makes her veins ice over. It feels so… final. Like licking the tab of an envelope sealing her fate.

"Then don't get married. What you want comes first." Rina says this with all the confidence of someone used to being in charge of her life. Lulu's whole life has been dictated by her family, and she's had no space to just be herself, whoever that is.

"Easy for you to say," Jane says. "Everything always works out for you."

Rina is offended. "I've worked hard for everything I have."

"Yeah, yeah," Jane says, and Lulu can tell she's refraining from rolling her eyes. "Nobody works harder than you."

Even though Rina and Jane worked at the same company, their goals in life couldn't be more different. Jane took her first opportunity to get out, while Rina's sole focus has been on getting to the top.

"You shouldn't have to go through with this wedding if you don't want to." Rina returns her attention to Lulu. "Say something now, before it's too late."

"It *is* too late," Lulu says, her voice a watery warble. "Peng Ayi visited a fortune teller to set a date. And my dad already committed some of our family's savings." Despite how limited funds are, Ba was insistent the Fei family contribute somehow. Lulu hasn't been able to send anything home since quitting, so her dad pooled together money from friends and his cleaning job. It's probably only enough to pay for the cake.

"Yeah, she can't call it off now. Think of all those red envelopes she's going to get as wedding gifts." Jane rubs her hands.

"Even marrying Zihao netted the two of us some serious cash." Her expression dims. "Not that I got to spend any of it."

"Yes, Ma keeps mentioning the money," Lulu says tightly. Because money is the only useful thing she can give her family. Not the money she makes on her own, but money by way of a wealthy son-in-law.

"Don't be so dismissive," Jane says. "If we stole all the red envelope money, you could use it to run away. It could help you disappear." She flutters her hand like she's performing a magic trick.

Rina laughs. "Steal the money? Do you have some criminal history you've kept hidden from us all these years?"

Jane faces Lulu. "What do you think, Lulu? This is your wedding, after all. How badly do you want out?"

Rather than the perfect wedding, this is the thing Lulu dreams of. Disappearing. Going somewhere far away from this life in which a purpose has been predetermined for her. But she's never had the means to leave China. "It doesn't matter what I want."

"Even if it means we could buy you a plane ticket out of here? You could visit all those places you've dreamed of." Jane seems to get more excited as she speaks. "We just have to make sure none of us get caught. Easy."

"Easy." Rina lifts her hair, fanning the back of her neck. "You're nuts."

As they talk around her, Lulu wipes her eyes with one of the napkins from the table. Rina may be laughing, but Jane has snagged Lulu's attention. The truth is, she's always felt guilty over the fine her family paid the government to keep her. She knows her dad had insisted on it, and that he'd worked extra hours so she could go to Shanghai for career school. She's always wanted to pay him back. If she could secure the wedding money without getting married, her family wouldn't be able to use her as a channel to the Zhus' wealth, but she also wouldn't be leaving them with nothing. She could do as Jane says and go somewhere else, figure out what she wants to do with her life. She could actually have a *choice*.

Jane taps her chopsticks against her plate, which Rina grabs out of her reach to stop her. "What would the payoff be? A million RMB?"

Lulu folds her wet napkin and sets it aside. "More like five million."

"That's over half a million USD," Rina mumbles. Even she sounds stunned.

"Wah, is the president himself coming?"

"No, but I do think Peng Ayi is going to invite the wealthiest people she knows." It's broad knowledge that the Zhus have ins with decision-makers, even Standing Committee officials, if rumors are to be trusted.

"We could totally do it," Jane argues. "Come on, don't you want this chance to metaphorically bitch-slap a rich family? It'll be fun!"

"*Fun* is getting a manicure. *Fun* is reading a good adventure novel. This is not *fun*." Rina lays a perfectly deshelled shrimp in Lulu's bowl, a clear entreaty to eat. "Speaking of books, Lulu, I picked up your copy of *Don Quixote* and saw that it was in Spanish. I thought you were learning Thai."

"I did learn a bit, but it's not so easy finding Thai books," Lulu says. "So I'm trying Spanish now." The used-book store she frequents often has castaway books in a variety of languages, and Lulu loves opening them and looking at the strings of symbols and letters. They are codes that unlock new worlds, if she takes the time to learn them. It's been hard lately, with wedding planning sapping all her energy.

Jane bangs her hand on the table, unwilling to be distracted. "What we're talking about is way more exciting than some old bloke who fancies himself a knight! We could totally do this and not get caught. Rina, even if the Zhus suspected us, you could flee the country. I can't, but I'd take the risk. What does that tell you?"

"Nothing. You're reckless," Rina answers.

Jane takes this in stride. "And you're too careful. But if we combine forces, think of what we could accomplish. We could bring down the patriarchy."

"This isn't some John Woo film. We're not going to go in there with fists swinging and claim justice."

"It's not. Because we're women. And possess a level of finesse that men do not." Jane flutters her eyelashes winningly. "Rina, aren't you tired of it? Being at the whims of all these fucking men? You can deny it if you want, but I worked at the same place as you. The people deciding whether you deserve to be in the same room as them are a bunch of slick men in expensive suits, and at least one person is going to mention your childbearing probability."

Jane sighs, then turns to Lulu, who flinches at the intensity of her expression. "Lulu, you see the potential, don't you? We could walk away with one million RMB each—if we were to bring on two extra people—and get on living the lives we've wanted. I get a new face. Rina can work a little less. Or not. Overtime does give her a hard-on. But Lulu, *you* get out of marrying a privileged prick while getting your money-grubbing family off your ass. Even if they don't deserve it."

"I owe them," Lulu says emphatically, even if her friends have often tried to convince her otherwise. They could never understand.

"Right, and they were so merciful not to drown you when they discovered you were a girl." Rina elbows her, and Jane adds dryly, "Well, that's a good reason for theft. Family. Anything for family."

When the bill comes, Jane grabs it before either of them can. Over their protests, she says, "I'll cover this one, and in exchange, I want the two of you to actually think about this. This might be our chance to seize what we want from the world, if we aren't chickenshit about it." She nudges Lulu. "Instead of reading about an adventure, you could be living one."

As they exit Hotpot Palace, Rina tugs on Lulu's arm. "Don't worry," she says quietly. "She'll forget about it by tomorrow."

But Lulu doesn't. Back at her and Rina's apartment, she sits on the edge of her small bed and looks at the shelf of torn foreign language paperbacks she's accumulated in her five years in Shanghai. She's always paged through them with the knowledge that she will never visit in real life, never experience the infinite textures, colors, and customs so different from her world. She's never dared to dream outside of the lines her family has drawn for her, to explore who she is outside them. But Jane's comments tonight have made her wonder.

5

8 months to the wedding

JANE

JANE FEELS A HEADY, reckless exhilaration as she punches in the code to her apartment. It's all that red meat she consumed. Oh, and the possibility of plotting a heist. She knows Rina and Lulu will expect her to drop it, but the prospect is too tantalizing. This is the solution she's been looking for. A new face, a new future.

She just needs to convince the others. Rina scoffed at the idea because she lacks imagination and associates heists with action movies and slick men in sunglasses. But Lulu is already halfway there. She's a romantic, and Jane can see how desperately she doesn't want this wedding. She'll get Lulu onboard first, and once they have a structured plan, something that makes it more tangible, Rina won't be able to deny its potential.

"Where were you?" Zihao asks as Jane walks in. He should be asleep, but he's sitting at the dining table, a glass of tea beside him, the water so clear it must be his fourth or fifth steep.

"I came home early from work and was planning to take you to dinner."

Dinner? Since when did he take her to dinner? Is it because he wants to have sex? She wouldn't be opposed. Her spirits are high, and his tie is loose around his neck, his unbuttoned shirt exposing his shadowy collarbone. She would never admit it to him, but a loosened tie does things to her.

Jane pours herself a glass of water, composing herself. "You know Friday nights are for the girls. We were talking about Lulu's wedding. It's in May."

"Am I coming?" he asks. He sounds uncertain, a far cry from the authority she hears in his voice during his work calls. Since their xiāng qīn, Jane's realized Zihao is a very different person at work than he is at home.

Jane had showed up to their blind date aware that Chen Zihao was from an unknown rural family with an extremely smart son. But despite dressing like someone's underpaid secretary, he had actually tried to get to know her. He asked questions about what she liked to watch, her thoughts on working in Shanghai. Tired of all the rejection, of acting the way she knew she was supposed to, for once Jane didn't hold back. She didn't censor her answers to fit what most men wanted to hear.

She'd thought he was just being polite, but then he'd wanted to meet again.

"Finally someone who values a house more than a pretty face," her mom had remarked afterward, reminding Jane there was something in this for him, too.

Without her apartment, Zihao would probably be paying sky-high rent on some tiny space in Pudong, and knowing his philosophy toward spending, that would've galled him every day.

"You're my husband. Of course you're coming to the wedding." They might be a poor match, but they have to keep up appearances. Weddings are hotspots for gossip, and she doesn't need questions making their way to her parents. Jane leans against the counter and catches up on her WeChat messages. After further thought, she decided to crawl back to MianHua888 and agree to the terms of her deal. Though the woman's smugness still prickles, it's unlikely she'll find a similar opportunity for a while.

"Jane, can you stop looking at your phone and talk to me?"

She exhales dramatically before glancing up. "What do you want?"

He shifts his weight and holds her gaze even though she's trying to burn him to a crisp with her eyes. "You're being unnecessarily cold."

"This is how I've always been," she says. He isn't the first person to accuse her of it. It's how she protects herself. She'd rather someone call her a bitch than pity her for being the one standing alone at the club. Keeping people at a distance, Jane has learned, is the only way to stop them from looking too closely. Of all her friends, only Lulu and Rina have fought through those walls, bringing Jane into the fold of their friendship as the others drifted away. When she'd shared her insecurities with them, they might have tried to soothe her, but they didn't turn away or downplay them.

Zihao puts a hand on his torso, his wedding ring flashing. "I rushed home from work because I thought we could eat together."

Jane huffs. "Not work again. You seriously can't go five minutes without mentioning how hard you work."

"I'm doing it to support our family. And our future children, if we decide to have them."

Jane shudders at the mention of kids. No way can she be a mom. Her kid will inherit her unhappiness, along with her looks. "And I'm just the useless housewife who cooks and cleans. I know." As she says this, she proceeds to the kitchen, slamming a pot on the counter. She fills it with water and sets it to boil, then tosses a packet of instant noodles on the table in front of him. "When there are bubbles in the water, put this in. Noodles first, then sauce."

Zihao glares at her. "I don't need your help to make instant noodles."

"Fine," she says, shoving her way past his chair. "Don't set off the fire alarm again."

In the bathroom, she brushes her teeth and starts her skin care routine, carefully exfoliating, patting SKII toner into her cheeks, trying not to focus on her full face.

Society has never let her forget how she looks. Not when she had to submit a headshot with her CV and got rejected from more places than her similarly qualified female classmates, or when she goes to a bar, and men regard her as the barrier between them and her more attractive friends. When she was younger, she would lie in bed with her eyes squeezed shut, praying to be made pretty.

If she could get surgery, the hours of poring over fashion magazines, agonizing over the perfect outfit, acquiring handbags, and becoming a master at makeup will simply be a way to express herself rather than hide what she hates.

Zihao comes in, and she's momentarily distracted by the reflection of his muscles contracting as he tugs his workout shirt over his head. They both run, but never together. There's a treadmill at home, and Jane would never let herself be seen sweaty and red, running on the Bund alongside her unflustered husband.

He steps into the shower, and despite the irritation she feels toward him, she entertains the notion of stripping off her robe and joining. He would probably fall over in shock.

Jane cackles to herself.

"What are you laughing at?"

Water streams down the sides of his neck and over his chest. His hair is inky dark and dripping. It infuriates her that Zihao is conventionally good-looking. It doesn't matter that *she* has a world-class education, that *she* knows how to conduct business in Mandarin, Canto, English, and Japanese. When people see them together, all they wonder is how someone who looks like *her* ended up with *him*. They don't see the man who stews over forgetting to scan a coupon at the grocery store.

She thinks she gets his stinginess, sometimes. Things must have happened quickly for Zihao. One minute he was studying in some dusty school, the next he's getting offers from top companies in Shanghai. He must still be trying to hold on for dear life to what he's achieved, believing it may disappear in a blink—

"Jane." Though it is taxing for him to speak English, Zihao insists on calling her by her English name rather than her Chinese one. It's the name she chose when she enrolled at Oxford, and she'd told him it fits her better than what her parents came up with. But she doesn't understand why he makes the effort. "Jane," Zihao repeats. "That noodle brand was no good. It was bland." He puts a miniscule amount of soap on his loofa before lathering himself.

"It's not the brand that's the problem," she says, rolling her eyes. He definitely put too much water in again.

She finishes all the skin care steps in silence and then situates herself on her side of the bed. A few minutes later, she can smell his bodywash and toothpaste as he gets in. Perhaps tomorrow, when her annoyance has faded slightly, they'll have sex. It will be with the lights out and enjoyable, but not so much that she goes looking for it again.

"If you're still mad about the money," Zihao starts, and her ears perk up. Maybe he's had a change of heart.

"You could create a budgeting plan. I can help you."

After more than half a year of this, why had she even gotten her hopes up? Jane flips onto her side, facing away from him. "You're so right. The problem all along has been how irresponsible I am."

He doesn't respond, doesn't reach for her. They maintain the invisible barrier between them, the way they always have.

As Jane stares into the darkness, she thinks of red envelopes bulging with cash and the Zhus, who are flush with wealth while she, Lulu, and Rina accept the meager allowances life gives them.

For the first time, they have the perfect opportunity to take what they deserve.

6

8 months to the wedding

RINA

RINA LIES AWAKE, listening to the unhappy gurgles of her stomach struggling to digest spicy oil, when her phone rings. It's ten at night, but Luo Ren has never believed in "working hours."

She presses the phone to her ear and sits up eagerly. "Luo Zong."

"Rina." He betrays no emotion. "I'm sure you can guess what this is about."

Rina's insides flip. People only ever ask you to guess because they don't want to be the first to say something ugly. "This is about the engagement manager role."

He waits for her to continue and fill in the blanks herself. That's how Rina knows for sure. "I didn't get it."

"I wanted to call ahead so it doesn't take you by surprise tomorrow." He makes it sound like he's doing her a favor.

A good employee would accept the news in stride. Follow-up questions are reserved for business meetings, not performance reviews. But Rina hears herself ask, "Luo Zong, why didn't they think I was good enough?"

There's a pause. Then, in a mildly exasperated voice, Luo Ren says, "You're good enough, Rina. But there are some things that will naturally work against you."

She sucks in a breath and poses the question she already knows the answer to. "Like what?"

"You've improved a lot since you first joined us..." A Chinese person who'd grown up in America, she knew her behavior had rubbed some people the wrong way. She was more outspoken than they were accustomed to. Once, she'd asked Luo Ren for a heads-up if he needed her to work longer hours, and he had looked at her like she'd grown two heads. Even Jane had known not to act that way. "But you're thirty-two now. When are you going to get married and settle down?"

She squeezes her eyes shut, trying to stay composed. It's so unfair he can ask such an invasive question, and she's powerless to do anything but answer.

After a beat, she opens her eyes and says as evenly as she can, "I've always prioritized work over my personal life."

"We've seen it from other women your age. They meet someone, get married, and immediately start having children because they don't want to miss their window. Then the quality of their work suffers." Rina grew up abroad, interned at an American firm where it was taboo to discuss personal matters. But here, anything that can affect a worker's output is fair game. "It's unavoidable, Rina."

At least one person is going to mention your childbearing probability. Jane's words echo through her skull.

"This job has always come first. You know that." Her fingers itch for her planner, where she's written everything out. Engagement manager this year. Associate partner in two. Partner in four. In five years, start dating with the intention of getting married and having kids. At that point, she'll have enough saved up to invest in her children's upbringing, in all the nannies, summer camps, and special classes they'll need. Plus a senior leadership position would make her harder to fire.

Her plan has always been to front-load her life, maximize her youth and energy to achieve the best results, before people think she, as a woman, is too old to be useful. But apparently, she's already too late.

Luo Ren is politely apologetic. "I wish I could give you better news, but you know how it is."

"Thank you for informing me." Even though she'd like to tell Luo Ren he can go fuck himself, she must remain professional. Getting a promotion might be hard, but looking for a job after being fired would be even more difficult.

"Maybe next cycle, huh?" He hangs up, probably moving on to the next task on his list.

Rina slowly puts her phone down.

There's a plummeting sensation in her chest, like she was reaching for something but only managed to brush her fingertips against it. She was *so close*. If only she had worked a few more Sundays, maybe things would be different.

She doesn't lie back down. There's no way she'll fall asleep now. She pulls on a pair of sweats and pads into the kitchen to make tea.

Once she's poured tea leaves into a pot to steep, Rina sits on the couch and debates calling her mom, until she recognizes it's too late. She texts her instead, reminding her she wants to drop off fresh ginseng from the neighborhood herbalist. The recent cold weather is no good for her mom's health.

She can't just sit here and stew over Luo Ren's news. But she also can't bother Lulu. When they got home, Lulu went straight to her room and has been there ever since. Rina remembers the tears, the helplessness plain on her face. In Rina's opinion, Lulu shouldn't do anything she doesn't want to. But she has always been trapped by other people's expectations, unable to stray too far before she's yanked back again. She came to Shanghai to be

independent, yet she obediently sends money back home whenever her mom asks for it. She canceled a vacation to Hangzhou
with her coworkers because her mom found out and scolded her
for using money so frivolously. And when her brother caught
a cold, Lulu refused the better shifts at work so she could dutifully go home, lugging sacks of ginseng and jujubes with her
to make him soup.

Rina gets up and grabs the eraser next to the whiteboard she
uses to scope projects and erases everything with wide, frenzied
strokes. The work she does is fulfilling, but it galls her that it's
going unrecognized and unrewarded.

The blank board looks strange now, the white glaring in its
emptiness. Rina sets aside the eraser and uncaps a marker. She
writes *Steal wedding gifts from Zhu wedding* at the top. From there,
she writes her name, Jane's, and Lulu's. She draws a rectangle,
and inside writes *Pre-event checklist*. Before she can stop herself,
she's connecting boxes and creating a list.

They'd need a blueprint of whichever venue Peng Ayi chooses
to determine how to get the money out, and most importantly,
they'd need to figure out how to keep the three of them from
suspicion. Lulu will have to put on her best performance up
until the very end.

Rina keeps writing until Lulu is suddenly there, lightly pushing her back from the board. "Rina? What's wrong? Rina, talk
to me."

The boxes and diagrams blur. When she blinks, tears roll
down her cheeks. Lulu plucks the marker from her fingers and
ushers her to the couch. A warm cup of tea is placed into her
hand.

As she sits on the edge, Lulu's hand rubbing her back, the
shock finally catches up with her. "I didn't get it," Rina mumbles. "I did everything, and it still wasn't enough."

Lulu doesn't respond. Rina looks up and sees her phone to
her ear. "Jane? Rina heard back. It wasn't good news. Oh, you

want to do video? Okay." Lulu joins her on the couch and holds the phone so they're both captured in the frame.

On the other side, Jane is perched on what appears to be a toilet. Her eyes bulge, and she's waving a plunger in the air, enraged. "I'm going to stab that bastard's eyes out with chopsticks and feed them to the pigeons!"

"Jane!" They hear Zihao's voice. "It's the middle of the night."

"My friends need me!" There's furious whispering, then Jane's face comes back into view. "I'll be right back. Apparently my husband needs a bedtime story and warm milk before he'll fall asleep again." She says this loudly enough that they know Zihao is hovering nearby. The screen goes dark.

Lulu wraps an arm around Rina and angles her head toward the whiteboard. "So, what is this?" she asks carefully.

Rina lifts a shoulder. She's separated the white space into a grid. *Pre-wedding, during, post.* There's an arrow pointing at a number: *5 million yuan.* It beams down at them like a beacon, full of promise.

They're silent as Lulu removes her arm and drapes her long Hello Kitty shirt over her knees.

"I really don't want to get married." She plays with the hem of her shirt. "But marrying Harv is what my family wants. I feel like it should be what I want too."

Rina wishes Lulu wouldn't always wait for others to validate her feelings. That's how she ends up getting swept along in other people's currents. It's how she ended up engaged to Harv. She'd been lukewarm about their first date but still gave in to her mom. At first, Rina thought maybe her feelings had changed, but after her breakdown at Hotpot Palace, Rina can only see this marriage making Lulu unhappy.

"You know yourself best," she tells her. "I know things happened fast—" *fast* is an understatement "—but could you love him?"

Lulu seems to absorb this like it's a totally foreign concept.

"Ma said that it's more important to consider whether he'll support me."

Sometimes, Rina feels like she and Lulu talk in circles. She decides to state it outright. "You deserve more than just someone who will pick up the bill."

At that, a change seems to come over Lulu. Her spine stiffens, her eyes narrow. "Your fertility appointment. Didn't that depend on your promotion?"

"Yes. But there will be another way." There isn't. Egg freezing carries a large upfront cost, and Rina hasn't saved enough to cover the airfare, lodging, and procedure. And there's the annual upkeep of the eggs, which adds up. But Lulu doesn't need to be burdened with this problem.

"You've come up with the other way," Lulu says, pulling back to consider the board. "Right here. This is how we get you your money, so that you don't have to spend another six months waiting for a promotion."

"Money isn't everything." Rina hears the lie as she says it. Of course it is. Money opens doors, the same way it keeps some shut. "If we stole from the Zhus, they would hunt us down. Especially if it went missing in such a visible place. Everyone will know, and they wouldn't accept that humiliation."

"Does it matter if they never find out who did it?"

"That's a big assumption."

"Who cares. Let's do it. The heist."

"What? Lulu, no—"

"Peng Ayi told me we're going to receive the wedding cash in a password-protected safe. It can't be that hard to get it out. It's possible, isn't it? What you've written here—it's a plan."

The objection rises up Rina's throat, but she swallows it. Before today, that promotion was her only shot at freezing her eggs and getting ahead of her doctor's warning. This seems like a second chance. The Zhus, with their wealth and status, can withstand the loss. "I won't do it if there's any possibility you'll be hurt in the process." Resolve hardens her voice. Her sweet friend, who leaves Rina Post-it notes saying *jiā yóu* and makes sure she eats when she gets home late from work, must be protected.

"I won't." Lulu gives her a soft smile. "Even if they think I did it, you and Jane will help me go somewhere they can't touch me. Ideally, the weather is nice and I can stay awhile, too. Won't you?"

Rina nods, one single, emphatic motion. "That will be more important than anything else." She can't believe she's actually considering this. But written out on the whiteboard, the whole idea seems more solid. There's a way out. All they need is a team and an airtight plan. She feels that familiar thrill of starting a brand-new project, knowing its solution is hidden, that she will make it reveal itself to her.

Lulu refills her tea. "You always worry about me, Rina. Thank you."

"I'm your Jie," Rina replies. "It's my job."

Both of their phones suddenly go off with a video request from Jane.

Rina picks up, and there's Jane, in her bathroom again. At least the plunger has been put away. She speaks more quietly this time. "Are we plotting how to murder your boss?"

Lulu reaches for the phone, like she's afraid Rina will suddenly back out. There's a tremor in her voice as she says, "What we talked about at Hotpot Palace. Let's do it."

Jane looks like she can hardly believe it. "Am I dreaming?"

"No," Lulu says. This time, she's firm.

Jane pauses, like she's giving Rina a chance to pop in and say, *Just kidding!* When Rina doesn't say anything, she releases a quiet whoop. "Yes, bitches!"

"We'll talk more later." Rina ends the call before they say something that could get them in trouble. Nowadays, there's always someone listening in.

Lulu turns to Rina, eyes alight. It's the first time she's seen her friend like this since the engagement. "This is exciting, isn't it?"

Rina stretches her fingers as she scans the to-do list. There are far too many consequences to this decision for her to feel anything but apprehensive, but there are consequences for doing nothing too. She gets to her feet, uncapping her marker. "We should set rules about communication now. We can't text about this, and we can only talk about it at home or Hotpot Palace. If anyone gets suspicious at all, it's over. Especially for you. With how much time you're spending with Harv and Peng Ayi, you'll have the most acting to do."

For a moment, there's only the sound of her marker squeaking against the board. Then Lulu says, "You know, this is a wild idea, but with you and Jane leading the way, I think it might actually work."

7

7 months to the wedding

LULU

AS LULU STANDS on the steps of Jing'an Temple, her dad calls.

"Nǚ'ér." His voice is affectionate, though worn and cracked like leather left too long under the sun. "What are you doing?"

She looks up at the ancient temple, absorbing its grandeur. "I'm waiting for Peng Ayi. We're asking the gods for their blessing before our marriage certification."

In the month since they agreed to the heist, Rina and Jane have been busy planning. Lulu still can't shake the sense of fiction. It's like something out of an adventure novel, a quest that Sun Wukong would take on in *Journey to the West*. Jane and Rina, with their years of working on big, million-dollar problems, have tackled this one with their usual ruthless efficiency.

"Sit back and watch the magic happen," Jane had said, a laptop tucked under her arm, a fierce expression on her face.

Within a few hours, they came up with a color-coded spreadsheet of a hypothetical wedding schedule pending Lulu's acquisition of the real thing, along with a timeline for who they needed to recruit and task milestones leading up to the wedding day. The speed with which they worked and tossed out ideas made Lulu's head spin, so she focused on keeping them fed and hydrated, not wanting to slow their momentum by asking questions they already knew the answers to.

"And are you looking forward to the wedding?" her dad asks. "Only seven months away!"

Before, Lulu would've had to lie through her teeth. But now, thinking about what's in store, she smiles. If all goes well, there will be money, happiness, freedom. "I am."

"You sound happier," her dad notes. "When you first started dating that boy, your ma seemed more excited than you. Wah, to be like you, living in a big city, spending time with intelligent people with fancy names. How that might've changed the way I saw the world when I was a young man." Wistfulness threads through his words.

Growing up, she could always count on her dad to listen. When her brother and his friends would gang up on her, she would retreat into the corners of their house and read. If her mom discovered her hiding, she would kick her out and complain Lulu was getting underfoot. But her dad never did that. He would sit next to her and ask, "And what new places has my daughter discovered?" And even if Lulu didn't fully understand all the words in a book, she would use her own imagination, and her dad would act enthralled.

Her dad's yearning makes Lulu feel guilty, but she spots Peng Ayi coming up the steps, Harv not far behind. "Ba, I have to go. Make sure you use some of the money I sent home for a new blanket. The one you're using is too thin."

"Sure, sure." There's a lull, then her dad says, "I can see that you are happy, so I am happy. Once you're married, your old Ba can worry less."

It's on the tip of her tongue to apologize. If he knew what she was planning, he would worry more, not less. But Lulu holds back. All he needs to know right now is she's happy, even if it's not for the reasons he believes.

"Lulu!" Peng Ayi exclaims as she reaches her. "How long have you been standing here under the sun? Are you wearing sunscreen? We must hurry because we have venues to visit later. Come!"

While Rina and Jane arrange for the rest of their crew, Lulu's job today is to push the date of the marriage certification to after the wedding. Because running away will be hard enough without being legally married to one of China's wealthiest heirs.

Harv tugs Lulu to his side and hugs her. He's wearing a cream-colored button-up tucked neatly into the waistband of his tailored slacks. Lulu has never seen him with a hair out of place. More than ever, she can't imagine a life by his side. She would never be able to attain the level of polish and composure needed to fit into his world. He holds a plastic bag up. "Boba?"

"No drinks in the temple," the bored guard at the entrance says.

Harv hands her something that looks like cash, says smoothly, "We'll be good."

She accepts it and waves them through without another word. Harv tries to give Lulu the boba, but she politely refuses it. Even if Harv bribed the security guard, Lulu doesn't want the monks to catch her breaking the rules. It seems...disrespectful.

Besides, she's got a plan to carry out. Lulu yawns, and Peng Ayi spins around to glare at her. "What's wrong with you? Āiyá, were you staying up late on your phone again? You'll get eye bags."

It's as good as a cue. She rubs her eyes. "I had a bad dream."

"Bad dream?" Harv asks, stopping next to her. He squeezes her hand. "What was it about? Were you using the diffuser I got you? It's supposed to reduce stress."

Lulu nods, not mentioning the pungent lavender from his diffuser keeps her up rather than helping her sleep. "I dreamed of a piece of paper and a red book. I saw the ink leaking from the page, then a turtle tracking it everywhere. The ink was red. Like blood. Then I woke up." Lulu's voice quavers as she recites the lines Jane gave her, hoping her mother-in-law doesn't sense the lie. "Do you think it's a bad sign? Like…maybe we shouldn't be here today?"

"Don't say silly things like that!" Peng Ayi says, but Lulu doesn't miss the horror in her face. "Just make sure you pray a little longer today, ah?"

"Ma, dreams are reflections of real life." Harv turns to Lulu, who's surprised he spoke up. "It's probably stress over the wedding. How about you take a break from the planning and we book you a spa day?"

"She doesn't have time for that," Peng Ayi snaps. "Neither do you, if you're going to handle the new Former French Concession property and help with wedding planning."

Harv pulls at his collar. "Then why are we here? A temple visit seems like the last thing we need to do right now."

Peng Ayi folds her arms. "What, you don't respect what your Ma wants now?" Her eyes are narrowed, and Lulu is thankful she isn't the target of Peng Ayi's aggravation for once. "Am I less important than your father?"

"That's not what I'm saying." Harv lowers his gaze, contrite. "I'm trying to make everyone happy here."

Peng Ayi clicks her tongue. "Then come along!"

As they walk past Lulu's favorite room, Guanyin Hall, she gets a brief glimpse of the austere goddess standing on her lotus-shaped base. Next comes the massive Buddha in Mahavira Hall, where multiple people kneel on pillows, praying for everything from good health to high scores on the gāokǎo.

Peng Ayi ushers them into a hall much smaller than the others. In front of the lines of prayer pillows is a statue of a fat Buddha, glowing a brighter gold than last month, when Peng Ayi brought Lulu here to pay their respects. He's a big favor-

WOMEN OF GOOD FORTUNE

ite of the Zhu family. It's mainly their money that pays for the extra coating of gold he gets every year.

"Lulu," Harv murmurs to her as they kneel side by side on red pillows. "I have a favor to ask."

"Now?" Lulu looks at the jolly Buddha peering down at them.

"Ma mentioned the FFC property, but she doesn't know how much Ba's counting on me to make it a success. It's a lot of work. So I need you to deal with Ma. Anything she wants, give it to her." His eyes are earnest. "Can you do that?"

Lulu gulps. "But—but you should be involved in the wedding planning too, shouldn't you?" She wishes Harv could be there more to shield her from Peng Ayi's tyranny, even if that means he's another person she has to deceive.

"You can handle it. I believe in you." There's conviction in his voice, or maybe it's desperation.

Peng Ayi directs them to press their foreheads to the floor. Lulu closes her eyes, and even though she's supposed to be praying for good fortune on their wedding day, she wonders what would've happened if she wasn't working when Harv came to Scarlet Beauty for lunch that day. Someone else might've served him tea and watermelon cut into perfect cubes. Another beautiful woman could have caught his eye, like her friend Jiang Hui, who Lulu had been filling in for.

Jiang Hui could be in her place right now, brimming with gratitude at being chosen.

"Āiyá, Peng Ayi! Is that you?" Jane pokes her head into the room as they rise, mouth stretched into a wide smile. She's wearing a bright red peacoat and dangling gold earrings, like she coordinated her outfit to match the temple. "What luck!"

Peng Ayi swivels around on her pillow, agitated. "Jane? How did you find us?" She shifts her body, like she can block the Buddha they've been praying to from Jane's view.

Jane grins, walking right up to the icon and giving him an

affectionate pat on his head. "What do you mean? I come here all the time. With how gold this guy is, he must be full of luck."

Peng Ayi looks scandalized as she realizes the coating of gold she donates to the temple is being enjoyed by the rabble. "That's—he's—we don't come that much."

Lulu tries to appear unmoved as Jane comes and kneels beside her mother-in-law. "You don't mind if I pray for some good fortune for my husband, right? After all, I didn't marry a rich man!" She sends Peng Ayi an exaggerated wink.

Peng Ayi is unsettled, but she can't leave Jane alone with her beloved Buddha. "Yes, let's," she mutters, gesturing for Lulu and Harv to get on their knees again.

Silence falls, and incense clogs Lulu's nostrils with its cloying scent. How many times has she seen her mother in the exact same position, praying Lulu would find a rich husband?

After a few minutes, Jane gasps, wrenching all the peace out of the room. "What is that?"

Peng Ayi's eyes fly open, and she glances at the Buddha, as if she's expecting him to come alive and speak to her. Then she follows Jane's finger to where a tortoise plods toward them, its wrinkled head pointed at Peng Ayi.

Lulu knows Peng Ayi's superstitious brain is working, connecting the tortoise's presence to some higher power. In Chinese superstition, tortoises are signs of longevity, but because of how slowly they move, it's also believed that owning one slows down business. And little is more important to the Zhus than business.

"Maybe it's a sign you have a long life ahead of you, Peng Ayi," Jane says politely. "Are you sure you don't want to take it home with you? It seems to like you."

"Make it go away!" Peng Ayi flaps her hands at the tortoise, even though she's several feet away. "Shoo!" Beyond slightly retracting its neck, the tortoise continues to make its way over.

Jane presses a hand to her mouth. Lulu almost buys it. "Peng Ayi, call me superstitious, but the gods must be trying to tell you something. Maybe they'll come to your dreams with a clearer message."

Peng Ayi shakes her head like she can dispel the bad news they're giving her. "Āiyá, Lulu had some silly dream about paper and blood."

Lulu sucks in a breath. "It couldn't be related, could it?"

Jane grabs her shoulder. "I know another friend who dreamed of three fours the night before her wedding. She ignored the death premonition and still went through with it. Then after she got married, her uncle, grandpa, and father-in-law died within a month!"

Peng Ayi's mouth drops slightly, and she stands up from her pillow, trying to distance herself from this sort of misfortune.

Harv lifts Lulu to her feet. "Ma, I told you. With everything happening with the new property and the wedding, there's too much at risk. Let's push the certification back. I'd rather do it after the wedding, once everything's calmed down. We can't be ignoring divine signs." He looks utterly serious. Lulu can't believe they've succeeded. If only she could tell her dad. He would laugh at the ruse they've managed.

Peng Ayi regards the Buddha as if he might offer his opinion. "We will discuss after the wedding. I suppose there's no rush." After she pushes a wad of cash into the donation box, she chases behind Harv, who's gone off to take a call, nagging him about a suit fitting.

"Nice job," Jane says, revealing the lettuce she'd been wiggling behind her back and feeding it to the tortoise. "You actually looked terrified. Very convincing."

Lulu bends down to watch the tortoise nibble. "Where did you get him?"

"Tortoise marketplace on WeChat. This little guy would be soup if not for us."

"Is what you said about your friend true?"

Jane gets to her feet. "The only friends I have are you and

Rina. I read it through some viral article, then it turned out the uncle and father-in-law were fine, and the grandpa only came down with a cold. That's why you shouldn't believe everything you hear." She executes a tiny little bow to the Zhus' Buddha. "I hope you enjoyed the performance, O Eminent One."

8

7 months to the wedding

JANE

JANE INHERITED HER appreciation for nice things from her mom, master of assessing bags and dresses. Just one look, and she could calculate how much someone's outfit was worth, like a walking price scanner. From following her mom around stores as a child, to navigating them on her own, Jane has learned how to build outfits that are cheap but look like they cost thousands of yuan. It's the one good thing her mom taught her.

If only Zihao understood fashion is more than a superficial, expensive hobby. For Jane, it expresses who she wishes she was. Someone elegant, stylish, confident. Beautiful.

"I haven't been here in forever," Rina notes as they descend the steps to the sprawling underground mall.

The stores are plastered with giant signs advertising discounts of 99 percent off, large bins outside them stacked high with tote bags, socks, underwear. They walk past eyeglass stores offering cheap exams, cluttered electronics stores promising "verified" iPhone repairs. It's a weekend, and there are plenty of people shopping, haggling with store owners and flipping through racks.

But today, Jane's not here to search for the best fits. Since planning started a month ago, she's racked her brain nightly and is certain the key to getting the red envelopes out of the safe resides in this mall.

"Are you sure about this?" Rina asks uneasily as Jane leads her down a dark hallway. "Should we really be recruiting a scammer?"

"The woman we're about to meet is an *artiste*. Nobody even knows her real name." She pauses as someone squeezes between them. "She goes by Michelangelo."

Rina stares at her blankly.

"Because Michelangelo used to be an art forger. You know, before he became a famous sculptor and painted the Sistine Chapel." Jane rolls her eyes. "Someone didn't pay attention in art history."

"I don't think art history really applies here," Rina says.

Jane stops at the stairs up to Michelangelo's store. There's a rusty gate across them. Like a gate will keep out her ardent fans.

"It doesn't seem like we're supposed to go here," Rina says unhelpfully.

"If you think this is dodgy, wait until you see where I get my knockoff sunglasses from. Stop gawping and give me a hand."

Rina refuses to touch the gate with more than the tips of her fingers, but Jane puts her back into it and they shove it open with a screech.

On the windowless floor upstairs, it's a lot quieter. Jane's been to Michelangelo's store countless times and confidently makes her way toward the queue stretching out from her tiny storefront. Many of the women in line wear sunglasses or surgical masks to obscure their faces, and they speak in whispers.

Jane marches directly to the front door. She's a loyal customer, not some new recruit to the counterfeit whisper network. No way she's waiting.

"This isn't like a sex dungeon or something, is it?" Rina whispers urgently as she takes in the blacked-out windows.

Jane shushes her and pushes open the door, ignoring the security guard who rises from his seat, along with the muttered complaints from the women in line.

Unlike the cluttered counterfeit stores that litter the mall, this one could almost pass as a luxury operation. Instead of bags piled up to the ceiling, there are at most two or three arranged on each surface. The walls are painted gray, and the shelves are a muted ash, lit from behind with a sophisticated, gentle glow. A life-size replica of Michelangelo's *David* stands in the corner, his appendage modestly covered with a fake Burberry silk scarf.

Jane spots the fully white hair first, cut into a stylish pixie. "Michelangelo!" she exclaims, giving the name a Chinese accent. She waves at the thin woman, who's busy showing a set of rose-colored cross-body bags to a family dripping in luxury brands. "Your favorite customer is here!"

Michelangelo crosses her arms but gestures for her bouncer to back down. "How many times have I told you to call ahead?" she scolds Jane.

"Please. You always have time for me." Jane smiles, basking in the feeling of being back here.

This is her domain. Rina, on the other hand, scrutinizes the bags on display with suspicion. She wouldn't be able to tell a good knockoff from a bad one. She dresses boringly, with a limited selection of plain blazers, slacks, and blouses tailored to her slim, tall figure. The gold bracelet Lulu gifted them is the only accent she wears.

Which is why Jane's expertise is needed.

After Michelangelo finishes up with her customers and sees them out, she locks the door and strides to a gongfu tea set on the shelf above one of her display counters. "Tea?" she asks as she moves the tray to a small area at the back with plush chairs. She puts a kettle on, motioning for Jane and Rina to sit. "You really should have made an appointment. I thought business would die down when I switched from online to brick-and-mortar, but news spreads fast."

Jane digs out a paper bag from her fake Neverfull. "I know, but I wanted to drop this off! Fish oil from the States."

Michelangelo lowers her glasses, peering at the label. "Kirkland?"

"Yep, the real thing," Jane says proudly. "Straight from American Costco." Every time Zihao travels to America for work, he returns with a whole suitcase of products Chinese people love. Bottles upon bottles of fish oil vitamins, Ralph Lauren polos, and sacks of Ghirardelli chocolates. Twice a year, he'll visit his friends back home and dole them out with an air of benevolence like some kind of wholesale god. Jane can't help but note the hypocrisy of this spending habit, but at least this time it's come in handy.

Michelangelo gathers the bottles and slips them underneath the coffee table and out of sight. "How are you liking the Saffiano? I have a larger version in sage. That's a popular color this year."

"Really?" Jane asks, looking around. "Where is it?"

"It's on back order. It's pricier than the others, but I think it's a worthy investment. I know how attuned you are to trends."

"Oh, you," Jane coos. Michelangelo has mastered the art of the subtle sell: flattering people into thinking they deserve to purchase something expensive. That's why she's cultivated a loyal audience of middle-class Chinese women who don't want to buy counterfeits that are overtly cheap, but can't drop the money on the real thing. Jane has learned more than a few things from her over the years.

Michelangelo's eyes slide to Rina's bag, a years-old camel-colored Céline classic it took more than six months to save up for. "Very practical. Your style is understated and elegant. But you must be frustrated by how easily that calfskin scratches. I have a couple reps that are identical but much hardier. No need for leather conditioning, and much less than what it cost you to buy that bag."

Interest slips into Rina's expression.

"She's good, right?" Jane asks, and Rina reluctantly nods. "Michelangelo, this is Rina. But she's not here to buy a bag either." She glances about the room. "You don't have cameras in here, do you?"

Michelangelo scoffs. "You think I want to be watched? I'm still paying off the fines those Louis Vuitton people laid on me! They think what I do is beneath them, yet they fine me anyway!"

Even though the counterfeit industry is thriving in China, luxury brands have been coming down harder lately. It's why Michelangelo had to temporarily dismantle her online store.

"What if we had a business venture that could help you pay off that fine?" Jane begins.

Michelangelo squints at them. "What are you suggesting?"

"There's a big wedding in seven months. It will probably be the biggest, most expensive wedding in Shanghai this year, if not in the past decade. And an expensive wedding means expensive gifts from the guests. Five million RMB, there for the taking..." She lets that number hang in the air, her own excitement probably clear on her face. She'll get the best nose job money can buy.

Michelangelo lifts the teacup to her lips and takes a tiny sip. Jane has already downed hers. She has no idea how it's possible to drink from something the size of a thimble for more than ten minutes.

"And what do you need me for?" Michelangelo finally bites.

Jane decides to be direct. Michelangelo will see through anything else. "We need a counterfeiter. Someone who can make an identical copy of anything." Originally, they thought they could remove the envelopes from the safe and bring them elsewhere. But Jane's had ample time to tease apart this strategy while cooking dinner and folding laundry, and she's concluded a decoy is critical. They'll swap the real safe for a fake one so that even overly suspicious Peng Ayi, who might check on the safe once it's in storage, will find nothing amiss.

"Hmm." Michelangelo grabs the ends of her shawl and gathers them at her waist. "But I do such good business. Eventually, I will pay the fines off."

Jane opens her mouth, but Rina says briskly, "You must have interest in expanding your business. Hiring good people, importing more goods… Maybe you've entertained the idea of leaving this behind and starting anew. There are only two ways to accomplish that. More time, or more money. And I'm sure your time is very precious." At some point, she's discarded her skepticism, perhaps because she recognizes a fellow businesswoman in Michelangelo. Michelangelo doesn't talk much about her life outside of work, but Jane suspects she eschewed a more conventional profession because it didn't give her the same autonomy as doing something of her own.

Michelangelo tilts her head like a curious bird. "Why would you think I want to leave this business behind? People will always desire counterfeits. That's what these luxury brands don't understand. As long as they survive, so will I. When my customers move on to the real thing, more imposters will take their place."

Jane shifts slightly, feeling targeted by the statement. But Rina is undeterred. "In all your years of hawking fakes, you must have spent enough time studying the real thing to have considered making your own originals. Your name, after all, is Michelangelo. And we all know he wasn't known for forgery."

"True," Jane pipes up, the familiar sensation of working a client side by side with Rina returning. Together, they are un-

WOMEN OF GOOD FORTUNE

defeatable. "You and I joke about opening a shop together all the time. You the designer, me the salesperson. Michelangelo, when are you going to sculpt your *David*?"

Still unconvinced, Michelangelo points at her tinted window. "Do you see that line outside? Those people are here for me. For my products. I've already made a name for myself."

Jane shrugs. "Fine. If you're satisfied with hiding behind a fake name in the bowels of Shanghai, suit yourself. We'll find someone else for the job. Come on, Rina."

Rina grabs her bag, making a *what now* face at Jane.

Jane has thought this through. They could recruit another counterfeiter, but that would lower the success probability of their plan. Michelangelo is Jane's luxury goods shīfù. The woman taught her how to check the stitching on a bag, count the pockets, look for date stamps to verify authenticity. Anything in her store could be mistaken for the real thing, even by a trained eye. There is nobody more detail-oriented, nobody better. They need Michelangelo.

Jane knew Michelangelo might be too shrewd to be swayed by vanity, so she has one more angle to try. "By the way, are you familiar with Zhu Development Group?" she asks.

"Intimately. They are the reason my favorite black market was demolished." Michelangelo shudders. "It's probably now home to some socialite with five shedding cats."

Jane takes the opening without hesitation. "The groom is the son of the CEO."

Michelangelo refills her cup carefully. "I see. And you're not worried about being caught?" She raises an eyebrow.

"Not with this genius on our team." Jane pats Rina's shoulder. "This woman's moved billions in assets." No need to clarify that by *move*, she means given strongly worded PowerPoint presentations recommending new financial management practices.

Rina glares at Jane, but she doesn't object to this inflation of her qualifications.

Michelangelo gazes at the women lined up outside. One of them puts her hands on the window and presses her face close, like that might help her see inside better. "I'll consider it," she says, her focus still on the crowd.

"You're not curious about what you'd need to counterfeit for us?" Jane asks.

"No matter what it is, I will make a copy that is just as good as the original. Never better, because then it would not be identical. But before I agree to anything, you have to answer a question. Why do you want to do this?"

Jane's about to explain, but Michelangelo shakes her head. "Not you. I know you. I want to know why *she* wants it." She looks at Rina, waiting.

Jane expects Rina's usual answer about freezing her eggs, maintaining her independence, winning at her career. It's aggravating sometimes, how Rina believes wholeheartedly that being successful in a company full of men is the only way for a woman to claim her place in society. Although Michelangelo is unmarried and an entrepreneur, Jane's not sure she's ever had to climb a corporate ladder, or that she'll be moved by Rina's appeal.

But Rina proves she knows how to adapt her message to her audience. "I want to balance the scales," she says firmly, defiance in her eyes.

Michelangelo seems satisfied by this answer, though she does not smile, only sips from her cup. "I'll be in touch."

9

6 months to the wedding

RINA

LULU'S ENGAGEMENT DINNER is on the rooftop of a luxury hotel overlooking the Bund. As she hustles over in her double-breasted blazer and suede pumps, Rina impatiently shoves past people who've stopped to ooh and ahh at the reflection of lights on the river and snap pictures of the glowing spheres of the Oriental Pearl Tower.

On the roof, numerous heat lamps protect against the evening chill. Fairy lights line a walkway leading to a long table laid with flowers and jade candleholders. This might be a social gathering, but Rina will have to keep her eyes and ears open for any details about the wedding. They still need Peng Ayi to commit to a venue so they can recruit the rest of their crew.

At the table, Lulu greets all their guests. She hugs Rina hello before whispering apologetically, "You'll have to sit next to Yaqing."

Ever the good sport, Rina makes eye contact with Harv's dour sister and offers a friendly smile that is ignored. "Who's on the other side of me?" she asks, gesturing at the empty seat. She's already unforgivably late because a meeting ran over. Work has been nonstop the past month. After discovering a guy three years younger than her had been promoted, Rina's been hell-bent on showing Luo Ren he made a mistake.

All that said, whoever is supposed to be sitting there is just plain rude.

"Leave that open for Vic," Peng Ayi calls from much farther down the table, probably catching Rina's question with her bat-like hearing. Harv is one seat away from her, consulting the extensive wine menu with a server, the chair between them ostensibly reserved for Lulu.

Rina groans quietly. Not him. Anyone but him.

"He might not even show up," Lulu quickly assures her. "You know it's usually a fifty-fifty chance."

Harv suddenly jumps up. "I picked him up from the airport this afternoon. He said he needed a nap, but he should be awake now."

Peng Ayi yanks him back down. "You're the groom! You have to talk to your guests. Make someone else do it. Rina, would you mind getting him? He's got a suite here. Lulu, talk to Hong Ri over there. Her mom owns Cuicui Chicken."

Lulu mouths *sorry* as she drifts away and attempts to find commonality with the chicken empire heiress.

Stalling, Rina drapes her coat and bag over her chair. "Hi, Yaqing. Good to see you again."

Yaqing tips her head up, eyes running over her outfit and face, then sniffs and turns away without saying a single word.

Rina bites back a sigh and heads into the hotel to search for the best man. According to Peng Ayi, Vic's room number is 888. Figures. Eight in Chinese sounds similar to *fā*, the word for wealth, so it's usually reserved for someone willing to pay for it.

She exits the elevator to the penthouse floor, and hears loud voices coming from inside room 888. Only one is male.

She stops, mentally preparing herself to deal with Vic Shan and his brand of easy confidence that sets her off every time she's in his presence. Even before Econ 100 at Stanford, she'd heard of him. The guy who parked his sports cars in the professors' lot, who famously tried to create a boycott of finals by offering fellow freshmen a free trip to Cabo. Then she met him and discovered the face matched the reputation.

Knowing her former classmate, there's an orgy happening on the other side of the door. She should just let him run his event to completion. He'll show up when he shows up.

She pivots to leave when her phone buzzes with a text from Lulu.

Peng Ayi says everyone needs to be seated before the appetizers can be brought out. Please hurry!

Rina lowers the phone, massaging her forehead. She's learned enough about Harv from classmates to form an opinion of him and his family. His mom is involved in every decision he makes, from the clothes he wears to the food he eats, and it doesn't help that he still lives at home. She fears what Lulu will suffer with Peng Ayi as a mother-in-law.

All Rina can do now is avoid upsetting Peng Ayi further. She knocks on the door.

The talking ceases, and she has a moment to steady herself before the door opens and Vic is peering down at her, his arm propped on the doorframe. "You're not room service," he drawls. He's wearing a black beanie that says FUCKKK upside down, in big white letters.

"You're very late to dinner." She determinedly keeps her eyes on his, not allowing them to waver to whatever pandemonium is happening behind him.

He's got aggressively defined cheekbones and eyes the color of her favorite mocha frappuccino. He fixes them on her face, his smile making a dimple in his right cheek. "It's been a while, hasn't it? Six months since the proposal?" Rina remembers when Harv got down on one knee in the restaurant. She'd suspected something big was happening, given the audience of friends and family, but it was still shocking he'd proposed in under a year, especially when they hadn't been an arranged couple. The only people who'd been warned beforehand were the parents, and apparently Vic. He'd winked at her from across the room, like he already knew how much more they'd be seeing of each other. "You missed me so much that you had to fetch me personally?" he asks now.

She ignores him and checks her watch. "Everyone's waiting on you."

"I'm in the middle of something." A hand comes under her chin, and her gaze catches on the ink on his arm. Lotuses, drawn in xiěyì, a freehand Chinese brush technique that characterizes ancient watercolors. Rina knows people who would sneer at a guy with flower tattoos, but the art captivates her. It's intricate and beautiful, so at odds with the man whose arm it covers. "Eyes up here." His voice is amused, but he examines her closely. "You look tired."

"Vic, what are you doing?" calls someone in Shanghainese.

Rina hurriedly pulls her chin from his grip as a woman totters into view. Rina stares, her brain short-circuiting. The woman is a granny, at least eighty, with folds around her eyes that crinkle when she smiles. Is this Vic's type?

"Wah, who is this? She's so pretty! Invite her inside!" the woman insists.

"I will, Liang Nainai," Vic replies good-naturedly, his Shanghainese impeccable. "We'll join you in a moment."

"No, we won't." Rina tries not to let her annoyance leak through. "Nainai hǎo," she says politely to the old lady beside him. "My name is Zhou Rina. I'm here because Vic promised his friend he would be at dinner tonight, and we're already very late."

"Āiyá, Vic! You didn't say that you had something tonight. We could have rescheduled." Liang Nainai pats Vic's cheek affectionately.

What is the relation between these two? Rina can barely process the scene before her. Are they on a date? Is she his sugar momma? Of course it's becoming more common for older women to date younger men, but this age difference is a bit extreme...

Vic smiles impishly. "How about you join us?"

Rina takes a step back, even as Liang Nainai's face lights up. "Are you interested, dear? We always welcome new members!"

She's about to give them a very firm rejection when they move aside, and she sees the table behind them, where two other grannies are seated. The green mat is covered with white tiles.

"You're playing mahjong?"

"What did you think we were doing?" Vic smirks, like he can read every single thought racing through her head.

She looks at her watch again. She already wastes enough time at work dealing with undisciplined men. She needs to get him to dinner *now*. But it seems he isn't going to leave easily. Rina decides to offer him a deal. "I'll play. If I win, you come with me."

"If you lose, you have to play strip poker next with us."

Rina hopes for the grandmas' sakes that he's bluffing. "Fine," she mutters before stalking toward the mahjong table. Liang Nainai graciously lets Rina take her spot. She greets the others and wonders how Vic even found this group.

"Xǐ pái," Vic commands, sliding into a seat. He's several heads taller than the grandmas, and that obnoxious grin is still on his face, like he's already won. Rina's never seen him anything but smug. Like that time he didn't show up to any of their group project meetings but emailed her an eloquently written paper about food price volatility thirty minutes before their assignment was due.

They push the tiles around the table, mixing them up before arranging stacks in front of themselves. Vic glances at one of his tiles and tosses it into the center of the table.

The grandmas titter, and one of them smacks him in the shoulder. "Bad luck!" she says, pointing to the green *cái* on the tile, the Chinese character for *rich*. Throwing out that tile first is equivalent to throwing away your riches.

Vic asks cordially, "Do you think bad luck is why you owe me a thousand yuan, Wu Nainai?"

Wu Nainai snatches her hand back. "A newborn calf is not afraid of tigers," she says.

"I'm neither calf nor tiger. I'm a dragon," he says wryly, then to Rina, "Your turn."

Mahjong is mostly luck, and it seems like the gods want Rina to drag this infuriating man to the engagement dinner. She starts with a strong hand and continues to draw good tiles as the game progresses.

Finally, Vic tosses out the last tile she needs, and she grabs it triumphantly. "Hú," she announces, flipping all her tiles over.

"Wah!" the grandmas exclaim as she scrapes her chair back.

She glares at Vic. "We're leaving now."

He doesn't look upset. Instead, he seems highly entertained. "You earned it."

They bid goodbye to the grandmas, who are merrily discussing which of their other friends to invite over. As Vic is about to leave, Rina blocks his path. "The hat is not coming," she tells him. She can already envision Peng Ayi's disapproval over Vic's attire, which is going to make the dinner even more painful to sit through.

His eyes locked to hers, he slips off the offensive beanie. Black hair spills out, and in an act that could only be out of pure malice, he plops it over her head, his curled fingers brushing against her temples.

She catches the briefest, earthy scent of patchouli before she rips the hat off and chucks it into the depths of his room. She hopes it doesn't accidentally hit one of the grandmas.

10

6 months to the wedding

LULU

JUST AS LULU is about to go off in search of Rina and Vic herself, they finally appear. Rina power walks to her chair in her work pumps and collapses into it with visible relief.

"Vic, ah!" Peng Ayi exclaims from Lulu's side, a forced enthusiasm pulling at the corners of her mouth. "We almost gave your seat to one of the waiters!"

"I would never miss the chance to spend time with you, Peng Ayi," Vic says as he breezes past her to kiss Lulu's cheek. "How are you, Lulu?"

"I'm well." Lulu smiles at him. Vic's presence always makes everything livelier. Even though Rina hates him, some grudge from their college days, Lulu likes his contagious, carefree attitude. "How were your travels?"

"Enlightening," Vic said. "Harv, you should've come and seen some old friends. Audrey owns an esports team and won some big competition recently. Remember when she used to yell at you for being bad at *Mario Kart*?"

Harv seems to deflate slightly. "I couldn't have. The wedding. Ba's got me busy, too."

"Next time then," Vic persists. "You won't be busy forever."

"Yeah, next time," Harv says noncommittally.

Vic glances at Peng Ayi, who's staring at them with suspicion. He murmurs to Harv, "You don't have to play perfect son all the time. We miss you."

Harv opens one of the menus, avoiding Vic. A muscle pulses in his jaw. "You should find your seat. You haven't eaten since the flight."

Vic seems disappointed. He gives Harv's shoulder a squeeze, and Lulu watches him go to the other end of the table and take his seat beside Rina, who stabs her tofu, an expression of pure suffering on her face.

Lulu came to this dinner considerably less worried now that she won't actually be getting married, but Harv's stress is impossible to ignore. "You could spend more time with him. I wouldn't mind," she says.

"Times are different. I have responsibilities now," he says.

Once, when Harv picked her up for a date after her shift at Scarlet Beauty, Vic tagged along, and they had a drink while they waited. The entire staff was mesmerized. The waitresses fought over who got to serve their table, and Harv even convinced Lulu's manager to let her join them. She'd sipped rice wine and listened to their stories. Since the engagement, though, she hasn't seen Harv go anywhere without one of his parents.

Lulu doesn't push the issue further.

When the servers bring out their entrées, Vic stands. "A toast!" He raises his glass of whiskey toward Harv. "To my best friend, who's finally found the love of his life." The candlelight sparkles in the crystal as he tips it to his lips.

Rina pops up next to him. "A toast to Lulu, who is a true catch." She gives Vic a flinty-eyed stare before draining the entire glass.

"Then I must toast you," Vic says, unwilling to let Rina get the last word. "For being Lulu's best friend and a constant presence in all of our lives."

Rina doesn't sit down. "You know what? I'll drink to that too."

Everyone loses interest in their competition and returns to their conversations.

Harv's mouth can't help but twitch into a smile. "Vic always loves a challenge." Lulu refills his water, and Harv looks at her strangely. She realizes it's because she should've let the server do it. He angles his head toward her. "Have things with Ma been going smoothly?" he asks, serious again.

"They've been great," Lulu says, and she actually means it. Ever since they all agreed to Jane's idea, things have been looking up. They have a strong plan; they onboarded a fourth crew member. Even Peng Ayi isn't so bad these days, now that Lulu knows she isn't actually going to be her mother-in-law. "We chose stationery together the other day. It took a few hours to choose between blush and crepe, but I think Peng Ayi is happy with the final color."

"I'm sorry," Harv says, startling her. "I wish I could be there more. It's been so busy at work." He runs a hand through his hair. "I was the one who asked Ba to take a chance on me. I can't fail. If I do, I won't be worthy of being his son."

That pressure to show his parents he is worth the investment they made in him… Lulu understands it. "He can't exactly fire you, can he?"

Harv shakes his head slowly. "It would be worse than that."

"Ní hǎo," their server says, approaching Peng Ayi. "There's a woman here saying she's looking for the wedding party? Says she's the bride's mother, but you never mentioned someone like that being on the guest list?"

"Because there is not," Peng Ayi says, deeply offended. "She must have the wrong place."

Her mom is here? Lulu vaguely remembers inviting her, but she had complained how far Shanghai was and how it had already cost her so much in time and money to make the journey for the proposal. But now that she thinks about it, her mom never outright declined the invitation either. "I'll get her," Lulu offers, dread sinking in.

"Shall I come with you?" Harv asks. He sets his napkin aside.

"No," Lulu says quickly. She doesn't want him to be there when her mom inevitably scolds her for starting without her. There's no need for him to see the tension that exists between her and her family. After all, she has to make sure Harv still wants to marry her and that they make it to the wedding.

Her mother is in the lobby, wearing a quilted coat that looks out of place in the splendor of the hotel. Her hair is drawn back into a messy bun, and her glasses are crooked on her nose. She's arguing with the concierge, flustered. "I know someone, I swear I do! Fei Lulu, check your list again."

"Ma!" she calls out from the elevator.

She turns, relief crossing her face, followed by irritation. "See, that's my daughter," she shouts, darting toward Lulu, who holds the elevator doors open. "Why didn't you tell them I was coming?" she whispers furiously when she reaches her. "How embarrassing!"

"Ma, you didn't confirm. And Ba—"

"He'll be fine for a few days without me. I dropped my things off at your apartment, by the way. Are you still living with that Zhou Rina girl? That *shèngnǚ*?"

"Ma! Don't call her that. She chose not to get married."

"Sounds like an excuse. She isn't as beautiful as my Lulu." Her mom rubs her arm tenderly.

No matter how many times she tells her mom that Rina is actually far too successful and intelligent to settle for anyone, her mom refuses to believe a woman would choose to be single.

"Have you eaten?"

She disregards Lulu's question, pinching her face critically. "Āiyá, your chin is looking sharp. Make sure you're eating fruits and taking care of your skin. You don't want to do anything that will make Harv change his mind! You *are* treating him well, right? Lulu, if you let this one slip away, you are disrespecting the sacrifice your Ba and I have made for you. His family has their own website! How many people can say that about themselves?"

"I'm grateful," Lulu protests softly. "I know what you paid for me to come here." Her mom will never let her forget it.

Her mom moves Lulu's hair over her shoulder, her tone gentle as she says, "I know you love your Ba more than me. He likes to fill your head with dreams and grand desires. But be realistic, Lulu. This is as good as it gets, so don't ruin things. Now, I've come a long way. What's for dinner?"

By the time they make it up to the rooftop, the party has moved on to dessert. From the doorway, Lulu's mom grimly watches servers parade past with fruit cut into animal shapes.

"We can order you something to go," Lulu assures her. She wishes her mom hadn't shown up. There's no telling what she might say or do tonight, whether her actions might inadvertently offend Harv or Peng Ayi.

"Chen Jie," says Peng Ayi, standing up with all the appearance of warmth. "I had no idea you would be coming today! Our table is very full, unfortunately. Perhaps we can seat you somewhere else?"

Lulu swiftly intercedes. Her mom has always sought Peng Ayi's approval, and despite her issues with her mom, it makes Lulu's stomach clench to see how Peng Ayi still treats her with such obvious disdain. "That's alright, she can take my spot."

"She can take mine," Harv says, scooting back his chair. "We can't split Lulu up from her mom."

Peng Ayi looks peeved. "I suppose we can see about squeezing in a chair."

"Sorry about the trouble," Lulu says to Harv as the servers wedge in another chair.

"I should be apologizing. I should have made arrangements for your mom to attend." Harv gives her a reassuring smile. "You must miss home, living so far away. I'm happy to call a car to bring your parents to the city if you ever feel homesick."

"That's very kind of you. Thank you." Harv's generosity always takes her aback. It's so easy for him to offer her things, with no cost to him.

Once they're seated again, Harv asks a server to bring her mom some of the roast duck from earlier. As her mom eats, Peng Ayi calls from her other side, "Lulu, ah." Lulu leans closer to hear her. "About the invitation list. I will work on it myself, then we can talk about who you'd like to invite."

"Um," Lulu says, remembering that Jane and Rina mentioned they need to keep a few spots open for other crew members. "I want to make sure there's enough space for—"

Peng Ayi waves her off. "Zhu Shushu has some very important business associates that we want to prioritize. We can talk about it more when we address the invitations together."

"But—"

"Peng Jie, you always have the smartest suggestions. Who needs a wedding planner with you around?" Lulu's mom asks. Under the table, Lulu gets kicked in the leg. *Don't be a nuisance,* she can almost hear her mom saying. *Just go along with it.*

Stay out of the way. Don't be a bother. Let the adults talk. Lulu fights to control her expression. She feels like she's back at the dinner table at home, her mom and brother admonishing her into silence.

Peng Ayi reluctantly accepts the praise. "Chen Jie, you are too kind with your compliments. But it's true. I can't let such an important event be managed by someone who doesn't understand the intricacy of it! All of my friends offered to connect me with wedding planners who have wait lists hundreds of names long, but I told them all no. Only I understand my son well enough to arrange his wedding."

"If that's true, maybe we can just invite twenty people and do it at home," Harv remarks.

There's a brief pause, then Peng Ayi bursts out laughing. Lulu's mom joins her a second later. "Wah, my son!" Peng Ayi exclaims. "So funny."

Peng Ayi rises to go argue with the servers over the temperature of the pudding, and Lulu's mom watches her leave before she tugs on Lulu's elbow. "Lulu," she says. "I came because I wanted to talk to you. About Gege. He's having a hard time and could use your support."

Lulu thinks of their last call, her brother obliviously chewing on his chicken leg while his wife cleaned up around him. Although Lulu only sees her sister-in-law when she visits home for holidays, she knows she's far too kind and tolerant of him. "He is?"

"Everything you give us helps."

Lulu lets her hold her hand. Of course only so much time would pass before her mom would start looking for money again. Her mom has a way of asking her for things as if she's already said yes. "Ma, I sent you my last paycheck, and I'm not working anymore. Have you spent everything already?" Harv gave her enough money to pay a whole year's rent after she quit her job. It was hard enough to accept, and she refuses to ask for more.

Her mom shushes her, checking that Harv is engaged in conversation with someone else. "Āiyá, have some decency! Don't speak of it so loudly. I'm your mother. Are you really going to hold out on me like this? Why did I raise you?"

"If Gege could get a job, he could help out." She doesn't mean to sound bitter, but she doesn't understand why all of the expectations have fallen upon her shoulders. The last time she visited home, her brother went out every night to meet friends for cards and didn't get back until morning, which he then slept away before repeating the routine again. And her mom didn't say a word.

"Why are you so eager to blame your brother? Just look at how much Peng Ayi is spending on your wedding! And Harv spoils you. He won't object." Her mom deals the final blow. "Is it really so hard to do this small thing for your family?"

Lulu hates this, how effectively her mom preys on her guilt. She wants to tell her she refuses to enter this marriage, to be trapped further in a life that's not her own. But she must keep up pretenses. When Lulu sends her mom her portion of the gift money, an amount far larger than anything she has ever received, maybe it'll finally be enough. But for now she just says, "I'll see what I can do."

11

6 months to the wedding

JANE

WATCHING VIC AND Rina across the table is better than watching television. They're both drunk, though a casual spectator might not be able to tell. Jane would bet Vic is slightly drunker. Rina has had too much training drinking at business dinners. Her tolerance is superhuman.

Yaqing leans over Rina, basically smooshing her boobs into her face in an attempt to get Vic's attention. "Are you still running that investment fund?" she asks, fake-sweet.

"You mean, am I still wasting money? Of course, I am." His eyes dance. "You should tell your brother to get in on it with me. Way more fun than the family business. Let's not talk about my boring job, though. You're in consulting, aren't you?" He directs the question at Rina, propping his chin in his hand. "Maybe I can consult you on something. I've got this company I'm thinking of investing in. I really identify with their values, but I'm not sure about the returns."

Rina ignores him, and Yaqing asks, "What industry is it?"

"Sex toys."

Yaqing gasps and Jane snorts into her soup, but Rina continues spooning hers into her mouth mechanically. Farther down the table, Harv glances longingly in their direction while Lulu gets trapped in conversation with the moms. Jane feels a surge of distaste, especially knowing what Harv has asked of Lulu. He might be rich, but making Lulu deal with Peng Ayi on her own is like dropping a baby into a tank with a great white shark.

On the other side of Jane, a couple other women Peng Ayi has roped into Lulu's bridal party gossip with haughty expressions and skin that looks like it's never seen the sun.

"My husband took me to Hawaii and when we landed, he surprised me with a Tiffany necklace!" one of them brags. "Can you believe such a thing? He's so foolish. I can't believe he managed to hide such a purchase from me!"

"Wah," another replies. "Mine is such a cheapskate. He told me he won't buy me any gifts over five thousand yuan!"

Jane mashes the lotus seeds in her soup with her chopsticks. She feels drab in her Dior cropped jacket she had to fight tooth and nail for, especially when most of these other women are wearing haute couture.

"Jane," one of them says, not noticing, or maybe caring, that she's been busying herself with the food to avoid them. "You and your husband married quickly too, didn't you? You must have been so in love. Tell us what it's like!"

"Just perfect," she says, all saccharine. "The other day, he bought me a Cartier ring, and I told him, 'Lǎogōng, I don't have enough fingers for all the rings you've bought me!' He's worried I'll divorce him for the next man who comes along who's eager to satisfy my tastes."

The women's eyes widen, and Jane sits back, picking her teeth behind a napkin. Let them chew on that.

"Āiyá." It's Hong Jie, one of Peng Ayi's friends who somehow got invited despite not being part of the bridal party. "You young people have it so good. Yet you are always looking for the first reason to get divorced. Things have been too easy for you."

"And what's wrong with that?" Jane says, unable to resist contesting Hong Jie, with her imperious, know-it-all attitude. "Doesn't a woman deserve the right to chase her own happiness?"

"I'm not saying that." Hong Jie gives Jane a patronizing look. "Too often, I'm seeing these young women look for an escape, and they think divorce will solve all their problems."

Yaqing speaks up, probably bored of trying to insert herself into the Vic and Rina show. "Jie, sounds like you are a supporter of the cool-down period!"

Hong Jie nods. "Young people are too eager to act these days. Having thirty days to really consider their decisions is not just good, it's necessary."

"What if it's an abusive relationship? You still think that's a good idea?" Jane challenges. The cool-down period, required for any couple considering a divorce, is controversial. Jane will have to take it into account when she decides when to break the news to Zihao. Should she do it after her surgery so he can see what he could have had? Or before so he'll have no way to recognize her on the street in the future?

Hong Jie peers at her. "My, Jane, you are very passionate about this topic. Was that joke you made about divorce actually real?"

All the women swivel their heads around to Jane.

Jane realizes her butt has risen a few inches above her seat and sits back down. "Of course not. We're extremely happy together." Even as she says it, she flashes back to their latest fight about her getting too many deliveries, triggered when she rushed downstairs to collect a package of activewear at 11:00 p.m. She can get packages whenever she damn well wants.

"Where *is* your husband?" Hong Jie asks, making an exaggerated display of scanning the table like Zihao might be hiding under the pudding. She's sensed a sore spot that can be prod-

WOMEN OF GOOD FORTUNE

ded further. "Surely he wants to spend all the time with you that he can?"

"He's at work." She wouldn't have invited Zihao, anyway. He would've been out of place here, caught in mutual dislike with all these rich exhibitionists.

"He's working at that big security firm, isn't he?"

Another woman jumps in. "Security is so important to this nation's infrastructure. Just the other day, someone's daughter got mugged in the street! But the police immediately found the culprit using CCTV. Do you know they can scan faces in minutes?"

"Crime has no place here," Jane agrees. She's already been snooping around Zihao's office for anything that could help them disable security at the wedding. Sadly, she has a feeling most of that knowledge lives in his head, and to get it, she'll have to bring up his job in a way that seems natural when she's never demonstrated any interest in it before.

By the end of dinner, Jane is sick of all these women and their sparkly, shiny possessions. Her irritability propels her over to Lulu's side of the table, wineglass in hand. "Wonderful dinner, Peng Ayi," she says, clinking her glass against Peng Ayi's. "The food, the service—your attention to detail always amazes me. With you handling Lulu's wedding, I have no doubt it'll be magnificent."

Peng Ayi smiles self-importantly. "It isn't work when you do it out of love!"

"Speaking of," Jane says, wedging herself into this opening. "Where have you landed for venues?" The last time she, Lulu, and Rina met to discuss their plan, Peng Ayi had been considering the Shangri-La, Shanghai Yacht Club, and the Ritz. Naturally, the insufferable Peng Ayi had found issues with all of those venues. But with six months left before the wedding, she must have chosen somewhere, and they need to know to create blueprints and figure out how to disable the security system.

"It hasn't been easy, but we're doing it at Sun Island, which should afford us the space and privacy we need. The hotel staff is very amenable to me making any modifications to the property as I see fit."

"Sun Island?" Harv looks at his mom. "I thought we were still considering other places. I liked the Ritz."

"I liked Sun Island, so I put down a deposit," she says, an edge to her voice. "This wedding isn't just yours, you know! We've got so many friends and business associates who have been waiting for the day our only son is married."

Harv scratches his neck. "So you keep reminding me."

"I've never heard of this place." Jane redirects the conversation. "It must be a good find."

"It was an hour from Shanghai proper in my private car, so not too far. I'm not surprised you haven't heard of it. It's better this way, so we don't attract too much undue attention. We'll completely transform it for the wedding." Peng Ayi flutters her hands like some fairy godmother making dreams come true. "I'm thinking crystals dripping from the ceiling, flower arches, gold-tipped fans in each place setting, silk lanterns… We'll have space for at least five hundred, if not more."

Five hundred. Just thinking about the amount of money that could be harvested from that many people makes Jane want to chortle with glee. "That sounds like the perfect place for a wedding, and I know your creativity will bring it alive. I'll help in any way I can, Ayi."

"Lulu is so lucky to have friends like you and Rina," Peng Ayi says warmly, like Jane's pretend awe at the venue has suddenly made them best friends. "China is a hard place for women. So much pressure, and men are so fixated on beauty! But you, my dear, have done so well for yourself despite it all." She says this affectionately.

Having entrapped a man with her unfortunate looks is apparently her standout achievement.

As everyone files out of the restaurant at the end of the evening, Jane pulls Lulu and Rina aside. "Can we please bitch about how excruciating that meal was?"

"At least we know where the venue is now," Lulu says. "Sun Island wasn't even on Peng Ayi's initial list. I wonder why."

Jane has a guess. "It's probably not as well-known as the other spots, which could be advantageous for us. Security might not be as tight."

"Should we talk more tonight?" Rina asks.

"I have to take my mom home," Lulu says apologetically. "She's staying over."

Before Rina can respond, an arm throws itself around her neck, and Vic says, "Rina, my Rina, when am I going to see you again?"

She shakes him off. "Not until the wedding, if I have anything to say about it."

He gives a despondent sigh. "Why do you despise me so much, my Rina?"

Rina turns to face him, her heels bringing them almost nose to nose, her expression fearsome enough for Jane to be afraid for Vic. "You were later than me tonight, and you didn't even have a good reason. It's disrespectful, and if you do this at one of Lulu's events again, I'll show you no mercy."

Vic mouths *wow*. "How can you expect me to stay away when you talk to me like that?"

Rina stalks off, the conversation finished. Vic smirks, then salutes Lulu and Jane before jogging off.

Jane watches Vic, an idea forming in her head. She might not have money or looks, but she still has her own brilliant brain. "We're going to make this wedding our bitch," she says to Lulu. "And I have just the plan."

12

5 months to the wedding

RINA

RINA'S FINISHING UP her work for the day when her boss comes by her desk. Luo Ren's in his midforties, a master at maintaining a stoic expression, and she suspects he dyes his hair; there's no way it's still completely black with the pressure that comes with this job.

"I'm sending those files to you now," she says quickly, hoping he's not here to drop something else on her when she's got somewhere to be. Now that they know the location of the wedding, it's time to recruit their driver, the person who will whisk the money away from the venue to a secure place where it'll be stored until it's safe to withdraw. Jane's ideal candidate was someone "who you wouldn't trust with your life, but who would get you somewhere on time." Rina only knows one person who meets that specific description.

"You've been working hard. Why don't you head out early today?" Luo Ren suggests.

Rina senses a trap. It's not going to look good if she leaves now. It'll seem like she took his offer, when the correct move is to politely turn it down. "That's alright. I can get started on that new case proposal."

Luo Ren nods approvingly, then lowers his voice. "I can tell you're committed to the firm, and I wanted to assure you that the extra energy you're devoting to us isn't going unnoticed. Keep it up, and I can guarantee you'll be considered next cycle."

Rina smiles pleasantly at him, but she hears Jane in her head. *If he really wanted to promote you, he would've done it already.* All Luo Ren is doing is keeping her hopes up to ensure her work product isn't impacted by her disillusionment.

Because of Luo Ren's drop-in, Rina ends up staying another hour to make progress on the proposal she mentioned, so that she can send him a draft before she leaves.

On the way to her destination, she catches up on her text chain with her mom, who's been refusing her repeated offers to drop off ginseng because she doesn't like the taste. Rina threatens to take the train all the way home and personally put it in her mom's tea. They arrange to meet next month.

An email arrives from Lulu with the official schedule for the wedding. It's five pages long. Rina imagines it can't be much different from the schedule of a diplomat visiting a foreign nation. At least all the activity will keep guests distracted as the crew performs their work—

The taxi driver grunts, and she hurriedly puts her phone away. They've arrived at her aunt's house on the outskirts of Shanghai.

Before she even has a chance to ring the bell, the door swings open to reveal her aunt's eager face. "Rina, ah, come in! I thought you were going to be here earlier! Wah, you look like such a professional. Have you eaten? Xiaoyi has been making a pot of yān dū xiān and it's almost ready. You will have a bowl."

"Xiaoyi hǎo," Rina greets her aunt. "I'll have one after I see Mei." Before today, she wrestled with the ethics of what she's about to do. But the conversation with Luo Ren has only assured her there will be no promotion in the near future. She needs that wedding money.

Rina surrenders her things to Xiaoyi, then steps into a pair of fluffy house slippers.

"Xiao Mei!" her aunt hollers. "Quit sulking and come out here to greet your cousin!" She lowers her voice. "We're not letting her leave the house without us while she's here for winter break. Yale put her on academic probation. And the other day, she stole Xiaoyifu's car and drove it through Shanghai! We only found out because he checks his security cameras every day."

"You mean she returned the car without a scratch?" Rina asks.

Her aunt frets. "Your uncle imported that car from Germany! If she crashed the car, we would have so much trouble!"

Owning a car in Shanghai is a luxury, and anyone who wants to register one has to bid for a license plate. Beyond the expense of an imported car, Xiaoyifu must have spent a couple months' salary on the plates. The problem, at least for her parents, is that Mei, who learned how to drive completely on her own, has a knack for finding her way behind the wheel of any moving vehicle. It's incredible she hasn't managed to injure herself or damage the many cars she's "borrowed." A very useful skill for a getaway driver.

Rina needs to escape her chatty aunt and get down to business, so she says, "I'm going to make sure she's reflecting on her bad behavior." She slips down the small hallway to Mei's closed door, which is covered in stickers of anime boys. She knocks loudly. "Hey, Mei. It's Rina. I'm coming in."

A voice shrieks out, "Wait!"

She pauses and hears a bunch of shuffling behind the door.

"You can come in now," her cousin says after a minute.

When she opens the door, Mei is sitting primly in her chair in a ratty T-shirt that says Adidus, breathing kind of hard. The whole room has a musty smell, and there's a pile of clothes on her sagging mattress. The desktop behind her is on its home screen.

Rina looks suspiciously at her computer. "Did I interrupt something?"

"No," Mei says, folding her hands in her lap. Her legs are long and skinny, like a foal's. "What's up, Rina Jie?"

Rina enters and gingerly lowers herself onto the edge of Mei's unmade bed. "How was your first year at Yale?" Everyone was surprised when Mei, who had a habit of hitting boys who provoked her and talking back to teachers, got admitted to an Ivy League school. Even Xiaoyi had no idea that Mei applied abroad, a testament to how good she was at keeping secrets.

"Pointless." Mei spins her chair in a lazy circle. "The rich kids are obsessed with themselves, and the poor kids work too hard and are boring as a result. Also, why's everyone so obsessed with hooking up? Don't people understand that the *cuffing* in 'cuffing season' refers to handcuffs? Why would you want to be handcuffed to anyone?"

"Did you like being in the States, though?" It's been so long since Rina's been to California, the place she grew up, attended school. When she moved to Shanghai, everyone said she was moving "back," like being born here meant it was her true home. But even after years of learning how to live in this city, sometimes Rina still feels like a transplant, attempting to grow in foreign soil.

Mei shrugs, oblivious to Rina's nostalgia. "I thought college in the States would be fun and new. But it's the same social games in a different environment."

"You have all that space, though. And didn't you say you wanted to meet other ace students beyond the ones in Xiao A?" Before college, Mei had been active on asexuality forums, something that constantly worried Xiaoyi and Xiaoyifu. Her online behavior could get her in trouble, especially with the lack of legal protections for the queer community in China. Rina had encouraged Mei to study overseas, hoping she'd find a safer space to explore and meet others. "At least compared to here, people are more open-minded," Rina adds.

"True," Mei concedes. "I tried more drugs there than I have my entire life! College really did open my mind."

"That is *not* what I meant." Rina's fairly certain Xiaoyi had spent a small fortune at the temple, praying her daughter would get into college. Now she probably spends that same fortune praying her daughter doesn't get kicked out. While Rina could never be as bold as Mei, she sort of admires her fearlessness. "Why is it that I only hear about the bad things you've done?"

Mei rolls her eyes. "Like they'll do anything besides give me a slap on the wrist. The Dictator doesn't understand." At Rina's confused look, she says, "That's what I call Ma now. She keeps trying to control my life."

"And you think stealing your dad's car will make her stop?"

"It's better than staying home, being bugged all day long to clean my room. Although, the Dictator said she was cutting my allowance back until I stop getting Cs." Mei blows her overlong bangs to the side.

Rina surveys Mei's messy room, colorful posters of anime characters plastered on the walls. Everything here exudes youthful carefreeness. One day, Mei will discover that punishment can certainly be worse than a slap on the wrist, but Rina hopes that isn't anytime soon. "Was it fun?" she asks.

This brings a grin to Mei's face. "It was awesome. Horsepower was lacking, but it's better than my scooter. Do you want to see the route I took?" She pushes her chair next to the bed and pulls up a map of Shanghai on her phone. The screen is cracked, and Rina has to angle her head to see. "I started at Gaoqiao and went all the way to Songjiang, then back. It usually takes an hour, but I did it in forty minutes. That's because everyone would tell you to take the S20, but I happen to know that this local road—" she taps a spot on the map "—has way less congestion."

"Does that apply during rush hour?" Rina tests her knowledge.

Mei scoffs. "Of course. If you know which local roads to take and don't change lanes like a pussy, you can always decrease your driving time." Despite the resentment Mei holds for her mom, she's inherited the same inability to sit still. She keeps shifting her posture, drumming her fingers on her knees. "This one time, I went all the way to Jiashan. The Dictator saw where I was and freaked out."

Rina studies her cousin, whose grin has become borderline maniacal. Either Rina can let Mei get into trouble all on her own, or she can enlist her help and monitor her. "Your dear Rina Jie might be able to get you out of the house more, but you'll have to swear yourself to silence."

Mei is dubious. Because of how often Xiaoyi talks up Rina as a successful career woman, Mei hasn't ever taken much interest in her. "Keep talking..." she says.

"My friend Lulu is getting married, and we need a driver to transport a very important package from her wedding."

"And you want me? I don't own a car. Why not ask Ba?"

"Xiaoyifu only likes taking pictures of his car. He doesn't actually drive it. We'll get you a car. That's not important. What we need is someone who knows the streets of Shanghai and can drive fast. And knows where the fewest cameras are."

"Fast? Cameras?" Mei's unplucked eyebrows rise with intrigue.

"I need your promise not to say a word of this to anyone."

"It sounds like you're up to something criminal." Mei props her arm against the back of her chair, smirking. "What would Dayi think?"

Her mom is lax on most things, but Rina's pretty sure she would disapprove of her bringing her young, impressionable cousin along on a criminal endeavor. "That wouldn't end well for either of us."

"I mean, I could use the rest of my break to help you out. But is that really the best use of my time? I could be watching anime…"

Mei is being difficult just because she can, but Rina knows how to play this game too.

"I guess you are a bit young." She gets up in the direction of the door, injecting regret into her voice. "I won't drag you into something so dangerous—"

She hears the squeak of wheels, then the sound of Mei's feet hitting the floor as she hops out of her chair. "Wait! I'm in."

Rina hides her triumph. The word *dangerous* has the same power over Mei as the term *value add* has over Rina. "Good. Meet us at Hotpot Palace next Friday at nine. I trust that you'll figure out how to leave the house without your mom knowing."

"Who's 'us'?"

"You'll see."

"Rina Jie, you're being very mysterious." Mei considers her. "Have you finally decided to be less boring?"

Boring is hardly an insult coming from Mei. Rina smiles placidly. "I'm trying harder for my favorite cousin."

"I'm your only cousin." By the time the One Child Policy was lifted, Xiaoyi thought herself too old and too tired to try for another child. It was probably for the best. She had her hands full with Mei anyway.

Rina pats her on the head. "I like your skepticism. You should wash your hair, by the way."

She leaves Mei to peacefully resume whatever sketchy stuff she was doing. Jane and Lulu might question the sensibility of a college student joining their crew, but Rina knows better than anyone that age isn't a determinant of skill.

In the hall, Xiaoyi ambushes her and forces her to stay for a bowl of yān dū xiān. Her aunt doesn't drink any herself, but sits across from Rina, watching her eagerly. "Rina, remember when you visited us after you arrived in China? You tried to cancel, and Xiaoyifu and I were so offended! Then you came to our house and asked to drink iced water! You were so *American*."

"Xiaoyi, we don't need to talk about that." Rina remembers her first year in China with plenty of embarrassment. She'd broken so many social rules. She'd been overwhelmed and not in the headspace to see anyone when she first arrived, so she told Xiaoyi she couldn't make it to her house. Her mom had called her the very next day, scolding her for being so rude to her aunt. Now, she knows better than to cancel any plans, and when she's thirsty, she drinks hot water instead.

Once she finishes slurping the salty, hot broth, flavored with ginger and ham, she folds her arms in front of her and says to her aunt, "Mei's going to shadow me every evening during her break. Pick up some practical skills. I'll put her to work."

"Oh, that's wonderful! You are such a good influence, Rina. I'm so happy you're close," she says gratefully.

If her residual anger at Luo Ren and work wasn't still simmering, Rina might've felt bad about deceiving her aunt. But this is probably only the first of many lies, and she'll have to get comfortable with that.

She lifts her soup bowl and drinks it clean.

13

5 months to the wedding

LULU

❖ ❖ ❖ ❖ ❖

THE SPECIAL TODAY at Hotpot Palace is rice cakes in the shape of bunnies. Lulu eyes the plump white forms on other people's tables. They actually look good, which is never the case with the specials. "Maybe we should order one," she says, but Jane sends the waiter off with a list of dishes for the table.

She turns to Lulu. "Did you say something?"

"No, it was nothing." The waiter was just here, and who knows if the others joining them even want rice cakes? Lulu regards the two empty seats between Rina and Jane. They had to move to a larger table to accommodate their new additions.

"Before the others arrive, I want to share some updates," Jane says. Rina is busy texting, and Jane clears her throat.

"Sorry."

Rina puts her phone down. When it buzzes again, Jane tosses a napkin over it. Lulu's been engaged in a lively group chat with her old Scarlet Beauty coworkers, but it's nothing compared to Rina's constant mobile activity.

"Anyway," Jane says, "I realized that besides Lulu, we need another insider at the wedding. Someone who has the trust of the best man." Jane emphasizes *best man* as she leans in, hands on the table. "Lulu will obviously be busy getting married, and I am taken, so..." She twists toward Rina. "The duty falls to you."

Rina freezes. "I'm not sure I get what you mean."

Even though Jane hadn't clued Lulu in beforehand, she catches on quickly. It'll be useful to have someone keep tabs on the man who'll be watching over the safe. But no matter how Jane spins it, Lulu knows Rina's going to have a problem with this. Lulu tries to spell it out gently for her. "She wants you to seduce Vic."

At that, Rina nearly tips her chair over crossing her arms in front of her body. "No. No way. I'll do anything else," she says. "I'll map out escape routes. I'll learn lockpicking. I'll set myself on fire as a distraction. Anything but this."

"It's tradition for the best man to guard the safe. We need a distraction for when we move it. And you two already have a relationship that we can leverage."

"A *relationship*?" Rina sputters. "That's really pushing it."

Lulu sips her water. Jane will have to do the convincing this time. She's not the one who has to live with Rina.

"Nobody else can do it but you," Jane drawls.

Rina shakes her head vehemently. "I'm not going to stoop this low."

"Are you really going to let your pride get in the way of the plan?"

"It's not my pride," Rina says haughtily. "It's a matter of *principle*."

Jane laughs. "The principle of saying no because you don't feel like it? Way to be a team player."

"You never have a problem saying no," Rina retorts. "With no justification, either."

"Lulu, what do you think?" Jane says, roping her in.

Rina stares at Lulu, only slightly dialing down the fieriness of her gaze. Personally, she does think they need an in with Vic.

She knows Rina hates him, but the depth of that hatred seems a bit extreme.

"Vic's not that bad," Lulu says. "I really like him."

"That's because you see the good in everyone. Look, there's Mei. Oh, and Michelangelo." Rina stands and waves over a short, surprisingly young girl with straight bangs. A well-dressed, older woman follows closely behind. Neither of them is what Lulu anticipated, but she trusts her friends and knows they would only have chosen the best people for the job. "Mei and Michelangelo, this is Lulu. The bride."

"Congratulations," Michelangelo says. "Marriage is a big step. Sharing a home, assets, secrets." She gives a small shudder. "Certainly something I never wanted to do."

"Me neither," Mei chimes in. "You're pretty," she notes before taking a seat. "Can I eat? I'm so hungry." She doesn't wait for a response and starts to remove a red chunk of beef from its plate, oblivious to Jane's glare.

"Rina, you've brought a child," Jane says, like this was a simple oversight.

Mei holds a fish ball in front of Rina's mouth. "Rina Jie, eat this. I know how much you like fish balls."

Rina accepts the fish ball into her bowl. "Trust me, Mei is a better driver than most adults."

"What do you know about driving?" Jane asks Mei.

"Enough to drive circles around you," Mei responds coolly.

Jane looks miffed she's not being afforded the respect due her. Lulu expects her to put Mei in her place, but she barrels forward. "Thanks all for coming to our inaugural gathering," she says to the group. "Today, we'll be doing a walk-through of the plan."

Lulu hands Jane the brochure. They move plates and silverware so she can unfold the map of Sun Island before them. Sauce stains the paper, creating big oily circles, but Jane ignores it, jabbing her finger in the center.

"In five months, our lovely Lulu will be getting married.

Out of all the luxury properties out there, her mother-in-law has chosen this fake island for reasons we don't quite get yet." Around them, the din of the restaurant persists, no risk of being overheard.

"It's because the staff is more flexible," Lulu explains. She's figured out that when Peng Ayi says "flexible," she means as long as she pays, they'll make changes to the property however she wants. This includes installing a floating platform on the lagoon for the ceremony and pruning the bushes to be in the shape of cranes. The grandness will surely appeal to the Zhus' wealthiest connections, and Lulu knows that's Peng Ayi's number one goal.

Jane nods in acknowledgment before continuing. "We're expecting five hundred guests, all bearing red envelopes stuffed with cash as wedding gifts. Five million yuan, if not more." Jane lets this sink in. After a moment, she smiles, all professional. "Now Rina's going to run us all through the schedule of events and everyone's expected role."

Rina gulps down water, then straightens her blazer like she's about to give a work presentation. "There will be three main events on the wedding day. The tea ceremony, the official ceremony, and the banquet. Wedding gifts will be collected in a safe at the beginning of the banquet, and as food is served, the safe will be moved elsewhere in the venue. We need to find out where it is, swap it for a counterfeit, and maneuver the real safe out of the venue without being seen. Get it into someone's car and transport it to a secure spot."

"Why not move the cash out first so we don't have to deal with the safe?" Mei asks.

"Time will be tight. And Vic—the best man—will be sticking close to it until after the first dance, which is when it'll go into storage and they'll start serving food. We'd also need a lot of hands to extract the cash, and it's unlikely that all of us are going to be able to be in the same place without our absence looking suspicious. We'll remove the safe, get Lulu out of the country, and the rest of us lie low until it all blows over."

"Out of the country?" Michelangelo asks Lulu. "Where are you thinking?"

"Oh," Lulu says, surprised to be in the spotlight. There is a whole world spread out in front of her, and it still feels surreal that she'll get to explore it.

"Make sure to choose somewhere with relaxed visa requirements," Michelangelo advises. "Just in case you need to stay longer than anticipated."

Jane taps the map. "We can chat travel plans later."

"Sorry," Lulu says.

"Rina, Lulu, and I will have responsibilities as part of the bridal party. We've got to pose for pictures, be front and center for the ceremony, and participate in the door games. Mei and Michelangelo, you'll be less visible. You'll get the money into the getaway car. Nobody will recognize Mei, and Michelangelo, we'll get you a disguise."

"Ooh, I want a disguise! Can I be an heiress? Or a queen?" Mei bounces in her seat.

"What does the safe look like?" Michelangelo asks.

"Uh…" Jane hesitates. "We don't know yet."

The group goes silent.

Michelangelo taps her fingernails against her water glass, an impatient *click click click*. "You don't know what it looks like, and you're asking me to make a counterfeit. What shall I do then, get it designed based on my imagination?"

Lulu's about to reassure Michelangelo that they'll work it all out. She's seen Jane haggle the upholstered sofa now in Lulu and Rina's living room down from an exorbitant price, witnessed Rina plan a packed day in Hangzhou for them down to the minute and execute it flawlessly. They have what it takes.

Jane cuts in as Lulu's about to speak. "There's no need to get snippy. You'll see the safe when it's ready. Anyway, moving on.

I'm taking care of tech. Surveillance is our biggest threat. Everything we do will be monitored, that's for damn sure. Luckily, I'm married to a man who works at one of the leading security companies in the nation, and I'm betting he'll tell me how to disable a security system." Lulu tries not to react to this blatant lie. Jane isn't exactly a sweet talker, and her relationship with Zihao is lukewarm at best. But she sounds confident, and if it doesn't work, they'll find another way.

"What's Rina Jie doing?" Mei inquires.

"Why, I'm glad you asked!" Jane exclaims, her eyebrows doing a little wiggle. "She's going to be busy—"

"Busy drawing the blueprint," Rina finishes.

"Uh-huh," Jane says, smirking.

They're caught in a staring contest, so Lulu decides to pick up where they left off, not wanting their back-and-forth to derail the conversation. She offers Mei a smile. "So you're the one driving the safe away from the venue. You've got the most important job of all."

Jane resumes her spiel. "Zhongxin Bridge is the only way across. Transport aside, Mei also will help with communication on-site. Notes, keys, gossip. We need someone with her ear to the ground. Nobody will be texting anything besides emojis. Phone calls are banned. You never know who's listening."

Mei considers this. "If I'm going to drive, I'll need a car. Where am I going to get one of those?"

"Michelangelo, don't you have a car?" Jane asks.

"It's a Mini Cooper."

"Oh. Yeah, that won't work. They'll know it's you right away." Jane hums. "My husband has a car, and he's coming to the wedding. I'll pass you the keys."

"Isn't that going to make Zihao a suspect?" Rina asks.

"Yeah, so?" There's a hard glint in Jane's eye.

"That's ice cold." Mei chomps a piece of spam. "Why's he your husband if you hate him so much?"

Jane gives Mei a condescending smile. "There are always reasons besides love to get married. Why do you think we're all here?"

Lulu watches the chilis dance in the broth, feeling exposed. Even if Lulu went on those dates with Harv at the behest of her mom and agreed to marry him, Jane's comment makes her sound coldhearted and mean, like Lulu is using him. The thought unsettles her. But it's not like he'll miss the money, and there will be a whole throng of women lining up to marry him.

"He doesn't have to get in trouble if you get another license plate on the car," Michelangelo says. "The cameras identify cars based on plate, after all."

Jane shakes her head. "A different license plate? That will cost way too much, and a fake one would get police on us right away."

The government keeps tabs on every single plate that gets sold. There's a limited number, driving up prices. Lulu's parents could never afford one. Any time she visits home, her dad has to arrange to borrow a neighbor's car to pick her up at the train station.

"Steal one. A swap during the wedding. It should be easy enough with a screwdriver. In fact, if this wedding is filled with rich people, they'll have vanity plates. You know, ones that give you special privileges." They've all heard about plates like those. Military plates that allow someone to drive through red lights and in bus lanes without retribution. Harv's dad recently got outbid while trying to buy one.

"Wow," Jane says. "You came up with that idea way too easily."

Michelangelo meticulously adds four rings of green onion to her dipping sauce. "I like to keep things simple."

"I can do that!" Mei seems ecstatic at the prospect of doing something illegal. "I can plot out routes, too. I just need a practice car."

"Xiǎo yātou," Jane says, and Mei's eyes narrow at being called *little girl*. "Slow down. Let's start with you plotting out those routes, then we can discuss whether you deserve to be in front of the wheel."

Mei sneers. "What is this, an internship? Also, what is *she* doing?" She points her chopsticks at Lulu in a way that makes Lulu flush.

"Lulu is keeping an eye on our biggest threat." Jane pauses theatrically before she says, "Peng Ayi. For those of you who are new, Peng Ayi is an absolute snake of a woman. If you gain a pound, she'll say something about how *healthy* you look. You think I'm a bitch? Peng Ayi will slap you in the face and say it's because there was a mosquito on your cheek."

"That's a tad overdramatic," Rina says.

Lulu would disagree. Of everyone, Peng Ayi will be the quickest to suspect something is wrong. Plus she's keeping an iron grip over the wedding planning. The other day, Lulu had been daydreaming about all the places she could go after the wedding and unthinkingly agreed to having place cards on cream-colored paper.

"Lulu ah, you are useless if you are distracted," Peng Ayi had said, and Lulu realized the question had been a test. "Cream! That will clash with the ivory invitations!"

Since then, Lulu's been much more vigilant. One wrong move, and Peng Ayi will catch on.

"Besides managing Peng Ayi, Lulu and Rina will visit Sun Island in the coming weeks under the guise of wedding planning, enough so that we can draw up a blueprint of the place and identify security blind spots. We all need to be familiar with the layout if we're going to transport the goods out in the most covert way possible."

"So…she's just doing what she already would've done," Mei mutters. "Guess it pays to be the bride. Literally."

"Mei!" Rina says sharply, but the words are out there now.

Mei makes a good point. Everyone else has a job, but Lulu's is to sit pretty and pretend everything is normal. She wants to contribute in a more meaningful way, so that when they get the money, she'll feel like she's *earned* it. Keeping an eye on Peng Ayi is a passive task, and Rina will probably take over most of the blueprint drawing.

"What about our backup plan?" Lulu asks. "I can work on that. In case anything goes wrong."

"Lulu, you don't have to prove anything to us." Rina's voice is gentle. "You're the one getting married, and you're leaving afterward. Plan for that instead."

Even after the conversation's moved on, Lulu notices Rina glancing concernedly in her direction. When they're alone, Rina will probably advise her not to let Mei's comment get to her. Sometimes, she is too attentive, and Lulu wishes she knew how to tell Rina to worry less about her without pushing her away.

But sitting here, surrounded by these women, Lulu is hit by a sudden surge of gratitude. Despite any misgivings, despite the risks, they all showed up, and she feels like she has to acknowledge that somehow. She stands. "I'm glad we're all here," she says before Jane can end the meeting. "All of us—we each bring something special to this. And that's why it's going to work."

Jane begins clapping. "You tell them, Lulu."

Part 2:

THE PLAN

14

4 months to the wedding

RINA

A FEW WEEKS LATER, Rina gets off the subway at the People's Park stop with a dread that only multiplies as she heads toward the park, joining crowds of elderly people moving in the same direction. Things have been so busy. There's work, but she's also been spending time with Mei on a regular basis, familiarizing her with the wedding schedule and providing feedback on the driving routes she's mapped out. If she'd had more time, she would've convinced her mom to meet somewhere else.

Rina spots her at the edge, a cup of coffee in either hand and a contemplative look on her face as she takes in the pandemonium.

When she reaches her, her mom silently passes over one of the cups. It's from a café that sources the same beans she used to buy in California. After she returned to Shanghai, Rina forced herself to become a habitual tea drinker to stop the memories of home that flooded whenever she smelled coffee. But today, she gratefully wraps her hands around the warm drink. Its aroma reminds her of a small house in the San Francisco suburbs, with a backyard she could run around in and plates of Bisquick pancakes doused with syrup. Nowadays, she rarely has time for breakfast, and the coffee machines at work are broken half the time anyway.

"Thanks. How are you feeling today?" She always starts with that question. Even as she waits for an answer, her eyes rove over her mom for signs of tiredness, new wrinkles, a hint that she's sick. She can't help it. Because of all her grinding toward that promotion, she hasn't seen her mom in person since shortly after Lulu's engagement.

Her mom waves her off. "Fine, just like for the past nine years. Let's walk."

They proceed toward the center of the park, leaving their safe observation post to stroll down the rows of laminated sheets, as grandparents clutch their grandchildren's profiles in their hands.

The Shanghai Marriage Market is notoriously popular among the elderly, who have nothing better to do than hawk their unaware granddaughters and grandsons in a desperate maneuver to see their great-grandkids before they die. It's like a farmer's market where all the fruit is rotten. Years of accomplishments distilled to lines on a single sheet of paper. Everyone knows the marriage market is not the place to actually find a suitable match, but apparently this fact hasn't deterred them.

An elderly lady comes up to her. "Méinǚ are you here for a match? I have a grandson who is single! He works at an investment firm right now and is 180 centimeters tall! Very handsome."

This brings Rina's mom to life. "Really? My daughter here is single. She's thirty-two and has a very good job at a consulting firm."

The smile immediately drops from the woman's face. "I think we better end our conversation here," she says with an awkward laugh. "My grandson is too young for her." She backs away, and Rina's mom gives her a look, like *see?*

"Did you just bring me here to make me feel bad about myself?" Rina asks. She knows that if she'd told her mom about the failed promotion, her mom wouldn't have subjected her to this. But despite the texts they've exchanged, Rina's held back from sharing this news. She's embarrassed to admit everyone else was right, that she pushed and pushed and still failed.

"This is your reality." Her mom gestures to their surroundings. "You know, I bet some of these folks would be interested if I told them you're twenty-five."

"Ma, that's a seven-year difference."

"You can explain that after you're married."

"I'm not going to lie to a guy until I get married!"

"Why not? He should love you for your personality, not your age."

"He won't love me because I'm a *liar*."

This back-and-forth is just her mom's way of warming up for the question she asks every so often. "Have you given any more thought to going back to the States?"

Rina focuses straight ahead, though her grip on her coffee tightens. "As long as you're here, I have no plans of going back." It saddens her to say it, but it's a truth she accepted a long time ago.

"Even if you don't get that promotion you were telling me about?" The wound is still fresh, and her mom's sharp eyes don't miss the falter in Rina's step. "You didn't get it. I know this is not what you want to hear, but this is the result you should have expected. Do you think your manager believes in equality? You are a woman, so he sees you as a risk. This isn't America, Rina. There are no special efforts to hire or promote women."

Rina stops and faces her mom. "Can we not talk about this?" She knows she disappointed her when she followed her parents back to Shanghai immediately after college. They had gotten married young in China, and Miranda had been pressured by her mother-in-law to quit her job and have Rina. They'd immigrated to the US so her dad could take a better job. Her mom, too busy dealing with a small daughter and trying to learn English, never worked again. But Miranda's never forgotten the women she met who were driven more by career than marriage. She wants Rina to have the opportunity she didn't.

"I don't want to be one of these people," her mom says, tucking a loose strand of hair behind Rina's ear. "I don't want to have to brag about how you studied overseas, how you have a Shanghai hùkǒu. Because you are more than those things, but in China, those are the qualities that people will use to evaluate you. Companies here follow very different rules than American ones. You are working five times as hard. Aren't you tired?"

"I'm not," Rina says, but it sounds weak to her own ears.

Her mom gazes at the bustle around them. "I can guarantee that most of the men advertised here can barely stomach a wife who is more successful than them."

"That's why I'm not dating yet. I'll find someone eventually. It'll just take time." Rina knows it'll be difficult to find a man who understands the tensions between her Chinese and American identities, but she doesn't have time to worry about that these days.

"Even if you freeze your eggs, someone's got to fertilize them, Rina. I read an article the other day that San Francisco is one of the places where people get married the latest. Men there would probably be more open to starting families later. It's ideal for you."

Her mom reads more news about America than she ever did while living there. In San Francisco, she clung to the weekly issues of *The China Daily*, bootlegged DVDs of *My Fair Princess*. When they got their first desktop computer, her mom spent hours scrolling through endless blocks of Chinese text on *Wenxuecity*.

"What's ideal is staying near you," Rina says, starting to walk again.

Her mom matches her pace. "I'm old now, and China's always

been where I saw myself spending my old age. But it doesn't have to be your home. At least, not at this particular point in time. I don't want you so caught up in achieving things at work that you forget to reflect on what actually makes you happy." Rina's mom sips from her coffee. They've done two laps around the park already.

Before Rina can respond, there's a surge in one direction, and they are swept along in the current of excitedly babbling grandmas.

"So handsome! So tall, too! Studied at Stanford!"

Rina and her mom dodge the flow and end up deposited on the edge of a large crowd. Apparently everyone is attempting to get closer to one man. Rina feels a brief flash of pity for the grandson of the person who thought it would be a good idea to bring him in person.

"I have a daughter you would love! She modeled for a while. Here's a picture!"

"Xiǎohuǒzi!" another woman calls to get the guy's attention. "How about my daughter? She's very smart! She's getting her master's in Machine Learning right now."

"Why don't you all get in line?"

Rina recognizes that voice instantly. It burrows under her skin, making her whole body feel itchy. "Time to leave," she says to her mom, as the people around her actually begin to form a *line*. The crowd now organized, she spots Vic, who happens to be looking right in her direction. Fuck.

He doesn't even hesitate before making his way over. "Of all the places I would expect you to be, this was not one of them," he says with a shit-eating grin.

"Can't say the same." Seeing him brings Jane's proposal front of mind. She's been wrestling with the idea for the past month. She really is their best option for distracting Vic, but every time she considers asking Lulu for his contact information, she's found a reason to put it off.

"You wound me. I'm here to entertain my grandma." Vic steps aside, revealing a small gray-haired woman. Although she's similar to the mahjong grannies in size and dress, she isn't familiar. "Nainai, this is Zhou Rina."

Rina reins in her hostility to say "Nainai hǎo." It feels like déjà vu. It's almost as if Vic knows more octogenarians than women his age.

"Ah, are you looking for a match here, too? How do you know my grandson?"

Rina quickly shakes her head before replying in Shanghainese, "No, no, my mom and I are just here…for a stroll. Vic and I were classmates in college."

Her mom introduces herself. "You have a very handsome grandson, Nainai."

"Yes, he is my pride." Vic's grandma is tiny next to him, but her smile is as charming as his.

"So is my daughter." The two of them begin chatting about recently opened restaurants and new property development.

Despite the line of elderly women trying to corral Vic, he turns his back to them, coercing Rina into conversation. "If you wanted a date so badly, you could've just let me know."

Rina glares at him. "I'd rather chew off my own leg." Lulu's voice is in her head now, promising Vic isn't so bad. She nudges it away.

"Rina, ah," her mom says, her cajoling tone immediately putting Rina on alert. "Nainai and I were talking. You said you're visiting Sun Island on Sunday. That's far. Vic will drive you. Just give him your WeChat ID, and you can coordinate."

Rina's jaw drops. How did her mom manage to come to this arrangement in a matter of minutes? "I was going to call a car."

Her mom tsks. "No need to waste money when there's someone offering to take you."

"I insist," Vic says, an utter gentleman. "I was already planning to drop by and speak with the staff so they make sure to take good care of Harv."

Rina knows this is her chance. Her mom and Vic's grandma have done the hard work for her, and all she needs to do now is accept. "Okay." She'll spend time with Vic so she can find out where the safe will be stored and be the distraction they need her to be. She must do it for the plan.

Vic's grandma pats his arm. "It's good for you to spend time with others your age. I keep telling him he should visit me less, but he won't stay away."

"I can't help it if you're more fun than everyone else." Vic's eyes crinkle at the corners as he smiles down at his grandma like she's the center of his universe. It makes Rina feel funny. She doesn't want to see this Vic, doting on his grandma and wearing a fuzzy cardigan.

"Well…" Rina observes the anxious line of aunties and grandmas waiting for a moment with Vic. "I suppose I'll see you later."

"Wait," he says, holding up his phone. "Let me scan you."

Reluctantly, Rina lets him add her on WeChat. "Would you look at that." Vic waves his phone at her. "We're friends now."

"Shuaige, add me too! I have a much cuter daughter." A woman in her fifties thrusts her phone in Vic's face.

"That boy is handsome," Rina's mom comments as they walk away.

"You and the rest of China seem to think so," Rina says, gesturing at the throng they're leaving behind. "He's insufferable."

"I thought the same thing about your dad." There's a spark in her eyes that Rina does not like.

15

4 months to the wedding

JANE

THE CLINIC IS FANCY. No peeling medical chairs with crinkly paper that barely disguises unsanitary surfaces. The cushioned white armchair has a massage function. Jane's looked forward to this moment since she booked the appointment months ago, but now that it's here, she's nervous. Maybe the doctor will tell her she's beyond saving, even if she does have the money for it.

"Tian Juyi?" the doctor asks from the doorway, eyes on his clipboard, Rolex peeking out from under his sleeve.

"That's me," Jane says.

He lowers himself into a rolling chair and crosses one leg over the other. Dr. Yu is a very average-looking, middle-aged man, a stark contrast to the beautiful women working the front office. And that makes Jane feel more comfortable.

"Let's chat about what you're looking to get out of your procedure," he says. "What is it about your appearance you're hoping to change?"

She pulls up a picture of herself, one she's fiddled with for hours on Meitu, reshaping her jaw and minimizing her fore-head. "Anything that makes me look as close to this as possible. I'm thinking facial contouring, eyelid lift, some kind of rhino-plasty? I know I have features that are far from the beauty stan-dard. I want to make myself...easier to look at."

Dr. Yu makes a *hmm* noise as he studies her phone. "You came prepared."

"I've been thinking about this all my life." She'd once asked her mom if it was true, that she wasn't pretty. In her heart, she'd wanted to be gathered into her arms and told everyone was wrong, that Jane was beautiful. But her mom had merely responded, "People will always say things like that to you. Get used to it." This was one way she wouldn't have to.

"Let me ask you a more general question." Dr. Yu adjusts his thick-framed glasses. "How would you like to feel after this procedure?"

"Happy. Proud." Jane swallows. "Beautiful."

"I can help you with the *beautiful* part." Dr. Yu scribbles some-thing in his notepad. "However, it will take multiple procedures and require months of healing, and it will only transform you on the surface. I find that many of my patients who believe plas-tic surgery is the key to a happy life, that it will help them keep husbands or get jobs, end up disappointed. It's important to be realistic about what you're hoping to achieve, and if your main goal is emotional satisfaction, a therapist may be a better fit."

"I don't need a therapist. Can you help me with what I want or not?" Jane says. She did not come here to be psychoanalyzed.

Dr. Yu gives her a long look. "I can."

"Great. Then let's do it."

At the end of the appointment, his cold fingers skim her face impersonally as he indicates where to expect swelling and bruis-ing. And then it's over.

As she reviews the contract for the procedure in the waiting room, her mind drifts back to a comment Dr. Yu made that she may not be satisfied, that she may have to come back for more work, that this will not change her into someone else—

Jane brushes her uncertainty aside and picks up the pen. The deposit will drain most of the checking account she's kept separately from Zihao's for a rainy day. She could've used it to buy a new outfit, but this is a worthy sacrifice. The receptionist hands her a business card with her appointment date six months from now and asks who's going to accompany her on the day of the surgery.

She gives them Rina's phone number because Lulu will probably be off drinking from a coconut somewhere. She'll confirm with Rina next time they see each other, and Rina will say yes, but not before asking Jane if she's *sure*. She'll never understand how desperately Jane needs this. But in the end Rina will still take time off from work to be there for Jane, and it'll be nice to wake up from surgery to a friend.

On the train ride home, Jane forces herself to focus on the challenges ahead. She still hasn't gotten details on how the security system at Sun Island operates, and it's a very crucial part of their plan that they disable it. Maybe they could just break the cameras. Maybe it isn't too late for her to pick up hacking.

Or maybe she could just talk to her damn husband.

Jane groans. She withdraws the appointment card from her bag and stares down at the date written across it. Only she has the power to make this happen.

Back at home, she shoves the card into her wallet, which she tosses into her handbag. Zihao returns shortly after, and she meets him in the doorway. "Welcome home!" she sings.

Zihao is in the middle of taking her discarded shoes and carefully putting them on the shoe rack next to his newly polished loafers. He raises his head, brow wrinkling. "Are you alright? You sound funny."

Jane can work with this. "I got caught up watching a karaoke competition. That's why I haven't made dinner. Do you want to order takeout?"

"Let me look at Dazhong Dianping, see if there are any deals."

"Okay," Jane replies, refraining from rolling her eyes. Zihao has spent half an hour debating between two brands of rice at the store; he's probably going to look through all hundred neighborhood food joints to find something that hits his standards of price and quality. They're not going to be eating until late.

She follows him to the living room, where he leans against the wall, scrolling through options. "This dumpling place is doing twenty dumplings for ten yuan. Oh, but wait, this place is doing thirty for fifteen and they've got a shrimp filling…"

"How was work?" she asks, dropping onto the couch.

Zihao looks up. "*Work? My* work?"

His reaction is no surprise to Jane. She had resolved never to bring up his job after having to hear about it so often from his parents, who used every opportunity to flaunt his qualifications during the marriage negotiation, from his gāokǎo score to all the offers he received after graduating from Fudan, like Jane had struck gold. In China, men like Zihao are dubbed phoenixes, geniuses who burst free from their humble rural upbringings to advance their great nation.

But today, the circumstances call for it. She swings her legs up, narrowly missing the tea set on the coffee table. "Yeah. Didn't you mention some government contract a few weeks back? That's right, I've been listening. You didn't think I was, did you?" *Government contract* are the only two words she remembers from that conversation, but bullshitting has always been one of her superpowers. Jane widens her eyes to appear interested and approachable. It feels unnatural.

"It's good, I suppose," Zihao says, but he's stiff, like there's more he wants to say.

"I'm your wife, aren't I? You can tell me anything."

Zihao is regarding her like she's found day parking in the city. "It's confidential."

She pats the couch forcefully. "Come sit next to me."

Gingerly, Zihao sits beside her. He smells like public transportation and the mints he likes to pop into his mouth to stay awake during work.

Jane scoots closer. "I won't tell a soul," she promises, trying to sound genuine.

He sighs, and something in him gives way. "They want us to collaborate more with our Shenzhen branch."

Her ears perk up. "Does that mean you'll be traveling to Shenzhen more often?" The company will probably put him up somewhere nice. Maybe he'll let her come. She's had her eye on some navy sateen pillowcases at a bedding store in Shenzhen, and picking up in person would save her the shipping fee.

Zihao nods, but his jaw is clenched. Jane's cohabited with him long enough to read this body language. She considers leaving him to sulk when he leans forward, elbows on his knees. "What you said a while back, about privacy. It's something I've been thinking myself. Before, the money was enough for me to look the other way. Now, I'm not sure…" He runs a hand through his hair.

Now is really not the time for Zihao to begin philosophizing over the moral ambiguity of his job. If he quits, Jane will lose her only lead. She doesn't even dare search *how to fool a security camera*. These days, there's no telling what the Ministry is keeping tabs on. Whatever information she gets will have to come straight from Zihao.

"I don't think you need to cast the role of surveillance as one that's all negative. The other day, my virtual wallet wasn't working and all I needed to do was scan my face to get my coffee."

Zihao scratches at the stubble on his chin, a sign that he's been rushing through shaving. He must be stressed. "I don't know, things are moving pretty quickly. We're working on an

AI-powered update that brings error down to insignificant levels. Leadership is breathing down our necks to ship it, especially because they have coverage goals they're trying to hit."

This is concerning. Jane needs to find the flaws in these systems, and Zihao's just giving her more reasons not to mess with them. She channels Rina, her care when it comes to asking sensitive questions. "Aren't you afraid that moving too quickly might leave some of your technology vulnerable?"

"That's one of my concerns, actually. Everyone's so focused on this new update that they've drawn away resources from maintaining our legacy systems. That leaves our customers vulnerable to attacks."

"Like hacker attacks?" Jane asks faintly.

Zihao's lips twitch, like he's trying not to laugh. "Not even that. It could be as simple as purchasing a jammer to disrupt frequencies or cutting the right wires."

Jane files this knowledge away, though she has no idea what a jammer is, or how to cut wires. Would that require special scissors?

"You should feel powerful," she declares, buttering him up. "You're the orchestrator of all this."

Zihao's brows draw together. "I just want to be paid."

He always sees the world in such transactional terms. Do a job, get paid. Marry this woman his parents insist on, live in Shanghai for free.

Jane assumes the conversation is over and Zihao will skulk off to read industry textbooks, but then he says, "What about you? How was your day?"

Jane's mind flashes back to signing the agreement for her plastic surgery. Dr. Yu's cool, probing fingers.

"I got fitted for my bridesmaid dress," she says. He doesn't need to know the fitting was yesterday. "Pink isn't usually my color, but I think it'll work this time. Oh, and I mended some of your shirts."

"I think you look nice in any color." He touches her shoulder and smiles.

This throws Jane off. Did he actually just compliment her? Before she can respond, Zihao says, "You could buy a few new shirts for me. I'll give you the money. You're right. My clothes are getting a bit worn."

"Really?" She's wanted to replace Zihao's wardrobe forever. This is a major concession on his part. "I'll look up some options right now!" Zihao has no idea how much his style is about to advance.

"Don't go overboard," Zihao warns, but Jane barely hears him as she pulls up all the menswear sites she knows of. "I'm going to order the dumplings and get some work done." He rises from the couch but hovers for a moment. "This was nice."

"Yes," Jane agrees, adding a polo in a fantastic olive color to her cart. "Yes, it was."

16

4 months to the wedding

LULU

LULU IS DEEP in a travel blog about the benefits of being an expat in Thailand when Rina gets home. She tosses her tablet aside. This is an exercise she prefers to do in private, something she needs to decide on her own. This heist has given her hope, but it all still feels like a story that lives only in her head.

Rina drops down beside her with a huff. "I just spent all morning running errands because work sucks away all my time during the week. I can't even complain about it to my mom because she just asks me why I don't get a job back in the States."

Lulu hums sympathetically, even though she agrees with Rina's mom. She remembers back when they'd first connected on an online language app a decade ago, how much Rina loved her internships in San Francisco. Even if Lulu's English wasn't the greatest then, she could still hear the enthusiasm in Rina's voice. But ever since Miranda got sick, Rina's lived in constant fear it could happen again, that she may not make it in time. Lulu wonders what it must be like to have that kind of relationship, one of love with no strings attached. She can't remember the last time her mom contacted her without making some kind of request.

Rina reaches for Lulu's tablet. "Ooh, this is a nice beach. Is this where your honeymoon is supposed to be?"

"It's not. I got distracted," Lulu admits. All of Harv's specifications—ocean view, private pool and balcony, twenty-four-hour butler service, and at least two hundred square feet of living space—made her head spin.

Rina checks out the article. "Thailand. Is this where you want to go after the heist? It's a good choice. Did you choose it because of Wu Laoshi?"

Lulu is touched. "You remember what I told you about Wu Laoshi?"

"How could I forget? That photo she gave you is still right above your bed," Rina says, still scrolling on the tablet.

Even now, Lulu can conjure up an image of Wu Laoshi. Her hair cut close to her chin, glasses with red frames, a patient smile as she helped Lulu with her English pronunciations. Of all the teachers at the rural school she attended, Wu Laoshi had actually cared about her students. She'd had a giant photograph in her classroom of Thailand's aquamarine water and sand white as a sheet of paper. It'd taken her years to save for the trip.

I hope your dreams take you far, her teacher had said when she gifted the photo to Lulu at the end of the school year.

The past few years, Lulu's financial situation has limited her ability to explore what that means, but sometimes, she wonders if it's more than that, if there's something inside her holding her back too.

"Sometimes, I want to dive into that photo and onto that island," she says. It's not just the place, but the way Wu Laoshi looked as she described it, a joyful memory that nobody could take away. Lulu longs for something of her own, for that perfect play of the light upon the waves. "I still remember its name. Ko Lipe."

"Then that's where we're sending you," Rina says simply.

Lulu picks at her nails. "My mom always manages to sniff out any unspent cent."

"You won't be withholding money. You'll give them the amount they need to fix up the house and get their lives together. Honestly, this might be what your family needs to learn how to fend for themselves."

"You're probably right." She's not sure she believes it, but she's also not in the mood to be convinced. Lulu shifts the conversation to a different topic. "By the way, did you and Jane see the wedding schedule I sent you?"

"Yep, thanks for sending it along. Jane and I are going to meet to discuss it."

"Maybe I should be there too, in case you need more details."

"No, we're good—" Rina's cut off by Lulu's phone. It's Harv.

Lulu scrambles to pick up. "Wéi, Lulu?" Harv says on the other end. "The invitations are here, and Ma wants to address them. She's sent the car for you."

"Don't explain all that! Just tell her that it's *urgent*," Lulu hears Peng Ayi command in the background.

There's silence on the other end, and when Harv speaks again, it sounds like he's in another room. "Sorry, Ma was being loud. I was going to handle the invitations with her and leave you out of it, but all this work has suddenly come up, and—" There's a pause. "I could really use some extra help, that's all."

"I'll be right there."

Lulu gets up from the couch. She knows she has to keep Peng Ayi happy. Hopefully the car isn't already here, or else she'll show up to almond cookies, tea, and a lecture about punctuality. "I have to go help with invitations," she tells Rina, heading toward her room.

"The safe was supposed to arrive last week, wasn't it?" Rina calls as Lulu looks for something appropriate to wear. She can't go over there in her sweatpants and oversize T-shirt.

"That's what Harv said."

"Make sure to ask to see it. Michelangelo needs at least two months to create the counterfeit. We can't delay any longer."

"Okay." After Mei's comments at their first dinner, Lulu's committed to playing her small part flawlessly. "Do you want to call a cab to Hotpot Palace together later? I should be back in time." At least, she hopes so.

"No, you should head straight there." There's a weird note in Rina's voice that she doesn't have time to puzzle through. "I have something beforehand that might run late."

Twenty minutes later, Harv greets her at the doorway of the Zhus' luxury apartment in Century Park. "Sorry for calling you over here so abruptly. Have you eaten? I can ask Ling to prepare a snack."

"I'm okay." Lulu smooths the skirt of her chiffon dress. "You sounded stressed on the phone."

Harv gives her a weak smile. "Ba's handed me a lot of paperwork for our new property, and it's an immense responsibility. I just wish the timing were better. Honestly…" He glances over his shoulder and lowers his voice. "I'm not sure if we should do the wedding this year anymore."

There's a swooping sensation in Lulu's stomach. Months ago, she would've rejoiced over this hesitation, but not now, when they need this wedding and the money it'll bring them. "Wouldn't you lose the deposits if you postponed?" she asks shakily.

"A few hundred thousand, probably," Harv says with a shrug. "But it might be worth it."

Lulu fails to see a scenario where losing that much money could ever be "worth it," but she tries another angle. "I… I want to get married this year."

Harv looks taken aback. "You do?"

"Of course!" Lulu modulates her tone. "I want us to start our life together as soon as possible."

Harv's surprise melts into pleasure. "I thought all of this was moving too fast for you. I'm...really happy to hear that."

Lulu's smile feels strained. She has to try harder to convince Harv she wants this wedding, she realizes. Otherwise, there's a risk he'll get too overwhelmed and postpone things. "Let's get these invitations sorted."

That's how she finds herself sitting beside Peng Ayi, her dress sticking to her back as they painstakingly seal invitations into their red envelopes, gilded in gold with the double symbol for *xǐ*, happiness. Harv is farther down the twelve-person table, working on his laptop. He addressed five invitations before announcing he had more pressing work to do, and Peng Ayi accepted it without question. Apparently, his mere presence is enough for his mother.

"Āiyá, your handwriting is not good!" Peng Ayi shouts at Lulu. "Didn't your mother ever send you to school for calligraphy? Here, let me demonstrate." Next to her, Peng Ayi draws her pen in elegant strokes along an envelope. "Our Harv has beautiful handwriting." She motions toward the scrolls of calligraphy on their walls. "Harv, you will have to teach your wife a good deal after you're married! She'll be starting from scratch."

Harv shuts his laptop. "Ma, calligraphy isn't very practical. Ba said himself that I should've spent that time learning about taxes instead. Also, you'll probably finish the invitations faster if you don't lecture Lulu so much."

Peng Ayi flutters a hand dismissively. "If I'm so distracting, go to your office!"

Lulu catches Harv's eye, hoping he'll take her with him, but he just squeezes her shoulder on his way out.

Peng Ayi adds another envelope to her growing stack and continues her sermon. "After you get married, your job will be to uphold the household, to take care of Harv and your future children, and us. Even if Harv looks elsewhere for happiness, you must stay by his side and observe quietly."

Lulu can't believe Peng Ayi is hinting that Harv will cheat before they're even married. It's a relief she isn't actually marrying into this family, where she'd be expected to silently accept these transgressions. "Yes, Peng Ayi," Lulu mutters.

"It took me a long time to gain the respect of this household, and it will take you longer. Living in that awful place in the countryside, you must not have gotten a proper education."

"H-how do you know where I'm from?" Lulu's mom always told her to be vague about her origins. City dwellers are masters of a different sort of math: one where they can calculate your worth through a combination of where you live, what you do, and where your family's from. The less they knew about Lulu's family, the better, especially now that she needs this wedding to happen.

Peng Ayi sets her pen down, stacking the invitations neatly before casting her gaze on Lulu. "I can't have my son marrying just anyone. It was strange to me why he insisted on you when there were many better options. Of course I looked into your family. Such short lifespans, and a no-good brother. With your looks, you probably would have commanded a very good bride price with some peasant man. When I met you, I realized why we could accept you into our family." Lulu is almost afraid to breathe. "You're obedient, soft. And the benefit of coming from a background like yours is that you'll be grateful for everything you get."

Lulu was surprised Harv's parents didn't attempt to block his marriage to a girl who wasn't rich or from some notable family. In fact, she'd almost hoped they would. Here, then, is the truth: she was chosen because she is weak.

She's been digging the nib of her pen onto the same place for too long. A pool of ink bleeds through, staining her fingers. As Peng Ayi returns to her task, Lulu forces herself to relax her grip and musters up an enthusiasm she didn't know she had. "Ayi, didn't you say the safe would be delivered today? I would *love* to see the design. Didn't you say the glass was hand-blown in Qixian?"

"Ah, of course! We haven't even opened it yet." Luckily, Peng Ayi never passes up an opportunity to show off. "Ling, bring it here."

The Zhus' maid, Ling, wheels a giant box into the room. Peng Ayi jumps up, abandoning her invitation list on the table. "Our custom-made safe! Ling, grab some scissors. No, not those—are you stupid? We use those in the kitchen! Get the ones we have for opening packages."

Once the right scissors are in hand, she cuts through the tape. Lulu and Ling lift out the safe, Peng Ayi screeching at them to be careful, and position it on the dining table.

The safe is made of clear glass with a red chrome top engraved with a gold double *Xĭ*. Below the surface of the glass are frosted images out of a Chinese watercolor, depicting swirls of clouds and cranes in flight.

"Beautiful," croons Peng Ayi as she circles the safe. "The glass exterior was my idea. It will give our guests a little pressure."

"It's lovely," Lulu marvels. "But it's so see-through. Is that safe?" She's used to big metal boxes with no way to see inside, not this work of art.

"What, do you expect someone to steal it? Don't touch the surface, you'll leave fingerprints."

Lulu withdraws her hand nervously, then remembers Peng Ayi just doesn't want smudges on the glass. Of course nobody would dare steal from the illustrious Zhus, whose wealth and guānxi protect them from all the world's ills. They'll just have to stuff the fake safe with red envelopes too.

Her reaction strengthens Lulu's confidence. "Can I take a photo? The design is so lovely, I have to share it with my friends."

She's snapped one photo to send to Michelangelo when Peng

Ayi says, "That's enough. Don't give all our secrets away. Ling, put this in my husband's office." She places the key to Harv's father's office in Ling's hand.

Lulu's eyes follow Ling and the safe as they disappear into Zhu Shushu's office.

"How does it lock?" Lulu asks, pretending to fill a cup of water on the table as she tries to get a better look through the doorway.

"Four characters typed into the keypad. Harv can probably think of something clever." Peng Ayi resumes copying names from her list.

As Ling exits again, Lulu gets up and approaches her. "Ling, could you heat some water for our tea?"

They both head into the kitchen, and once her back is turned, Lulu pauses for a split second, debating if she should act. They'll need a backup option if the photo isn't sufficient for Michelangelo.

It's now or never. She takes the office key Ling has abandoned on the counter and hides it in her fist. There are no pockets on her dress, and Ling has hung up her bag somewhere in the depths of this giant apartment.

She's sure Peng Ayi can see the sweat on her forehead as she squeezes the key and walks back to resume her place at the table. Slowly, she grabs an invitation and writes Michelangelo's address on the envelope with a fake name. Her eye on Peng Ayi, who leans over her papers, she slides the key inside and seals it, then inserts it into Peng Ayi's stack. She hopes Michelangelo will be able to work with the photo. She's supposed to be a counterfeiting genius, after all. But if not, Lulu will have to get her into Zhu Shushu's office somehow to view it in person.

Peng Ayi is still focused intently and doesn't notice any of this. It's strange; she hasn't criticized Lulu once in the last five minutes.

"Do you want help with that?" Lulu asks, curious why Peng Ayi is giving this one page so much extra attention.

"These are our most esteemed guests, and I can't have you addressing them with your atrocious handwriting. Go help Ling cut some fruit." A dismissal.

Lulu goes back to the kitchen, where she slices honeydew before bringing it to Harv's room.

"The invitations are done?" he asks, accepting the plate. "Ma didn't give you a hard time after I left, did she?"

"No," Lulu lies. What's the point in being honest? There are so many roles for her to play: meek daughter-in-law, eager bride-to-be, capable friend. None of them feels like her. "Everything is going perfectly. I can't wait."

17

4 months to the wedding

RINA

RINA CONSIDERS STANDING Vic up but knows Jane would somehow find out and howl about it. Besides, she has to do what's best for the crew. Lulu wasn't able to come because Peng Ayi's got her occupied, so it's up to her to gather the information they need.

She can only hope Vic stays true to his unreliable nature and doesn't show. She'll be able to concentrate better on creating the blueprint of the venue without him looming over her.

But at the exact time they agreed on, an incredibly shiny, sleek sports car pulls up to the curb in front of her. The paint is an obnoxious matte chrome. A group of aunties leaving her building visibly slow so they can ogle the car and its handsome driver.

No, not handsome. Treacherous. He's come ready to antagonize her, promising mayhem in that car of his. Also, is that a *hoop* in his ear?

From his eyesore of a car, Vic calls, "Right on time. Do I pass?"

Rina reluctantly walks over, but as she reaches for the door, it opens upward. Of course.

She climbs in the car, and Vic says, "Thanks for coming. My grandma always loves a good Marriage Market date story."

"You actually go on dates with the women you meet through there?" She's so horrified by the idea that she forgets to remind him this is not a date.

"Why not? You should see the looks on these girls' faces when I come to pick them up in this car. I'm a walking red envelope." His tone hardens at the end, and she searches his face for signs of resentment. It's impossible to read him through his designer sunglasses.

A couple exits from the front entrance and stares at the car. Rina has to get Vic out of here before she becomes the topic of choice in the building elevator. "I'm on a tight schedule, so let's make this quick."

"My driving will shorten your trip by twenty minutes at least," Vic promises. "I'm *very* good at it. Among other things."

Then she's pressed back against her seat as he floors it.

"If you get pulled over," she says evenly while clinging to the grab handle, "that two-hour buffer you promised me will become zero."

In response, he speeds up. They zip perilously close to another car as he cuts in front, and Rina feels her heart stop for a brief second.

"Nobody's going to pull me over," Vic says, totally at ease. "Besides, girls always like a thrill."

"Don't lump me in with all the girls you've dated," Rina protests.

Vic performs a risky merge. "You say that, but all girls seem to enjoy nice clothes, jewelry, and surprise trips to Paris."

"Because you don't bother sticking around long enough to know them any better."

"True."

He's quiet for a few minutes, which gives Rina time to re-assess. Is she really going to let her distaste for the man prevent them from gaining an advantage on the wedding day?

The answer is instantaneous. Absolutely not. If there's a way to use Vic, it is Rina's duty to leverage it. She has to get on his good side.

"So why do you need to go to Sun Island anyway?" she asks, to make conversation.

"Harv might say he isn't picky, but he needs an open bar with his favorite plum wine from Kishu and round tables because he hates sharp corners. As his best man, I'm responsible for making that happen."

Rina is impressed by this attention to detail. She shivers slightly. It must be the leather seat, cold through the thin fabric of her pants.

Vic seems comfortable with the silence, but she pushes on. "So you really think the marriage market is the best place to pick up women?"

"Not really, but it's how I get my grandma out of the house. She knows half of the old biddies there. She would've been at mahjong night, but I got her an iPad and she's been binging Chinese operas."

"Right, it's definitely not because she wants you to settle down." Elderly people here have too much free time not to have ulterior motives.

"I've told her that I'm taking things at my own pace. When I want to settle down, it'll be easy enough."

"I suppose you're right. Your eggs aren't going to expire by the time you're forty."

"I don't feel strongly about kids either way."

She raises her eyebrows. "What, you don't want someone to carry on the Shan line?"

"Having kids isn't something you should do for legacy alone. Me and Harv are suffering the consequences of parents who have kids with no idea how to raise them." The car bumps over Zhongxin Bridge. It's narrow, Rina notes. It'll be an absolute shit show to cross the day of the wedding. If the getaway car doesn't leave before all the guests, it'll never make it. "Remember when my dad disowned me in college?" he says. "All because I didn't give a shit about his business."

"That explains the one time I saw you eating in the dining hall." Rina rarely encountered Vic around campus, but she remembers him once sitting in the middle of the dining hall, head in his hands over a bowl of unidentifiable mush. She'd assumed he was hungover.

Vic winces. "Congealed tuna salad. My tastebuds tremble from the mere memory. Questionable cafeteria fare aside, I don't regret it. Family, job, friends… If they don't make you happy, ditch them."

The mention of work has Rina tensing. "I disagree." This is exactly the attitude that made her avoid Vic Shan in college. He's the sort of person who will fling you out of his orbit when he's tired of you. "Some would call that shirking responsibility."

"It's optimization, something I'm sure you're familiar with." Vic taps on his steering wheel. "Anyway, let's talk about something else. Did you know I outbid Harv's dad for my license plate?"

Rina gives a startled laugh. "That was you? He was so mad!" Lulu told her Harv's dad had broken a Qing Dynasty vase, cursing out wealthy brats who only knew how to spend money, not make it, the day he lost the bid.

"I know." Anger creeps into Vic's voice. "And because he couldn't take it out on me, he took it out on Harv instead."

The picture Vic is painting makes Rina even more determined to rescue Lulu from Harv's family. She wonders if he feels the same protectiveness toward Harv that she does for Lulu. "Then why did you do it?"

"Because Harv's dad is a dick, and my dick is bigger."

Rina determinedly keeps her eyes from flicking to Vic's

crotch. "How special are these plates? Do they let you break laws?" Maybe they can just jack Vic's plates during the wedding.

"My plates don't provide any advantages beyond bragging rights. Besides," Vic says with a cheeky grin, his dark mood already dissipated, "I break hearts, not the law."

True to his word, they are in the driveway of the Sun Island resort in under an hour. Rina reaches for the handle automatically, then almost falls out as the doors rise.

Sun Island is comprised of Tudor-style buildings set against generously watered grass lawns. With a pool, golf course, and manmade beach, it allows overworked Shanghainese to fool themselves into thinking they're away on vacation, not still in the city.

A veritable gang of people accost them at the entrance, likely having seen Vic's flashy car. "Huān yíng guāng lín!" the uniformed staff chorus as they hold the doors for them.

Inside, Rina scans the foyer, with its faded gold trimming and dusty-looking lantern chandelier hanging from the ceiling. The management must be offering a lot of concessions, if Peng Ayi chose this place over the Ritz. In every corner, she detects a black void monitoring her. Cameras, but the building seems old enough that their security system can't be that advanced.

"Are you staying with us tonight?" asks the lady at the check-in counter, looking Vic over appreciatively. "We have some lovely couple suites here that you could take advantage of."

"No," Rina answers for him. "I'm here to get a tour of the venue. The reservation should be under Fei and Zhu?"

The woman's eyes light up with recognition. "You don't mean Harvard Zhu?"

Vic gives one of his characteristically loud laughs. The woman jumps while Rina stays stonily still. "Sorry," Vic says. "His full name gets me every time."

"Yes, him," Rina says. Baby Harv did not escape the brief but appalling trend of parents naming their kids after Ivy League schools, a side effect of China's glorification of an overseas education. She'd thought it was funny back in college, but now she just feels bad for him.

"Certainly, we can give you a tour." She marks something in her book, then guides them over to the waiting area.

Rina paces, scanning the foyer, trying to memorize as much as she can.

"You're twitchy as always." Vic watches her from one of the cushy sofas, the pinnacle of relaxed.

"You don't know anything about me." At least he's keeping the attention off of her. Everyone has their eyes on him. China has developed dramatically, lifting people out of poverty and making others very rich. Nowadays, in a city as cosmopolitan as Shanghai, people are skilled at detecting wealth, and Rina is pretty sure Vic's sweat smells like money.

A different woman ushers them toward the ballroom where the banquet will be held. Without decorations, it's bland and beige, but Rina knows the whole island will be unrecognizable once Peng Ayi has her way with it.

"Are the two of you thinking of a wedding anytime soon?" the woman asks, clearly the venue's salesperson. "Our Gold Package is a favorite among couples."

Rina is about to correct her when Vic cuts in. "Sorry, only Diamond is good enough for me and my fiancée." He grabs Rina around the waist, making her gasp.

As the woman gawks, his arm remains there. The nerve. He's messing with Rina and enjoying it far too much.

"Bǎobèi," she says in a saccharine voice, "you speak so sweetly, yet you still haven't even bought me a ring!" On a whim, she slides her right hand under his cardigan. Even though there's a shirt below it, she can feel the heat of his skin, the hardness of his abs.

The woman zeroes in on Rina's bare ring finger. And because Rina is now playing Vic's game, all she can do is stare into his eyes and will herself to stay still as he lifts her hand and softly presses his lips to every single knuckle.

He finishes with one last kiss on the tip of her ring finger. "How can I kiss my fiancée wherever I want with jewelry in the way?" he asks as he releases her hand. "Now, this is all very nice, but how much am I going to have to pay for you to get top-shelf liquor for the open bar?"

The woman coughs delicately. "We have a specific agreement for bev—"

"Let's not get all tangled up in legalese," Vic says smoothly. "We're bringing a lot of people here, after all."

As Vic convinces the woman to let him overhaul their entire alcohol selection to Harv's liking, Rina lags behind, digging in her purse for hand sanitizer. But she has to admit, Vic is being unexpectedly useful; by asking all these questions, he's created an opening for her.

Once she catches up to the two of them, she asks, "As my... partner mentioned, there will be a lot of important guests here. How secure is this place?"

"We've got a state-of-the-art surveillance system." The woman mentions a name unfamiliar to Rina. "I can ask my manager for more information about the model we're using if the two of you require it." The woman looks eager to help. Rina takes a moment to delight in how easy this is turning out to be. Who knew that being here with Vic would actually be the right move?

"Have you heard of Jianshi Group?" Rina asks, seeing an opportunity to give Jane a hand with her part of the plan.

"If they don't already have Jianshi installed," Jane had warned her, "we need to convince them to do it. Otherwise the information I get from Zihao won't be very useful."

The woman nods. "Who hasn't? They're all over China."

"I'm a consultant, and we recently worked with Jianshi on the launch of their algorithm-powered surveillance system. Their technology is highly trusted. It'll be able to identify a face in minutes, even recognize an individual based on how they walk." Rina makes a show of looking around, then angles forward as if to confide. "Maybe you can't afford them, but a family like the Zhus is *very* demanding, and you wouldn't want something to happen if you didn't put the appropriate measures in place. At the very least, your manager would appreciate this advice."

"I see," the woman says, and Rina notes the small wrinkle in her brow with delight. She's planted the seed, and now she just needs this eager employee to pass the warning up the chain. If this doesn't work, they'll have to impersonate a Jianshi sales associate and sway the hotel that way. And if *that* doesn't work, they could pay off a security guard to shut off the system for them. But Rina hopes it doesn't come to that; things are delicate enough without bringing another person into the mix.

"Baobei," Vic says, coming up behind her and reclaiming her hand. "Don't worry. You're utterly safe with me." He lowers his voice. "I see what you're doing, asking all these questions."

A chill runs down her spine.

"Trying to close on some business for your friend's husband," Vic continues. "This is the kind of back-scratching they don't teach you at school."

She conceals her relief. "It *is* the leading surveillance company in China." Jane's told her about the new AI update, and its accuracy in identifying criminals is honestly frightening. But better that the surveillance technology is produced by a company they have an in at, rather than one whose operations are a total mystery.

He squeezes her hand. "Always thinking business. I like it."

"The two of you are so sweet," the tour guide says once they're back in the foyer. "Please think of us when you start planning your big day!"

She extracts her hand from Vic's once they've exited the sliding doors. "I've got cavities from that show we just put on." Even as she says it, Rina realizes she should tone it down, use this opportunity to her advantage. "Anyway, you should be concerned about security too. Aren't you in charge of guarding the safe where everyone's going to be dropping their red envelopes?" she prods.

"Oh, that," Vic says lazily. "It's going to be in the center of the banquet hall. If something suspicious happens, everybody will see."

Rina's pulse quickens, and she has to make a concerted effort to keep walking. Their plan was hinging on the safe being placed out of sight, where they could more easily swap it with the counterfeit. "The center? Isn't it customary to move it somewhere after everyone's seated?"

"Yeah, but according to Harv, his mom balled out for some expensive custom-designed safe and wants everyone to see it."

Back in his car, Vic leans over to buckle her seat belt. She smacks his hand away and leans her head against the rest. She feels lucky to have found this out now, while there's still time to change the plan. She knows Lulu is exhausted and stressed from Peng Ayi's constant demands, and Jane's got her marital issues. She won't worry them with this, and besides, she can handle it on her own.

What else might Vic know that could help them? A tip from him could be the difference between failure and success. Rina needs to stick close. "You're in charge of planning the bachelor party, right?" she asks. "What if we planned something together? A joint celebration."

Vic is about to start the car. "You're volunteering to spend more time with me? What's really going on here?"

Shit. She's come on too strong. Rina casts around for an explanation. "I want Lulu to have the best celebration ever, and what better way than to bring you in to elevate it? You knew about the Diamond Package, after all."

This seems to satisfy Vic. As the car shakes to life, he says with a smile, "Oh, my Rina. There's so much I want to show you. There's *always* a Diamond tier."

18

3 months to the wedding

JANE

JANE CATCHES HERSELF humming as she rolls dumpling dough. With the plastic surgery in her calendar and a tentative truce with Zihao, things are looking up. And there's nothing like making dumplings to keep her disciplined. The natural rhythm of kneading dough, rolling it into perfect disks, then pleating it neatly around a pork and chive filling is a ritual familiar and dear to her. She taught herself in order to escape her mom's terrible cooking, and it's a process she's grown to enjoy.

Today, the dumplings are supposed to be a distraction so she can hack into Zihao's computer. She's gotten some general information from him, but she needs to find out whether Rina's tip worked and the installation is actually happening, and what model of the security system Jianshi plans to use. That's the only way she'll know which type of jammer to buy.

She's hears Zihao's telltale footsteps in the hall, then the front door open. He usually walks past her and toward the dining area, but today, he stops at the kitchen counter.

She lifts her head and sees him holding a bouquet. It's small, but the flowers are tulips in shades of orange and pink. Her favorite.

"Happy anniversary," Zihao says, resting them on the counter.

Their anniversary. Between arranging her plastic surgery, assembling their crew, and formulating this scheme, Jane totally forgot. She remembers lying in bed a while back, unable to fathom how this marriage would survive a whole year. But since they agreed to this plan five months ago, that feeling hasn't returned.

Zihao sees her floury hands and says quickly, "I'll put them in water." There's some clattering as he locates the one vase in their house, and then carefully places the flowers in the center of their dining table.

Jane stares suspiciously at the tulips. What is up with Zihao? She never thought he was sentimental, but something about their anniversary seems to have altered his brain chemistry. That, or he's possessed.

There's an awkward beat, then Jane says, "Thank you. For the flowers."

"It's the least I can do. You're making dumplings, and that takes far more time than buying some flowers."

He thinks she did this because of their anniversary. Jane laughs nervously.

"Let me help." Zihao rolls up his sleeves and reaches for a circle of dough, grabbing the chopsticks stuck in the mixture of meat and veggies. Jane watches as he spoons far too much filling into the middle of a circle. He stretches the dough so taut over the giant ball that it threatens to explode.

"You keep folding your dumplings like that, and just one will be enough to fill you up."

Zihao looks offended. "I know how to do it," he insists, focusing intensely on the task at hand.

He may have bought her flowers, but she needs to get him

out of here. The whole point of making dumplings was so she had an excuse to commandeer the kitchen and get her hands on his laptop. Usually, he moves his briefcase into his office after he showers, so the window for her to act is narrow.

"Go shower." Jane shoos him away. "And stay out of my way. I need twenty minutes."

"You'll have to teach me how to do it so I can help you next time," he says.

When she hears the shower, she wipes her hands and darts over to the dining table, drawing his laptop out of his bag and hunting through the pockets for the VPN key that connects to his company network.

There's a prompt for a PIN. Jane panics slightly. She tries his birthday. It fails. She tries his mom's birthday, which she remembers from helping Zihao buy a birthday gift last year. Also a fail. Shit, she really should've thought this through. Out of desperation, she types in her own birthday.

The laptop unlocks.

Zihao manages software updates for all the systems installed in the Shanghai region, so he must have a map of Jianshi's installation locations somewhere. There aren't any leads in his email, but when she opens up a browser, it redirects to the company's internal home page. She opens the hamburger menu and sees *heat maps* listed. She clicks. A heat map of Shanghai blooms over the screen, and she draws in an excited breath.

The water shuts off. Jane hurriedly zooms in on the area surrounding Sun Island. There's a dot. A pop-up indicates the model of the security system queued for installation. Jane commits the serial number to memory, then closes all the windows, putting the computer to sleep before she unplugs the VPN. She curses as she notices spots of flour on the laptop and grabs a damp towel from the kitchen to wipe it down before blowing on the surface to dry it.

The doorknob of their bedroom turns, and she positions herself between the table and the doorway, screeching, "What did I tell you about staying out of the way?"

"Okay, okay!" The door shuts again, and Jane resumes breathing as she zips everything into his bag and double checks nothing is out of place before racing back to the kitchen.

The dumplings are bobbing on top of the water and the table is cleared when Zihao emerges cautiously ten minutes later. Jane's heart beats fast as he walks to the table. He peers at the briefcase oddly, but just then the dumplings boil over, the water sizzling on the stove and diverting his attention. "Do you need help?" he asks, meeting her at the stove. He holds the pot as she scoops out dumplings onto a plate.

Once everything's on the table, she sinks into her chair with relief, her body still catching up with the stress of the task.

She waits for Zihao to do the same, but instead of pulling out his own chair, he comes around behind hers and lays his hands on her shoulders, right at the base of her neck.

Does he know? Is he going to strangle her? She didn't really think he had it in him, but most men are repressed in some way.

Then, to her surprise, he starts *massaging* her. His thumbs knead the muscles, the gesture so foreign that Jane only grows tenser.

"Thank you for doing this. And for those clothes you bought me. They do feel a lot nicer than the other things I own."

Jane blinks at the spread of untouched food in front of her. This was not something she could've anticipated in a million years. She tries to turn around, but Zihao's hands keep her in place, and she realizes the massage is as much a distraction for him as it is for her.

"I've neglected you, and I'd like to do better."

"Maybe we can talk about this after we've eaten..." This isn't a conversation she's prepared to have.

Zihao doesn't make any move to go to his seat. "I'm not finished." The determination in his voice stops her from picking up her chopsticks. He resumes the massage. "When you think of a successful marriage, what comes to mind?"

"I can't be philosophical on an empty stomach."

"Jane." His grip slackens.

She finally faces him. "My parents, I guess? They've been together for thirty years."

"But are they happy?"

She's silent. Her parents presented a united front when it came to reprimanding her for bad grades or setting the ultimatum that unless she got married, they would disinherit her. They were collectively disappointed that their only daughter was unwanted on the market. But she's never seen them show any affection toward each other. Jane knows her mom's shopping is a survival instinct developed to deal with her own unsatisfactory marriage to a man who is never home. They are simply together because it would be more work to get divorced. Maybe there was love once, but Jane has a feeling that all those years of living with each other's imperfections and co-parenting her have dissolved what little there was.

"I don't think my parents ever loved each other." Zihao sits next to her. "If the generation before us wants us to be better than them in income and circumstances, why can't we apply that same mentality to marriage? Even if our parents arranged this marriage, we can still make it better than theirs."

Zihao is being overly idealistic, as if he's forgotten their whole history. "How can we make something out of a marriage that was basically a transaction? You married me because of the assets I owned. Not because of—not because of me."

Zihao pauses, and she can see the truth of it. "I won't pretend that I entered this marriage without selfish reasons," he admits. "But don't you want to try to make something of it, to make it better? I have no desire for us to become my parents, and I think we still have time to change." His face is sincere. Usually, they sit at opposite ends of the table, with a distance that feels insurmountable between them. But there's an openness to Zihao—plus he bought her flowers—that makes Jane want to meet him in the middle.

Briefly, she wonders what it would be like if he had been in love with her. Maybe every day would've been like this: flowers, gentle touches, him listening to her like he actually cares. Cooking for him and asking questions about work because she wants to, not in service of a secret plot. "Okay. We can try. But can you please eat the food? It's getting cold."

He nods, smiling hesitantly at her.

Jane fills his plate with dumplings.

"By the way," Zihao says. "We signed a new, big contract with Sun Island today. Isn't that where Lulu's holding her wedding?"

19

3 months to the wedding

LULU

"WILL AN HOUR be enough time?" Lulu asks Michelangelo as they wait outside the Zhus' penthouse for Harv to unlock the door. It turned out that the single, blurry photo Lulu took of the safe was not sufficient. The design is quite elaborate, after all.

Michelangelo folds her arms, hands cupping her elbows. "Do you think I'm some amateur?"

Lulu feels childish next to the elegant, poised woman in her houndstooth jacket, a silk scarf tied around her neck. She decides not to ask any more questions about Michelangelo's process.

"So they own this entire floor?" Michelangelo tsks.

In the lobby, Michelangelo had admired the bamboo fountain, gentle spa music, eucalyptus-scented air. The complex where the Zhus live is a far cry from the cramped structures Lulu is used to, and she'd had the same reaction the first time she visited. With all the space they have, it's no wonder Harv hasn't been in any hurry to move out.

When Harv slides open the door, Lulu makes quick introductions and explains Michelangelo is here to help choose ribbons for the bridesmaid bouquets.

"Don't you need Ma here to help you?" Harv asks, squinting.

"Oh, um, I wanted to save her some time," Lulu says, hoping he buys this explanation. She purposefully chose today because Peng Ayi's supposed to be picking up some expensive seafood delivered from Japan. "At least narrow it down to a few choices."

Thankfully, Harv accepts this excuse. "That's nice of you." He looks tired, his hair not even gelled. But he's polite and makes small talk with Michelangelo as he brings them through the hallway that leads into their living room.

"Are you coming to the wedding?" he asks Michelangelo cordially.

Michelangelo's smile is appropriately remorseful. "I'll be out of the country, but I hear it'll be quite the spectacle."

"An unfortunate product of having a mother who's been thinking of this day since I was born." Harv refocuses his attention on Lulu, concern entering his voice. "Are you getting enough rest? Ma's been running you ragged. Let me take you out this weekend. There's a private club that I'm a member of, and they do great sound baths. Very relaxing."

Lulu's not quite sure what a sound bath is, but she has a feeling she won't find them as relaxing as Harv does. "I'm okay," she demurs.

When they get to the living room, Lulu almost doesn't recognize it. Every square inch of the normally immaculate space is covered in boxes and tissue paper.

"What—" She catches a strap of leather sticking out of one of the boxes in a tower and yanks.

Out comes a small red backpack with Ls and Vs, its gold hardware covered in plastic wrap.

"Louis Vuitton," Michelangelo says instantly.

Lulu sweeps her gaze over the clutter. It's like the bags are worthless, the way they're just stacked atop each other. Jane's eyes would fall out of her head at the sight.

Harv rubs his forehead as he surveys the mess. "Party favors. Ma and Ba want to impress our wedding guests. I tried to talk them out of it."

Even before this engagement, Lulu knew Chinese weddings are more than just a celebration of two people; they're a union of families. That sort of pressure has made them expensive, so much so that Rina's firm actually worked on an advertising campaign emphasizing that weddings don't have to be such elaborate affairs as part of some government effort to counter falling birthrates in China.

Unsurprisingly, Peng Ayi is not heeding this guidance. Lulu makes a mental note to tell Rina and Jane about the goody bags. Maybe they could be useful.

Harv toes one of the bursting boxes out of his way. "They said there's no price on good connections. And I suppose they're right. All this fanfare might come in handy when we need one of our guests to accelerate our visa process for travel to Europe or get us a prime spot at the Grand Theater."

It astonishes Lulu, the way Harv talks about access like it's a fact of life, not a rare privilege. "Are these things really that important?" Lulu has never gotten much pleasure from cutting the line. It assumes a level of power she would never feel comfortable wielding. She'd rather earn what she has, even if it isn't much.

Harv considers her, a faintly confused look on his face. "I... Yes? Are they not important to you?"

"Michelangelo, maybe you can look for the box of ribbons?" Lulu points at a farther corner where there seems to be a stack of newer shipments before redirecting her attention to Harv. Michelangelo gets the hint and wanders off. Once Harv leaves, they can sneak off to the safe.

"Not really," Lulu answers. "I've never really had those sorts of options. I guess that's where we're different."

Harv frowns. "Are we? That different?"

She can't believe he's asking her that, like it's not obvious they come from completely different layers of society. At the same time, she can't answer him honestly. He'll realize how incompatible they are.

"You're not rethinking getting married to me, right?" Harv is watching her intently.

Lulu's struggles to keep her features smooth. "Wh-why would you think that?"

Harv shrugs. "Because everything is happening too fast. Because I'm nothing special. Because Ma is putting you through so much, and I'm buried in the work for this ground-breaking ceremony. It's the first time I've been entrusted with something this big, and if I don't manage to sell off all the apartments beforehand, Ba won't trust me to handle any other business again."

Lulu is shocked that Harv is being so open with her. Knowing she has to play concerned fiancée, she lays a hand on his arm. "I'm sure you'll do a great job. He trusted you with this responsibility, didn't he?"

Harv laughs humorlessly. "He gave this to me so that I could fuck it up." His defeated tone gives her a pang of pity. "I'm going to get back to work. Let me know if you need anything."

When he's gone, Michelangelo circles the bags like a shark scenting blood. "This must have cost a fortune. There's probably a backlog at all the LVs in this part of China because of the size of this order."

"The safe is in Zhu Shushu's office. Did you copy his office key?" Michelangelo had returned the key to her a few days after receiving it in the envelope, and Lulu had placed it in the chopstick drawer on her next visit to the Zhus, mentally apologizing to Ling for the verbal thrashing Peng Ayi must've given her for losing it.

"Don't ask such obvious questions." Michelangelo walks to the door and unlocks it with the duplicate key.

Zhu Shushu's office is more a museum exhibit. A giant oak desk occupies most of the room, a tea tray positioned at the center with a purple sand tea set. Lulu watched a documentary about how these teapots retain the flavor of the tea steeped within them. Limited quantities are handmade every year in Jiangsu. It's a special piece to have.

It's impossible to miss the safe, placed behind his shiny, gigantic desk. Michelangelo knocks on the glass creation, draws a finger down the keypad. "Glass is easy enough, though this shape is unique." From her pocket, she pulls out a protractor, then begins measuring the angles of each part of the apparatus. She scans the double *Xǐ* engraving with her phone, magnifying the texture of the gold. On the back of a crumpled napkin she withdraws from her pocket, a sketch takes shape.

While Michelangelo works, Lulu runs her eyes over the room. She goes to Zhu Shushu's desk and tugs on the drawers. They give easily, but they're empty. She pokes her head out of Zhu Shushu's office. Harv's door is still firmly shut. If he comes out, she'll have to pretend she was showing Michelangelo to the bathroom.

"I'm going to check on something," she says to Michelangelo. "Will you be okay?"

At her nod, Lulu heads into Peng Ayi and Zhu Shushu's bedroom. She's never been in there before, and her skin prickles as she enters. The bed is neatly made, and unlike Lulu's room with all the postcards and pictures of foreign places she's collected, the walls are bare, save for a large framed wedding portrait. Zhu Shushu and Peng Ayi stare down at her, judgmental even in their static state.

Her heart is thudding so hard she feels light-headed. She could leave here knowing she completed the task assigned to her: get Michelangelo inside to see the safe. But Peng Ayi's list of notable guests could mean even more security for all of them. More money than they've planned for.

Where would Peng Ayi keep it? Tiptoeing to the nightstand, she opens one of the drawers. There's a map of Sun Island with copious notes, like *floating island?* written over the pool and *tea ceremony tent* nearby. Lulu snaps a photo to show Rina later.

"What are you doing?"

Lulu jumps a few meters and hurriedly pushes the drawer shut. Michelangelo leans against the doorway with her arms crossed.

"You're done? Can you help me?" Lulu asks quickly.

"You want me to go nosing through a complete stranger's things with you?"

She almost withers, but she knows she'll regret it if she doesn't act now. "Yes, please."

Michelangelo sighs dramatically and shrugs off her coat, draping it on the bedpost. "What are we looking for?"

"A list of names." Lulu scans the bedroom, its ironic sparseness making it seem like the Zhus don't have many possessions. There has to be somewhere Peng Ayi stores all their valuables.

Her eyes land on the door next to their giant bathroom. It leads into a massive walk-in closet. Piercing lights illuminate long rows of shoes and bags, arranged by color. It smells like Peng Ayi, lightly herbal.

Michelangelo joins her in the closet, sticking her hands down coat pockets. "This is just lovely," she murmurs as she caresses the sleeve of a camel-colored trench. "Do you think she'll notice if this goes missing?"

"Definitely," Lulu says, hurrying her along. "I'll check the bags." But there are so many bags, and for all she knows, Peng Ayi has already thrown that list in the trash. There's a chance the list might be on her phone, but Lulu would rather fight a tiger than attempt to steal Peng Ayi's phone.

"Instead of checking each one, maybe try to remember which bag she used last time you saw this list." Michelangelo's calm, sensible tone makes Lulu step back and search the depths of her memory.

"It was black," she remembers. "With small handles. And a gold clasp." She searches the rows of bags. "I don't see it here."

"Was it Hermès? Louis Vuitton? Céline?"

She wishes she had Jane's talent for identifying luxury brands, but they all look the same to her. "I... I don't know."

"Harv?" A familiar, unwelcome voice reaches them. "The doorman said Lulu checked in. Where is she?"

"She's back," Lulu says, alarmed. They stumble out of the Zhus' bedroom, rushing to the dining room just as Peng Ayi enters. On her arm is the handbag Lulu just described.

"Lulu?" She glances at Michelangelo, who's putting her jacket back on. "Who's this?"

"Um... A friend. From the restaurant. I thought I could use her advice on the ribbons." Lulu hopes her shakiness isn't too obvious. If Michelangelo isn't disguised at the wedding, Peng Ayi is definitely going to recognize her.

"Ah." The moment she learns Michelangelo is from the restaurant, Peng Ayi's demeanor changes, her chin lifting and her politeness vanishing. "I would have appreciated a heads-up that you were bringing a stranger over. You may be marrying Harv soon, but this house is not yours."

"Sorry, Peng Ayi," Lulu mumbles.

"I'm going to wash my hands. The store was filthy. That's the last time I go without Ling."

Peng Ayi heads to the bathroom, and Lulu leaps into action. "It's in that bag," she says to Michelangelo. "I'll cover you. Look for a slip of paper with names on it."

As Michelangelo floats over to Peng Ayi's abandoned bag, Lulu positions herself in the doorway of the bathroom, where Peng Ayi bends over the sink, washing her hands thoroughly, then drying them on a monogrammed towel. "Have you spoken to your family lately?" she asks, noticing Lulu in the mirror.

This takes Lulu off guard. Since she sent money from Harv to her mom, it's been quiet. She'd assumed that meant her mom was satisfied, not plotting new ways to get more of the Zhus' wealth. "Not recently."

"I see." The two words are loaded with meaning. Clearly, Lulu is meant to continue this conversation.

"Why do you ask?"

"Your mother called on me. She went on and on about how lovely it would be when our families are officially joined together," Peng Ayi says, lip curling. "I can tell she is looking forward to it."

What is her mom thinking? She has no idea how precarious everything is, and how her involvement threatens this wedding rather than helps it. Peng Ayi is already determined to cast her as someone whose sole motivation is money.

"I'll be honest," Peng Ayi says, squirting lotion onto her hands, rubbing it in with focused care. "I wish my son had better taste."

"Ma!" Harv's sharpness clears the humiliation that has clouded Lulu's vision. He's standing outside the doorway of the bathroom, Michelangelo hovering behind him. "You can't say that to my fiancée."

Peng Ayi becomes soothing. "Erzi, you weren't meant to hear that."

"What, and that's supposed to make it better? That if I didn't hear this, it didn't happen?" Lulu's never seen Harv angry before, but he's gripping the doorframe like he's going to break it. "Is this how you've been treating Lulu when I'm not there?"

"Erzi," Peng Ayi says, and there's a slight tremble in her voice. "It was just a long day, and I didn't mean it. Lulu knows, don't you, Lulu?"

Lulu nods automatically, mostly because she doesn't want to be caught in the middle of this.

"I'll walk the two of you out," Harv says, giving Peng Ayi another furious glare before putting an arm around Lulu.

WOMEN OF GOOD FORTUNE 149

"Why don't you two head down first?" Michelangelo says. "I'd like to admire this foyer a bit longer."

In the elevator, Harv puts his hands on Lulu's shoulders. "I'm sorry you had to hear that. I don't want you to feel like you're facing Ma alone. I'm in this with you."

His regret is genuine. Before she can doubt herself, she says, "Those apartments your dad wants you to sell. Have you considered selling them to your parents' VIPs?" The names on that list hold so much wealth. Originally, she was considering enlisting Rina and Jane to figure out how best to use it. After all, she's a nobody.

But Harv could help her. It wouldn't be strange for him to reach out to them, and it would benefit him, too.

Harv seems startled, like he never expected Lulu to talk to him about business. To his credit, he doesn't dismiss her. "Those are my father's business partners. He doesn't want me anywhere near them." The sadness in Harv's voice reminds Lulu of the last dinner she attended with the Zhus and their connections. Afterward, when the men stayed in the room to drink and smoke, Zhu Shushu ordered Harv to leave with the women.

"But what about their kids? You know, the people our age?" Lulu asks as they exit the elevators. The fù'èrdài occupy a unique place in the fabric of Chinese society, born into money while a mere generation ago, their parents might have still been struggling in poverty. She only needs to look at Harv to observe this pressure to uphold the family name, the fear of parental disappointment waiting at every corner. That pressure to lay claim to something, to prove their worth...others in Harv's position must feel it too. "They're probably looking for ways to spend their money."

And if they can present these heirs a good business opportunity, Lulu's confident they'll see far more red envelopes at the wedding.

"That's an interesting idea. Vic is doing that now. Everyone's been going to him, now that he has his own fund and will invest in anything that feels viable and forward-looking." Harv smiles. "It's working out for him."

The elevator doors open again, and Michelangelo breezes through, her face impassive. "Lulu, we should go."

Harv squeezes Lulu's arm. "Let's talk more about this. You might be onto something."

Michelangelo seems eager to get out of there, but once Harv is back in the elevator, Lulu asks, "Can we sit?" She needs a moment to process everything. Peng Ayi's insults, the fact that she has impulsively roped Harv into her plan.

They sit on a bench surrounded by gardenias. The perfume of the white blooms makes Lulu's head ache.

"Michelangelo, did you choose to be a counterfeiter? Or did you fall into it?" she asks, buying time to steady herself.

Michelangelo considers her question. "I've spent my life surrounded by women desperate to fool themselves with something that can only ever approximate the real thing. And I wondered— why shouldn't someone get the admiration she craves, simply because she cannot spend a ludicrous sum on a pile of leather? I wanted to make their dreams feel a little closer."

"You help them lie to themselves," Lulu says, watching as a bee floats around a gardenia before landing on one of its creamy petals.

"There's good money in lies. Too often, we let people around us inflate our views of something that might be objectively worthless. This subterfuge is getting tiresome, though. Once I pay off my fine, I think I'll do something different. Create something I can call my own."

"That's good, that you know what to do next." Wisps of hair blow into her eyes, and Lulu brushes them away. Rina, Jane, even Michelangelo are so sure of what they want. Right now, Lulu only knows that she wants to escape. To go somewhere she doesn't have to give everything to her parents, or feel guilty about buying a single book every month. "I've thought about running away. But I don't know what comes after. What my purpose is." She loves to read and explore new cultures, but what is she supposed to do with that? Maybe this lack of vision is what makes her the weakling Peng Ayi believes her to be.

"Purpose is something you choose. You can't rely on others to give it to you." Michelangelo takes her hand and opens her fingers, which is when Lulu realizes they were balled into fists. She tucks the list of names into Lulu's grip. "Don't underestimate yourself. After all, you remembered the bag correctly."

20

3 months to the wedding

RINA

SOMETIMES, BEING THE most organized member of the Leftovers can be to Rina's detriment. It means ordering a thousand
red envelopes online to fill a fake safe, drawing up blueprints,
and now, having the unenviable task of planning the bachelorette party, with Harv's sister, no less.

At least it's a good opportunity to ingratiate herself with Vic,
who's been remarkably responsive to her texts about setting a
date for the bachelor-bachelorette. Luckily, Rina hasn't uncov-
ered any other unexpected developments. She still hasn't worked
out what to do about the safe being in the middle of the banquet hall. The only idea she's come up with so far is to pull the
fire alarm and evacuate the venue, but that would be too messy
and Vic or an overly committed hotel staff member might run
to rescue the safe. But she'll figure it out. She always does.

On the train to meet Vic and Yaqing in Xintiandi, she reopens
the spreadsheet she created last night to work out the logistics of
egg freezing. She's got a prioritization matrix for clinics and a

tab for estimated costs, plus alerts tracking flights to San Francisco. Every time she sees the amount she'll be paying, she has to take a deep breath and assure herself they'll get the money. And isn't it worth it, to stop this terrible feeling of time slipping through her fingers?

Stick to the plan, she reminds herself. Steal the money. Freeze your eggs. Then she can focus on advancing her career without worrying about her declining fertility. And when she is in a place to start dating again, she won't have to settle because her biological clock is ticking.

Xintiandi, like a lot of Shanghai, is a mix of modern and ancient, where old streets contrast with glass-paned boutiques that house shoes and bags centered in golden spotlights. Its very name means New Heaven and Earth. Yaqing chose a café in the South Block, where more of the upscale, high-end stores are located. As Rina makes her way there, people much younger than her occupy al fresco dining areas and bars. Radiant girls with fingers wrapped around the stems of martini glasses laugh as they lounge under the sun. It reminds Rina of her college days, when she didn't have to worry about anything but getting good grades. When career, marriage, and caring for her parents seemed worlds away.

The café features a mouthwatering display of cakes in a glass case. A diverse food scene has risen in Shanghai where any craving can be satisfied at any hour of the day. Rina and Lulu have ordered sesame noodles at 3:00 a.m. more than once.

One small cake with a dusting of matcha powder seems especially tasty, and there's only one left. She's so busy deliberating that she doesn't notice Yaqing and Vic already sitting at one of the tables behind her until Yaqing calls her name.

"I was just telling Vic that if this ends up being like those vulgar American bachelorette parties, it's your idea, not mine," Yaqing says with a sniff as Rina takes a seat.

"If you want to invite strippers, let me know. I've got a couple

I can call." Vic sticks a forkful of chocolate cake into his mouth without a care in the world.

There are a million things she'd rather do than hang out with these two, but this is the best way to both appease Peng Ayi and get time with Vic without seeming suspiciously eager. "No strippers, please. Let's keep it classy."

Vic stands. "Not as exciting, but we can discuss. I'm getting some bourbon to go with this cake. Do either of you want anything?"

"No," Rina immediately replies, though she eyes the cake again. Someone's approaching the case, and she hopes they don't buy it.

"Champagne for me!" chirps Yaqing.

Vic comes back with the drinks and a beautifully packaged box dangling from his pinky. He hands Yaqing the champagne, then puts the box on the table in front of Rina. She looks up, confused.

"They only had one more of this flavor left, and it's their best one," he says. "Also, I stole this right from under that guy's nose. He was about to pay."

"You thief," Yaqing giggles. "How'd you manage that?"

"I asked if he'd seen the limited-edition cheesecake. You get them distracted looking for something else, and you can take anything from them."

Yaqing's giggles fade into the background as Rina hones in on what Vic's just said. *Get them looking for something else.* Of course. How else do you steal something in plain sight? *Get them looking for something else.* They don't need to pull a fire alarm. Rina and Lulu just have to divert the guests' attention onto something else to create an opening for Michelangelo and Jane to take the safe.

"Rina." Vic's voice cuts into her thoughts. "Take this to share with Lulu. Don't make me eat a whole cake at home by myself."

"The cakes here are very delicious," Yaqing says, her face all twisted up. "But fattening."

"Thanks," she says to Vic, catching up to the scene before her. Lulu is going to love it, but accepting this cake from him makes her feel like she's in his debt.

They dive back into the party planning so she can get out of there and focus on brainstorming the right distraction for the wedding. "I was thinking we could rent out a restaurant somewhere. A big room, with activities that we can do together."

"What if we use my yacht?" Vic suggests.

Rina's lips thin. They're probably permanently white from the pressure she's exerting on them. "Your yacht?"

"Yeah, I've got one that we can launch from the International Cruise Terminal. Makes it a lot easier than trying to find something to rent that'll have all the amenities Peng Ayi expects. I'm thinking we can do an evening cruise along the Huangpu, have some drinks and a buffet dinner. There's a game room with baccarat, poker, mahjong. It'll be fun."

"Yes! Let's do it!" Yaqing cheers, then sips her champagne.

Rina's still stuck at the part where Vic casually mentioned he has a yacht. She tries to focus. "That does sound…nice. Do you need help getting everything set up?"

"Nah. I've got a whole team to do that. Don't worry your pretty head."

She stares at him in suspicion. Peng Ayi sees her as the leader of this whole thing, so if anything goes wrong, it's *her* head. The last thing she needs is to lose Peng Ayi's trust. "Have you ever planned a thing in your life?"

Vic presses a hand to his chest, his expression comically distressed. "Rina, I'm the king of throwing parties. And I am committed to giving my best friend the best night of his life. At least, the best night until his wedding night."

Yaqing is looking between the two of them, seemingly unable to decide how to contribute to the conversation.

Rina asks whether she needs to get catering or pick up decorations, but Vic keeps deferring to the supposed team at his beck and call. It must be nice to be so rich that there's someone to wipe your nose when you sneeze.

After an hour, Rina has gotten enough information about Vic's vision for his yacht party that she feels comfortable letting him and Yaqing go. Yaqing will handle communications with the guests, Vic will do the venue, and Rina's going to make sure the whole thing doesn't blow up with her well-honed project management skills. Peng Ayi would approve.

"I'll call you a car," Vic tells Yaqing as they get up to leave.

Before he can offer Rina the same, she says, "I'm taking the subway."

"I'll come with you."

"Didn't you drive?"

"Even I don't dare find parking around here."

Once Yaqing is shut into the cab, Vic slides the cake off the table and holds it carefully as he and Rina head to the station.

The evening train is packed, a mess of elbows and backpacks, rough edges bumping Rina and digging into her sides. She shoves her way forward through the sea of people until she's found a tiny pocket of space. There's no hope of grabbing on to anything, but she's ridden public transportation enough to surf the intermittent stops.

She thought she'd lost him, but Vic is right behind her. He easily reaches for one of the poles, the expensive watch on his wrist catching the light, his other hand still gripping the cake. Rina tries to maintain some distance between them, which brings her as far as someone else's armpit.

"I'll be gone for the month before the party," Vic says, looking down at her. "Scouting out something in Singapore."

"Don't you think you should be here to oversee the plans for your giant boat party?" This is just classic. Vic is incapable of staying in a single country for more than weeks at a time, and now she'll be the one coordinating with his team, something she definitely doesn't have time for. She'd planned to host the bachelorette party at a venue that would handle all the logistics.

"Are you asking me to stay?" He smiles down at her, and she realizes belatedly that she fell into his trap. He registers her stress and reassures her, "My team will take care of it. Don't worry. I'll give you my event manager's WeChat."

The train jolts, and she nearly stumbles right into his chest. His hand shoots out, bracing her shoulder. They're so close she can see the small freckle near his eye, and a single thread of silver amid the thick mass of his black hair. She takes a tiny, steadying breath.

"You can hold on to me, Rina," he says softly, his voice somehow audible over the noise.

When the train arrives at her stop, she rushes out.

Vic exits alongside her.

She spins to face him. "This isn't your stop," she says accusingly, even though she has no idea where he was planning to get off.

He holds out the box. "You forgot your cake."

She's supposed to be the one manipulating him, but he's making her feel wobbly. She needs to flip this power dynamic back. Before she can question herself, Rina raises herself up and places a single kiss on his cheek.

Vic, for once, has nothing to say. His eyes are liquid and dark. She takes the box from him, keeping her voice from shaking as she says, "Thank you."

Then, she flees.

21

3 months to the wedding

LULU

✥ ✥ ✥ ✥ ✥

"YOU SAID YOU had information about the first dance," Jane says the moment Lulu sits down at their table at Hotpot Palace. "We still don't know how long the whole thing is going to take, and that's messing with the schedule."

"Jane, calm down. Let her eat something." Rina pushes the condiment container toward Lulu so she can assemble her dipping sauce.

Lulu's grateful for the moment to collect herself. She'd rushed over from wedding waltz practice and can still hear the instructor admonishing her lack of rhythm.

She and Harv have been meeting regularly after each rehearsal too. His surprise when she shared the list had sent a warm current of pleasure through her. "Ma never parts with this thing. She and my dad think I need to create my own network before I can use theirs, which is ridiculous. Why shouldn't I benefit from what my family already has?" He seemed to realize his voice was rising and gave an embarrassed smile. "How did you even get this?"

"I had an opening," Lulu replied. His comment had been entitled, but it wasn't her business to correct him. "You won't tell her, will you?"

"I won't." His eyes were fixed on the list, and she could tell he was already thinking about what he could do with it. "This is great, Lulu. Now that we have these names, we can research their heirs. Would you want to help with that?"

Lulu had nodded fervently.

A server comes by. "Are you interested in our special today?" he asks, jutting a laminated card in Jane's face. "Boba hotpot. The perfect dessert to finish off a spicy meal!" The picture is of a brown liquid, frothing with boba pearls and food that does not belong in sweet broth, like radishes and mushrooms.

Jane wrinkles her nose. "No, thanks."

As he leaves, Lulu says, "Peng Ayi has been working with a choreographer and visual artist on the first dance. There'll be a stage engineer and band too." She'd wanted to tell Jane and Rina about the list, but she holds back for now. She knows they won't like the idea of relying on Harv.

Jane barks a laugh. "I didn't realize your pop star debut was happening on the same day as your wedding."

"Wait," Rina says. Something has shifted in her expression. "So you're saying this is going to be a whole production? And everyone's going to be looking at the stage?"

"Anyone who wants to see me attempt to waltz, I guess," Lulu says. Harv winced the first few times Lulu stepped on his feet, but now he barely reacts, like his facial muscles have tired of flinching every time it happens.

Rina presses her hands to the table, bobbing slightly with excitement. "This is it! This is how we get around the safe being in the middle of the banquet hall the entire time. The trick is to have everyone focused on something else."

"Hold on," Jane says, raising a hand. "What the fuck did you say? The safe is in the middle of the hall the entire time?" She looks over at Lulu. "Did you know about this?"

Lulu shakes her head slowly. This could change a lot. With how observant Peng Ayi is, how can they hope to get the safe out now? "You shouldn't have kept this information from us," she blurts out. "We all need to be in the loop on what's happening. And we're friends first, aren't we? Rina, even if you're capable of doing a lot at once, you should feel comfortable asking us for help."

"I just—" Rina groans, frustrated. "I don't want you two blaming me for not doing my part. You told me to get close to Vic, and I have, and now it's paid off."

"Good lord, Rina," Jane says. "We're not evaluating your performance like the cunt who's disguised as your manager."

"It doesn't matter now," Lulu says. She knows Rina didn't want to worry them. "Rina, how were you thinking of getting the safe out then?"

"We could tell people there's a message in the visuals. Or a specific dance move to watch out for. They'll be too busy staring at Lulu and Harv to watch the safe. We'll have to move fast, though, especially since we'll be in the open. Jane, this is your realm of expertise. What's something juicy we can spread?"

"I can get Peng Ayi to dim the lights," Lulu adds. "We could bring the cake out to obstruct the view when you move the safe."

Rina points at her. "Great idea. Jane, what do you think?"

"Yeah, that could work. Maybe we spread around a pregnancy rumor or something. People love speculating over that shit." Jane's arms are still crossed.

"Yeah. Let's do that." Rina swirls a piece of meat in the broth, and an uncharacteristic quiet settles over the three of them.

After a few minutes, Jane breaks the silence. "Well, I'm glad you came around on Vic. If anyone can resist his charm, it's you, Rina. The rest of us don't stand a chance." She cracks a small smile.

Lulu grabs on to this topic, glad for a break from the tension. Every day is like walking a tightrope. She's terrified she'll say something incriminating, Peng Ayi will catch on, and everything will fall apart. "Harv used to joke that I'd run away with Vic. Apparently he's had girlfriends who've tried to do that."

"How are he and Harv even friends?" Jane asks. "They're so different. Like putting a rosebush next to a tornado."

"They were roommates until Vic dropped out of Stanford. I think his parents cut him off, and Harv let him stay in his apartment while he figured things out. I feel like they balance each other out, though." Lulu knows that people who are very different can still be the best of friends. Just look at the three of them.

"Huh. I wonder what it's like to be friends with someone for that long." Jane fishes limp spinach out of the pot. "Feels like I've drifted apart from everyone I knew in childhood."

"Not us," Lulu says. "You could never make us leave you alone. Right, Rina?" When Rina first introduced her to Jane, she'd been caught off guard by her brusqueness, but now she appreciates how straightforward Jane is. Lulu knows that anything she says, she means, whether it's an effusive compliment about a new scarf, or a caustic remark about a book that Lulu liked, but she hated. Unlike Rina, Jane would never soften the truth just to spare her.

"Right," Rina says, scooping out a mishmash of seaweed, tofu, and beef. She offers it to Lulu and Jane, who select their favorite pieces before Rina dumps the rest in her bowl. "We're stuck with each other."

That coaxes a grin out of all of them, and Lulu sighs inwardly with relief. Things had been weirdly strained, a far cry from the days when it seemed like them against the world. They have three more months. They just need to hold everything together until then.

22

3 months to the wedding

JANE

❖ ❖ ❖ ❖ ❖

IF ZIHAO SOMEHOW discovers that Jane is sneaking Rina's bratty little cousin into their garage and taking his car out for a joyride, it will definitely shatter the newfound peace between them. After investing in both car and license plate, Zihao mourned the hole in their bank account with ten-mile runs. For months, he wouldn't even let the car leave the garage, which was a big problem for Jane, who'd harbored dreams of driving to an outlet mall on the city outskirts and filling the trunk with shopping bags. Now, whenever Jane uses the car, Zihao always inspects it for scratches or scuffs, and she doesn't trust this teenager is as smooth of a driver as Rina claims.

"Wow, this place is pretty nice. How'd you afford it?" Mei doesn't even say a polite "Ayi hǎo" as she tromps past Jane and into their apartment.

Jane glares at Mei's back. "A gift from my parents for getting someone to marry me."

"So your bride price." Mei picks up the golden monkey resting on one of the floating shelves in their entryway. It's Zihao's zodiac sign and a wedding gift from one of his relatives who believes owning the gaudy object will bring luck. Jane only feels unlucky having something so tacky on display. "Whoever marries me better be paying *me* for the honor."

"Put that down." Jane grabs Zihao's car keys from the dish they keep near the door. "I guess Rina didn't come through for you on the *Lotus*." Rina's going to kill her, but it serves her right. Jane's still irked she kept the development about the safe's location from them. Sure, she came up with a pretty good way to get around it in the end, but what if she hadn't? Rina's pride could have brought this whole thing down.

Mei tosses the monkey from one hand to the other. "What Lotus?"

"You didn't know?" Jane asks innocently. "Your cousin's been hanging out with a rich guy. Look, this is him." She opens Vic's WeChat profile.

Mei tucks the monkey under an armpit. "Whoa, he looks like a bad boy! I didn't know that was Rina Jie's type."

Jane smirks. "Your Rina Jie's full of surprises."

Mei hands her phone back. "Ugh, what a bummer! I asked if she could rent me a nice car, but she said I should practice with something more expendable."

Expendable! Oh, Rina's going to get it next time Jane sees her. "You better not drive our car thinking it's expendable."

"Of course not," Mei replies dismissively. "What kind of car is it again?"

"An SAIC electric."

Mei nearly drops the monkey. "Are you serious? You want me to drive that piece of junk as our getaway car?" She places the monkey none too gently back on the shelf, making everything else on it shudder. "This sucks. I should've stayed home and done homework."

Jane, who was about to pass her the keys, yanks them back.

"According to your cousin, you're a part-time student who's barely hanging on. Something tells me you're not doing homework. Besides, this car is compact and easy to park." This is the exact argument Zihao made when she asked why they couldn't get a Benz or some other German car. "If you keep whining, you can go home and stare at a wall instead. See if I care."

Mei crosses her arms and scrunches her face dramatically, but she trails Jane obediently to the elevators.

"We need to get back in an hour, by the way," Jane says as they descend to the garage. "I have to make dinner."

"What's the point of getting educated if you're going to end up stuck as a housewife?"

Jane's heard that one before. Some people find it hard to accept that housework is preferable to inflexible deadlines and bosses with no respect for personal boundaries. But after spending too many late nights making slides for men who talked shit about her in the break room, she's glad she's left that life behind. "Because I get to spend half my day shopping and watching TV."

"That does sound pretty awesome. I wish I could do that without my parents getting on my ass."

They walk down the row of expensive European cars. When they arrive at Zihao's, Mei slips into the driver's seat and gets busy adjusting the mirrors and examining the clutch. "Wow, a manual? It's been so long. Everyone in the US drives automatic. Losers."

Jane climbs in beside her, and Mei starts the car. She immediately backs out of the spot, braking with a force that hammers Jane's head into the seat before peeling out of the garage, narrowly skating by an incoming BMW.

Jane swears, lunging for the grab handle. "Are you sure you know how to drive stick?" She hopes Mei will say *no*, and they can find another car that doesn't belong to her husband.

"I just did that to freak you out." Mei cruises onto the main road. "Besides, this is such a boring car. I have to make it fun somehow."

Mei is a ruthless but effective driver. She cuts people off and eases into tiny gaps without looking the slightest bit bothered, and she manages to hold a conversation with Jane the entire time.

As they drive, Jane notices the number of SAICs on the road that are the same make and model. She's always known using this car as their getaway vehicle puts Zihao at risk. Even with the swapped license plates, it could be recognized. But this car is apparently so popular that the likelihood of the police being able to trace it should be low.

"Jane Jie, you seem pretty different from Rina Jie. It's like, you tried hard and realized it wasn't worth it," Mei says, heading toward Zhujiajiao.

On the way back, they'll visit their established blind spot thirty minutes north of Sun Island. Rina had suggested the detour to Zhujiajiao because the tourists and constant traffic will provide extra cover. There, they'll observe traffic patterns and stoplights to nail down the amount of time Mei has to pull over, replace the license plate, then merge back into the flow of traffic.

Mei's voice softens. "Do people ever make you feel bad about your choices?"

Even if he didn't protest her quitting her job, sometimes Jane still thinks she sees accusation in Zihao's gaze. Her practical husband would've wanted her to keep working so he didn't have to share as much of his earnings. Rina would never admit it, but she disapproved too. She thinks Jane committed the ultimate crime, giving up her career to be a housewife. Jane's parents were the ones who had no problem with it.

"What is it with women suddenly all wanting their own careers?" her mom had asked once. "Why would you want to work when you don't have to?"

"At some point, you have to do things for yourself," Jane says to Mei. "You'll understand once you've been worked like a dog and can't even keep track of which days you've showered." She doesn't tell Mei she's still figuring out how to let the negative comments slide off her back. When people judge her for her choices, Jane finds herself questioning them too.

Mei takes this in. "It's so weird. You get good grades in high school so you can get into a good college. Then you go to a good college so you can get a good job. I thought that was the endgame."

Jane laughs. "That's the endgame of your youth. Then you start learning all those things you were working so hard for don't actually make you happy—hey, that's a red light!"

Mei slams on the brake. "Whoops."

They drive a while in silence. Jane finds it hard to relax with Mei's reckless style and tries to come up with things she can ask the kid to distract herself. "Are you ready to head back to school?" she finally says.

"Ugh, no. I'm not excited to sit in a bunch of classes I don't care about or hear my classmates simper after preppy boys who own too many sweater vests." They swing around Zhujiajiao, and Jane glimpses the sunlight sparkling off the river. "All of that is so overrated, you know?"

"What would you rather do instead?"

"*So* many things. Walk in a Pride parade. Watch all one thousand episodes of *One Piece*. Try to fit twenty marshmallows in my mouth." She taps on the steering wheel. "I'm really glad Rina Jie invited me to do this heist. Being home with my parents is reminding me why I wanted to study abroad. Ma's a total dictator, and ever since I told them I'm ace, they always want to know where I'm going."

"They're trying to keep you safe. China's not the best place to be open about queerness." Jane admires Mei's bravery for telling her parents. According to Rina, Mei's mom spent time on the phone with Miranda Zhou every night for two weeks, alternating between crying and fretting over whether she ever knew her daughter. Eventually, she came around, but she's extra vigilant any time Mei is home.

As they approach the intersection where the license plate swap is supposed to occur, Mei says, "Jane Jie, I think you're pretty cool."

Affection for Mei spreads in Jane's chest. This little brat's got more going on below the surface than she lets on. "I'm here if you ever need to talk about anything, but so is your cousin. Ask all your questions while you're still young."

"I do have something else to ask."

"Okay…"

"Can you drop me off at KFC? I'm craving something greasy."

Jane laughs. "That, I can do."

Back in her kitchen after their drive, Jane happily checks on her braised chicken. She's found herself anticipating the evenings when Zihao returns from work, enjoying the discussions they have over dinner.

"Dinner will be ready in ten!" she says as the door opens.

But when she looks up, there's a sour expression on Zihao's face. "Did you drive my car?"

She knows there's no use in lying. "I did. How did you know?"

"It was a couple inches too far from the line."

No wonder he keeps getting promoted at work. Such attention to detail must not go unnoticed. Jane says evenly, "You said it was fine for me to drive it if I needed it."

"You should still give me a heads-up. What if something happens to you while you're driving it?"

She puts a hand on her hip. She should've paid more attention while parking. "'What if something happens *to the car* while I'm driving it.' That's what you *really* mean. You think I'll get into an accident because you don't think women can drive."

Zihao steps toward her. She doesn't budge, maintaining her stance by the stove. When he's close enough, his hands hover, like he wants to touch her but is unsure if she will attack him. Then he seems to come to a decision and brings her into his arms. It's an unfamiliar gesture. His shirt pressing against her cheek, his body folded around her. "You're right," he whispers into her hair. "It was wrong of me to think that."

She slowly moves away, even though a traitorous part of her wants to sink deeper into his hug. The thought flusters her. "I'll plate everything if you set the table."

Once they're seated at the table with the soy sauce–braised chicken, smashed cucumbers, and fish fragrant eggplant, she says, "So are you still on track to install Jianshi before Lulu's wedding? I remember you said you'll be using your temporary product since it's such short notice." Over the past few weeks, she's slipped in small, innocuous questions about his job to get him comfortable talking about it. She's already sourced a jammer based on the security model she scraped a month ago.

Zihao exhales heavily. "We were going to, but we might wait. Management has paused new installations as they shift all resources into the new AI system we've been developing."

Jane sits up straighter. If some other security company is operating the system on the day of the wedding, they won't be able to disable it. "Why do you have to wait? Won't you risk losing business?"

"I agree with you. The sooner we install our system, the less likely they'll back out of a partnership."

"So tell them that."

"It's not my decision to make." Frustration simmers in Zihao's voice. "In fact, I rarely get to make any decisions."

"You can influence them. It's your work they're using, and they won't want to lose you over something so minor. If you let them have their way, they'll think it's easy to push you around."

"You're right. The health of our Shanghai accounts is my priority. I'm going to talk to our head of partnerships about getting the interim solution installed at Sun Island as soon as possible."

It's a testament to how much Zihao must trust her now that he's actually taking her advice. A month ago, they couldn't exchange two words without getting into an argument. Jane goes to refill their water glasses, thirsty from all the talking.

When she sits back down, Zihao is studying her closely. She thinks he's about to ask why exactly she's so interested in the politics of his workplace. Instead, he says, "I like that you're interested in my work."

It's brief, but she feels it nevertheless. A sharp spike of guilt.

23

3 months to the wedding

RINA

MEI'S EYES BUG out of their sockets. Though they're parked a few feet from where she stands, it's very easy to read the *Oh my fucking god* she mouths.

Her eyes grow even wider as the doors on Vic's Lotus go up and Rina steps out and over the curb.

"I thought Jane was joking when she said you knew someone with a Lotus," Mei bursts out. "Holy shit. Can I take a photo with it?"

Since Jane let it slip about the Lotus, Mei's been threatening to tell Xiaoyi everything if Rina doesn't introduce her to "her hot side piece." Eventually, she caved and made a bargain with Vic: she'd buy a month's supply of frozen buns from his bun lady in Zhujiajiao if he allows Mei to drive his car. She'll have plenty of work waiting for her back at the office, but it's a small price to pay for Mei's silence. Plus this outing is a chance to confirm bachelor party details before Vic flounces off to Singapore.

Vic gets out of the car and gives Mei a little wave. Mei returns it bashfully. "Oh my god, way to *go*," she hisses at Rina. "Whoa, look at the tattoos on him!"

Rina positions herself to block Vic from view. "I thought you didn't find anyone attractive."

Mei shoves her aside so she can continue ogling. "I might be ace, but I have *eyes*. It's like how I can appreciate Dylan Wang or Yang Mi without wanting to bone them. Does Dayi know about this guy?"

"Ma's the one who set us up," Rina says, mostly for the shock factor.

Mei shakes her head. "Respect, Rina Jie. Respect."

Vic saunters over. "Nice to meet you, little Rina. You're too cute to be the menace your cousin makes you out to be."

Mei crosses her arms, assessing him. "The name is Lin Zhou-mei. I'm not a *little* anything."

"That's really no way to treat someone who's considering lending you these." He dangles his car keys from his finger, and Rina can almost see Mei salivating.

"I take it back." She grabs the keys. "I'm at your service, Gege." With a whoop, she runs around to the driver's seat and throws herself inside. There's the rumble of the engine, then the bass thumping with some Douyin song Rina's heard way too many times.

Vic smirks at Rina. "She called me big brother. I'm already part of the family." He's wearing a short-sleeve tee with a worn collar, his tattoo peeking out from beneath the sleeve.

Rina quickly diverts her attention. "Thanks for doing this. I don't think Mei will ever forget this ride." Mei's returning to school tomorrow after convincing Yale's academic office she needed an extended winter break for "family matters." She and Rina *are* related, after all, even if said matters include staking out roads and plotting escape routes.

She'll be back for summer break right before the wedding. Rina will miss her.

"As long as that means she'll never forget me, too."

"Sadly, she won't," Rina mutters as she climbs into the back.

Once they're all buckled in, Mei guns the engine eagerly. "I'll try my best not to wreck your car."

"I'll just buy another one if you do."

Mei releases a delighted peal of laughter, already half in love with Vic before they've even left the curb.

"So you're at Yale?" Vic asks. "How's that?"

"Super boring."

"You can always drop out. Like me."

Rina reaches over the headrest and fists a clump of Vic's hair. "You will do no such thing."

"My parents always told me to be more like Rina Jie," Mei says. "They've said that less lately. They're terrified I'm going to end up a shèngnǚ like her. Little do they know that that's goals for me."

Vic's eyes meet Rina's in the rearview, and his hand lands over hers, loosening her fingers from his hair. "I don't think I've met a more appetizing leftover."

"Ew!" Mei squeals as Rina yanks her hand away. "That's kind of cute."

While Mei focuses on driving, Rina grills Vic about the party. "Are you sure you have everything ready? There's nothing I can help with?"

"I told you, I have people to handle every little detail."

"But for you to have people to handle details, you'd have to know what details require handling."

"I was almost expelled for throwing a party that half of the school attended. Organizing an epic celebration is the only thing I know how to do."

"Chill out, Rina Jie. He sounds like he's got this."

"Listen to your cousin. She's wise for her years. Also, you're doing plenty already. You gave feedback on the decorations and picked out the menu, and unlike me, you have a real job. Leave the rest to me."

"How did you and Rina Jie meet, anyway?" Mei asks.

"That's a fun story," Vic says, and Rina prepares to shut him up quickly if necessary. "As you know, Harv and I were fast friends at Stanford because we were the only rich, handsome Chinese guys there."

"You were both annoying and could find nobody else to tolerate you."

"Your cousin and I worked on a group project. Well, she worked on it. She scheduled ten meetings. I went to none of them."

Rina seethes. "Worst. Teammate."

"I turned in my work, didn't I? Anyway, then we just kept running into each other. On campus, during dinner with our families, at the same internship interview..."

Vic was late for that interview, like always. His ink was covered, but he forgot about the piercing in his ear. He still managed to get an offer, but declined in favor of a three-month jaunt through all the islands in Europe.

"Imagine my surprise when I see her at my best friend's lunch. Almost ten years later, in a whole other country." Vic swivels his head to look at Rina, a playful smile on his face. "Fate."

"That's great, but are you good enough for Rina Jie?" Mei challenges him. "She's *very* accomplished. She might not have time for you."

"I'll free up my schedule to match hers."

Rina knows it's all talk, but she feels her cheeks flush.

Luckily, Mei has moved on. "So are you sure you didn't drop out of school because it was too hard?"

Vic laughs. "I dropped out because it was too easy. So many rules about which classes I should take and how to behave. I wanted to take risks, not have someone put limitations on my every decision." This prompts him to impart bad advice about how to cram for tests the night before and get out of turning in mandatory assignments, while Rina attempts to dissuade Mei from following his example.

They arrive at Zhujiajiao, and Mei miraculously finds a parking spot. As promised, Rina buys them all pork buns. She bites into hers, the soft white bun giving way to piping hot, candied meat. Instantly, the tension leaves her body. Mei is already halfway through hers, grunting happily.

Vic says with great satisfaction, "Today, I've shown both of you what are undeniably the best buns in the world. But there's one more thing we're going to do. A boat ride."

Before Rina can stop him, he leans over the bridge and calls in Chinese to one of the boatmen rowing along the river, waving to tourists and offering tours. "How much?"

"I'll give you a deal if your two pretty friends are coming too!" the man calls back.

Vic raises his head to Rina and Mei. "Looks like you're both coming." He puts his arms around them and urges them down the stairs. Before long, they're gliding down the river. There's something about the sound of the water, the shining sun, the happy chatter coming from the souvenir shops along the banks, the ease of Vic and Mei's conversation, that makes Rina feel safe. There is no one demanding anything of her.

Their guide tells them to call him Lao Wang. "If you come four more times after this, I'll give you a free sixth ride." His grizzled face holds an almost childlike playfulness. "Perhaps I'll even sing to you. I could've been in the opera, you know!"

Vic laughs, and Rina cracks a smile. "I had no idea the waters of Zhujiajiao held such talent."

By the time the trip is over, Lao Wang has convinced them all to visit again.

On the drive back, Rina lets the wind flow through her hair. She's glad Vic insisted on that boat ride. She needed it, the chance to close her eyes and get lost in the rhythm of the oars hitting the water. When she rolls her window back up again, she realizes Vic is watching her through the side mirror. He doesn't look away, and neither does she.

"Thanks for letting me drive your car." Mei reluctantly hands over the keys when they arrive at her house.

"Anytime, Meimei." Her name, doubled, means *little sister*, and Vic says it with affection as he opens his arms wide and gives her a tight squeeze.

"See you around, Gege." Mei skips to Rina's side as he gets back in the car. "I don't know how long you plan to keep him around," she says out the side of her mouth, "but he definitely has a six-pack." Before Rina can point out all the problems with that statement, Mei sets her hands on Rina's shoulders and steadies her gaze. "Rina Jie. I know you're using him, but you should enjoy yourself more. Who knows, maybe you'll miss him when he's gone."

An odd pang goes through her as the Lotus leaves the curb. Vic has always flitted in and out of her life, usually to her annoyance. Even though they went years without seeing each other after college, she still heard about his exploits from old friends. Then, after that lunch with him, Harv, and Lulu, he began dropping by their apartment infrequently to deliver flowers or trinkets from Harv. Rina would hide in her room until he left, but on the occasions she had to answer the door, she tried to make their interactions as brief and neutral as possible. Now, the grudge she's harbored all these years seems ridiculous.

"Oh, take this before we go in for dinner." Mei withdraws a map from her back pocket. Colored lines run across it, linking Sun Island and the internet café together. "These Xs are blind spots," she says, stabbing at different locations. "Red means lots of traffic. Blue means working cameras at all intersections. I'll lose them here. High traffic area."

"Don't forget to ditch the decoy plates, too. In case they try to stop you and search the car."

Mei folds the map away. "I won't forget."

"Mei..." Rina stares at her cousin, surprised by her maturity. Perhaps this crime has forced her to grow up. Rina feels a trickle of regret. Should she have let Mei be a child for longer? "I shouldn't have involved you in this."

"Are you kidding?" Mei's solemnity melts away. "This is the most fun I've had in ages."

24

1 month to the wedding

LULU

WITH A MONTH to go until the wedding, and a one-way ticket to Thailand booked, Lulu feels like she should be spending her time saying goodbye to family and friends, to the city she's called home, all the nooks and alleys she's discovered over the years. The other day, she finally got together with her Scarlet Beauty coworkers for dinner.

But now, she's at Cartier.

She and Harv have managed to carve out two hours after their jewelry appointment to meet with the VIP heirs, and she's nervous. She can hardly concentrate as she sits upon a plush sofa in one of Cartier's private rooms, watching the sales associate set various kumquat-sized jewels in front of them.

"Gorgeous," Peng Ayi says, holding a thin chain that drips with diamonds to Lulu's neck. She looks over at Harv for his reaction and frowns. "Erzi, why are you fidgeting so much?"

Peng Ayi had been delighted when Harv said he would attend the ring fitting. Ever since he heard his mom berate her,

Harv has made a concerted effort to join Lulu at wedding planning activities, a blockade between her and Peng Ayi. Little do they know that by the end of the wedding, Peng Ayi will dislike Lulu so completely that Harv will have no way to protect her.

"Too much coffee." Harv drums his fingers on the rectangular velvet box housing rows of men's wedding bands. The past few weeks, they've been busy strategizing this meeting, and she can read the nervousness running through his body.

If this meeting goes as intended, it'll prove him worthy of handling the Zhus' business. He'll be able to tell his dad he's created outsize demand for his properties before they even hit the market. He'll inch one step closer to being the perfect son.

She knows his dad won't react well when the wedding gifts go missing, but she hopes these two things cancel each other out.

Peng Ayi clicks her tongue. "I told you coffee's bad for your qì."

"These were on loan to Dilraba when she accepted her Best Actress award." The sales associate swoops in with a new necklace.

Peng Ayi smiles at her. "Ah, these are all wonderful! So hard to choose."

"You can always layer them."

"You're trying to upsell me, aren't you?" Peng Ayi says sternly. Then she laughs. It's a laugh flushed with the giddiness of dropping millions on something that will likely never leave its box more than a few times. "It's working!"

Lulu's mom would've loved this. Being able to touch and wear all these sparkly baubles. She's been texting Lulu daily, bugging her to send pictures of the preparations so she can forward them to her friends. It's a constant reminder of how upset her mom will be to learn the wedding is a sham.

"Ma, are we almost done?" Harv asks impatiently. He glances at Lulu. "Did you find a necklace you liked? Ma, let Lulu choose something. You're the only one who's been saying anything about these necklaces."

Lulu gives him an appreciative smile.

"What about you? You still haven't chosen a ring!" Peng Ayi exclaims.

Harv points randomly at a ring. "I'll take that one."

Lulu knows he's trying to hurry things along. If this appointment overlaps with the arrival of the VIP heirs, they'll have a lot of explaining to do.

"Silver?" Peng Ayi frets. "At least get the platinum."

"Fine," Harv says, relenting.

That settled, more necklace options are paraded out. After pretending to care about Lulu's opinion, Peng Ayi lands on a white gold necklace of diamonds woven together in a lattice shape. It sits on Lulu's collarbone like a stone block, but she's just glad to be done. This was the last wedding errand on their list, which means no more Peng Ayi, and now she and Harv can focus on the more important task at hand.

They accompany Peng Ayi to the front of the store to handle the bill. When the Zhus' car pulls up outside, as planned, Harv says, "Ma, Lulu's going to help me look at cuff links for my groomsmen. You go ahead."

Peng Ayi purses her lips. "You and Lulu? Are you sure you don't want me to help you decide—"

"No, no." Harv almost pushes her out the exit. "You have that hair appointment, don't you? You said your grays are showing."

Once she's gone, Harv checks his watch and motions their sales associate over. "We have a few friends joining us. Please direct them to the salon."

Back in the private room, Harv sinks into one of the couches, brow furrowed. They wait in silence, towers of tea sandwiches and cakes untouched in front of them. "This is scary," Harv admits. He laughs slightly, like he finds himself ridiculous. "Days like these, I wish I had a brother. Someone like Vic, so this legacy isn't just mine to bear. My parents never put any of this pressure on Yaqing."

"You're not doing this alone," Lulu assures him. She and

Harv both need a dose of confidence. "We're in this together." Anyway, it's true. She's probably spent more time huddling with Harv the past two months than with Rina and Jane, drafting emails and searching people's contact information.

The guests trickle in one by one. Each is vetted by security Harv has stationed at the door. The youngest, most entitled billionaires in China.

There's Jiang Zhufeng, son of a tech mogul, who built a mini mansion for his Samoyed, complete with butler and gold-plated toilet, though netizens insist a dog that spoiled can't be potty-trained. He's brought Baobao, and the first thing she does is pee on the carpet. Yue Tingting, daughter of a cosmetics company CEO, whose video of her twenty Rolls-Royces went viral. Ye Sijia, who tried and failed to develop vending machines that sell Botox. There are others, too, but what links them together is they have spent their inheritances irresponsibly, and that's why Lulu and Harv think they'll be receptive to what they have to offer. They'll be eager to get back into their parents' good graces, and how better than investing in something that actually promises returns?

When they've made themselves comfortable, sprawling across chairs and selecting sandwiches for their porcelain plates, Harv stands.

"Thank you for coming. Lulu and I invited you today because your parents are our most esteemed wedding guests. They've amassed the sort of fortune that everyone else envies us for. But the responsibility is on us to grow their wealth."

Lulu's clammy palms rest on her knees. Even though she's beside Harv, blending right in, she feels an acute sense of being separate from everyone else in this room.

"We'll be unveiling a new property in the Former French Concession next year," Harv says. There's a visible shift in attention. Jane once told Lulu that property in Shanghai is hotly contested, with prices rising astronomically each year. The number of houses one owns is the best indicator of status. "You all know how quickly property appreciates in Shanghai. Especially a brand-new home. It's an empty canvas."

"I'm interested," Feili blurts, before Harv is even finished. According to their research, she's the daughter of a dean, recently caught spending ten thousand dollars on a shopping spree for her and her friends in London's West End. Lulu has a feeling her home life isn't too great right now. "What do we need to do?"

Harv holds a hand out, a warning for her to rein it in. "I will give you time to assess your finances and come forward with your best offer. And I hope we can finalize matters after our wedding."

The others start asking questions, eyeing one another viciously as they recognize their competition is in the room, possibly coveting the same floors and apartment numbers. Lulu relaxes. Everyone is reacting exactly as expected. When Harv mentioned wanting to maximize the bids on the properties, Lulu had suggested waiting until after the wedding to confirm who'd won which bids. It was perfect; everyone would gift lots of money at the wedding to get into Harv's good graces, which meant more to steal.

The meeting drags on as each guest corners Harv to discuss details and potential offers. A few approach Lulu to make casual conversation, probably hoping she'll put in a good word for them. Then Feili struts over, the sparkly beads on her miniskirt clacking with each movement.

"So the two of you are getting married?" she asks, angling her chin toward Harv. "You don't act like it. When my second husband proposed, we couldn't keep our hands off each other!"

Lulu gives a forced smile. Feili doesn't need to know there isn't love between them. "We just aren't public about it."

Feili seems to accept this. "Your skin is so clear," she marvels, putting her face very close to Lulu's. "What products do you use? SKII? La Mer?"

"Um. Water and a cloth?"

Feili laughs. "Fair, you look like a natural beauty. I'm doing a face mask night with these snail jelly masks that just came in from Korea. You should come, and we can hang out. Who knows, we might be neighbors soon! Here, let me scan your WeChat!"

Eventually, one of the Cartier staff members comes in and announces the store is closing. Harv accompanies the last stragglers out before he returns, dropping down beside Lulu. "That was exhausting but successful."

Lulu takes a sip of tea, and with its warmth comes a sense of accomplishment. Harv might've done most of the talking, but this was her idea. She can't wait to tell Jane and Rina. "You put together a convincing presentation."

"It's what I was raised to do," Harv says. "You know, Ba doesn't let Ma in on any of his business. For the longest time, I thought it was because she didn't have the brain for it."

Lulu thinks about Peng Ayi, her frightening attention to detail when it comes to every aspect of the wedding. "I don't think that's fair. I think he just never gave her the chance to show what she could do."

·Harv considers this. "Then he missed out." He pulls a cracker from the tower of snacks. "I like this. Us working together."

His comment gives her pause. At first, this side project was mostly about proving to herself that Peng Ayi was wrong. Her remarks about Lulu's weakness still sting. But Lulu hadn't realized how desperately she wanted to prove she isn't like her mom, happy to sit back and benefit from the Zhus' wealth. She doesn't want that to be the impression she leaves. When the Zhus inevitably hate her in the end, she wants it to be for the right reason.

Slowly, she nods in agreement. Gaining Harv's respect is unexpected, but it just shows how convincing of an act she's put on. "We make a good team."

25

1 month to the wedding

JANE

THE SUN ISLAND parking lot is bustling. Operations are underway to create Peng Ayi's perfect wedding. As she sits in the car waiting for Rina and Lulu to arrive—yes, she gave Zihao a heads-up this time—Jane watches people carry everything from bamboo planks to basins of floating lotuses into the lobby.

They need to do a final pass of the venue to make sure they haven't missed anything, and Jane also wants to use this opportunity to confirm the jammer she acquired on the black market actually works. She's thinking about the best place to test it when she gets a video call request from her mom.

She immediately tenses. She despises talking to her mom. The woman made her style-savvy, taught her how to choose the best dresses and colors for her figure, but it was so she could get Jane out the door, not out of love.

Everything inside her screams not to pick up. But because there's the slimmest possibility something could be wrong, Jane ignores the impulse. Her mom is wearing a sleek white blazer, her dyed black hair twisted into a chignon, and she taps away at her keyboard. Probably writing a scathing review for the last restaurant she visited or anonymously posting nationalist commentary on Weibo. She isn't even looking at the camera.

"What?" Jane asks.

"That's no way to greet your mother, Tian Juyi."

Jane rolls her eyes. "It's not time for our quarterly call." Talking to her mom usually requires breathing exercises and a lot of mental fortitude. Advance preparation. "Is there something wrong?"

Jane's mom addresses the camera. "You don't notice anything new about me?" She angles her head, and Jane squints.

"Did you get a new nose?"

Her mom beams. "I also lost ten pounds. There's this all-fiber diet I've been doing. You know, Juyi, there's nothing in this world you can't have without a little diligence and money. Just look at that friend of yours. She's already accomplished what you couldn't. If we had sent her fiancé a photo of you, I bet he would've immediately marked it as spam." She clicks her tongue. "There are some doors that only beauty can open."

"I'm getting work done soon, too," Jane blurts before she can stop herself. She had wanted to keep it a secret until the day she could show up on her mom's doorstep, and her mom would finally acknowledge she was beautiful. "My appointment's scheduled for three months from now."

"Oh?" Her mom is more attentive now. "I'm proud of you, Juyi. Are you nervous? Don't be. Anything they do will be an improvement."

Her mom is incapable of completing a sentence without an insult, and Jane automatically snipes back. "Like your new nose? It hasn't improved my opinion of you."

A gasp. "How dare you speak to your mother this way!"

The air in the car is stifling, and her mom's voice is like a swarm of bees in her head. "I've got to go. Next time, give me a heads-up if you're going to call." She hangs up and pops the door open, gulping cool air down. This woman raised her, yet Jane still hasn't figured out how to desensitize herself to the words that still get under her skin. Her own fucking mom doesn't seem to accept her, so why would anyone else?

Once she doesn't feel so much like she's going to explode, Jane gets out of the car and walks toward the hotel. The man who sold the jammer to her said it had a feature that would light up if connected to the right wireless frequency, and that it's matched to the one on Jianshi's heat map, but his accent was so thick that Jane isn't sure. All she knows is she paid extra for this alleged feature and that her supplier doesn't do repeat customers, so she won't be able to get a refund.

At the entrance, she glances down at the jammer. It doesn't light up. Fine. She might've been scammed on the light thing. It hadn't come on when she tried it at home either. The salesman said the light sometimes didn't work the first time, but it definitely jammed her home network. Zihao had made a number of vexed calls to their internet provider, arguing for a discount, and it had required all her willpower to hold in her laughter as multiple operators transferred him around.

To avoid suspicion, she takes a seat on one of the couches inside and reaches into her purse for her lipstick. When she's withdrawn it, a green blink catches her eye. The jammer's light. It's then she remembers something Zihao said, that outdoor cameras are often on another network because of weather, which means they operate on a different system. This is a problem. Jane has only accounted for interrupting the indoor system frequency.

That's how Lulu and Rina find her, staring angrily beyond the lobby doors, unable to believe she missed this detail.

Lulu bends toward her, places a hand on her forehead. "Are you okay, Jane?"

Rina gives her shoulder a firm shake. "You look like the world is ending. Either that, or your mom called."

"Both," Jane says glumly. In a lower voice, she explains the current debacle. "We've got less than a month left. That isn't enough time for me to source a second jammer. What are we going to do about the external cameras?"

"Can't you hack them or something?" Rina asks.

"Oh, right, let me use the hacking abilities I never told you about."

Rina seems to be thinking hard before she says, "Yeah, I don't have any hackers in my network. If we needed a banker or lawyer, though..."

"More importantly," Lulu says, "what did your mom say?"

"The same old stuff that still manages to piss me off." Lulu opens her arms, and Jane gets to her feet and hugs her, grateful for this opportunity to hide her face for a few seconds. Lulu's smaller, but her hugs are big and comforting. "You're hard to pin down these days," Jane says once they've pulled apart. "I'm still waiting for pictures of that posh jewelry you picked up at Cartier last week."

Lulu twists a loop of hair around her finger. "Sorry, I've been helping Harv with some business things." Her smile seems strangely secretive.

Lulu has no business experience, and the fact that she's been hanging out with Harv is even weirder. Jane feels a flash of concern. There's no reason for them to be getting chummy, not if Lulu's going to ditch him at the altar. "What, like which caterers to hire?"

"No, catering is already finalized. Why don't we just cover the cameras?" Lulu suggests. "Like...with decorations or something? Peng Ayi is planning to have flowers everywhere. I can tell her the theme should extend over the whole property, including the parking lot."

"The hotel's security might have a problem with that," Rina says.

"They'll accept it if the directive comes from Peng Ayi," Jane says. "Seriously, has anyone said no to that woman and lived to tell the tale?" The hotel staff will relax any of their rules for Peng Ayi. She's paying for them to. "Even if we do this, we have to know where the cameras are. Since Rina left them off her blueprint."

"Because you never said anything about outdoor surveillance!"

"Let's fix it now," Lulu says. Before either of them can respond, she walks over to one of the receptionists, totally unfazed.

"What's up with her?" Jane asks Rina as Lulu and the receptionist begin chatting like they're long-lost friends. "She seems oddly...lively."

Rina's brow wrinkles. "We did buy her ticket to Thailand the other day. It must be dawning on her that she's actually leaving."

"She's that excited to leave us?" It's so soon, Jane realizes. Soon, she won't be able to get a Lulu hug when she wants one. They won't have their regular Hotpot Palace dinners, where Rina freaks out about work and Lulu backs up Jane as she tells her to chill the fuck out. She won't be able to see Lulu whenever she wants to watch a show together and analyze the characters' relationships.

Rina frowns. "She's not leaving forever. Just for an extended period."

"Like you're not going to cry alone in your room when someone takes her place in your apartment and doesn't bake you cookies or print you the slides you forgot."

Rina's frown deepens. "That's unfair. I only forgot my slides *once*."

Before long, Lulu returns with her new friend. "Weiyi is going to take us around, and we can look at where the best places would be to put up decorations."

Weiyi guides them around the perimeter of the main building where most of the wedding festivities will take place. At every step, Jane pauses to search for the telltale black screens of a camera. They aren't easy to spot, but she absolutely can't risk missing a single one. Rina and Lulu keep a running commentary of nice areas to loop garlands or pin flowers.

When they're standing outside the entranceway of the hotel at the end of the tour, Jane spies additional external cameras nestled where the tall walls of the foyer meet the roof. "This area looks bare," Jane says, gesturing upward.

"Maybe balloons?" Lulu says.

"Yes, red ones," Rina agrees. "A lucky color, and the balloons symbolize reaching for great heights."

"What do you think, Weiyi?"

Weiyi beams, chuffed to be included. "If you need the heights of our roofs to pass to your decorator, I can provide them."

"That's a wonderful idea," Lulu says effusively. "Thank you for the tour."

Weiyi goes back inside, and the three of them power walk to Jane's car. They mark the areas where they saw cameras on Rina's map.

Jane reclines her seat. This lapse has given her a good shock, and she realizes how precarious all of this is. One misstep, and that's it. No plastic surgery. No divorce. Same sad life. Potentially sadder, because she'll be in jail. "That was close."

"You caught it in time, and that's what matters." Rina slumps in the seat next to her. "Is this actually happening? It doesn't feel real."

Lulu answers from the back. "It's happening, and it is real."

Jane pumps her head up and down. Hell if she's going to be the one who screws everything up. "Let today remind us that we've got to remain diligent. A single mistake will destroy us." Briefly, she thinks about Zihao. If they aren't careful, he could be incriminated too. "Who's going to explain this sudden need for more decorations to Peng Ayi?" She turns to Lulu. "I assume you've got it."

Lulu tucks their map away carefully. "I'll handle it."

"Are you sure?" Rina asks. "I can help if you want."

"I can ask for more decorations." Lulu pats her pocket, smiling. "I am the bride, after all."

26

1 month to the wedding

RINA

Rina: Did you get enough food for a group of 20?

Vic: the food is enough to feed a small country

Rina: People might get bored. Is it too late to get some entertainers?

Vic: i'm the entertainment. i guarantee that if i take off my shirt and wiggle my butt around, all eyes will be on me

"SORRY, JUST SOME important work emails," Rina says to her friends as she puts her phone away. They don't need to know how often she's been texting Vic. Though he's in Singapore, it's like he never left Shanghai. She'd realized his grandma must be lonely without him and even offered to take her to a qigong session at the local cultural center. She'd needed a break from work anyway, especially after her recently promoted male colleague started trying to "manage" her.

His reply had been instantaneous. *I'll send you her address. just warning you that my grandma's the master of asking invasive questions*

Rina had indeed been asked about everything from her blood type to which high school her parents went to, but it had been nice to spend the day with someone who knew Vic so well, who shared funny stories from his childhood but also the harder ones he didn't boast about, like the way he struggled to balance jobs with the weight of his parents' abandonment.

Shaking off the memory, she refocuses on Michelangelo's store, where they're about to view the fake safe. She can practically hear the work piling up for her back at the office. But after the scare with Sun Island's security system, she needs to monitor things more closely from here on out. Luo Ren and his incessant demands will have to wait.

"I'm excited for this bachelor-bachelorette party," Jane says, wiggling her eyebrows. "Well, Rina? Is his boat as big as he says it is?"

Rina takes a seat on the couch next to Lulu. Her friend has been oddly buoyant, confident lately, and sometimes Rina catches Lulu looking at her with a dazed smile on her face. Rina's glad Lulu is so ready to leave for Thailand, and she's kept her sadness to herself. It's going to be tough being apart for so long, but the three of them will work hard to stay in touch.

Disregarding Jane's comment, she says, "It'll be a great event. Also, Jane, we didn't talk about it at Sun Island, but it's amazing they actually installed the Jianshi cameras. You got Zihao to do exactly what you wanted."

This seems to wipe the smugness off Jane's face. "Yeah. I guess I did."

Rina and Lulu exchange a look. "What's going on with you?" Rina says.

Jane swallows once. "With all our fiddling around with security...you don't think they'd fire Zihao, do you?"

Now that Rina thinks about it, Jane hasn't complained much about Zihao recently. Any hesitation so close to the wedding isn't good. Putting in all this work and then quitting would be the worst outcome. "Don't forget what you're getting out of this. What we're all getting out of it," she reminds her, patting her knee in a rare show of affection.

Jane seems to pull herself out of it. "Yeah, the money comes first. We've got a month to go. I'll save the guilt for after."

Michelangelo finally materializes through a heavy velvet curtain at the back of her store, rolling a safe that looks identical to the one Peng Ayi commissioned.

They crowd around, and Lulu runs a hand down the design, awestruck. "You even captured the dew on the cranes' wings."

Michelangelo examines her fingernails. "The art was bothersome. I had to consult a connection who makes fake Swarovski. Fortunately, cloud and crane motifs are very popular, so plenty of imitations exist."

"And the lock?" Rina asks.

"You installed the keylogger I got you?" Jane seems pleased with herself. "I've sourced so much sketchy surveillance stuff I could run my own black market."

Michelangelo points at the screen on top of the safe. "Yes, it's programmed with a keylogger. If you can get Harv to type the password for the real safe onto this one during the wedding, it'll capture the code and send it to our phones so we can open the real safe."

"You've outdone yourself," Jane says.

"It's art," Lulu agrees.

Rina is impressed, too. Maybe she was wrong to be suspicious of Michelangelo. Rina admires her attention to detail and commitment to excellence. She's never bought anything counterfeit, but she might consider purchasing a Michelangelo bag someday.

"It was nothing. I even had time for some other…projects."

At this, Lulu sits up straighter. "There's an update I wanted to share—"

She's cut off by Rina's ringtone. Rina groans when she sees it's Luo Ren.

"I have to take this." Retreating to a corner, she whispers, "Luo Zong, what do you need?" Across the room, Jane mouths *Asshole boss.*

"Rina!" His voice is jovial, which immediately raises her hackles. "If you're not too busy, could you head to the office? We need slides for a client meeting that just got scheduled. It's not far for you, is it?"

"Of course not. I'll be right there." She's on the opposite side of the city from the office, and it's 10:00 p.m.

"They're making you work this late?" Jane demands when Rina hangs up.

"I have to go." At the end of the day, she still has her real life to attend to. This money will pay for her to freeze her eggs, but it definitely isn't enough for retirement. She rushes out to call a car. Knowing Luo Ren, there's a good chance she'll have to work until the morning.

When Rina finally arrives, the office is dark and empty. The email from Luo Ren pings into her inbox, and her dread rises as she scrolls through his notes. This is going to take three hours, at least.

At midnight, she drops her head onto her desk. A creak makes her snap up. After the noisiness of the mall, the silence here is unnerving. She wants company. Someone to fill the space. Jane would probably just rail about Luo Ren, and Lulu needs to prepare for Thailand. She could call her mom, but there's going to be an *I told you so* in that conversation, and Rina can't hear that right now.

That leaves one person. Rina hesitates for a minute before hitting the call button.

He picks up. Of course he does. Hooligans don't keep regular hours.

"Is this a booty call?"

She hangs up.

Her phone buzzes instantly, and she waits a couple rings before putting it on speaker. "Are you going to greet me properly this time?" she asks him.

Vic's throaty chuckle vibrates down her spine. "It's late. I got excited."

It might be exhaustion, but she blurts out the truth. "I'm at work. It's lonely."

"And you thought to call me? I'm honored." His voice is low and intimate, like they're lying next to each other in bed.

"I'll be here all night because my manager has shirked all responsibility." Frustration leaks in, and she closes her eyes, trying to collect herself. There are so many times she feels on top of the world at this job. When she secures a deal, when she answers a client question better than any of her male colleagues can, when she's shopping and sees a brand she worked on. It's rewarding to have a career. It's offered her independence in a way marriage never will. But there are times like this when she questions how long she'll be able to keep it up. If she's naive for wanting more than the world may be willing to give her.

"Bastard. You should quit. Be my secretary. Bring me coffee and tell callers I'm too busy to meet with them. I can already imagine it." Vic's tone turns velvety. "You'd call me Shan Xianshen."

"Dream on."

He chuckles again. "Oh, I will. But I've wondered myself—why did you come back? You could've worked in San Francisco. There's better work-life balance there, if you look for it. I've funded some companies there that offer very generous reproductive policies for women. You want kids, right?"

Rina blinks into the darkness, surprised. Most men wouldn't pay attention to women-centric benefits. "Eventually."

"Imagine the sort of kid we'd raise. My good looks and your ruthless ambition. A superior specimen."

Rina does not want to think about a hypothetical baby with Vic Shan. "I came back because it made the most sense," she says.

"But *why*? Tell me. I don't care if it's a long story. I'm interested." He waits, and Rina finds herself starting to talk.

"After we immigrated to the US, my parents always talked about returning to China. They moved back when I got accepted to college. In my last year of school, my mom got sick. A viral infection. We thought we might lose her." Rina takes a second to breathe. The horror of waking up to the WeChat message from her dad still lingers to this day. Of her world falling apart while she could do nothing but sit on a plane, telling a flight attendant what she wanted to drink. "I spent twenty hours on a plane, praying she wouldn't die before I reached her. That's why I decided to move here. So I won't be too far away if something happens."

"I feel the same way about my grandma." She makes out the rustle of sheets and imagines him propping himself up on his elbow, his phone on the pillow next to him. "I can't imagine losing her. But death is the one thing we can't control. No matter if you're rich or poor, it comes for everyone."

Rina rests her chin on her hands, watching the timer on her phone count each second of their call. The horrible part is that sometimes she wonders about an alternate universe in which her mom did die. She might've convinced her dad to move back to the States. Sure, she might still be grinding in some job, but at least she'd have a fairer chance at getting somewhere. "Aren't you afraid something will happen when you're not in Shanghai?"

"I can't be by her side every waking minute of my life. Neither of us would be better for it." She can almost hear his shrug. "Besides, I hate staying in one place for too long."

"Commitment-phobe." She doesn't understand the sentiment. When Rina identified the right place for her, she grew roots. It was painful to yank them out of San Francisco. She'd said goodbye to most of her friends, the coffee shops she frequented, the familiar paths she walked. Her sense of security and belonging. Vic is a dandelion seed drifting wherever the wind will take him.

"I go where I want to be. Do you?"

"I go where I'm needed." She thinks of Jane, crying before her wedding because she knew her husband didn't love her. Lulu, the look on her face as she dutifully sends her paycheck to her family each month, leaving very little for herself. Rina's mom, her exhaustion in the months after her illness. They need her to look out for them, to help carry burdens that are too much for a single person.

"I know." The way he says it is unbearably tender. "Do you want me to jump on a flight back to Shanghai and hang out with you? It'll only take six hours if I bribe customs."

"No. You should go to sleep. The party's in a few weeks, and you definitely won't be getting any rest then."

"I'll stay on with you."

Tomorrow, she'll blame her tiredness. But tonight, she accepts.

"Okay."

27

1 week to the wedding

JANE

❖ ❖ ❖ ❖ ❖

"ARE YOU SURE you don't want to come?" Jane asks Zihao as she flips through clothing in their walk-in closet, searching for the dress she bought. She browbeat the other five women she's splitting it with to let her be the first person to wear it. No way was some little girl overruling her this time. The dress is a burgundy Gucci midi, with metallic dots down the length of the skirt and enough give in the belly area that she isn't uncomfortable. It makes her feel like a sexy fish.

"No, you know I don't do well in places like that. Rich people flaunting their excess." Zihao shudders slightly. "You'll have a better time without me." He's in shorts and a gray T-shirt, about to go for a run, but instead of leaving, he takes up residence on their bed, watching her.

After she's slipped into the dress, Jane positions herself in front of the mirror hanging on the closet door. She eyes her body, running a hand down her side. She feels self-conscious even though she's been naked in front of him millions of times.

"Why do you do that?"

"Do what?"

"I've noticed that when you look at yourself, you never look at your face. You consciously avoid it."

Jane stiffens. "No, I don't." She sits at her vanity to put on makeup, hoping he shelves the subject.

He doesn't. "You do. You do it every morning. Also, you never take selfies. Which is strange, because it seems like that's all people do nowadays." As Jane draws on eyeliner, Zihao asks, "Why do you act like you don't like your face?"

Heat washes over her. The second worst thing to someone judging her face is someone judging her for judging her face. Hating herself is supposed to be a private activity. "I don't know what you're talking about."

He gets up and walks over, but before she can rise, he has one hand on the chair and another gripping the edge of the vanity, boxing her in. In the mirror, their eyes meet, and he asks, "Why do you treat yourself like that?"

Her breaths quicken, and she averts her gaze from his. Nobody has looked at her like this in recent memory.

Zihao removes his hands, but it's to lay them on her shoulders instead. "I'm not letting you leave like this. I've noticed this for the longest time, and I hate it. I see how you hide from yourself, and it's not healthy. You should like who you are, Jane."

Who she is? What does he know about who she is? She gives him a shove. "How am I supposed to do that when my own husband thinks I'm ugly?"

He staggers back. "I never said that."

She jumps up, starting toward him. "I heard you." He's going to think she's pathetic for bringing up something from more than a year ago. But she's held the memory inside for too long, revisiting it in the moments she feels the most ashamed. Now, she unleashes it, her greatest weapon. "Talking to my parents.

Telling them you didn't care that I wasn't pretty, that I would *do*. Like some shitty add-on you had no choice but to take."

"That's not what I meant." He reaches toward her again, then drops his arm pathetically.

"Cut the shit. You didn't marry me for my face, just like I didn't marry you for your wealth."

Zihao combs his fingers through his hair. "Honestly, I can't even recall exactly what I said, but I'm sorry, okay?"

Jane holds her makeup brush so tightly she's surprised it doesn't snap. Of course he wouldn't remember.

"I *am* sorry." His voice is emphatic. "Jane, your parents...they drove me insane with the way they talked about you. Like they couldn't believe anyone wanted you. I was so sick of it, of them and my parents asking me if I was sure. I said what they expected to hear. I'm sorry that something I said to shut them up bothered you for this long." He swallows, like he doesn't know how to get his next words out.

Jane shakes her head, trying to stop the burn behind her eyes. For so long, she has buried her feelings, terrified of letting others witness the real depth of her pain. "You meant it," she whispers.

"No. I didn't want a supermodel. I wanted someone who wasn't afraid to be honest with me, to be open about the things she likes. You seemed like that sort of person." His lips twitch. "When you took my money and spent it on a handbag that looks like a takeout box, I knew you were."

Her makeup brush falls to the ground, and she starts to cry. Is it possible she married the one man in the world who doesn't care about appearance? Tears roll down her cheeks. Damn it, she doesn't have time to redo her makeup.

"If you're lying to me, I'm really going to kill you," she sobs as he pulls her into his chest.

Zihao dabs at her eyes with the bottom of his shirt, paying no attention to the stains her makeup leaves. "When I look at you, I see someone who challenges me like nobody ever has. Someone fierce. Beautiful."

Jane presses her nose into his neck, breathing in his scent. Their entire home smells like him, and she wonders now if it's the reason why her muscles loosen whenever she enters the apartment. He is her own special kind of aromatherapy.

He strokes her hair. "I respect you for speaking your mind. Even if I don't always agree, it makes me think about ways I can do better."

"If—" Jane chokes a little. "If you respect me, why do you disapprove so much of everything I do?"

Zihao's hand pauses, resting on her head. "Because shopping is superficial and wasteful. I don't get why it makes you happy. It makes me think you're compensating for something you think you don't have, and it frustrates me to know my money is being spent on something pointless."

"It's not pointless to me," she says quietly. She doesn't know if he'll ever get it. Even if he accepts her, the rest of the world still won't. A woman's appearance will always be the first thing people see.

She feels his chest lift. "I'll try harder to understand. If you do the same for me."

Slowly, she nods.

He curls his fingers around her chin, tips it up, and kisses her.

They've kissed before, but it's always felt more like a chore. A demonstration of their marriage to an invisible audience. But something about this kiss is different.

The proximity of the bed makes things easy. The mattress is soft underneath her as Zihao struggles to get her dress off.

"Wait, stop!" If he rips something, she's going to have to pay back all the other girls who put in money to buy it.

He observes her with half-amusement, half-arousal as she shimmies out of the dress, until she's down to matching bra and underwear. Then he tugs off his shirt, and she takes a moment to appreciate the view before crawling back into bed beside him.

He brushes her hair back, and she turns away into the pillows. She's aware of the freckles on her forehead, the wideness of her cheeks that will seem more pronounced at this distance.

In the past, sex was done in the dark. Lights off, curtains drawn, her mind in some other place. That wasn't the case now, with the light shining in from their windows and her senses full of him.

"Let me look at you," he whispers. At first she hesitates, but his voice is so gentle that she grits her teeth and complies. "Qīn'ài'de," he says into her ear. *Beloved.* This is the first time he's called her that. Something inside her gives way as he skims his fingers up her thigh, up to that most intimate spot, applying pressure in a way that makes her gasp. "Can you still say I don't find you beautiful?" he asks.

After, when she's reapplying her makeup at the vanity, Zihao drapes his arms over her shoulders and flips the mirror away from its magnification setting so she's looking at her face. She manages it for a minute before her eyes dart away.

"It will get easier," Zihao tells her as she puts on her shoes, missing nothing. "But you have to keep doing it." He grabs the collar of her coat and draws it tightly around her. "Stay warm."

As Jane marches toward the subway, feeling like she's just bathed in fire, her phone buzzes in her purse. Probably Rina and Lulu, wondering where she is. She digs for it, but her fingers land on something coarse—the card from her consultation. She'd put the appointment in her calendar but forgotten about this paper reminder. She stares at it until her phone buzzes again, then shoves the card into her wallet and out of her mind.

28

1 week to the wedding

LULU

LULU SHIVERS AS she and Harv greet their party guests on
the dock. Her baby blue cape dress is too thin against the breezy
spring.

"You're going to catch a cold," Rina declares upon arriving.
She looks chic in a long-sleeved, sapphire blue jumpsuit with
silver bar earrings. "Are you sure you won't get seasick?" she
whispers as she drapes her jacket around Lulu's shoulders. It has
the faint smell of perfume, something delicate and citrusy that
she recognizes, a sample from the bottle Harv had gifted Lulu,
one of his many presents since their engagement. Lulu's learned
that's how he shows affection. What Harv doesn't realize is his
excessive gift-giving, maybe welcomed by women he's dated in
the past, makes everything seem transactional to Lulu.

"I'll be fine," Lulu says, refusing her coat. "Thank you for
planning so much of this." This whole party is about playing pretend, but of course Rina still made it come together flawlessly.

"She's right, you can't get sick before the wedding. The two of you should head inside," Harv says as he returns from greeting a friend. "Go have fun."

As they start up the ramp to the boat, Rina stifles a giant yawn. Lulu heard her on the phone late last night. They've all been working hard for so many months; it's difficult to believe the wedding is only a week away. It's real, it's happening. When all of this succeeds, she will have earned it. They all will have.

Inside, Vic hands out flutes of champagne in a floral shirt with three buttons undone. "Get any sleep last night?" he asks as they approach.

Rina smiles at him. For a moment, they hold each other's gaze.

"Some," Rina says, and continues on through the room.

Vic's watches her as she disappears.

"Thanks for lending us your boat," Lulu tells Vic. "And for being there for Harv." And she means it. She's grateful for Vic. For his loyalty as best man. At least, when she's not there anymore, Vic Shan will be. Though she doesn't love Harv, she's come to understand him better, how he's doing his best trying to satisfy everyone around him, just like she is. He deserves family and friends who support him.

"It's the least I can do. I'm the man's best friend, after all." Vic's smile slips slightly. "Maybe one of his only friends."

"He cares about your friendship a lot." Something like uncertainty crosses Vic's face, and Lulu feels the need to reassure him. "Trust me, he does."

Vic casts his eyes downward. "Did he tell you? We've only fought twice. Once was when I told him not to go work for his dad, a few months ago when he was dead set on handling the FFC property."

The boat sways and she has to steady herself. "You did?"

"At least Harv's mom cares about him. His dad...well, he's an asshole."

"He's still his dad."

Vic rocks back on his heels. "I guess I've never understood that sort of attachment to people who never truly care about you. I think your real family is proven by actions, not blood. Harv is my family. No matter what, he'll always welcome me into his home, and I'll do the same for him."

It's moving, the strength of their bond. "What about the second time?" she asks Vic.

"What?"

"You said you've fought twice."

"Did I?" His expression is guarded. "I misspoke. Anyway, we're good now. You should get inside and try the caviar before it's gone. Some of the bridesmaids eat it like it's yogurt."

"What is that again? Fish eggs?"

"That's too pedestrian a word to assign to something so delicious." Vic gives her a nudge. "Go on. It's your party."

Lulu walks deeper into the cavernous interior of the yacht. It's outfitted in marble and steel, and there's a bar in the back with buckets of champagne and tins of caviar. The other twenty-some members of the wedding party mingle, too busy drinking and eating to notice Lulu.

Rina appears with a platter heaped with sushi, braised pork, and blanched vegetables.

"Eat," Rina instructs, tugging her to a plush bench. Setting aside the food, she says, "The doctor I requested at the clinic approved my appointment yesterday. It'll take at least two weeks for the hormone injections. I'll have to take a month off from work. I'm not sure they'll let me."

"It's on the calendar now, though. That's exciting."

A full smile stretches across Rina's face. "It is. God, Lulu. I felt so much relief when I finally booked it. I've been hoping I'd be able to do this for so long. I wasn't sure it would happen."

"What about Vic, though?" she asks, not willing to ignore the shift she's sensed between them.

Rina lifts her head, suddenly alert. "What *about* Vic?"

"You're wearing my perfume."

Rina gives herself a self-conscious sniff. "Sorry, I hope you don't mind."

Lulu decides to press harder. There's something going on between them. "Not if you tell me what happened with you and Vic."

Rina checks that nobody's in earshot, then leans toward her. "We've been talking a lot recently, while he's been away. At night. I'm incredibly sleep-deprived. He must be too."

Vic, despite being so cavalier, knows how to care for other people. Lulu has always appreciated this about him, even if Rina couldn't see it. "I don't think he would do that for just anyone," she says.

Rina plays with her bracelet.

"You could make it work." Lulu wants Rina to grab this happiness and hold on to it.

"He's Harv's best friend, Lulu. You know how much he cares about him. If we hurt Harv, we hurt him, too."

Lulu sighs. "I guess you're right." It's unfair there are expiration dates on their bodies. That the smartest person she knows still can't have everything she wants. Lulu's seen Rina furiously study clinics, registering them in her Excel, rating them based on results, efficiency, cost. The money from this wedding will help her achieve that. Lulu opens her mouth to tell Rina what she's been up to, the recent meeting with the VIPs and how they're going to get so much more money than expected—

"Where's Jane? The boat is going to leave without her." Rina pulls out her phone.

When Jane picks up, they hear the *whoosh* of the train in the background. "I swear I'm almost there."

"You're still on the train?!" Rina exclaims. "Jane, the boat's going to leave."

"I know, I know. But I have a good reason."

"What reason?" Rina says.

"I just had some of the *best* sex of my life!" Jane reveals, like she's reporting on breaking news. "Anyway, more later. See you soon." She hangs up.

Rina and Lulu look at each other. "That was a terrible reason," Rina says. "I'm going to warn the captain. Want to come?"

"No, I'll wait for you here." Lulu observes the festivities unfurling around her. The women cluster together, gossiping while balancing little crackers heaped with caviar. The men pour each other heavy shots from a bottle of amber liquid. Harv and Vic are clinking glasses of beer at the bar, their postures sweetly similar. Lulu hopes Harv enjoys this party, too. He's been working so hard, trying to be supportive of Lulu while appeasing his demanding parents. Lulu imagines him as a child, standing in the shadow of his demanding father. Always vigilant, wary of the world around him. How lonely that must have been.

She's on her phone, again studying her flight details, when her mom calls.

"Lulu," she says warmly. "Has your party started?"

"It's about to." Her mom has become increasingly excited about the wedding, the venue, the decorations, the colors of the place mats.

"Your Baba and I wanted to check in. You've made it so far, Lulu." She almost sounds choked up. "Āiyá." Her voice becomes distant, like she's stepped away to wipe her tears. "You talk to her."

Lulu's never heard her mom cry.

"Lulu, we are looking forward to seeing you soon," her dad says through the phone. He also sounds emotional. "Even if your Baba is sad that it will be the day you stop being only our daughter."

"Oh, don't say such things!" Her mom has returned. "Lulu, you will be so protected and well-off. And think about the security you are giving our family. Wah, when you're married, we can finally upgrade our house. Your Ba doesn't need to get back issues from always trying to fix things!"

"Back issues? Ba, is this true?"

"Don't worry about me, nǚér. I was working on our plumbing and pulled something."

"Ma, why didn't you stop him?"

"There were leaks and we didn't have money to hire someone! Lulu, don't you see? Once you are married, we won't have to worry about this anymore. Your husband will take care of all of us." She gives a watery sob. "Truly, a daughter is a blessing."

Lulu's throat is tight. Her mom is looking out for the good of her entire family, and what the Leftovers have planned will ruin all of that. Will she be able to live with this choice? That she put her own desire for happiness over what was best for her family?

"Enough," her dad says to her mom. "Let her enjoy the party. We love you, nǚér."

After Lulu hangs up, she digs her fingers into the velvet sofa beneath her, watching it turn dark where she clutches it.

29

1 week to the wedding

RINA

I LIKE HIM. The realization needles Rina as she heads toward the navigation room. Last night, they'd stayed up chatting on the phone again, and she felt the intimacy of those midnight conversations in the way Vic just looked at her on the ramp. She can't deny that her anticipation on the way here had been because of him either.

"Do you even know where you're going?" A familiar amused voice follows her down the hallway.

"The captain is always toward the bow." She did a bunch of research on boats on her way to the pier.

"Silly me to assume that was something you didn't know." Vic's stride is long and unhurried. "I've been enjoying our late-night chats, but I should confess that I'm beginning to feel like your dirty little secret."

You are, Rina thinks. Their interactions feel like a host of rash decisions at odds with who she's supposed to be. She should be focused on the value he can provide, not the connection that's developed between them. There are other things to look forward to. A trip to San Francisco. Sending Lulu off. Accompanying Jane to her appointment. Seeing her friends' dreams come true.

"You never finished your story last night. About the kayak," she says. They can't talk about this, not with the wedding looming so close.

Vic takes the bait and finishes his story of tipping out of his kayak while fishing near Sentosa Island by the time they reach the cockpit. Inside the small room, the captain is reading a copy of *The Three-Body Problem*.

"We have someone who's running late," Rina tells him. "Can we depart a little later?"

The captain looks at Vic.

"Whatever the lady wishes," Vic says with a shrug.

As they walk back to the main cabin side by side, Vic says, "This party's not bad, huh? I did a good job."

"Let's not forget *I'm* the one who confirmed the beverage selection and discovered you forgot to include water."

"I had everything else, though. And who would be upset about only being able to drink top-shelf liquor all night?"

As Rina is about to enter the hallway leading to the main room, Vic's fingers brush her elbow. "Let's take a detour." He beckons her toward a door she didn't notice before, cleverly painted with the same marble pattern as the rest of the interior.

She should say they need to get back. But Vic is looking at her so earnestly, and suddenly she can't find the resolve to say no.

The door opens to a windowless room, round lamps on the ceiling providing a soft glow. Rina gasps as she takes in the treasures. Watercolor paintings of gray hues of birds, forests, and rivers, each with a picture light installed above, line the walls, and carefully placed throughout are various sculptures and carvings. Rina stops to examine a particularly arresting painting of a man rowing a raft between imposing mountains.

"I pick up stuff whenever I travel. Pieces from local artists that will remind me of these places in a way that photos can't." Vic taps the skull of what might be a bull, its horns carved out of material that looks like jade. "I'm proud of this one. It was a steal."

"And before you were this rich, did you satisfy yourself with keychains as souvenirs?" she asks, eyebrow raised.

"I've never been not rich." Vic says it matter-of-factly. "Oh, except for when I dropped out of college. But I threw all my savings into investing, and it worked out."

She thinks about him sitting alone in the cafeteria, trying to choke down tuna salad, what his grandma told her about the many odd jobs he worked to support himself during his year out of school, when his parents cut him off. He'd used money from those gigs and got into day trading. While Rina and her classmates were studying for midterms, Vic invested his stock earnings in an early-stage gaming company that ended up IPOing in five years and led to more investments. At that point, his grandma had begged his parents to let him come back home. Unable to deny he'd achieved success, they'd agreed, though Rina has a feeling Vic never forgave them. "It worked out, but it must not have been easy."

Vic tilts his head as he examines the bull. The light glides across the angles of his face, getting lost in his black hair. "All the other international kids but Harv thought I was going to disgrace myself and stopped associating with me. Now they come to me for business advice. I'm used to being alone, though. My parents were never around when I was growing up in Hong Kong. Once my grandma passes, I'll have no more ties to Shanghai either." He steps out from under the sculpture. The lamps offer only a haze, and the room is all dark corners and shadows.

"You have Harv, don't you?"

"Once his dad hands over the business, I'll never get to see him." Vic sounds sad. "I can steer my life however I want, but Harv has to make his own decisions, even if he's damning himself."

It's sweet that Vic has this attachment to Harv. "Regardless

of what he does, the best thing you can do is be there for him."
Rina drifts toward a painting of lotuses, their petals white, the
tips tinged with pink. His footsteps trail after her. "Is this the
inspiration for your tattoo?"

"No, there was a giant pond near my childhood home. It
was so covered in lotus paddies that you couldn't even see the
water below. I got the great idea to walk on them once and almost drowned." Rina pictures a younger Vic and smiles. "My
grandma told me that some things must be appreciated from a
distance. Later, I learned the lotus is the gentleman's flower. It
grows in mud yet stays unstained." He's right behind her now.

"How many girls have you told that story to?" she asks wryly.

"You're the only one," he says into her ear. Rina spins around.
She refuses to let him back her against the wall, so she just stands
there as he leans in, brings his nose inches from her neck. Her
skin tingles, his hair tickling her chin. He smirks. "Perfume,
huh? You trying to impress me?"

It had been a spur-of-the-moment choice, to spray on one
of Lulu's perfumes. She knew he would notice. "I always wear
perfume."

"I don't think you do." His eyes are dark with intent, and
Rina knows if she does not get out of here now, something is
going to happen between them that she won't be able to take
back. All those late-night conversations, the way she no longer
wants to duck away from his touch...

He leans in a little closer, and fuck it. She reaches for him and
brings his mouth to hers.

Their lips move like it's a choreographed sequence, practiced
and built into muscle memory. One of his hands is pressed against
the wall next to her, and the other grips the back of her hair.

His fingers skim her waist just as they hear Harv call for him.
"Vic, we need a map of this place—"

Rina shoves him away, dragging a hand through her now-
messy hair as she gets the hell out of there.

She ends up in the game room, where rowdy guests play drinking games at a large table in the center. Lulu and Jane sit off to the side. Both of them are stunned at the sight of her.

As Rina joins them, Jane silently slides a shot glass over.

Rina downs it, her heart still beating fast. She sees the question on the tip of their tongues.

"Why were you so late?" she demands of Jane instead. "We almost left without you."

"You wouldn't have let that happen." The presumption in Jane's voice rubs against her already raw nerves. Is Rina just around to anticipate catastrophes and tidy everyone's messes? "Anyway, I was telling Lulu that before I left, Zihao and I had the best sex *ever*," Jane explains.

"I thought you were having sex regularly?" Lulu asks as Rina sits.

"Sure, but it was the vanilla kind that you do just so you don't have to masturbate that day."

Lulu scrunches up her nose. "Is that a thing?"

"I can guarantee you that it is," Jane assures her. "But this time, it was actually *hot*."

"What made it different?"

Jane's eyes glitter. "He called me beautiful."

Rina blurts, "That's it?"

Lulu seems to get it better than she does. "He said it like he meant it."

"We've always told you that," Rina says. Zihao is no Du Fu, but she'd expected something more poetic to sway her friend.

"I know, and I love you for it. But... It was different coming from him." She bites her lip.

Of course. A man waltzes in, says the words Rina's been repeating her whole life, and Jane's insecurity disappears with a poof. Rina breathes in deeply through her nose. No, she's happy for Jane. She's just projecting her own problems onto her friend.

"So you don't need the money anymore?" Lulu asks.

"One can always have more money," Jane says. "We go

through with everything as planned. I just may not get divorced after all."

She fluffs her hair. "Anyway, let's celebrate! We've worked hard, and we're about to send our dear friend off to a lifetime of happiness." She winks at Lulu.

Just as they're about to order wine, a groomsman barges in, face red and voice loud, wheeling a gigantic brass gong. "Everyone, stop what you're doing! It's time for Jígǔ Chuánhuā. Otherwise known as the Gong Game."

30

1 week to the wedding

LULU

THE GONG HANGS from a large wooden stand, occupying most of the game room. The groomsman who summoned them jumps up to grab the mallet from the frame and misses.

"What's the Gong Game?" Lulu whispers to Jane while the others pile up on the plush couches in the center.

Jane glances toward the exit. "You won't like it. It's such a childish game, and even if this whole event is a farce, we should find something else to—"

"Why aren't you sitting together?" someone calls. Suddenly, Lulu is airborne. She releases an alarmed yelp.

"Bo, put her down." Harv tries to control the room, but the groomsmen have other ideas.

"Don't be shy, Harv! The two of you will be getting a lot closer soon." A chorus of oohs rises around them.

"Come give your wife-to-be a kiss," Bo says. "Or better yet, a smack." He spins so Lulu's butt is in Harv's face. Her hands fly to her skirt.

Jane's voice cuts through the ruckus like a knife. "Put. Her. Down."

There's a brief silence, then Lulu gets dropped on a couch like a sack of potatoes, crashing into Harv.

Jane stomps up to Bo and pushes him hard. "If you can't put her down gently, you weren't strong enough to pick her up in the first place."

Lulu rights herself on the couch, then reaches for Jane, pulling her down beside her before she can get into a fistfight with Bo. "I'm fine."

Harv keeps the peace and says, "So, who wants to tell us how to play this game?"

"I'll get us started." Vic goes to one of the giant vases, this one blooming with peonies, and breaks one off its stem. He presents it to Rina with a flourish. "You can start," he says. Then he heads over to the gong. "I beat this gong as you pass the flower around. When the gong stops, the person holding the flower drinks."

Harv sits beside Jane while Rina takes Lulu's other side. Rina looks at her flower, then at Lulu, who has never really developed a taste for alcohol. "Can we play something that doesn't involve drinking?" she asks, but the words are lost as Vic hits the gong once. The sound is wide and echoing, like sea spray hitting rocks in a deep cavern.

"Let's goooo," another groomsman bellows, leaping to his feet. He almost headbutts Vic, who steps aside at the last second. The groomsman bangs the gong. The sacredness is gone, replaced by a head-splitting boom.

Rina hurriedly hands the flower to Lulu, who gives it to Jane. It makes its way around the circle of twenty people. When the flower returns to Lulu, the gong stops. Someone inserts a small flask of clear liquid into her hand. "Drink!" they crow.

The Maotai burns going down, fiery and corrosive. Her stomach responds with a gurgle of dissatisfaction.

The gong starts again. Once again, the flower stops with Lulu.

She searches the gleeful faces around her, only here for fancy fish eggs, champagne, and gossip. This whole thing is a sham, just like Jane said. Why does she need to subject herself to this? "I can't," she murmurs. She makes a motion to get up, wanting soda to gargle away the taste.

"She's escaping!" exclaims a bridesmaid in a distractingly sparkly diamond choker. "Lulu, don't be a wimp."

It's eerily similar to something her brother would say. If her mom could see her now, she would scold Lulu for bringing down the mood.

"I'll drink for her," Rina announces.

A groomsman with his hair in a greasy topknot snorts. "That's not how the game works."

"Shut up," Jane says. "This isn't your party."

Rina snatches the tiny glass out of Lulu's hands and tips it into her mouth before anyone else can protest. She aims a steely glare at the groomsman in charge of the gong. "Again."

The flower lands on Lulu once more, and this time, Jane picks up her drink, but not before scowling at Harv. "Hey, you. Shouldn't you pick up some of the slack?"

"Jane—" Lulu shakes her head. They aren't actually getting married. Harv has no obligation toward her.

Harv holds out his hand. "I'll take it."

Jane slams down the shot before saying disdainfully, "Do you love her at all, or did you propose because she was the first pretty girl to cross your path?"

The question sucks all the air out of the room. Lulu finds herself waiting for the answer along with everyone else. She knows why Harv's parents approved of their marriage, but she's never learned the reason he proposed so quickly.

"Well?" Jane demands. Without alcohol, she is already a force to be reckoned with, but the added drunkenness has loosened her tongue to dangerous levels.

At this point, Rina has probably had more than Jane, but she touches Jane's elbow placatingly. "Let's play another game," she says audibly so everyone else gets the hint.

Vic tries to back her up. "Everyone else is dying of boredom."

"Why does it matter why I'm marrying her?" Harv yanks at the collar of his shirt like it's strangling him. "She said yes."

"That's because she never had a choice." Jane folds her arms. "Women never do."

"I don't either!" Harv says, then takes a step back, as if he's surprised himself. His outburst startles Lulu too. She recalls his earlier doubts about the wedding, back when they were address-ing invitations. But that had been because of work conflicts, hadn't it? Not because he didn't want to get married.

There's a clatter. Rina rose too quickly and knocked a foot-stool over. She kneels, scrabbling, gathering the fallen glasses that toppled over with it.

Harv takes advantage of the distraction and pushes himself up. "I'm not feeling well. Please, everyone, enjoy yourselves."

"Harv. Don't go," Vic says. He helps Rina up, but his face is turned toward his friend, pleading.

Harv clenches his jaw. "You've got your hands full."

Lulu watches Harv walk away. What did he mean when he said he didn't have a choice either? "I'm going to find him," she tells the others.

Outside on the deck, it feels rockier. The boat vibrates subtly beneath her feet, a reminder that she is trapped far from land. She slows, keeping one hand on the wall as she makes her way to their honeymoon suite. She forces the queasiness away as she slides open the door. "Harv?" In the dark, she sees the shape of his back, the defeated curve of his neck as he sits on the bed. He looks fragile, a shadow that could dissolve into the darkness. "I'm sorry about what Jane said." Jane had only been trying to defend her, but there was no need to do it so publicly.

Harv's head dips lower. "She was right. You never really had a choice, did you?"

Lulu approaches him cautiously. "Not really," she admits. "From our first date, you had the power. I would always have had to say yes." It's the most honest thing she's ever told him.

Rina and Jane would say it's risky, revealing something like this so close to the wedding. But Lulu has grown to regard him as more than just the man she's stealing from.

"I should've defended you before Jane had to. None of those guys are really my friends anyway, except for Vic." Harv's hands are clasped tightly. "It's just—I don't know how to be gallant or confident in those situations. I don't have the sorts of qualities women look for."

"You're kind and generous. That's what women want." Lulu would not have thought that Harv, the most desirable bachelor in Shanghai, could think of himself as anything less.

Harv laughs. "Maybe you could explain that to everyone who dumped me in college because I wasn't exciting enough for them."

Lulu finds this hard to believe. "You said you didn't have a choice, but surely there were so many other women you could have chosen from."

"Women I can see myself being with for life?" Harv stares down at his hands. "My parents have been pressuring me to marry and have kids since I graduated. When we started dating, they went on and on about how you were dirt poor, how your family would suck us dry. That stuff doesn't matter to me, though. I've figured out that what I want in a wife is someone who's gentle, accommodating. From the moment I met you, I knew you would always ask rather than demand. Do you remember our first kiss?"

Their first kiss didn't leave much of an impression on Lulu. All she recalls is the apprehension afterward, knowing that the first kiss is usually the gateway to more intimate activities. They did have sex, once. Harv never asked again, and Lulu was secretly relieved. It just felt awkward with him. Around their friends, they held hands, sometimes exchanged a kiss, but the affection was never genuine.

"I don't," Harv says. "And that's what I want. Something simple that doesn't require extra work. My family, our business. They give me enough stress as it is."

"So you've never wanted to marry for love?" Lulu asks. She folds her arms, suddenly cold.

"No." The word brings with it a release. At least there will be no broken hearts left behind. "Not anymore. I've gotten too attached before, and it didn't work out. It was harder than anything I've been through, and I don't want to go through that again. Besides, a sustainable marriage isn't about love. It's about compatibility. I'll provide for you, take care of you and your family. I know how important family is. Whatever your parents need, they'll have."

Guilt unfurls again, her mom's words ringing through her head. As long as she's making so little money, her dad will think he needs to fix everything in that crumbling house himself, and he's far too old for that. Harv is offering in no uncertain terms to support her family for the rest of her life.

Lulu sits on the bed but keeps distance between them. "How can you be content with this? When you know there can be more?"

"You sound like Vic." Harv chuckles humorlessly. "He's an idealist. He really fought me when I said I was going to propose to you." *We've only fought twice*, Vic had said. Because Vic, who loves his best friend, doesn't want Harv stuck in a marriage that's basically a transaction. "I can't keep giving excuses to my parents. It's past time for me to bring heirs into the family and honor to the Zhu name. You've actually already helped with the latter, and I think because of the differences in how we've been raised… I'll be pushed to see the world in another way." He faces her fully now. They've edged closer to each other, their arms brushing. "When we're married, I want us to work together. We'll be a team, and I won't leave you out of matters the way my dad has done to my mom."

She wishes Harv hadn't told her all this. If he was only using her to prop up his family name, it would be easier to leave him. But he wants a true partnership, one where he would welcome her opinions and thoughts.

The alcohol from earlier travels up her throat, along with everything else—a bitter, acidic mixture of guilt, anxiety, fear.

Bewilderment replaces the anguish on Harv's face. "Are you—"

She bursts out of the room and onto the deck, just barely avoiding vomiting all over Vic's shiny boat. After, she grips the rail. The lights on the shore of the Huangpu aren't so far away. She spots the dots of people taking evening strolls and admiring the shimmering water.

Too many expectations. Too many people in her ear, saying they're not asking for *too much*. She gives and gives, but still it's not enough.

What she wants is to get off this damn boat. Swim to shore and disappear into the crowd. She is sick of this party and sick of the people, and now she might be seasick.

She pictures Ko Lipe from her poster, the inviting turquoise waves. Her dress flutters around her legs as she heaves one leg over the railing, then the other. On her tiptoes, she surveys the water below her. It's no Thai island, but it'll do.

She jumps.

31

1 week to the wedding

JANE

❖ ❖ ❖ ❖ ❖

JANE IS MAKING her way through a bottle of expensive Bordeaux from Vic's wine fridge when the groomsmen file into the lounge. Yelling at Harv was in poor taste, especially considering the embarrassment they're about to cause him. But she'd rather drink than brood over her actions.

The groomsmen cluster at the end of the bar. At first, it's easy to ignore them, but their voices rise with the stacks of their empty glasses.

"I can't believe how fast this engagement was, considering how long it took with that last chick. Harv mooned after her for months before he asked her out."

"That's because her family was actually important. You don't mess around with the people who sell ninety percent of bottled water in China."

"Poor guy, he was obviously damaged when she chose the dude who popularized toasters over him."

"I still think he moved too fast. This time, he didn't even bother to check if she had a personality first."

Jane couldn't care less about Harv's tragic romance, but there's no way she's going to sit back while they attack Lulu. She grabs her bottle by the neck and marches over to them. "Hey, assholes. Don't talk shit about someone at their own party."

As one, they turn to her. The man who was talking guffaws loudly. "Who are you to tell me what to do, you square-faced troll?"

Jane grips the bottle tighter as his friends laugh. Their amusement galvanizes the prick, who grins. "If I looked like you, I'd be angry all the time too."

Her arm moves. Light flashes against glass. The men's jeers fade at the sound of something shattering. The bottom half of the wine bottle is gone, and red pools in the carpet. Their stares follow her as she raises its broken head and points it at their gaping leader. Spit flies as he screeches, "You crazy bitch!"

"That's right," Jane says, low and vicious. "I'm crazy, and I'll fuck you up."

Then she releases the rest of the bottle and storms out, glass crunching beneath her heels.

On the deck, she clasps the railing and tries to calm her rage. Squeezing her eyes shut, she feels two hot tears leak out.

She shouldn't let herself be bothered by what they said. Those petty men with tiny dicks. What do they matter?

But the insults swarm her mind. Ugly. Unlovable. She has spent her whole life protecting herself against this, but after three decades that armor is growing increasingly heavy to carry. It confirms why the surgery is so important. This is about more than what one man sees when he looks at her. This is about what the world sees.

She almost misses the figure in a pale dress that nearly glows in the darkness. At first, Jane thinks it's some malevolent ghost, coming to end her misery, but said ghost swings a leg over the railing. The moon illuminates her face.

Jane's lips are forming her name when Lulu dives straight into the water. There's a splash, and her white arms plunge through it like she's swimming away. But with each effort, the waves keep bringing her back toward the yacht until she stops, bobbing up and down.

Adrenaline sharpens into panic, and Jane runs to the door that opens into the saloon on the main deck, yelling, "Someone help!" before slamming it shut again and searching for the lifesaver to throw overboard. She has no idea if she was heard over the sounds of the party, but she can't take her eyes off Lulu again and risk losing her. She speed dials Rina as she paces. Rina is always good at picking up. Part of being a hostage to work.

It goes to voice mail.

"Fucking Rina." Jane finally locates the orange-and-white-striped circle and throws it overboard. "Lulu, I'm coming for you!" she calls. Then she strips off her dress—making sure not to tear it—until she's in only the lacy lingerie she'd flaunted for Zihao just hours ago. Zihao. He'd know what to do.

She texts him. Send help.

Then she jumps in after her friend.

As she hits the water, the cold drills through her skin all the way into her bones and sobers her instantly. Jane surfaces and gasps for a few wasteful seconds to orient herself. Lulu is barely visible over the waves. Jane fights the current and swims closer. Lulu's eyes are shut, her hair sticking to her forehead.

"Lulu!" Jane slaps her cheek, and Lulu's eyes fly open. "What do you think you're doing?"

Despite the freezing water, Lulu almost seems serene. She stares up at the sky. "I wanted to go for a swim."

Jane hoists the lifesaver under Lulu's arms. "There's a pool on the boat, you ninny. Here, grab on to this."

As the two of them float together, Jane scans the boat for movement, teeth chattering. The waves smack her in the face, and she gags when she remembers how polluted the Huangpu is.

A few minutes later, the engine shuts off, and a host of anxious bodies appear at the railing. Someone drags the line in, and Jane and Lulu flop onto the deck like fish. The grooms-men from earlier loom above them. She shivers, aware of what she must look like.

Rina shouts for someone to bring towels before kneeling beside them, the water on the deck soaking into her clothing. "What happened?"

"Someone wanted to go for a dip," Jane says bitterly.

Harv comes bearing a stack of towels. He hands one to Jane before crouching next to Lulu and wrapping another around her. "Don't get cold," he says, drawing it tight in a way that reminds Jane of how Zihao had attentively tightened her coat collar before she left. "You should've told me you were feeling unwell."

"Thanks," Lulu murmurs as she takes the edges of the towel. Harv doesn't relinquish his hold, gazing at her with concern.

In the bathroom, Jane and Lulu change into clothes Rina has scrounged from the bridesmaids: another dress for Lulu and oversize sweats for Jane. Jane glares at Lulu as she pushes her legs through the pants. She wishes Zihao were here.

When they return to the blessedly warm game room, where everyone else has gathered, Vic hands them hot tea. The entire mood of the party dips into watchful sobriety.

"Don't smother us," Jane snaps at the people around them. "Go drink and party and whatever."

They send one another uncertain looks, but Vic decides to lead the charge. "There's a KTV room here. Harv, shall we?"

"Go," Lulu says to Harv. He hesitates briefly, then follows Vic out.

Slowly, the room empties until it's just Lulu, Jane, and Rina. Jane shuts the door behind them and turns to Lulu, channeling all the delayed fury into her body.

"You scared the hell out of me," she says.

Lulu hugs herself. "I was seasick."

Jane's mouth opens and closes. "And instead of, oh, I don't know, grabbing a bucket, you decided to *throw yourself overboard*? And you," Jane says, leveling a finger at Rina. "Why didn't you answer when I called?"

"I was on a work call." There's a flash of self-hatred on her face. "I shouldn't have answered."

Jane's phone buzzes, and she digs it out of her pocket. "It's Zihao."

She makes her way out to the deck, leaning against the yacht's rail. The dark waters of the Huangpu seem threatening now. "Lulu went overboard and I jumped in after her. Everyone's fine now."

"*What?* You know there's a button you can press for situations like these?" Zihao is frantic.

"I'm fine. And I didn't know about the button. We didn't exactly get a safety lecture when we boarded this thing."

"That's so irresponsible. Who's the guy who organized this thing?"

"His name is Vic, and he's rich beyond reproach. Save your breath."

There's audible relief on his end. "I don't know what I would've done if something happened to you."

"The house would've been yours."

"That's not funny." Zihao's voice is cross. "Sometimes, Jane, the things you say drive me crazy."

Crazy bitch. Just like that, the men's comments from earlier flood back. Those sorts of insults should've been left on the playground. But even now, she's not immune to the hurt they cause.

"I have to get back," she says. "Good night."

"Wait, Jane—"

She hangs up before he can finish.

"Lulu," Jane announces, marching back in as Rina rubs Lulu's hands to warm them up, "why don't you walk us through the thought process that went from being on a boat to jumping off of it."

Lulu's head dips in shame. "I don't know what I was think-ing," she mumbles.

"You weren't."

Rina gives Jane a warning look before saying, "What's on your mind?"

Lulu glances around the room, and Rina gets the hint. She connects her phone to the speakers, putting on Jay Chou. As his sorrowful crooning fills the air, Jane gestures for Lulu to continue.

Lulu stares down at her hands. "I feel so trapped," she finally says. "No matter what I do, I'll let someone down."

Jane softens and pats her wrist. Even after her plunge in the Huangpu, she's gorgeous. There's a pink flush to her cheeks, and her eyes sparkle with unshed tears. But what makes Lulu so irresistible is she's beautiful both inside and out. "You're getting the pre-heist nerves. Totally understandable."

"There's no need to be nervous," Rina adds. "We've thought through everything. There's nothing you need to—"

"That's not it!" Lulu kneads her skirt anxiously. "I just don't know anymore. About me, about Harv, about anything. How much of what I'm doing is because of someone else?"

Jane puts an arm around her shoulders. Rina mirrors her, and the two of them cuddle Lulu between them. Lulu is over-thinking. They just need to get past this hump. Once the wed-ding is here, there won't be any room for doubt. She'll do what they've planned.

"You won't be letting *us* down," Jane says. "Isn't that what's most important?"

"What if..." Lulu seems to choke up. Then she takes a great big rattling breath and says, "What if I don't want to do the heist anymore?"

32

1 week to the wedding

LULU

✿ ✿ ✿ ✿ ✿

LULU IS AWARE of how impulsive she sounds right now. A week before the heist, and she wants to back out.

Jane and Rina exchange looks, making Lulu feel like a child who's done something wrong.

"Let me clarify," Rina says. Her voice rises slightly. "You don't want to do the thing we've been working on for the past eight months?"

Lulu inhales through her nose. She flashes back to Harv's proposal, the moment everyone was waiting for her "yes," even though everything in her wanted to refuse. A lot has changed since then. "I'm starting to think that marriage with Harv could work." Yes, it means she would be bound to his side. Peng Ayi would be a fixture of her life, presiding over every decision. But Harv is a better partner than she realized, and they've come to care for each other over the past months. The more she thinks about stealing from him, the sicker she feels.

Jane tilts her head. "I don't get it. Did you stop needing the money? Didn't you want to get away? Damn it, Lulu, don't you want to be free?"

Before she can reply, Rina bursts in. "This is a critical juncture, Lulu. Think of everything we've done. You want to throw all that away?" She's appalled. There's nothing Rina hates more than having to dispose of hard work.

Jane leans forward, and there's an alarming, raw desperation on her friend's face. "There are things we need that money for," she says. "Something with stakes this high...you can't get away with being fickle."

The door bangs open. Bo, the groomsman with a knack for bad timing, stands there with a goofy smile. He tosses something at their table, and two dice clatter across the surface, one of them hitting Jane's forearm. "We're almost at the pier. Anyone up for a game of Liar's Dice before we dock?"

Jane jumps up, and her thunderous expression makes his smile drop away. "Get out of here before I shove those dice up somewhere you'll never see them again."

Bo scuttles out, the door slamming decisively behind him. Rina turns up the music that was playing.

"Seriously, Lulu, why would you do this now?" Jane doesn't bother to sit back down. "You had plenty of time to speak up before."

"I—I feel like I haven't fully thought through how this is going to affect my parents, or Harv," Lulu says. How will they react when she leaves them to deal with her mess? Harv will feel so betrayed after opening up to her, and her mom will probably never speak to her again. And she'll be abandoning her dad. "You're reconsidering plastic surgery because of Zihao, aren't you? Things have changed."

"But I'm still doing it."

"You are?" Rina asks, her eyebrows bunching together. "I thought—"

"Because," Jane says, cutting her off, "I'm not going to put what he wants for me before what *I* want for me."

"What if the money ruins something that was perfectly acceptable?" Lulu works to keep her voice from shaking. "Zihao isn't perfect, but he's trying. But you're still holding on to this idea that it's better to be desired by people you don't know rather than people you do."

She doesn't know where she found the audacity to pull Jane's flaws to the surface. Perhaps it's because she already knows how this conversation is going to end.

"You want to talk about what's wrong with me?" Jane asks, each word coming out with the force of a blow. "When you can't even see the bigger picture? You're being impulsive and childish when your decisions impact everyone. You knew what you were getting into."

A bout of hysterical laughter rings out. It's her. She's laughing. All this time, she thought her friends were smarter, more self-aware than she is. "Have you ever seen me as your equal? Or am I only meant to be your echo chamber?"

"Lulu, going through with this wedding isn't going to solve your problems. It won't miraculously help you figure out what you're supposed to do with your life." Rina's tone is even, reasonable. "I understand you're overwhelmed and uncertain. And you're not used to dealing with this kind of pressure or responsibility. But this is not the time to change your mind."

Her words sting, even more so because they're true. Even if Lulu has that ticket to Thailand, she has struggled to see herself boarding a flight and leaving everything behind with no idea what awaits her. At least here, everything is laid out clearly, even if it would mean a life of endlessly appeasing Harv, his parents, her own family.

She'd expected Rina and Jane to react differently. To display a little bit of empathy.

"I didn't know you thought so little of me." Tears trickle

down Lulu's cheeks. "I've always felt like I bring less to this friendship than either of you. So I listen because that's at least something I can give. I listen to your problems, even though it's *exhausting*. I am so *exhausted*." She gasps, her breath not quite catching up with her words. "I feel like I am being torn apart from all directions."

Remorse passes over Rina's face. "You're stressed," she says.

Lulu's eyelashes are sticky with tears. "Were you ever true friends? Would you ever have put me before the things you want?"

Rina is flustered. "How could you—of course I would."

"Then why was your first response to convince me to change my mind when I debated calling this whole thing off?"

Both of them are silent.

The vibration under their feet has stopped, she realizes. The boat is back at the pier. Soon, they'll have to disembark, and looking at Rina and Jane, Lulu knows there's no apology forthcoming. "I should've seen it sooner," she says. "That all of this would cost us something." Everyone is just selfishly watching out for themselves. She was the foolish one, to think their friendship would stay untouched through it all.

In the absence of conversation, Lulu hears the rap on the door. She turns down the music. "Lulu, we're getting off. Do you want to come back with me? My car's already here, and I don't want you to catch a cold." It's Harv.

Lulu pushes back her chair. She'd thought this conversation would make her feel better, but instead Jane and Rina are treating her like the enemy.

"Lulu," Jane says. Lulu stops, hoping she's about to say something that will fix all of this. "So, what does this mean? Are you in or out?"

Disappointment swells in her chest. "I don't know." She rises, goes to the double doors and opens them.

"Are you okay?" Harv asks, concerned.

She composes herself. "Do you think you could send Ling to get some of my clothes from home? I think it makes sense for me to stay at yours until the wedding."

Harv looks over her shoulder uncertainly before nodding. "Do you want to say goodbye to your friends before we go?"

Lulu glances back at the women she loves so dearly. She could go inside, laugh it off, pretend everything is still okay. But she is so tired of all of this, the constant juggling of everyone's expectations.

Rina stands, arm stretching toward Lulu, like she might draw her back. "Lulu—"

Lulu turns and steps out, closing the door behind her. "I already have."

33

2 days to the wedding

RINA

"RINA JIE, IF YOU keep clicking your pen like that, I'll throw it across the room." Mei's haughty voice cuts into Rina's thoughts. Mei's staying with Rina for the next two days, since they have a final meeting at Hotpot Palace and an early start for the wedding. Xiaoyi's under the impression Rina is spending their sleepovers teaching Mei about possible career paths and salary bands.

Rina starts to bite the cap instead as she silently rehearses the apology speech she's prepared to deliver to Lulu. It starts with "Not speaking in five days has made me realize..." With each day Lulu's absent, she's had to adjust the number.

They assumed Lulu had been staying at the Zhus', but Jane ambushed Harv outside his apartment and found out Lulu went home to see her family. In that time, Rina's constantly relived their conversation and the poor way she handled it. She'd been frazzled and not thinking straight after Lulu jumped overboard and the call from Luo Ren.

Mei wrestles away the pen and lobs it over the couch. "What's with you? Also, where's Lulu? I thought you said she was coming to Hotpot Palace with us."

"She's probably heading there separately," Rina says, looking at Lulu's closed door.

Everything will be fine after tonight. She and Jane will apologize, Lulu will forgive them, and they will all move on and focus on stealing those red envelopes.

She and Mei head downstairs to their cab. In the elevator, Mei says, "Rina Jie, you look like a zombie. I'm kind of afraid you're going to eat my brains."

"I'm fine, Mei. I just haven't slept much the past few days."

"Does it have anything to do with Vic Gege and the fact that you're not returning his calls?"

This gives Rina a jolt. "Have you been snooping?" She'd managed to avoid Vic during the disembarkation, but that doesn't mean she's been able to erase him from her thoughts. When she's not worrying over Lulu, her mind drifts back to all the little things she's learned about him over the past few months. His love for his grandma, his affection for Harv, his work ethic, the way he sees her.

Above all, she thinks about that stupid kiss.

"I added him on WeChat." Mei smiles slyly. "He has some shirtless pics from Singapore. Shall I send them to you?"

"No!"

"Your loss," Mei says as they get into their cab.

"Have you made any new friends at school?" Rina changes the subject, and gladly sits back as Mei talks about a girl she met through her women's studies class.

"The two of us skipped class so we could binge *Jojo's Bizarre Adventure* instead. It was awesome!"

At Hotpot Palace, Rina's spirits lift as she steps through its familiar, smudged glass doors. There's a constancy about the place that soothes her. Same peeling posters, spicy air that makes her eyes water slightly, the dull roar of too many conversations. If Hotpot Palace could survive this long, then so can their friendship.

Today's special is actually something edible: buns fried golden, paired with condensed milk. Lulu would like those. They'll have to order some.

Jane and Michelangelo are already there. Jane's hopeful expression dims as they approach. "Lulu's not with you?"

"She's probably just late."

Michelangelo's sharp eyes don't miss a thing. "Has something happened?"

"Nothing to worry about," Rina says. "Let's run through everything. We'll skip Lulu's parts for now. Michelangelo, you're still set to arrive at 9:00 a.m. with the safe?"

Two hours go by, enough time for two run-throughs of the plan. The buns Rina ordered for Lulu sit untouched, growing cold. A server comes by to collect her place setting an hour in, but Rina stops him. "We have one more."

The chair stays unoccupied. The hotpot broth empties of its ingredients, and Rina realizes that if Lulu had intended to show up, she would not have been this late.

"Cold feet, huh?" Mei asks.

Michelangelo folds her arms. "Ladies, I sincerely hope you haven't been wasting my time with this. How are we supposed to do any of this without the bride?"

"Relax. Just because she isn't here doesn't mean she's abandoned the plan," Jane says, but the statement lacks conviction.

Lulu has never stood them up for anything, especially without an explanation. If doubt was nibbling away at Rina before, now it's bitten a giant chunk out of her confidence. But she can't let that affect the others. "We're all nervous, and Lulu most of all," she says. "She probably just got wrapped up in pre-wedding stuff. Rest up, and I'll see you all in thirty-six hours."

Part 3:

THE HEIST

34

Wedding day, 8:00 a.m.

RINA

WHEN RINA AWAKES, Sun Island is utterly transformed. Each of the Bavarian-style hotel suites is decorated in climbing vines and silk lanterns, red roses blooming from every crevice like spilled blood. Flower petals cushion her steps. Apparently, Peng Ayi decided not to tear out the ugly lawn, but to bury it in fresh flowers. An extravagant waste, especially when Rina's not sure the bride is even going to show up. Every step rips petals away from the ground.

She and Mei arrived late last night, and she'd lain in bed unable to sleep, ruminating over all the things she's gotten wrong. Of her friends, she has always had the most choices. She's always believed this was solely a product of her own hard work, but now she understands her experiences and upbringing weren't the norm. Lulu was raised in a family that demands continuous sacrifice, and the party was probably the first time she was brave enough to ask for something for herself, which Jane and Rina threw back in her face.

As Rina walks the path toward Lulu's suite, she passes the mostly empty parking lot. Before the wedding ceremony starts, she'll have to break away from the bridal party and meet Mei and Michelangelo here to help sneak the fake safe into Rina's room. She tugs at the edge of her outfit, a rose-colored qípáo embroidered with gold. It's constrictive, and the high collar digs into her neck.

She expects an empty chair in the dressing room, much like the one left unoccupied at Hotpot Palace. But when she reaches Lulu's suite, Lulu sits in her perfumed dressing room, fussed over by Peng Ayi and a team of stylists. Her hair's already braided, and she's dressed. She probably has been here since six in the morning.

Lulu rises to hug her when Rina approaches, the brocade of her custom-made guàqún scratching Rina's arm.

"Lulu, I'm—"

"The plan is still on," she whispers, and Rina tastes her bitterness like she's bitten into an orange peel. Lulu has lost enthusiasm for the heist, but it'll be fine. They'll talk through her feelings on the way to the airport, when her reward for all this is in sight.

The other bridesmaids filter in, their chatter filling the space. Jane is behind them, looking terrible. The makeup artist gasps when she spots her.

"You look like you didn't sleep a blink," Rina says as they get their hair curled next to each other.

Jane digs her nail under the corner of her eye, chipping away some of the crustiness there. "Zihao insisted we get up early to beat traffic, and it's not like we turned in early last night." The prior night, Rina and Jane had stayed up late on the phone to determine if they could still execute the plan without Lulu. The answer to that was a resounding *no*.

"I see Lulu at least showed up to her own wedding."

Rina shushes her. "We spoke. Everything's still on."

"Thank god for that," Jane mutters, letting the makeup artist tug her away.

The hour drags on as they get ready and pose for photos with Lulu. They beam at the photographer with their arms linked, even though Lulu barely looks at Rina or Jane or says one word. Peng Ayi consults with the photographer, fiddling with Lulu's hair or the neckline of her dress between each shot. When it's time for the door games, she leaves to chat with one of the staff about the tea ceremony.

Harv raps on the door promptly at nine. "I'm here for my bride!" he calls, and the other bridesmaids giggle.

Rina sees Lulu's fingers curl into the diaphanous skirts under her guàqún. The jacket is hand-embroidered with gold thread and ends in red tassels. With the jade-tipped pins in her hair, she could be royalty. Just getting her hair into that complicated braid took hours. But along with the tightness of her mouth, the gesture betrays her nerves.

Yaqing opens the door. Rina follows the other bridesmaids into the hallway, forming a barrier between the men and the door. "We will allow you entry only if you complete a few tasks. Rina." Yaqing snaps her fingers, and Rina grabs a porcelain bowl with strips of slimy seaweed.

The men groan.

"No complaining!" Yaqing says, singsong. "Get in line." She gives Rina a none too gentle shove, enough for the fishy-smelling water to slosh against the sides of the bowl. "Rina, why don't you do the honors?"

Vic saunters to the front of the line. Rina holds a piece of slippery seaweed out to him, and he winks before bending his neck and grasping it with his mouth, his lips brushing her fingers.

Rina fights to stay composed. When it's Harv's turn, he misses, and the seaweed flops out of his mouth and onto the ground unceremoniously. "I don't have to pick that up, do I?" he asks.

"You have to finish the game!" Yaqing exclaims. "Otherwise, it's bad luck!"

"It's just a wedding. Let me see my bride." Rina steps aside as he opens the door to the suite. Lulu's forced smile is at utter odds with her luscious clothing. Like a queen who doesn't want her kingdom.

"You look beautiful," Harv says, eliciting a chorus of *awws*.

Rina ends up on the outer circle of the crowd as everyone gathers around Harv and Lulu for photos. Vic is right beside her, and the noise dulls as he dips his head. "Are we going to talk about what happened on my boat?" he murmurs. This is the longest they've gone without speaking in months. Rina has enough to deal with without the added pressure of confronting her feelings for him.

"Maybe later," she says before wriggling away. She's been avoiding him, and now is definitely not the time to have this discussion.

Harv is now supposed to accompany Lulu to the tea ceremony, but at the last minute, Peng Ayi enters in a striking lavender-colored qípáo, takes one look at Lulu, and screeches, "Āiyá, her lipstick is too dark!" She harasses the makeup artists while the bridesmaids and groomsmen hang back, fearful of getting dragged into the chaos. There's no question she's running the show, with a walkie-talkie in one hand and an antiquated key ring for all the rooms in the hotel in the other. Rina wonders how she convinced them to give her access to everything. Probably a mix of bribery and berating.

"Out, everyone, out! Harv, go there first and say hello to Yeye and Nainai," Peng Ayi says as she frets over Lulu's hair.

As everyone hurriedly exits, Rina looks for Jane, confirming that she's hovering around the photographer responsible for shooting the wedding party.

Their plan begins now.

Since the tea ceremony is only for the bride, groom, parents, and grandparents, the rest of the wedding party proceed toward the pool area, where the official marriage ceremony will be held in two hours. As caterers bring out lunch, the photographer Jane was speaking to earlier jogs up to Yaqing, and whispers something. Yaqing nods, then scans everyone in the party.

This is Rina's cue. She needs to do something annoying enough for Yaqing to pick on her. She pulls out the chair next to Vic and says brightly, "Anyone sitting here?"

His mouth curls into a smile. "I was saving it for you."

"Rina!" Yaqing says imperiously, her eyes narrowed at the two of them. "The photographer forgot one of his lenses. It's in the parking lot. Here are the keys. Go get it."

"Can Jane come with me?" Jane trots over at Rina's beckoning, looking more alive than she did earlier. The adrenaline is probably beginning to hit her, too.

"Yes, get out of here." Yaqing all but throws the keys at them.

"She's on a real power trip," Jane says as they grab a dolly near a service elevator and walk to the parking lot.

Michelangelo and Mei sit in Michelangelo's car, which she rented with falsified documents. "If you were going to be late, you should've told me so I could sleep in this morning," Mei complains from the passenger seat.

"It's not exactly easy hurling a camera lens into the bushes while a million people are around," Jane says.

The fake safe, covered by cloth, rests in the back seat. Michelangelo even put a seat belt over it. Rina glances at the overhangs of the surrounding buildings. They're covered in pale pink streamers, and glitter-filled gold balloons float in the corners, effectively obscuring any cameras. She feels another stab of guilt. Lulu has always done whatever's been asked of her.

Jane and Rina lower the safe out of the car while Mei keeps watch.

"Careful," Michelangelo warns. "I don't have another one of those lying around."

Jane grunts as she lifts it. "If I'd known all this physical labor was in my future, I would've hit the gym."

35

Wedding day, 10:00 a.m.

LULU

LULU FEELS LIKE she's nestled in a wild meadow as she kneels on a red silk pillow, pouring tea for the elder Zhus. Flowers crawl over the posts of the tent that's been erected to protect them from the sun. A soft breeze threads through the trees, making wooden chimes carved with double *xi* symbols emit a low melody. Everyone else is seated—Harv's grandparents, the Zhus, and Lulu's parents—while Lulu and Harv are on the ground as a gesture of respect.

There's a rattling sound, and Lulu looks down at the tiny teacups with their gold painted rims, too breakable in her trembling hands. She can't believe this day is actually here.

In the week since the party, she'd considered responding to Jane's and Rina's messages and calls. But she needed time to pause and think through everything, to process the conversations she's had with Harv, her parents, her friends—to process the past year of her life. She thought about all their hard work, about Mei and Michelangelo, who had placed their trust in her.

The heist would go on, she decided. But so would the marriage. It's the only way to please everyone.

She lowers her forehead to the ground, bowing to Harv's grandma after she's served her tea. The woman gestures to her maid, who carries over a black velvet box. Inside, a chain sparkles in the sunlight, a gold pig the size of her hand dangling from it. "For good fortune and many children," Nainai says. It is a precious, expensive gift, but all Lulu can feel is its weight as Nainai places it over her head.

Lulu's mom is busy shooting glances at Peng Ayi, shifting to mimic her posture, when it's her turn to accept Lulu's tea. Her father has to nudge her. "My beautiful daughter," her mom says as Lulu bends toward her. There's a giant red bow tied around her neck, and a lipstick smudge on her teeth. "You have finally made us proud."

Lulu barely hears her mother. She's too busy wondering whether Rina and Jane have met up with Mei and Michelangelo to roll the counterfeit safe into Rina's room. Even though they've rehearsed this hundreds of times and the risk of being seen is low this early in the day, Lulu's worried. She may be angry with them, but she doesn't want anyone to be caught.

After the tea ceremony, Lulu's mom fingers the gold chain around her neck. "Wah, how much must this be worth?" she marvels. "Are these eyes made of diamonds?"

"I thought Gege was coming," Lulu says, looking past her mom at her dad, dressed in an ill-fitting suit. Her brother is a loose cannon, but today his presence is important if things are to go right.

"Don't worry about him, ah. You'll see him next time you visit home."

All she can do is hope he does eventually show. In the meantime, she needs to put the other part of their plan in motion. Lulu leans close to her mom. "Ma, Peng Ayi seemed kind of unhappy that you weren't involved in much of the wedding planning."

Her mom's hand goes to her mouth, eyes darting to Peng Ayi in horror. "She's unhappy? With me?"

"Maybe you can help her today, make things easier for her." They'll need any help they can get to keep Peng Ayi occupied.

Her mom tightens her bow, straightening. "Anything for Peng Jie. I'll make it so she doesn't have to lift a finger! Ah, here she comes now."

"Lulu, are you watching the time? You must change into your second dress," Peng Ayi says briskly, one of the hotel staff in tow. "Come."

"I'm coming too!" her mom exclaims.

A golf cart brings them to a room located in the same building as the banquet hall Lulu will use for her many outfit changes.

There, Lulu carefully unbuttons the guàqún and puts it on a hanger. The pig necklace gets tangled in her hair, and Peng Ayi sighs when she sees Lulu struggling.

"Āiyá, useless!" She smacks Lulu's hands away and tugs the chain over her head, yanking out hair in the process.

"Peng Jie, guests are arriving. I'll greet them for you!" Lulu's mom's voice trills through the door. Peng Ayi had her stay outside to prevent anyone else from coming in.

If Peng Ayi cursed, she probably would have right then. "One second!" She flutters around Lulu, attaching the Cartier necklace and earrings. "Hair and makeup!" she barks into her walkie-talkie, swinging the door open.

All told, it takes more than half an hour to shove Lulu into the dress with all its layers of tulle and lace. They load her back onto the golf cart and head toward the beach area, moving at a crawl so the staff accompanying them can prevent her dress from touching the ground. She hears the faint strains of violin music, and her palms start sweating.

When she steps out of the golf cart, her dad is waiting on the false beach of Sun Island.

His eyes are glassy as he offers his arm. "So beautiful," he whispers.

The beach, a run-down sandpit the last time she saw it, has transformed into a fairy tale. Peng Ayi, who claimed the sand was too coarse, has replaced it with fine, white granules from an island in Australia. A walkway covered in red brocade runs from the sand and over the lagoon, where a floating platform awaits. The scent of gardenias surrounds them, the pungency sticking in her throat. Rows of white chairs line the sand, and everyone turns to watch as Lulu's dad leads her forward. Their gazes weigh her down more than the countless pins and combs in her hair.

Rina and Jane stand with the other bridesmaids on the left of the platform, lovely in their pink qípáo. They break into encouraging smiles when they see her. Jane mouths *hot* and Rina brushes away a tear. It's easy for them to be supportive now that Lulu has confirmed she'll still go through with the heist. They must assume she's come around to their way of thinking. Lulu tightens her grip on her bouquet of pink peonies.

She looks at her future husband last. Harv is under a circular arch decorated with dark red flowers, that gold double Xǐ looming overhead. He smiles hesitantly at her, and Lulu feels a sense of acceptance.

As they walk down the aisle, her dad leans in. "Lulu, wǒzhǐxīwàng nǐ néng dé dào xìng fú." His familiar smell, of cigarettes and cotton, makes tears prickle in her eyes. This is her dad's small rebellion. Whispering in his daughter's ear, moments before he delivers her to her fate, that the only thing he wants for her is happiness.

A candle drifts by in her periphery, fresh lotuses scattered around it on the surface of the water. The walkway bobs with each step. Peng Ayi pointed out that Lulu waddles too much, so she focuses on even strides, despite the fabric constricting her movements, and stares straight ahead.

Harv helps her onto the platform and links his hand with hers as the officiant tells an overly romanticized story about their first date, skipping over the fact that they met while Lulu was working at Scarlet Beauty.

When it's time, Lulu's mouth forms the words of their vows. She's rehearsed them so many times that occasionally she wakes up with them still on her lips.

They exchange rings.

"We're in this together," Harv says quietly as he slips on her ring.

"You may kiss the bride."

Harv closes the distance between them and plants a chaste kiss on her mouth. Her wedding dress squeezes her midsection as she receives it. Applause bursts out, and she turns to face the guests, mustering a faint smile, trying to ignore the tightness of the ring around her finger.

36

JANE

❖ ❖ ❖ ❖ ❖

AS THE GUESTS file into the banquet hall after the ceremony, Jane pretends she needs to pee and heads for the laundry room to steal a service uniform for Michelangelo. On her way there, she cuts through the kitchen, the greasy steam oozing into her skin, but the servers are too busy dealing with Peng Ayi's tyranny and prepping the ten courses to notice her. They have to swap the safes at twelve thirty, and every minute counts.

At the front of the laundry room, she peers into an abandoned cart but all she sees are dirty towels. Because the staff helping with the wedding have special uniforms, there wasn't a way to procure one ahead of time. They'd banked on finding unused ones here. She scurries around the room, even lifting a few suspiciously stained sheets off the washing machine. They smell like sweat and coconut body lotion.

In the movies, they would just knock someone out, take their clothes, and stuff them in a closet somewhere. But Jane doesn't know how hard to hit someone to knock them out. What if she accidentally kills them instead?

Best not to underestimate her own strength.

As she leaves the laundry room, wondering what the hell she's supposed to do now, she trips over a Starbucks cup on the ground. Brown liquid glugs out and stains the carpet before Jane rights it again. An idea strikes. Picking up the cup, she hurries back to the kitchen and scans the space for someone who seems like Michelangelo's size. She zeroes in on a willowy girl morosely sweeping the floor. Jane walks straight at her, bumping into her and splashing the old coffee onto her uniform.

"Āiyá, I'm so sorry!" She scampers off before the girl can get a good look at her, then stops and peeks around a corner.

The girl continues sweeping, apparently not worried at all about smelling like coffee, and Jane curses under her breath. She straightens and finds one of the hotel management patrolling the corridors, an uptight guy with slicked back hair. "You've got an employee with a stained uniform," she declares, pointing back toward the kitchen. "What if one of the guests sees?"

The man bows to her. "I will see to it that she changes. In the future, please stay in our guest area to avoid such unpleasant sights."

From a distance, Jane hears him reprimand the girl, who storms out of the kitchen in a huff and toward the staff bathroom.

Jane waits a few beats before following her. In the bathroom, the stained clothes are thrown over a stall door while she changes. Brilliant.

Jane's shoes are way too loud against the white tile. They're cute, impractical gold stilettos that she realizes now she should've left at home. She slips them off, pulls up her skirt so that if the server is paying attention, she won't be able to identify her by her dress. Then, with her heart pounding in her ears, she nabs the dirty uniform and buries it in her Neverfull, hearing only a shrieked "Hey!" before the door shuts behind her. She doesn't have the time to feel bad about it.

It's only after she's cleared that hallway and the next that Jane slows down and releases the hem of her dress, the uniform safely in her bag.

This part of the hotel, where the on-site workers stay, is deserted. The silence is refreshing as she straps her shoes back on. Even though it'd been all for show, when she saw Lulu coming down the walkway, she felt a bit teary. After all, this wedding is the beginning of the countdown to Lulu leaving for Thailand. With her refusing to talk to them, it feels like they've already lost her.

"Jane?"

She looks up. Zihao. There's an austere older man beside him, his black hair artfully arranged to hide his bald patch.

"Lǎogōng," she says, surprised. She'd left him to mingle with everyone in the banquet hall, intending to save him once she'd gotten the uniform to Michelangelo, who's hiding in Rina's room. "What are you doing so far away from the banquet?"

"I was actually searching for you." There's a strangeness to Zihao's voice. They'd kissed when he dropped her off, an affectionate smile on his lips. But now there's a hardness to his gaze, like he's erected a wall between the two of them. "You left your wallet."

He lifts his arm. Her pink Saffiano wallet is pinched between his index and middle fingers. There's a card sticking out of it, slightly crumpled, but very familiar.

The appointment card for Dr. Yu's clinic.

Jane feels the blood drain from her face. She lurches forward, retrieving her wallet, and Zihao withdraws his hand immediately, like he's afraid of her touch.

The man beside him coughs awkwardly. "Guang Zong, this is my wife," Zihao says stiffly, reminding her they have a witness. "Jane, Guang Zong is our Shanghai regional head at Jianshi."

Just when she thought things couldn't get worse. "Lovely to

meet you," she says, her brain short-circuiting as she absorbs the scene before her. The card. How had he— She must've forgotten her wallet in the car as she was rooting through her Neverfull this morning for concealer. Fuck, fuck, fuck. She should've thrown that card away—it's not like she needed it to remember the date—or at least hidden it behind a credit card.

"Ah, Jane!" Guang Zong interlaces his fingers and rests them against his stomach. "So this is the wife who you keep saying you must go home to. Your husband is working on a project very important to us. You should be proud to be married to a man making such monumental contributions to the country."

"I've heard all about the great work you're doing," she says as politely as she can. She'll have to explain the card to Zihao later. Right now, while he's here, she might as well get the valet ticket for when she retrieves his car for Mei in a couple hours. It's earlier than planned, but if he's mad now, who knows whether she'll be able to get him to hand the ticket over later, when he's had even more time to simmer. "Lǎogōng, I left something in the car. Can I have your valet ticket?"

"We can go together," Zihao says, narrowing his eyes at her.

"How can you leave Guang Zong?" Jane asks with false horror. "They're bringing out the suckling pig soon. Go get the good pieces." She sticks her hand out. Zihao, unable to refuse her with his boss watching, gives in. Hopefully, he'll be so busy catering to his boss that he won't remember to get it back from her.

"So nice to meet you, Guang Zong. I hope you enjoy the rest of the ceremony." She dips her head toward them and makes herself scarce.

On the trek to Rina's room, Jane thinks of ways to explain away the card. She just needs a good excuse, and Zihao will get over it. They'll laugh about it. By the time she reaches Michelangelo, she feels a lot better.

Michelangelo sits on Rina's bed, flipping through channels, the fake safe beside her, patiently waiting on its dolly.

"Seriously?"

Michelangelo shrugs. "Nothing good's on."

Jane removes the uniform from her bag and tosses it on the bed, along with a detergent pen. "You might want to do something about the coffee stains. I have to get back. The dance starts in twenty minutes, and the walk takes eight."

Michelangelo grimaces, lifting the edge of the shirt with a fingertip. "Are you saying I have to run? Jane, I do not *run*."

"I hope you wore comfortable shoes," Jane says. "See you in twenty."

She hurries back to the banquet hall. It's packed with round tables, and the arch from the ceremony has been moved to the stage at the center, where a table is set up for the bride and groom. Heavy burgundy drapes cascade from the ceiling while chandeliers glitter with a brightness that makes black splotches dot Jane's vision. On a gold tablecloth just a few steps from the stage, the safe sparkles like a diamond. It's crammed with red envelopes, and people sidle up to check it out as Vic looks on, no doubt trying to guess how much money is inside. Snobs.

Jane joins the bridesmaids' table, located slightly to the left of the safe, and instinctually searches for Zihao. She doesn't want to have to converse with the other guests about which elite university she attended, the latest limited-edition bag that went on the market, and which expensive private tutor was better at teaching children math. She's overcome by a general sense of being over this shit. Is this all her education and experience amount to? Asinine flexes and never feeling like she can keep up?

The lights dim before she can locate him. The first dance is about to start.

"Where were you?" Yaqing hisses. At her side, Rina takes a fortifying gulp of wine.

Jane gives her a jaunty little smile and sits back in her chair. "Causing trouble."

At a table nearby, someone says, "I heard that if he doesn't lift her, it means she's pregnant!"

"Wah, really?"

The auntie grapevine never fails to disappoint. The rumors they've planted the past few weeks have grown roots.

The other bridesmaids trade looks. "Do you two know anything about this?" one asks Jane and Rina.

Jane shrugs. "I don't share friends' secrets." Her nonanswer only makes them hungrier for details. Secret pregnancies are like candy to gossipy aunties, and at an event like this, news spreads fast. Now everyone's watching the dance intently, waiting for confirmation that a baby's on the way.

A spotlight shines down on the stage. Lulu wears a dark red qípáo that flares around her legs, a smile frozen to her face as Harv takes her hand.

Jane notes the time on her phone, then scans the entrance to the hall. If Michelangelo doesn't come now—

The cake enters, a multitiered monstrosity rolled in gold sprinkles. A peacock's piped green feathers hang down the sides, incredibly lifelike. Behind the cake, pushing the trolley along, is Michelangelo, trailed by a crew of kitchen staff.

Jane breathes easier. She wasn't sure Michelangelo had been able to seize control of the cake in time, but her commanding presence must have swayed the kitchen staff.

Michelangelo squeakily wheels the cake next to the safe and directs her entourage to transfer it from the cart to the large table that holds the safe. Grumbling arises among the people seated behind the cake, Jane included, its girth blocking their views of the dance.

"Āiyá, I can't see shit!" Jane exclaims. She dramatically tosses her napkin down and marches toward the stage. People follow her example, leaving their tables and clustering close.

From the corner of her eye, Jane sees Michelangelo dismiss her helpers and stand guard by the cake, ready to act.

Vic hasn't moved. He's still sitting by the safe, one hand on it like it's his pet dog.

Jane elbows Rina next to her in the crowd. "Time to work your magic."

Rina squares her shoulders, then walks toward Vic. His face splits into a grin as she tugs him to a dark corner of the hall.

Zihao also hasn't budged. He's at a table in the back, his arms crossed. He's looking straight at her. Even though he's upset with her, she knows he must be miserable here.

"You don't want to see the dance?" Jane asks, striding up to him.

His jaw is clenched so hard she's amazed he hasn't snapped a bone. "When were you planning to tell me?"

Okay, so they're going to do this now. "I only went by to check it out. You know how bored I get at home."

"You're lying. There was a date on the card," he says with disgust. "Did you honestly think I wouldn't notice if you came back looking different?"

"You're perfectly welcome to divorce me if you have a problem with me becoming prettier." This reaction is exactly why she was right to hide it from him.

"Are you fucking kidding me?" They're lucky that a musical crescendo muffles his raised voice. "I didn't marry you hoping you'd get prettier."

Jane mirrors Zihao and folds her arms defensively. "Stop pretending you married me for my shining personality. If that were true, you wouldn't have insisted your name go next to mine on our lease."

Zihao squeezes his eyes shut. Inhales audibly. "True, I barely knew you when we first got married," he says slowly. "But I'm *trying*, Jane. And I have demanded nothing from you. You're so focused on the past that you haven't noticed I've changed."

"I know you were trying. I was, too."

She's about to say more, to make him understand, but he says, "Bullshit."

The urge to explain herself deserts her. "Say that again."

"I call bullshit. You're stubborn, Jane. You're a childish kind of stubborn that makes me want to tear my hair out. I've tried to adapt, to be more generous toward you and recognize what you contribute to our marriage. They're small changes, but I'm making them. But you. You make all these demands while you resist change yourself."

"Plastic surgery is the biggest fucking change I could make!"

Zihao stabs at his forehead. "I'm talking about *up here*. How you see yourself. How you treat the people around you. What you believe you're entitled to. You have this obvious chip on your shoulder, and *that's* what makes it hard to look at you."

She recoils. This conversation needs to end now. "If I'm so hard to look at," she says quietly, "then leave."

Zihao's expression softens slightly. She knows she needs to get over to that cake, but for a second, she hopes he'll reach for her.

He rises. "I'm no match for the grudge you hold." Then he leaves, shaking his head.

Absurdly, she wants to cry, but Jane swallows the lump in her throat and hurries to where Michelangelo hovers by the cake at the edge of the crowd.

"I hope that was a nice chitchat," Michelangelo says bitingly as the two of them circle the safe. "You've just cost us some valuable time."

Vic and Rina are nowhere to be seen. The guests are oblivious, focused on Lulu and Harv's dance for signs while the famous singer Peng Ayi's hired croons that love is the answer to emptiness.

Still ruffled by Zihao's accusations, Jane nearly drops the safe as they place it on top of Michelangelo's empty cake cart. Michelangelo grabs a folded cloth from the cart and drapes it over the safe before they transfer the replica from the lower rung next to the cake on the table. Once it's positioned in the exact same spot, Michelangelo wheels her cart away.

Jane doesn't move. As Harv grabs Lulu by the waist and lifts her up on stage, a collective sigh of disappointment rippling through the crowd, Jane mentally charts Michelangelo's course through the grounds with their precious cargo. There's an empty wing near the kitchen where Michelangelo will wait until it's time to move the safe into the car in a couple hours.

The music fades, and Jane slides into her seat as everyone returns to their tables. Vic reappears and resumes his place, giving the fake safe a friendly pat. Jane's breath catches. But he's none the wiser.

"She looks beautiful, doesn't she?" Rina shows up beside her, a little disheveled as servers pour them champagne.

Onstage, Harv pulls a chair out for Lulu at their couple's table. The top and sleeves of her dress are dark red lace, and her curled hair, tied half up with a matching ribbon, frames her small face. She is radiant.

When Harv proposed, Jane's first thought was *of course*. Of course someone who looks like Lulu didn't have to do a thing to get him, while Jane had gone through endless rejections to arrive at the altar. What a thing to think about someone who's supposed to be her best friend.

Jane needs this money, but the whole reason she came up with the idea in the first place is so Lulu didn't have to end up like her, in a marriage she never wanted. Once she's on a faraway beach with a bulging bank account, Jane knows Lulu will understand. Lulu, like Zihao, will find it in her heart to forgive. That's the thing about kind people, people who aren't Jane; they will give you the space to make mistakes.

But in the time they sit there, Lulu never looks in their direction.

Jane imagines the thread of their friendship stretching thinner, fraying in the middle.

37

Wedding day, 1:00 p.m.

RINA

❖ ❖ ❖ ❖ ❖

RINA BITES HER LIP. Now that the food is being served, it's important for her and Jane to remain seated through the multiple main courses of meat and seafood. At two fifteen, there'll be a lull when people mingle again before the toasts. That's when they'll each leave separately, Jane to prepare the car and Rina to prepare Michelangelo and the safe. Their absence would be too conspicuous now, with all the guests at their tables.

Though they've successfully swapped the safe, Rina has a bad feeling, the sort of gut instinct that's woken her up in the middle of the night to check a client presentation, only to discover she never emailed it out. If she called off the heist now, would that change anything? She doesn't think so, not after the ugly words she said. How she basically accused Lulu of having no purpose or direction, like it's a failure of character. The thought makes her cringe.

"Are you sure you jammed the cameras?" she whispers to Jane.

"For the hundredth time, yes. I did it before the door games and tossed the jammer into a trash chute. Nobody can see us."

"But why hasn't anyone said anything about it?" She expected some hubbub when the hotel noticed their surveillance wasn't working, but she'd been so preoccupied the past four hours, and it's only now Rina realizes there's been nothing.

"If you're so worried, go check."

"Fine, I will." Yaqing is MIA and the other bridesmaids are happily drunk thanks to the many refills Rina and Jane have encouraged, so nobody protests as she gets up and leaves.

She takes off her heels—they're starting to cut into her feet— and walks cautiously toward the monitoring room.

A loud voice comes from within.

"I'm so hungry. There isn't even a water boiler in here for instant ramen. I should've gotten a serving job instead. Then I could be sneaking bites of food instead of watching everything like a pervert."

The door is slightly ajar, revealing a man in a security uni- form, focused not on the blinking screens in front of him but on his phone. The largest screen provides an unobscured view of the banquet hall.

As Rina continues down the hallway, her vision grows splotchy. The cameras are still on. Whatever Jane did didn't work.

They have to fix this. Rina's mind whirls as she heads back to the banquet hall. She doesn't know enough about security systems to craft a solution on her own. "Fuck!" She smacks the wall. The pain sobers her. She expected at least one thing to go wrong. And this is that thing. Unfortunately, it is a very, very big thing.

Her hand stings, and she takes a moment to collect herself. At least the security guard seems inattentive...

She hears a familiar high voice, followed by her name. It's Yaqing.

"You seem quite close with *Rina*." She doesn't sound far

enough away for Rina to outrun, and there's no room along this span of hallway for her to duck into.

"She's the best friend of my best friend's now wife." Great, Vic. A shiver runs through her as she remembers tugging him off into a dark corner, the surprise in his expression giving way to want right before she kissed him, Lulu and Harv dancing just meters away. She's not proud of what she had to do to distract him, but there was no other way to get Vic's attention off the safe.

"You should be careful with her. She's Lulu's friend, after all. If something happens between Lulu and Harv, you know whose side she'll be on."

Vic releases an easy laugh. "Give me some credit, Qingqing. I can think for myself. You really didn't need to ambush me during my bathroom break."

"I'm serious, Gege. You follow your heart. Women like Zhou Rina follow their brains. If anyone gets hurt, it will be you."

Yaqing seems almost protective. Rina doesn't like the woman, but on this point, she happens to be absolutely correct. He will be hurt. It's unavoidable.

The two of them round the corner. "Rina? What are you doing here?" Yaqing folds her arms, inching closer to Vic like she wants to shield him from her.

"I was looking for you two. Because… Lulu wants a photo with her maid of—"

"Why aren't you wearing your shoes?" Vic asks as Yaqing squints at her.

"Uh…my feet were hurting from the heels."

Yaqing scoffs. "They aren't even that high—"

She's cut off by Rina's yelp as Vic scoops her into his arms.

"Put me down!"

"No way. I saw your black-as-tar feet. This place probably hasn't washed their floors since the nineties. Yaqing, you should go ahead. Tell Bo I'll be back to take over guard duty soon. She's going to slow me down."

"Looks like it," Yaqing says disdainfully and strides away.

The buttons of Vic's shirt dig into Rina's arm, but his chest underneath is warm. For a few minutes, there's only the sound of his footsteps as he carries her down the hallway.

"Can you put me down now?" she asks, uncomfortable. What if someone sees?

"I've been wondering lately," Vic says, ignoring her, "how things could be different if I could see the world with someone by my side. If home, for me, is a person. We've been getting to know each other these past months, Rina. I know how much you want control, how you want to help everyone and do everything. But it's okay to lean on someone. Let me be that person."

Their surroundings blur. Rina's conscious of the thud of her heart.

Vic keeps talking, and she senses nerves. "I actually tried to text you after that group project ten years ago, but you blocked me. Then you show up as the best friend of *my* best friend's fiancée. We're destined to be part of each other's lives. You're starting to trust me, aren't you? You wouldn't have let me handle most of that yacht party otherwise."

Rina has barely begun to process her feelings for Vic, and he's already inviting her to run off together. She's accomplished her directive more spectacularly than she could've imagined. Jane would cackle if she heard this.

She squirms in his grasp. "Put me down first, then we'll talk." Vic sets her down gently, and she pretends to be busy sliding her feet into her heels. There's no future for them, but still she tests out the words, if only to live in them for a moment. "What if I wanted you to stay? No more jaunts anywhere."

"You want to clip my wings?" There's a lightness to the way he says it, but she can feel his eyes on her, intent.

"I'm only curious." His answer shouldn't matter. It would be impossible to remain in Vic's life with this gigantic secret hanging over them.

"I'll tell you the truth, as I know it right now. I don't think I could do that for anyone. I accept you for who you are. Can't you do the same for me?"

Vic offers his shoulder, but he uses the wall to balance as she slips on her shoes. If he can't promise to stay now, nothing will stop him from leaving later, when passion has fizzled away to responsibility. And if her missed promotion has taught her anything, there are enough things in her life she can't control.

She finishes putting on her shoes. Vic is right in her space, his gaze soft and beseeching. She still doesn't speak.

"Are you going to deny there's something happening between us?" he says.

She hesitates, conflicted about telling a truth she'll have to erase so soon. "I think about you more than I'd like." It's all she can give him.

His grin is instant. He leans toward her. Against her will, her eyes close, the anticipation of those lips touching hers, heating up every inch of her body, even as Yaqing's warning rattles in her head. She will hurt him, but right now, she nestles into him, holding on to the last few hours they have together.

38

Wedding day, 1:30 p.m.

LULU

AT FIRST, LULU THINKS the girl sauntering up to their table is the rich daughter of one of Peng Ayi's guests. A fancy bag is slung over her shoulder, and her lips are a striking red, matching her skintight dress. Her hair is streaked with purple highlights and goes all the way down to her butt. She's also the only one indoors wearing sunglasses.

She slaps her hand on the table and says in a pristine Beijing accent, "Do you see this?" She shakes her wrist in front of Harv's face.

Bewildered, Harv asks, "See *what?*"

The girl huffs. "I was dropping an envelope in your safe, and my bracelet fell in, and they won't open it for me. That bracelet costs more than my life! Is this how you treat the daughter of your vice premier?"

Harv stiffens at *vice premier.* He glances at the table where his parents sit, surrounded by well-dressed, important-looking people. "I'll get it right away," he says, rising from his seat.

"Make it fast." The girl drops into his vacated chair, lips in an entitled pout. When Harv is out of earshot, she starts scratching her scalp furiously. "This wig is so damn itchy."

"I had no idea it was you," Lulu says, awed. "The accent was a good touch."

"I'm not even the most ridiculous one here. Did you see that woman who looks like she's wearing aluminum foil?"

Harv steps down from the stage and walks toward the false safe. He exchanges words with Vic, then leans over it, typing in his password. Lulu's phone vibrates. That must be the text with the password, fed through the keylogger.

Harv seems to locate the bracelet Jane bought in some mall and returns to the table.

"Sorry about that," he says.

Mei lifts her nose high as she accepts the bracelet. "I'm going to have to get these diamonds cleaned, now that you've touched them." She tosses her hair, then stalks off to change before her next task. Unlike Lulu, Mei was very enthused about the number of outfit changes required today.

"Cheers," Harv says to Lulu, raising his small glass of baijiu. "Just a few more hours, and we can rest."

Lulu winds her arm around his, and they drink from each other's cups. Rest seems like a million miles away. They've got a long night ahead, then it's off to their honeymoon early in the morning. She feels like she's drowning in all the well-wishes.

"Ma will calm down after this too," Harv says. "She's been saying all these paranoid things—" He stops, expression guilty.

Lulu's skin goes cold. "What things?"

Harv hesitates. "She thinks Rina and Jane are acting strange. Apparently, Rina also asked a lot of questions about security when she visited the venue a few months ago. Not that I'm blaming your friends," he says quickly. "You know Ma and how she is."

Rina enters the banquet hall and heads toward their table,

looking stressed. They're in the middle of the meal, and she should've stayed put. Something must have gone wrong.

"Congratulations," she says to Lulu, holding her arms out for a hug. The smell and feel of her is so familiar, but Lulu doesn't let it lure her into a false sense of safety. Not when Rina is the one who told her she was confused, like she doesn't even know herself. If anything, these past few months have brought Lulu more in touch with who she really is. With every decision she's made, she's known exactly what she's sacrificing.

"The security cameras are back on," Rina whispers into her hair as they embrace. "We need to get into the room where the recordings are, but it's going to be locked. Can you get Peng Ayi's key ring so we can make copies? We also need to move Michelangelo somewhere safe while we try to deal with this."

Lulu nods, not liking the panic in Rina's voice. "If I get the keys, you can put the safe in my changing room. No cameras there."

Rina pulls out of the hug, but her hands float over Lulu's arms. Lulu can almost see the apology, hovering in the air between them. But what use is that now?

She speaks before Rina can. "Peng Ayi already suspects you. Be careful." Gathering her courage, she goes to Peng Ayi's table and cuts into a conversation between Peng Ayi and a woman in a bright red fur coat. "I need to change." It's half an hour early, but if they're still getting the safe out of here at three, she needs to act quickly.

Peng Ayi's eyes stray from her guest. "It's not time yet." With every dress change, her mother-in-law has become more irked, especially as each outfit is so complex.

"I just remember that we always had trouble with the laces," Lulu says.

Peng Ayi reluctantly tears herself away from her conversation partner. "I guess it can't be helped." She grabs the ring of keys from her purse.

Zhu Shushu stops her. "You're leaving again? My aunt wanted to speak with you."

"I'll be right back," Peng Ayi promises him, harried.

"Peng Jie!" Lulu's mom enthusiastically waves at them as they pass by. Even though Peng Ayi exiled her to a faraway table, her mom has barely sat down, too busy roaming from table to table like an ambassador of the wedding, while her dad has stayed put and befriended everyone at their table. "I've been introducing myself to all your friends! These ones are CEOs! Wah, so impressive!"

"Let's hurry," Peng Ayi says to Lulu. She sounds like she's gritting her teeth.

The evening gown is the most elaborate after Lulu's wedding ceremony dress. There's a lace-up back, and Lulu purposely gets her arm stuck in one of the sleeves for a few extra minutes, hoping it increases Peng Ayi's frustration.

Her hair is supposed to be in waves, which requires removing hundreds of bobby pins from the half updo that went with her banquet dress. Peng Ayi watches impatiently as the stylist picks up thin strands of hair to straighten. "Can't you go faster?"

"It won't be even."

Peng Ayi paces, the keys jangling in her hand. "I have to get back."

Lulu gestures at the jewelry boxes stacked on a table. "Do you want the room unlocked when we leave? It doesn't seem very safe."

Peng Ayi's phone buzzes, and Lulu can see her urgency increase. "I'll send Yaqing to get you and lock up."

Lulu thinks fast. She needs those keys to stay put. "I saw Yaqing in the gardens with Vic. It might take her some time to get here."

"Āiyá! That girl needs to stop mooning after a man who's no good for her. Fine." Peng Ayi throws the keys on a table. "Once you're done, lock up. I expect to see you in the banquet hall in fifteen minutes. If you're not there, I *will* come find you."

"Sorry about all this," Lulu says to the hairdresser after she's gone.

The hairdresser is sympathetic. "My mother-in-law is a lot, too."

"You're doing a wonderful job. Everyone has complimented me on my hair." She closes her eyes. "I just need a few minutes."

The hairdresser falls right into her trap. "I'll tell your mother-in-law this took a bit longer than expected."

"Thank you," Lulu says profusely.

The hairdresser packs up, and Lulu leaps up once the door closes behind her. Five minutes before she needs to report to Peng Ayi. The hairdresser might be able to buy her another five. She props open the door, a signal for Michelangelo that it's safe, then retreats back inside.

"This cart squeals louder than a toddler in a tantrum," Michelangelo says, rolling the cart in a minute later. Together, they maneuver the cart behind a bank of unused trash cans so that it's hidden from view. Lulu's last dress change is after the cake cutting, when the safe will already be in the getaway car, but if Peng Ayi decides to make a surprise visit before then, she won't go anywhere near some trash cans, and Michelangelo will come up with an excuse for being there. "Mei told me about the cameras." She surveys her surroundings critically.

"Can you make copies of these?" Lulu asks, passing the ring of keys to Michelangelo. "We need to get into the room with the security tapes."

Michelangelo squints at them. "You're really making me work overtime."

"It's because you're so good at what you do."

Michelangelo digs a lighter out of her pocket. "Don't overlook your role in all of this." She holds the flame under the teeth of each key, then extracts tape from her pocket. After pulling it away, the tape has a perfect imprint of each key.

Michelangelo strides over to the standing supply of beverages: sodas, beers, and a bottle of wine. She lifts a few beer bottles out by their necks. Then she systematically pops the caps off each with the side of Lulu's vanity. "Beer?" Michelangelo asks Lulu.

"No, thanks."

"You have scissors here, don't you?"

Lulu rifles through one of the makeup drawers for the scissors the hairstylist used to trim away her baby hairs. Michelangelo arranges the bottles to the side and lays out all the bottle caps she's collected. "I hope all of this finally convinces you how much power you have."

"Unless we get caught," Lulu says. They've still got so much more to do. "I'll let them know someone has to get the keys from you. After that, wait here until Rina fetches you."

"I'll keep myself busy." Michelangelo hands the keys to Lulu. "Rub the scorch marks off before you give them back to her."

The last thing Lulu sees before she leaves is Michelangelo gazing at the corner where the safe is hidden, a calculating look in her eyes.

39

Wedding day, 2:00 p.m.

JANE

THE BANQUET HALL is overflowing with privilege and pomp-ousness. As she scoops crab fried rice onto her plate, Jane over-hears a group of girls in sparkling dresses humblebragging about their airline status. At this moment, she'd rather be at Zihao's table, listening to him suck up to Guang Zong. But they're both currently pretending the other doesn't exist.

Fine. They can preen and prattle, and she'll take all their money.

"Jane," Rina hisses, scooting her chair next to her. "The se-curity system. It's up and running. I ran into Mei in the hall and sent her to warn Michelangelo. Lulu's going to get her and the safe into her changing room."

"What?" Automatically, she looks up into the corners of the banquet hall. Even though she can't see the cameras, now she feels like she's being watched.

As she's scanning the room, she makes eye contact with Peng Ayi, who's watching her and Rina. Quickly, she glances away.

Did Peng Ayi have anything to do with this? There's no way Zihao checked the security system, did he?

Suddenly, her encounter earlier makes sense. "The Zhus invited Zihao's boss to the wedding. He must've checked the security system and fixed it."

Rina rubs her elbow. "Lulu's getting the keys so Michelangelo can make copies. We can lock the security guard out of the live monitoring room, but the footage will be stored in a separate room."

"Wait. Let me think." Jane stress-eats a chicken drumstick. Screw being skinny; she needs calories to fuel her brain. She chews quickly, recalling everything she's learned from Zihao about Jianshi in the past few months. "All the data should be on a local device. There's a DVR recording the footage. If we get rid of the DVR, we're safe. You said Lulu and Michelangelo have the key copies?"

"I'll get them. It's not far." Mei struts over, holding a cup of milk tea. She's changed into a slightly less ridiculous getup, having traded her previous outfit for a more modest gold midi dress with cap sleeves. "By the way, Rina Jie, I was changing out of my earlier disguise and knocked down a lamp in your room. You might get charged for it."

"You were supposed to wait for me in the parking lot after you got the bracelet from Harv," Jane snaps. Michelangelo is scheduled to deliver the safe to the getaway car at three. It's already two fifteen, and she still has to handle this security fiasco before she can even think about retrieving and prepping the car. Time is running out, fast.

"You wanted me to wait for *so long*, and you didn't even leave me with any snacks or entertainment. I got thirsty." Mei slurps from her straw for emphasis.

Rina turns to Jane. "I'll distract the guard in the monitoring room. Can you take care of the DVR?"

"Yeah. Mei, get me the keys from Michelangelo, then go

straight to the parking lot. No detours, you hear me? I don't care if they're serving lychee ice cream with gold flakes, be there at two thirty. I'll get there as soon as I can."

"Whatever." Mei saunters off.

Harv's father rises to give a speech. "Welcome, everyone, to this marvelous celebration. I always told my son that loving a woman is how he knows he's become a man. I hope all of you drink and eat your fill today!"

"I can't stand another minute of this. I need to get out of here. I'll go first." Jane brings her champagne with her to the exit.

A few minutes later, Mei comes skipping down the hall, passing something cold into Jane's hand. At first glance, it appears to be a bunch of trash, but when Jane peers closer, she sees the shapes of keys cut around Tsingtao logos. Michelangelo must have traced the keys on hammered-out bottle caps before cutting them out. The woman's a genius and works like she graduated from a sweatshop. These will be as good as the real keys.

Jane goes back to the staff quarters. Things had been operating too smoothly. Well, other than Lulu's obvious discomfort. The suffering was plain on her face as Zhu Shushu went on about grandchildren and being joined together forever.

They'll get this damn train back on the tracks and Lulu as far away from this horrifying family as possible.

Jane finally finds a door with a sign that says Authorized Personnel Only. Score. Predictably, it's locked. She balances the ring of keys in her palm. "Tā mā de. This is going to take a while."

Luckily, she gets the right key on the fifth try and bursts into the room. It's several degrees warmer, wires everywhere. "Black box," she mutters under her breath, trying to remember what Zihao told her about optimal DVR placement when she was pretending to be scared of thieves breaking in and stealing her skin care fridge. After a minute, she spots it hidden in a tangle of wires.

The DVR is hot to the touch. She yanks out all its wires before setting it on the ground and jumping on it, the plastic crack-ing under her heels. *Suck it, Zihao's boss. Now what are you going to do?* She's thankful she had the foresight to wear satin gloves with her dress, otherwise she'd have to worry about fingerprints.

She gives it a few more good stomps, then whacks it against the wall until it's just a mangled pile of metal.

She's nearly sweating from the exertion. Abandoning the mess in the room, she pokes her head out, checking for potential wit-nesses. They'll discover the DVR eventually, but better than having it on her person. Hopefully Rina has been successful in locking out the guard.

By the time she's done, she's late to meet Mei, so she takes off for the parking lot at a fast clip. She should be there by now, the plates swapped. The car needs to be ready in ten minutes, when the toasts begin. The guests will be occupied through the toasts and cake cutting, and the staff will be busy clearing the plates, leaving an open path for Michelangelo. The bridesmaids are so drunk, Rina or Jane can easily make up a story about how they got caught up in the festivities and needed to run off to soothe their upset stomachs. Once Lulu cuts the cake, the first guests will start to trickle out to the valet, the earliest ap-propriate time for anyone to depart the wedding, and they'll lose their opportunity.

Her phone rings. It's Mei. They'd agreed no mobile com-munication.

"Mama?" Mei bawls. "Mama, please come get me! This man is scaring me!"

Jane freezes, alarmed. She's never heard Mei this screechy be-fore. "What are you on about?" she says into the phone.

Mei sobs grotesquely. "Just c-c-come. Please!"

Jane picks up her pace. In the parking lot, she spots Mei im-mediately. Her mascara is all streaky, and there's a suited man next to her looking very uncomfortable. They're standing be-side a glossy Aston Martin. Her mind races. Did Mei, bored out of her mind, try to hijack his car? Is he some nosy guest wondering what an eighteen-year-old is doing wandering around the parking lot?

Mei runs over and flings her arms around Jane, rubbing her messy face into her expensive dress. Resisting the urge to shove Mei's forehead back, Jane confronts the man. "What's the meaning of this?"

He scratches his head. "This is my boss's car. Your daughter was getting a bit too close."

"It was so cool!" Mei cries. "I wanted a picture with it!"

"Sorry," Jane says, trying to seem remorseful even though she wants to punch him for thinking she's old enough to be Mei's mom. "I don't know where I went wrong with this one."

"It's fine. Just don't do it again." He gets back in the car and rolls up the tinted windows.

"That could've been really bad," Jane hisses, dragging Mei toward the valet stand.

Unbothered, Mei fixes her hair. "I didn't know there was a dude in the car. Wait, stop here." They're two cars down from the Aston Martin. Mei squats, pulling her dress up around her hips. Jane can see her underwear. It's a thong. Well. Add that to the list of things Rina wouldn't want to know.

Mei lies on her belly, grunting. "I kicked it over here, it should be—aha!" There's a scraping noise, and she reveals two license plates. They're Shanghai plates, with three zeroes in a row. *Very* special plates, ones you could only get through high-up connections. She could kiss Mei right now.

Mei brushes the dirt off her knees, smug. "The moment I saw the zeroes, I knew he was our guy. You're lucky I cried so hard he didn't notice the plate was missing."

"You did good," Jane says begrudgingly, patting Mei on the head. She doesn't know who the plates belong to, but the owner should be important enough to shield their getaway car from consequences.

Mei shimmies the plates under her skirt, fluffing out the fabric so nobody can see their rectangular outline. "Where's that car you promised me?"

The non-VIP cars are parked elsewhere because the Sun Island lot is too small to fit everyone. Jane hands Zihao's ticket to the pimply valet, who brings their car around and retreats to his podium.

Jane pops open the trunk so it seems like she's retrieving something. "Screwdriver?" she whispers to Mei after she hands over the plates.

Mei reaches into her bra and withdraws a tiny screwdriver before going to distract the valet. "What's that you're reading?" Jane hears her ask.

Mei begins a rambling monologue about manga tropes, and Jane gets down to the task of swapping the plates. She removes the one in the front first, checking that Mei is blocking her from the valet's view before moving to the back. Her dress is strangling her midsection, and she can only bend at a ninety-degree angle rather than squatting like she'd prefer. As she's twisting in the last screw for the vanity plate, Zihao's real plates in the bed of the trunk, Mei says loudly, "Oh, hello, Shushu! Are you looking for Jane? She's getting something from the car."

Jane freezes. Of all the moments he could choose to take a stroll—

She tucks the screwdriver into her bag, smooths her hair, and rises. "Lǎogōng! I was going out of my mind looking for floss. The bok choy they're serving inside has such a habit of sticking in teeth. Have you toasted Harv and Lulu already?"

She moseys over to Zihao, but not before subtly transferring the car keys into Mei's hand. "Thanks!" she calls out to the valet, ushering Zihao away before he can realize she never returned the keys. As they walk, she scans the grounds, hoping they don't run into Michelangelo as she brings the safe to the parking lot.

She's nowhere to be seen. Hopefully, she's only a few minutes late. The toasts won't go on forever.

Zihao wrenches his arm out of hers as they enter the lobby. "You're hiding something from me. Something more than that appointment."

Jane nearly trips but rights herself in time. "Why are you so paranoid all of a sudden?"

He stops walking and turns to her. "Wouldn't you be, if you discovered your wife isn't who you thought? I mean, I knew you were obsessed with looks, but to actually want *plastic surgery*—"

"You never really knew me then." Over their short marriage, she's built a reservoir of reasons for divorce. His single-minded focus on work, which has made him incapable of seeing what she contributes to their household. It feels like they are back where they started. "What exactly do you want from me?"

"Cancel your appointment. *Don't* lie to me, Jane," he says, when she opens her mouth. "I want you to promise me you won't ever get plastic surgery. You want to buy fancy bags and waste time exchanging insults with strangers on WeChat? Be my guest. But I cannot abide by this."

"It's my face. What if I told you it would make me feel better about myself?"

His jaw hardens. "It doesn't matter. I'm your husband."

He sounds like every man who's ever told her she can't do something. Because in the end, he's her husband, and his wants will always eclipse hers. "If you feel so strongly," she says, her voice low and dangerous, "maybe you shouldn't be my husband anymore."

Her words hang between the two of them. His eyes glass over as he takes a moment to absorb them. "So you won't change your mind."

"If I do, it won't be because you told me to." Jane spins and stomps away. She has a damn job to do. If she does it right, by the end of the day, she will have no need for him or his opinion.

40

Wedding day, 3:00 p.m.

LULU

FACES BLUR AS Lulu and Harv make the rounds, stopping at each table to thank their guests and toast. The glass in her hand is filled with juice, a custom to protect her from getting drunk, but right now, Lulu wouldn't mind if it held alcohol.

At the fù'èrdài table, Harv fields questions about the new Former French Concession property. When it's time, Lulu has to pull him out of their clutches toward her Scarlet Beauty friends in a far corner of the hall.

Jiang Hui is seated alone, her hair braided, her makeup smokier than usual.

"You look lovely," she says to Lulu, hugging her tightly as Harv hangs back.

"You too." Lulu looks around carefully. "Where'd the others go?"

"They're around," she reassures Lulu. "Probably staking out the kitchen exit. We've never been invited to such a fancy event! Yunxi ate ten of those little dumplings they were passing around.

Oh, look, there he is." Yunxi, tall and affable, is busy charming one of the servers while he sneakily plucks two dishes of sweets off her tray. Lulu can't help but smile.

"I'm glad you're enjoying yourselves," Harv says, putting an arm around Lulu, drawing her away. She can tell all the festivities are wearing on him.

As they walk back to their table at the center, Harv says, "I'm ready to lie on a beach and sip a cocktail. Are you?"

"I am," Lulu lies as Jane sweeps in through the double doors, a dark cloud around her that makes other guests automatically move out of her path. Lulu stiffens.

"Is she okay?" Harv asks, concern in his brow. "She seems—"

"Jane's always fine," Lulu interjects. Surely, Jane and Rina have fixed the problem and the safe is on its way to the parking lot. "And isn't it time to cut the cake?"

Together, she and Harv stand in front of the towering cake and lift the knife. As it glides through soft buttercream, a voice calls, "I object to this wedding!"

Lulu feels Harv's arms tense against hers as she raises her eyes.

Her brother stands at the entrance of the banquet hall in joggers and his lucky crewneck, a bright orange shirt that's been patched multiple times because he claims it brings him good luck at mahjong.

"Gege," Lulu murmurs. He looks absolutely ridiculous, but he actually showed up. He took the bait.

The spotlight moves over to him, then darts away, like the operator is unsure whether this wedding crasher is worthy of it.

It seems like everyone holds their breath as her brother gestures at the chandeliers, the towering cake, the wide-mouthed guests in their luxurious clothing. "Fei Lulu, darling of the family." His voice is mocking. "You've tricked everyone with that spineless act of yours. But not me. *I* know the truth."

Peng Ayi, who was documenting the cake cutting across from them on her phone, now has her walkie-talkie pressed to her mouth. Her walkie-talkie crackles back. "He, uh, said he was the brother of the bride?"

The rest of the room is silent. All eyes are on Lulu's brother. Some people have taken out their phones to record the scene.

Two burly men arrive and start dragging her brother out the doors. He laughs hysterically. "Little Lulu, making us proud. You've learned how to play rich people games."

Harv tries to bring everyone's attention back to them. "To my wife!" He holds up a glass of champagne, and the room mirrors the gesture.

Lulu's mom gets up from her table and comes over as the atmosphere returns to normal, profusely apologizing to Peng Ayi. "Āiyá, my son must have been drinking again. I didn't expect him to—"

Peng Ayi ignores her and pinches Lulu on the wrist. She lowers her lips to her ear. "Fei Lulu, I will give you only one chance to speak honestly. Is there anything I should know? Any *games* I should be aware of?"

Lulu's knees shake beneath her dress, and she resists letting her eyes dart to Rina's and Jane's vacant seats. Peng Ayi, despite her contempt for Lulu's family, never overlooks a threat.

But Lulu manages to keep her voice even. "Why would I do anything when I already have everything I want?" As she speaks, she sees additional figures step up to the doorways, tall and stern. More security guards, far more than the hotel could conceivably employ.

"Lǎopó, you're not thinking clearly," Zhu Shushu says, placing a hand on Peng Ayi's shoulder. "What do you think she'll do, hack into our bank accounts? Harv married her for her beauty, not her brains, don't forget." He chuckles. "Security is here. They'll take care of everything. Don't look so put out, the guests will notice."

Peng Ayi releases Lulu, her mouth all twisted up. "People are always searching for an advantage. Poor people, especially." The accusation is pointed. "They forget that's all they will ever be."

41

Wedding day, 3:00 p.m.

RINA

THE SAFE WAS supposed to be on the way to the car right now. They're late, but after Lulu's warning, Rina stayed in the banquet hall a while longer to help offset Jane's absence. Now, Rina hovers outside the monitoring room, wondering if the best way to get the security guard out is to claim there's free food downstairs, when he rushes out without warning. The door shuts behind him. Something must have happened. She hopes it's not related to Jane's attempts to get into the recording room.

Stay focused. She will complete the task in front of her and figure out the rest later.

The door locks from the inside. She knocks to check there's nobody else within. Nobody answers. Good. She just needs to make sure the guard can't reenter and monitor any real-time footage. She withdraws her apartment key and forces it into the keyhole. Once it's nice and jammed, she holds her phone like a bat and smacks it hard. The top of the key breaks off, and she sweeps it from the ground. Nobody will be opening this door anytime soon. If Jane managed to destroy the recorded footage, there shouldn't be any evidence of their crime.

She rushes to Lulu's changing room, half an hour late to meet Michelangelo.

Inside, Michelangelo leans against her cart with a vexed expression, her plastic sneeze guard pushed up over her head while her surgical mask hangs from her right ear. A giant bucket sits on the top shelf, a tablecloth shielding the bottom rung where the safe must be. "I question why I agreed to this. The baker is out for blood because *someone* rolled the cake out earlier than scheduled. I may never leave this place if she finds out it's me."

"You're almost out of here." Rina hopes Michelangelo's irritability is not a sign she's going to hang them out to dry. "We're running late, but the car should be ready to go. If Mei followed instructions, she's waiting for you on the far right of the lot. You need to get there now before some people start leaving after the toasts." She peers over the edge of the bucket, then recoils at the dark sludge of congealed chili peppers inside. It smells strangely, tantalizingly, familiar.

"Hotpot oil that needs to get dumped," Michelangelo says, her lip curling. "You said I needed an excuse to wheel the cart into the parking lot."

Rina wrinkles her nose. The changing room is cramped and smells like beer. There are a few sweating bottles on the vanity, tools like curling irons and makeup palettes scattered everywhere. "Let's get you on your way."

She exits first. She's supposed to patrol the hallways ahead of Michelangelo, but almost immediately she sees Vic coming her way.

Quickly, she positions herself in front of the door so that Michelangelo doesn't try to leave. "It's you!" she exclaims. She feels the doorknob turn and reaches behind her, grabbing it to hold it still. As if they need more things to delay them.

"I abandoned safe duty to look for you." Vic crowds her back against the door, slips his hand around her waist. "You need to come back with me. A bit of an incident has happened in the banquet hall."

"An incident?" Her voice sounds unnatural. Did they see something on the cameras? Did they realize the safe was fake? Lulu. Lulu is going to suffer the most if they get caught. And she hasn't even mended things—

"Lulu's brother. He showed up and started saying she was some kind of evil mastermind." Rina stills. If Lulu's brother crashed the wedding, hurling accusations at her, the Zhus might actually believe she's responsible for the missing money.

Vic chuckles, not noticing her horror. "Lulu, of all people. You weren't there?"

Rina thinks fast. "I was…here. Waiting for you to get me."

"You're insatiable." He tilts toward her, his breath tickling her lips. "Pulling me away during the first dance, finding me in that hallway, now this. I've missed half of this wedding because of you."

Rina gulps. She can't deny she'd enjoyed kissing him, the heat of his fingers against the nape of her neck…

"I don't think I've been this horny since I bought my first VPN," Vic murmurs.

Rina gazes up at him in confusion.

"I used it to watch porn," Vic says, and she barely manages an eye roll. His perfect face is too close, and his breath smells of expensive whiskey. "When you put on the perfume, that was the first time I thought I had a chance. After this wedding—" He stops at her expression. "What's wrong?"

Rina nods, but she can't quite look at him.

He cups her chin, and she has no choice but to meet his eyes. "I noticed you and Lulu haven't really been talking today," he says gently.

She's relieved this is where he's brought the conversation, but the truth of it still hurts. At least this isn't something she needs to lie about. "We got into a fight."

"Believe me, as long as you both still care for each other, there's hope. A good friend is hard to lose."

His arms come around her and he presses her tightly to him, his hand cradling the back of her head.

They stay there, holding each other. Rina's mind quiets briefly, until she remembers there's a timeline and a plan that is running behind schedule, that a probably very pissed off Michelangelo is waiting behind the door.

She takes his hand and starts leading him back down the hallway. "We should get back," she says loud enough for Michelangelo to hear.

She sends a silent prayer upward Michelangelo can make it to the parking lot without her.

42

Wedding day, 3:30 p.m.

JANE

LULU'S BROTHER IS a tosser, and if Jane wasn't at a wedding with hundreds of people, she would've stomped right over to him and slapped him into silence.

The servers have set up stands with tea and sweets along each wall of the banquet hall. The dance floor is open, but most people remain in their seats, gossiping. They'll shit out all ten courses tomorrow, but this drama will keep them full for days.

Luckily that means no guests are in a rush to leave. Mei should have a clear path out of Sun Island despite the delay caused by the security setback.

Rina returns from locking out the security guard and escorting Michelangelo to the parking lot, her fingers interlaced with Vic's. She quickly drops his hand as they split up, Vic to his chair by the safe and Rina to the bridesmaids' table. Jane's eyebrows go up. Rina was only supposed to distract Vic during the safe swap, so what exactly is going on right now?

Before Rina's butt can even touch her chair, Jane pulls her

up. "Let's dance with Lulu!" she squeals. Both of their jobs are done now. It's time for them to display some normalcy. And why not celebrate a little, while there's still time left?

Peng Ayi and Lulu's mom are arguing onstage, and Lulu and Harv watch from their seats like it's a tennis match.

"We're going to steal her now that you're done with toasts," Jane informs Harv as they approach the couple's table.

Lulu doesn't get up. "Peng Ayi is expecting me to stay here for the last dress change."

Jane glances over at Peng Ayi, who's nearly foaming at the mouth as she points at the doors through which Lulu's brother had apparently barged through. "She's tied up at the moment."

"I'm not feeling well—" Before Lulu can finish, Rina's tugging her up and over to the dance floor. "It's done," she says as they move together, bouncy Chinese pop drowning out their words. "Michelangelo's en route. Mei should be leaving any minute. The drive to the internet café will take about an hour. We'll drop Lulu off at the airport tonight, and I'll check on the money tomorrow."

"Lulu, we did it!" Jane pokes Lulu, trying to get her to smile. "Can you believe it? We're getting you the hell out of here!"

"I never doubted the plan. The two of you can do anything." Lulu's expression is distant.

"You aren't still mad at us, are you?" Jane asks. "All that stuff about us parting ways—that was said in the heat of the moment."

Lulu steps back, and the lights strobing overhead illuminate the moisture in her eyes. "Haven't you felt like, this entire time, we've been drifting apart? This is something we were supposed to do together, so why did it feel like the two of you were constantly underestimating me?" There's an ache in her voice. "How did it become like this?"

"Like what?" Rina shakes her head. "Lulu, we're sorry about what we said. Can't we forget about that? Look at what we've accomplished together."

"You're still so focused on the heist." Lulu grows frustrated. "Sure, we had our meetings at Hotpot Palace. But did we really *talk* to each other? Did we see each other?"

"Of course," Rina replies. "I'm always looking out for you, Lulu, you know that."

"Rina, did you ever think about letting me handle things on my own?" Lulu's fists are clenched in her skirts. "Did the two of you even notice all the money in the safe? Did you wonder where it came from?"

"What do you mean?" Jane asks. "Didn't it all come from Peng Ayi's rich friends?"

"*I* did it. I got us even more. I saw a way, and I made it happen. But you never would've thought me capable, would you?" Lulu holds a hand to her stomach. "In our friendship, I always saw myself as lesser. I didn't go to a fancy school or work in a big skyscraper. You never gave me the chance to prove otherwise. I told you I would go through with the plan. But what I didn't tell you is I'm staying married. I'm not going anywhere."

Jane almost trips over herself. Lulu escaping was *part* of the plan. A big part. Jane knows joining the Zhus' household will crush her. "No," she protests. "You can't actually be serious." Thanks to Lulu's brother, the Zhus will now immediately suspect Lulu. They won't do anything to her family—that would be too embarrassing—but they'll make her life miserable.

"I can't leave my family. And Harv needs me, too. Peng Ayi is already suspicious of both of you. If I'm part of her household, I can protect you." There's a sheen of sweat on Lulu's forehead, and she looks unwell, like their conversation is physically making her ill. "We're getting our marriage certification in two weeks. After that, it's official."

Before Jane can say anything else, Lulu flings a hand over her mouth and runs for the edge of the dance floor. The guests around her manage to get out of the way right before she throws up all over the flower arrangements.

"Lulu! Shit!" Jane and Rina rush over, but Jiang Hui is already at her side, helping her up. Someone offers them a trash bag, and Lulu immediately sticks her face in.

They trail Lulu to the bathroom. A few others have followed, too, curious what happened to the bride. But they're not fast enough. Lulu and Jiang Hui quickly throw themselves behind the door and lock it.

"Lulu!" Jane knocks repeatedly. "Lulu!"

"Leave me alone!" Her voice is weak. "J-just leave."

The door opens, and Jiang Hui peeks out, her fingers daintily pinching her nose. "The bride has food poisoning. Please clear the hallway; she doesn't want anyone to see her." Then she slams it again before anyone can fight their way in.

The nearby guests immediately start speculating about which food item was responsible, backing away from the bathroom like it's radioactive.

"We have to wait here. She can't spring something like that on us and just run off," Rina says frantically.

Jane yanks at the door handle to no avail.

"God, this is all such a mess—" Rina says. Her phone starts buzzing. She looks up at Jane. "Yaqing."

It seems like the pile of shit they have to deal with is only getting bigger. "Put her on speaker."

"Rina, come to the lobby right now," Yaqing says. "Harv checked the safe. The money's gone."

43

Wedding day, 4:00 p.m.

RINA

SECURITY IS SWARMING the venue by the time Rina and Jane join the Zhus in the lobby. The counterfeit safe is at Zhu Shushu's feet, red envelopes scattered on the floor around him, their flaps open like empty mouths.

Zhu Shushu barks orders. "You! Get me security tapes. Bring the staff here for questioning. The incompetence of this place!" He gestures Rina and Jane over. "Ladies, show these men your bags."

Rina holds her breath as the men paw through their bags. The only incriminating thing in there is her broken key, crammed into the coin pouch of her wallet.

Beside her, Jane puts on a good show. "Seriously? How do you even know it's stolen?" Jane points at Yaqing. "Did you search her? I refuse to be searched if Yaqing and Harv haven't been."

Yaqing sputters, but her dad silences her with a look. "Everyone will be searched. Where's Lulu?"

"Puking up her guts," Yaqing says, eager to get back in her

dad's good graces. "They blocked off that whole hallway. It stinks."

Zhu Shushu throws up his hands. "This is a disgrace! Where is the bride's nitwit brother?"

"He left with his mother," Peng Ayi says nervously. "Lulu's father stayed behind. He was worried about her."

"That whole family is poisonous." Zhu Shushu plunges a hand into his graying hair. "A fucking embarrassment, all of this."

Harv tries to placate his dad. "Ba, don't worry. I'll fix this. I'll find whoever did this, and—"

"You are the reason for this." Zhu Shushu's voice thrums with barely restrained violence. "You couldn't find a decent girl with that weak personality of yours, and instead you bring this misfortune into our home. I did everything right, and somehow I still ended up with a son like you. Get out of my sight."

Harv lowers his eyes. "I'm going to check on Lulu," he mumbles, backing away.

"How could someone have done this?" Peng Ayi is aghast. "The safe was in the middle of the venue! We would've seen!" She whirls toward Vic. *"You,"* she says, forgetting her manners. "I knew we shouldn't have had someone so irresponsible watching it."

"I didn't know we had experienced thieves in our midst," Vic says, seemingly unaffected by her accusation.

"In our midst? What are you implying?"

"The theft was obviously planned." Vic taps the false safe with his toe thoughtfully. "I'm not even sure if this is the same safe we started the wedding with. Someone must have done their research. Who knows? Maybe it was one of us."

Rina swallows as the air thickens with distrust. Vic's eyes burn into her.

One of the hotel staff dashes over and whispers something into Peng Ayi's ear. She tries to regain her composure. "The valet said there was a car that left the lot half an hour ago. We'll reach out to the police for the plate number and get to the bottom of this."

Security finishes patting Jane down. Thankfully, nobody else but Rina sees the renewed alarm on her face. "These two are clear."

"Now that we've confirmed Rina and I are innocent," Jane says huffily, "are we free to go? I need to find my husband before he drives off without me."

"Fine," Zhu Shushu says, waving his hand.

"Rina—"

Vic cuts Jane off. "Rina and I need to talk first." A dangerous current runs beneath his words. "Let's take a walk," he says.

"I came here with Jane," Rina objects.

"I'll take you back if that's a problem."

It most certainly is, but everyone is staring at them now, and they can't risk coming off suspicious.

"I've got to go," Jane says. She mutters to Rina, "We'll meet in front and call a cab. I'll tell Zihao to find his own way home." Then she escapes.

Rina follows Vic, reluctance weighing down each step. She anxiously checks her phone, a nervous habit from work. Her email inbox is overflowing, which only makes her stomach tighten.

Outside, security has set up a makeshift fence between the lobby and the parking lot, and three extremely long lines of people slowly file through it. Everyone's gossiping about the disappearance of the bride and the supposedly empty safe. The wedding is over early, and the lot is choked with traffic as everyone tries to leave at once. Mei should've swapped the plates back at their blind spot by now and should be well on her way to the internet café. All Rina wants to do is call to make sure she's okay, that whoever Peng Ayi sent won't catch up to her. But it's too early, and there are too many people around.

"It's interesting, isn't it?" Vic muses. "The things people do for money."

Rina doesn't look at him. "It's a means to an end. Happiness. Choices. Freedom."

"Freedom?" He stops walking. They're somewhere on the path Rina took to get to Lulu's suite that morning. It's covered in wilted, torn-up flower petals. "Is that why you did it?"

"I don't know what you're talking about."

"You're lying to me." Vic forcefully tugs his tie loose. Steps closer. "I'm headed to the States after this. You could come with me. Leave this all behind. I'll take care of you."

He's telling her to give it up. Give up the money for Harv's sake. Follow Vic into the unknown.

It costs him nothing to say any of that.

They are *so* close. All she needs is Mei to confirm the safe has arrived, and their heist will be complete. There's no turning back now. If she follows Vic, she will have to rely on *his* money, *his* influence, to get her where she wants to go. But Zhou Rina does not rely on anyone. Because she's determined. Because she works hard. With the money from today, she will make a life for herself on her own terms.

"I can't." It's a ragged whisper. There's no need to deny it. He won't be able to prove anything anyway. The Zhus might keep a close eye on her for a while, but they'll move on. They have better things to do, more than enough money, and so does Vic.

"Just tell me," Vic says, his voice strained. The veneer cracks, and she glimpses the depth of his pain. "Did you ever believe there could be something between us?"

It's a precarious question, but what's the point in being honest? It will only break her heart and his. So she holds his eyes and says, "No."

It's like a switch flips. His expression dims, and in that moment, Rina knows Vic Shan is lost to her. "I see."

Vic turns. With his back to her, he says, "Wǒ shì zhēn xīn de." *I'm sincere. My heart is real.*

Of all the outcomes she should've expected from the heist, she never considered this one. That she'd get what she wants but still feel like she's losing.

He shoves his hands into his pockets. "I'm going to check on Harv. You should go."

There's a hole in her chest, growing wider with each breath she takes. But she can't focus on that. She has to get out of here. She must save the grief for later.

She chooses one of the security lines. People are complaining, asking why they're not letting anyone through.

"Rina!" Jane joins her, cutting in front of everyone. "Oh, shut up," she says to the people grumbling behind them.

"Hey, you were bridesmaids, weren't you?" One of the guests, a short man with a well-groomed mustache, inches closer. "What's this we hear about wedding money being stolen?"

Jane shrugs. "I have no idea. They don't tell us anything. Where'd you get that?" She points to someone's red Louis Vuitton mini backpack.

Now that Rina observes the scene around her, everyone seems to be holding them.

"Wedding favor! There were these guys inside handing them out with Chanel perfume and a silk scarf." The man sighs in disappointment. "The last wedding I went to, everyone got custom Rimowas."

"Oh, fun," Jane says. "I must have missed them. Rina, did you see them?"

"No," Rina says shortly, still dwelling on how quickly the conversation with Vic came and went. Things are over. Just like that.

"Sorry, everyone. To make this go faster, we request that you put your gifts into these boxes. We will give them back once you progress through security and your other belongings are inspected." A security guard brandishes one of the storage containers for everyone to see.

There's groaning. "I already opened mine!" someone calls.

"Who gave you these instructions? Nobody told us," another guard says to the man who made the announcement.

"If we have to look through every bag, it will take two hours for everyone to get through," he replies.

"Āiyá, two hours?" a man in a patterned red suit calls. "I'm in a hurry. I have a reservation at the Chop Chop Club. Do you know how impossible it is to get a table there?" He waves his goody bag. "Take it, take it! Just let me through."

People surge forward, tossing their goody bags in boxes, and the line starts to move.

An argument breaks out between a woman and a security guard as he hands her bag back. "This isn't the same one I got before!" she claims, thrusting it in his face. "This has logos. The one I got had a checked pattern!"

There's a kerfuffle when one man attempts to rush past security without being searched. They take his bag and direct him to the back of the line. The horror of having to repeat this wait subdues the rest of the guests, who from there on out obediently pass through.

Jiang Hui marches by them and up to the guards at the front with a bundle of Lulu's dresses. She gestures insistently at a few of the boxes. The guards step aside and let her lay the dresses in them before she sets the lids back on. She must be in charge of storing Lulu's outfits to be shipped home later. Once her task is done, Jiang Hui heads back into the hotel. Rina is about to follow her, but Jane grabs her arm.

In a low voice, she says, "I'm as worried about Lulu as you are, but going back for her now is only going to endanger all of us. And didn't you hear her? She doesn't want our help."

The situation on the other side of the security isn't much better, a mess of people harassing the poor valet and cabs blocking the driveway. It's 4:30 p.m. Mei should be calling any minute. Rina reaches into her bag and realizes she has twenty missed calls from Mei, plus a bunch from work.

Mei doesn't answer when she attempts to call her back.

Rina tries again, then again, her unease growing with each ring. At least it gives her something to do. It's either that, or be haunted by the look on Vic's face when she told him nothing between them had been real.

44

Wedding day, 5:00 p.m.

LULU

❖ ❖ ❖ ❖ ❖

THE TILES OF the bathroom are cold and hard as Lulu leans against the toilet, pushing aside errant pieces of tissue paper. Her stomach has finally settled. Somehow, they managed to get her out of her banquet dress before she ruined it further, though she still expects Peng Ayi to reprimand her lengthily about this later.

Jiang Hui helped Lulu into the fifth dress after assuring her the others had been packed away. Peng Ayi was least pleased with this one, but it's Lulu's favorite. The material is soft, maroon velvet, and it's tied in the back with a tassel. Lulu is almost sad she didn't get the chance to wear it.

"You know, I never would've expected this of you," Jiang Hui says.

Lulu joins Jiang Hui at the sinks, washing her hands carefully. There's a paper cut on her finger that stings as the water hits it. "What, for me to marry a rich man?"

There's a tentative knock on the door. "Lulu," Harv calls. "Are you feeling better?"

"I always knew you'd catch the eye of some rich guy. But agreeing to marry one you don't even love?" Jiang Hui shakes her head slowly. "Come on, Lulu."

Lulu narrows her eyes. "What else is out there for me?"

Jiang Hui dries her hands, then adds the paper towel to the layers of tissue and trash bags piled into the bin. "The whole damn world." She opens the door. "She's all yours."

Harv comes in, scratching an already red area on his forehead, and immediately starts talking. "Lulu, the money went missing. They searched everyone, but it's disappeared. You wouldn't know anything about it, would you?" He stops short, taking in her pale face. "You don't look too great. I'm sorry, I should've come to check on you sooner, but the money..."

She knows his parents are probably furious and that he's caught in the crosshairs. "It's alright. Of course that's more important."

Harv smiles slightly. "I knew you'd understand. I know we had our honeymoon scheduled for tomorrow, but we're going to have to stay. I have to help Ba investigate."

Lulu swallows. "Okay. I'll stay out of your way."

"You're coming home with me. If there's anything else you need from your apartment, Ma will send someone to get it for you." Harv rubs his forehead again. "With the scene your brother made, the things he said... Even if I believe you didn't do it, Ma won't let you leave."

They're locking her away. She expected this, for the suspicion to fall on her, but knowing she will be trapped in the Zhus' apartment before they move into the home Harv's parents bought for him, makes her lungs contract.

"I think I left my passport in the changing room. Let's stop by there first so we don't have any problems tomorrow."

Harv is in the middle of unlocking the changing room door when Zhu Shushu comes raging down the hallway. Peng Ayi scurries behind, clenched with worry.

"You," he says, his voice snapping like a whip when he spots

Harv. "I give you the FFC property to handle, and you go behind my back? What is all this I've heard about you meeting
with the children of my business partners?"

"Ba, it was a surprise for you, and it *worked*. It drove demand—"

"I don't want to hear it. You've embarrassed me in front of
all our guests."

"Ba," Harv pleads. "What about the license plate? Surely,
with that—"

"Do you know whose plate that was? One of our provincial
leaders." Zhu Shushu is basically snarling. "You're telling me
that a government official stole our money? Would you like me
to accuse him to his face?"

"No. That's not what I'm saying." His eyes dart to his mother,
then Lulu.

"Look at me!" Zhu Shushu slams his hand against the wall.
"Don't look at her! A weak man blames his woman for his problems. All you do is follow people around. First me, then that
pompous friend of yours, and now your wife. You are a disgrace,
and I never should've spent a single cent on you."

"That's enough!" Peng Ayi shouts, putting herself between
her husband and Harv. Harv is shaking, and Lulu feels like she's
witnessing something she shouldn't. "He's still our son."

"He is no son of mine." Zhu Shushu storms off.

Peng Ayi lays a hand on Harv's arm. "He's just angry. He doesn't
mean it."

Harv brushes her away. "Stop covering for him, Ma. Did he
not mean it any of those other times too?"

Lulu shuts the changing room door.

The place is a mess. The trash cans from earlier lie on their
sides, a few empty red envelopes crushed beneath them. Makeup
palettes and brushes are scattered across the vanity, and there's a
dark, shapeless mass on the ground that looks like Mei's wig. She
tidies up as best as she can as she gathers her stuff into her duffel bag. On the way out, she catches sight of the gold pig from

Harv's grandmother, glinting on the counter next to a mountain of bobby pins. She picks it up, and after a moment's pause, tucks it into her duffel bag.

Peng Ayi is gone when she emerges into the hall. Harv waits for her, his expression closed off. "The car's not here yet, but your dad wanted to say goodbye to you." Together, they walk toward the exit.

"Harv." Vic approaches them, waving to his friend.

"You're still here?" Harv sounds tired.

"Yeah, I wanted to check on you. And say goodbye." Vic's tie is gone, his carefree smile missing.

Something in Vic's voice makes Harv take notice. "Are you okay?"

Vic gives a self-effacing laugh. "Just brokenhearted, that's all. I'm headed back to the States tonight."

Rina. Something must have happened between them.

Harv's face falls. "I thought you'd stay longer this time."

Vic shrugs. "I'm tired of this place." He looks at Harv like he wants to say more. Then, he grabs his friend's shoulder. "If shit hits the fan at home, I could always use extra hands. We're looking into real estate." He nods at Lulu. "Take care of him."

They leave through the glass doors, and Harv gently nudges Lulu toward where her dad stands on the curb, wringing his hands. He rushes over when he spots her. "Lulu, ah," he says, and presses a palm to her forehead. "Are you well? I'm sorry about your brother and the trouble he caused."

"Ba." Lulu's eyes well. She wonders how often she'll get to see him now that her life will be governed by Harv's family. She hands him her bag. "Will you clean my clothes and put them back in my closet? It's something I can only trust you with." Her dad has always done their laundry, painstakingly clipping each article of clothing to their worn clothesline, folding shirts into neat squares while cross-legged on the floor. She knows he'll discover the pig.

"They'll be there next time you visit," he promises.

"I love you," she says. Her dad will be able to pawn the pig for a good price. Enough to pay someone to fix the house. Once things calm down with the Zhus, maybe Lulu can get him a doctor for his back. As softhearted as he is, he won't let her brother spend that money. Not when the Zhus are already suspicious of him.

She hugs her dad one last time.

"Be happy," he whispers.

45

Wedding day, 5:00 p.m.

JANE

❖ ❖ ❖ ❖ ❖

IT TAKES FOREVER, but Jane and Rina manage to call a taxi. Zihao had informed her via text that he was riding home with his boss. He'd called Jane twice while they were in line, but she ignored him, assuming he'd finally realized she never returned his valet ticket. At least he was still trying to communicate with her.

The middle between them is empty, a reminder that Lulu was supposed to be here. They should be on their way to the airport, buzzing with excitement and accomplishment, but the air inside is heavy with defeat.

She groans as she settles into her seat. "This day feels like it'll never end. Has Mei returned your calls?" She tries Lulu on her cell, but unsurprisingly, nobody picks up.

"They're going straight to voice mail now. Her phone must be dead." Rina's tone is flat as she continues to scroll through her phone.

Jane catches a glimpse of her old firm's logo. "Are you seriously reading work emails right now?"

Rina starts drafting a reply. "There are a lot to get through, and they're easier to think about than my missing cousin."

Jane snatches Rina's phone away. She's worried about Mei too, but she refuses to believe that little brat got stuck in a situation she can't get out of. "It'll be okay. Why the hell are you wearing a seat belt?"

"Reflex."

"After all these years? My friend, you are an American at heart. Forget your parents and go back to your old life."

Rina's laugh is bitter, but she looks beat down. "You're not the first one to voice that opinion."

"Everything will be fine," Jane assures her.

"It's not just that. Some other stuff happened at the venue, too. With...with Vic."

Jane recalls her and Vic walking back into the banquet together, how Vic whisked her off before they could leave.

No way. It was funny to watch the two of them joust, but for it to have led to something more—

She brought those two together, knowing this would be the ending. Had she not been paying enough attention to Rina's changing feelings all these months?

The taxi slows as they near Fangsheng Bridge. Even though it's a tourist destination, Zhujiajiao is never *this* crowded. "What the hell? Shifu, what's going on?"

"We're stuck," the taxi driver says unhelpfully. "Something going on near the bridge."

Jane exhales, frustrated. They're still so far from the city center. "We'll just get out here."

The sun is beginning to set, and the lanterns along the river bob in the breeze. There's a crowd near the bridge entrance, police in bright yellow vests. Yellow tape surrounds the area.

An officer blocks them when they try to approach. "You'll have to go another way."

"Understood, Officer. What happened here anyway?" Rina asks, angling to get a look over his shoulder.

Jane doesn't bother playing nice. She ducks under the tape, ignoring the shouting from behind her.

As she steps onto the bridge, she sees it. Popped wide open, the river lazily flowing around it. The safe. Its once spotless exterior is now covered in river grass and mud. The password Harv chose flickers on the digital screen. 不可兼得. *You can't have it all.* It feels like some sort of celestial irony, especially when Jane recognizes the safe is empty.

There's yelling from farther down the river, and Jane makes out someone waving a rectangle covered in mud. It's only when she notices the yellow numbers through the dirt that she realizes it's a license plate. The one Mei stole.

If things had gone according to plan, that safe should've been in the storage locker at the internet café, waiting for them to unlock it tomorrow. Not here, discarded and totally vacant.

Rina's made her way to Jane's side, and she inhales audibly at the sight. "But Mei—why can't I reach her? She dumped the license plate, but why the safe too? And if she actually made it to the internet café but her phone died, she would've found another way to get in touch. You don't think she's—"

"Dead?" Jane offers, and Rina lets out a tiny squawking noise. "Come on, let's get out of here before they actually take us to jail."

Who could it have been? Who betrayed them?

The only others who knew about the plan were Michelangelo and Mei. Mei is crafty, but she has no reason to make off with that amount of money, and she respects Rina too much to betray her like that. It can only be Michelangelo, who is a trickster by trade. Jane's fists clench. She never should've trusted her.

Rina is fully freaking out now. "I need to ask the police if they've seen Mei."

Jane grabs Rina by the shoulders. "Absolutely not. Do you think they're on our side? They'll be investigating who did this, and if any of us get implicated, it's over. We got away from the venue, which was hard enough. We can't do anything that puts us back on the Zhus' radar."

Rina drags a hand down her face. Breathes in. "Okay. Okay."

They walk down the river, away from the commotion. Even from afar, Jane catches the beams of flashlights as officers continue to search for evidence.

As the sky darkens, Zhujiajiao becomes even more romantic. The lanterns, the relaxing sound of the river, the welcoming entrances of the quaint buildings that line the riverwalk. It's a steep contrast to the emotions coursing through her. This situation has gotten wildly out of control. This whole thing was reckless.

Michelangelo betrayed them. Mei is missing. Their friendship with Lulu is in pieces. Zihao is mad at her. And the money is gone.

Rina nearly trips over the paddle of an old man whose small boat is up against the riverbank, one of the many boatmen who offer rides to tourists. In the dark, they seem more like ghosts, overlooked by the police and Shanghainese used to refusing their loudly marketed tours.

Jane is about to move along when the man says in a croak, "Xiao Na?"

Rina stops. "Lao Wang?"

The old man tips his straw hat. "You made it. I've been turning away business for over an hour, waiting for you! Your cousin sent me."

Rina is speechless, so Jane tries to confirm for both of them. "Yeye, are you talking about Mei? Gangly, straight bangs, disrespectful, kind of chubby in the cheeks?"

Lao Wang laughs heartily, but it ends with a hacking cough.

"I may be old, but I don't forget a face! I was rowing to where this river connects with the Dianpu when I saw her. She told me to dump some of her things upriver, then pass a message to you."

Hope enters Rina's voice, now that someone else has seen Mei. "Lao Wang, where is she now?"

"She said she had to park the car at home."

"My place," Jane says. "Let's go." Zihao could be home or off with his boss, but it's a risk they have to take.

"Thank you," Rina says with gratitude. "I would appreciate if you don't mention this to anyone."

Lao Wang spits into the river. "I took this job because I like to talk to young people, but it seems they would much rather ignore me and talk to each other. But you and your Vic were different. Thank you for keeping an old man company."

Rina's eyes are glassy. "We were happy to do it."

They head toward the main road, and Jane opens her phone to call another car. Hopefully Mei has stayed put. "Fuck, the Didi queue is over an hour long. Wait, what are you doing?"

Rina is slipping her heels off, shoving them into her bag. "I'm not waiting around. Let's take a bike, at least until we get somewhere less busy." Rina jogs to a bank of shared bikes, scanning the code to pay before stepping on, but her qípáo prevents her from extending her legs more than a few inches. "Shit!" With both hands, she grabs the ends of the slit up her thigh. The sound of fabric ripping splits the darkness.

"Wǒ cào," Jane says in admiration. "You badass bitch."

Rina pulls her bag over her head cross-body, then jumps onto the bike. "Let's go get my cousin."

Jane follows her lead. They pedal onto the main road, honks trailing them as they get onto North Street. Finally, around Qinghua Pavilion, they disembark and manage to get a taxi.

The moment they arrive at Jane's apartment complex, Rina bolts out of the car and races toward the garage.

Jane runs after her. The gate opens, and Rina darts down the rows of cars. In their designated spot, Zihao's car is parked perfectly within the lines.

"Mei!" Rina sprints to the car, checking inside. Her voice quakes. "She's not here."

"What?" There's no way Mei went up to her apartment when she only had the garage code. "Where else could she have gone?"

The garage door opens again, but it's just another resident's car entering.

Rina has her phone out, panic-stricken in the headlights. "I don't care anymore, I'm telling her mom—"

A black blur barrels into Rina, and when Jane's brain catches up, she sees Mei, her arms wound tightly around her cousin. "Rina Jie! Omigod, I'm so glad you made it. I was so scared, then Zihao Shushu—"

Fuck. Zihao stands there, still in his suit. His arms are folded, and there is a thunderous expression on his face that makes Jane certain this time, there will be no forgiveness.

46

Wedding day, 7:00 p.m.

RINA

THE FIRST THING Rina sees as she enters her apartment is their planning whiteboard, the pink heart Jane had drawn around Rina's and Vic's names. She ushers Mei into the shower, then grabs the eraser and wipes the board clean.

She texts Lulu, asking if she's okay, but doesn't get a response. She hasn't heard from Jane either, who they'd left with an angry Zihao. Rina doesn't know him all that well, but she could tell he was furious.

"When I pulled into the garage, he was already waiting for me," Mei admitted on their ride home. "Should I have run him over?"

"Don't joke about that."

"Jane Jie looked like she wished I'd done that."

Gazing at the smudges left behind on the board, Rina feels like a fool. Did they actually think they could pull this off and come out on the other side unscathed?

Her phone rings, and she snatches it, hoping it's Lulu. Instead,

Luo Ren's name appears on the screen. Her boss always seems to find the worst moments to bug her.

Reluctantly, she answers.

"Rina, I called you multiple times. We had an emergency today we needed you for." His voice is clipped, impatient.

"I was at my best friend's wedding. Remember? I told you I wouldn't be around," she reminds him. It's been so long since she's taken vacation that if she's ever offline, people assume it's because someone she knows has died. She gets a lot of joy out of her work, but this job is sucking her dry.

"Yes, but you still had your phone on you, didn't you?" He isn't sorry at all for demanding things on her day off.

An exquisite calm washes over her as Rina realizes what she needs to do. "I guess I'll tell you now—I quit."

The other end is silent. This is her chance to rescind her words, but Rina does not backtrack. She should've made this choice much sooner.

Luo Ren says evenly, "There are hundreds of people who want your job. I thought you were smarter than this."

"Then you should have no trouble finding a replacement. I'll pick up my things on Monday."

She hangs up and sinks into the couch. She's done it. She's quit, with no safety net, no money, no prospects. Vic would be proud. The thought makes her heart ache.

Her dread has just begun to settle in when Mei emerges from the shower smelling like Lulu's cherry blossom shampoo. "So Lulu's actually going to stay married?" she asks as she drains Rina's tea before placing it back on the coffee table. "And you're not going to do anything about it?"

Rina studies the dregs of her teacup. She's always viewed Lulu as a little sister to protect, but maybe Lulu never wanted an older sister. "I don't think it's my place to get involved."

"You know, the situation reminds me of this group project I did with this volleyball athlete. My group thought she only knew how to play volleyball so we tried to keep her out of the project. Then she totally flamed us one day for stereotyping her and rage quit. Felt bad. Shows that you can't step all over someone and think they won't notice."

Any other time, a comment like this would've prompted her to scold Mei for making a bad thing worse, but right now, she's too tired. "I just want her to tell me she's okay."

"You worry too much about everyone else around you, Rina Jie. Sometimes you can sit back and let people make their own mistakes." Mei reaches over and taps Rina's shoulder lightly. Rina is about to tell her how mature she's being, when Mei starts talking fast. "I wasn't sure that license plate would work, but I did an illegal U-turn by a police car and its lights didn't even come on. It was like a free ticket to break every law. I ran so many lights!"

Rina massages her temples. "I'm glad you're safe."

"So where's the money?" Mei's grin disappears as she takes in the look on Rina's face.

Embarrassment seeps in. She doesn't know how to answer this question. "Mei, when did you realize the safe was empty?"

"Michelangelo had it covered with cloth when she dropped it off. I took the cloth off once I arrived at the blind spot, and that's when I saw it was empty. I figured something in the plan had changed and that I had to get rid of any evidence, so I had Lao Wang help me dump everything."

If Michelangelo put an empty safe in the trunk, she must have removed the money in the venue. They should've kept a closer eye on her.

Mei releases a sigh. "There goes the money for my Funko Pop! collection."

Rina's doorbell rings, and panic flashes through her.

"It's not the police, is it?" Mei whispers, echoing her thoughts.

Slowly, Rina gets up and walks toward the screen displaying the apartment's entrance. If it is the police, she'll let them take her. There's no way she's endangering Mei again.

She relaxes when she sees the figure pacing on the screen. It's Jane.

A few minutes later, Rina opens her door, and Jane stomps inside. "That conniving bitch!" She drops on the couch with a huff, picking up Rina's refilled cup and downing it. "I looked her store up on WeChat, and the listing is gone!"

"So it was actually Michelangelo?" Mei asks with disappointment. "She was so nice. She gave me this mini Prada keychain that I put on my backpack, and apparently it was real too! I'm going to have to burn it."

"You don't have to burn something nice to make a point," Rina says.

"Don't listen to her. Burn it and curse it into the flames."

Rina wants to know what happened between Jane and Zihao, but she's afraid saying his name will only incite more fury. "Jane, are you staying here tonight?"

Jane punches the couch cushion behind her head. "The Zhus reached out to Zihao's boss about the security system not working. They don't have any records from the venue, but they got the local police to share footage from the bridge. Zihao recognized our car, even though the plates were swapped. He figured out I was involved. I denied it, obviously. Whether he reports us to his superiors is yet to be known."

"Do you think he will?" Rina has no faith any of this will hold up under scrutiny.

"He definitely isn't feeling very charitable toward me." Jane lies back and kicks her feet up. Mei scoots farther down the couch, annoyed to lose the space. "Honestly, we've lost everything already. What's a few days in jail?"

"I'm too young for imprisonment!" Mei says.

Rina's witnessed Jane's marriage improve over these months. She'd been so giddy at the yacht party, no longer wanted the divorce she'd been strategizing since shortly after her wedding. Even if Zihao's angry now, Rina suspects he's felt the same in that time period. Jane still has a chance to save her relationship, and her nonchalance pisses Rina off. "Jane, if you don't try to fix things with Zihao now, you're going to regret it forever."

Jane sits up. Her body is coiled tight, and there's fire in her eyes. "Are you trying to tell me what to do?"

She could tread carefully around this, arrange words in a certain way so nobody gets hurt. But she's tired of the mental gymnastics. If Rina wants to patch up the remnants of her life, she'll start tomorrow. "The things Lulu said…about us being selfish. We didn't just treat her that way. We did it to everyone in our lives."

Dimly, she remembers Mei is perched there, spectating, but it's too late to censor what's about to be said.

Jane grips the arm of the couch, her red nails stark against the white fabric. "Zihao's the selfish one! Have you not been listening, all those times I asked him for—"

"I've been listening. That's why I know you haven't complained about that in the past three months. And yes, you think he resents you for quitting your job, but maybe it's because he didn't want you to lose something you worked so hard for. I know you're angry. Your parents are awful people, and they didn't raise you with love. Lulu and I hate seeing the way it holds you back."

"You didn't hear the things he said—"

"Jane. You're not perfect all the time. How can you expect him to be?"

Jane stands. "I knew it. You've always looked down on me for my decisions. You think I chose the easy way out, when I've been struggling my entire fucking life."

Rina knows Jane is right. She did judge her for trading her career for marriage. She dismissed her complaints about Zihao, housework, and didn't really bother to try to understand. She'd been too busy feeling sorry for herself after losing a work ally, someone who truly understood what Rina was dealing with because she was experiencing it too. "I was wrong." The admission is hard to make, and Rina almost wants to snatch it back. "I guess, at some point, we all stopped listening to one another."

Jane doesn't sit back down, but she doesn't leave either. "Fine. If we're being honest with each other, I want you to hear this. I think you held a grudge against Vic all this time because his spontaneous approach scares you. You stay here because you somehow think that'll help you control the course of your mom's life." There's no anger when Jane looks at her now. Only sadness. "You think everything will happen on a timeline you've decided. For all your emphasis on being rational, you may be the biggest dreamer of all of us."

Rina laughs. "You certainly don't pull any punches." What's wrong with planning out her life? That's what keeps her on track. That's what allows her to achieve her goals.

The doorbell rings again, and Rina becomes conscious of how both their chests are heaving.

"Mei, *please* tell me someone's here because you ordered dumplings or something."

Mei shakes her head slowly.

Rina approaches the screen for the second time. In the lobby, there's a grumpy-looking woman wearing a yellow shirt that says SHANGHAI KUAIKUAI EXPRESS. Rina watches as she hits the buzzer again like it's personally offended her.

"I'm going to answer it," says Rina.

"What?" Jane snaps. "Do not answer!"

"If it's actually the police, they're going to get us eventually. Mei, hide behind the couch." There's no point in delaying the inevitable.

Mei glares at her, but even she must be distressed by Michelangelo's betrayal. She obeys, flipping off the back of the couch and out of sight.

Rina answers the buzzer.

"Wéi? I've been ringing you for the past five minutes," the delivery person complains. "We're dropping off event supplies like we were instructed."

Event supplies? Rina mouths to Jane, who crosses her arms, and mouths back, *Do. Not. Let. Her. In!* She glares at Rina.

"Okay, I'll buzz you in."

"Xièxie." Her *thank you* sounds more like a *fuck you.*

"Why are you letting them in?"

"They're probably delivering Lulu's stuff. I can't exactly leave it outside, can I?"

"Seriously?" Jane hisses.

"If you're so scared, get behind the couch with Mei."

Jane rolls her eyes. "Like that'll save us."

At the door are a group of men dressed in sunny yellow uniforms, captained by a scowling woman.

"Where do you want it?" the woman asks brusquely. She waves behind her, and that's when Rina sees all the stacked boxes.

"Um..." Rina drags the coffee table closer to the couch, leaving more space in front of the TV. "Will they fit here?"

The woman grunts at her posse, and they shuttle the boxes in.

Rina's racing heart slows slightly. They really are just dropping off boxes, although Rina doesn't know why here, rather than at the Zhus'. Across from her, Jane observes the workers, her jaw clenched.

"For the record, I quit my job," Rina says. "It's pretty fucking scary to be unemployed." There's no plan this time. She'll have to figure it out as she goes.

Jane stares at her. Then, she says, "Good. They sucked. This time, choose a place that actually deserves you."

"I'll be lucky if anyone gives me an interview."

"You'll find something."

The delivery people finish up. "Next time you call for us, don't make us wait," their leader declares. Then she marches out of there, leaving a mountain of boxes behind.

Rina opens one, and Lulu's wedding gown puffs out. Immediately, she shuts it again. It's only a painful reminder of a day she'd sooner forget.

47

Wedding day, 7:00 p.m.

LULU

ZHU SHUSHU STAYS back at the hotel to yell at the staff, and Lulu drives home with Harv and Peng Ayi. In the back seat of their car, Peng Ayi's arm presses against hers, and Lulu thinks of the plane ticket in her bag. She should've thrown it away.

"Those friends of yours," Peng Ayi says casually. "You're very close. You must have told them everything about our wedding."

Lulu's phone flashes with texts from Rina and Jane. Before she can read them, Peng Ayi extends her hand. "Let me hold on to that for now."

Her grip tightens, but Peng Ayi tilts her head. "Is there something urgent they need you for?"

Lulu knows she has to give Peng Ayi what she wants. Helplessly, she relinquishes her phone and watches as Peng Ayi turns it off, then slips it into her purse.

"We aren't really that close," Lulu manages to say. She must act this part out to the end. Peng Ayi had the resources to dig up everything on Lulu's background, and she doesn't want that sort of scrutiny on Rina and Jane. Even if Peng Ayi can't track down the missing money, who knows what she might find and weaponize against them? "I came to Shanghai without knowing anyone and needed friends. In the end, we're too different." Saying it aloud, the statement doesn't ring entirely false to Lulu's ears.

Peng Ayi sinks into her seat with a sigh. "Friends come and go, Lulu. We never stop growing, and sometimes that means our paths diverge. Your friends will never care for you the way that family does. And we are your family now. Right, Harv?"

Harv, in the front, says nothing. Peng Ayi frowns, but she doesn't admonish him.

When they get home, the living room is still a mess of boxes from the Louis Vuitton backpacks. Harv wades through the sea of tissue paper and cardboard and goes straight to his room—*their* room now, Lulu remembers—and closes the door behind him.

"Where are your dresses?" Peng Ayi asks from behind her. "They're supposed to be here. I got an alert they've been dropped off."

"I told them to deliver the dresses to my apartment," Lulu says. "I thought I was going back there."

Peng Ayi exhales, digging her fingers into her brow. "Nothing is going right today. Ling! Get me the hotel staff."

As Ling dials, Peng Ayi turns back to Lulu. Her voice drops, the civility she presented to everyone else gone. "I am tired of your sweet and naive routine. You are part of my household now, and you will follow my rules."

Ling brings in the phone, and Peng Ayi disappears into her bedroom, yelling about refunds. Lulu slides down the wall until her butt hits the carpet. Tissue paper crinkles beneath her. All day, she's resolutely pushed aside her fear. Now it hits her all at once. She's fully made an enemy of her mother-in-law. Peng Ayi, who was there as her family worked hard to rise in wealth and status, who will protect the place they have created for themselves in society at all costs.

"Lulu Xiaojie," Ling says. "This might help." She's come back with a tray with two bowls of tián tāng, jujubes floating on top of amber liquid. At first, Lulu thinks she's offering the soup to her out of solidarity, but Ling gestures toward Harv's closed door.

Harv needs her, and she is his wife now.

Lulu shakily accepts the tray. She knocks on Harv's door, then lets herself in. He's on the edge of the bed, his head dipped, hands clasped on his knees. "Harv? I have soup." She approaches him like he's a wounded animal. She wants to apologize, but doing so would mean confessing what she's done. All she can do is stay by his side.

Harv doesn't move, so she sits down carefully, placing the tray beside her. "Drink some. It'll make you feel better." She scoops soup out, blowing on it, before offering the spoon to him.

Harv takes Lulu's wrist, then lowers the spoon back into the bowl. His eyes are red. "I don't know how to stop being a disappointment."

Lulu squats in front of him and covers his hands with hers. He looks so lonely. Lulu can't bear to see him like this. "You've tried so hard. If it's still not enough, maybe it's not your fault."

"You don't understand what it's like to be raised with the sole purpose of being an investment."

She cradles his cheek. "Actually, I do." Lulu knows it will require more breath and energy than she has left to explain to Harv how even families who have nothing can still put expectations on their children.

Harv raises his face to hers. "This isn't what either of us wanted, and I'm sorry."

Lulu smiles sadly. She's never been someone to hold on to anger, and they've both betrayed each other, even if he doesn't know it. They are still just two lost children, forced together by their families, living in an impatient world. Husband and wife. In two weeks, this marriage will be officially registered. There will be nowhere for either of them to run. "I hope that one day, you give yourself permission to look for your own happiness." She knows, even as she says it, that there are no more choices left for her to make.

48

Wedding day, 11:00 p.m.

JANE
❖ ❖ ❖ ❖

AFTER RINA AND Mei left, Jane had waited for Zihao to make the first move so that she could prepare her defense.

"I saw the tapes," he'd said, and Jane opened her mouth, ready to lie all the way to the grave about her involvement. But all he'd followed that up with was, "I hope you drove safely."

She followed him silently up to the apartment, waiting for him to turn around and yell at her. He knew. It was obvious he'd recognized his own car, plus he'd found Mei in the garage. But all he did was head to their bedroom, where he methodically took off his watch, then his tie.

Finally, she couldn't stand it anymore. "What are you doing?"

He looked over his shoulder at her. "I'm going on a run."

She could've explained then, about what she had done. Asked for his understanding. Instead, she chose to leave too.

When she returns, there's a single light on in the hallway that illuminates the slippers lined up neatly on the shoe rack. She notices Zihao's slippers, so large they make hers seem like kids' shoes, are still there.

He isn't home. But he left the light on for her.

She slides her feet into her slippers and goes to the bathroom. Notes the bottles of her skin care products, organized on the counter. No matter how messed up she makes them—and she's tried—Zihao always rearranges them based on her twelve-step routine.

She shucks off her bridesmaid dress, showers, and gets into bed. The sheets are chilly, and she reaches her arm across them until it can't stretch any farther. There've been times she told herself how delightful it would be to have an entire bed to herself again. At this moment, she'd rather be a pauper on a tiny sliver of mattress, with Zihao's sleeping form centimeters away.

She opens their location sharing on her phone. Zihao's little glowing dot is near the Bund, steadily making its way down the pier.

When he's back, she'll say she's canceled the surgery. She can't afford it anymore, anyway.

No more plastic surgery, no more divorce. The thought doesn't upset her that much. Maybe this is what she really needed. A push to make her marriage better.

The door unlocks, and she shoves her feet into her slippers and walks into the living room.

"I came back," Jane announces.

Zihao goes straight to the kitchen to fill up a cup of water. "I can see that."

Jane trails him. "Talk to me," she demands.

He drinks the entire glass of water before plunking it down with force. "I don't even know where to start," Zihao says, his words measured. "Maybe we can talk about all the ways you have totally obliterated my trust."

Jane opens her mouth, then shuts it. For once, she has nothing to say. Before all of this started, she viewed her husband as expendable, someone whose feelings she wouldn't think twice about. Now, she's attuned to every part of his expression, the flatness of his mouth, the coolness in his eyes.

Zihao brushes past her and into their bedroom. He pulls out a large, threadbare suitcase, the same one he used to move all his things into her apartment when they got married.

"What are you doing?" Jane asks as Zihao begins folding clothes and stacking them in the suitcase. "What the fuck are you doing?" Jane repeats, blocking him from the closet so he has to look at her.

"Packing." He puts his hands on her waist, lifts her slightly to the side, then continues removing items like Jane is nothing but a pesky coatrack in the way.

"Packing for *what*? I haven't kicked you out."

Zihao starts rolling up socks. "I'm going to Shenzhen."

"Shenzhen?" The answer is too specific. "What for?"

Zihao ignores her as he assembles his socks.

"Don't treat me like I'm not here!" Jane grabs a bunch of the socks and throws them at the wall. They thump into the mirror, landing in a heap.

Zihao stops packing, and Jane steels herself. Slowly, he walks over to his socks and gathers them. There's only resignation on his face. "They're sending me there for work. In fact, they've wanted me in their Shenzhen office for a while now, but I kept telling them that I didn't want to leave my wife for months at a time."

"They can't just plop you in a whole other place like that! Tell them no!"

"What happened with the security system at Sun Island is because of my oversight. I should've checked on the DVR instead of only fixing the system when it was down. Whoever broke in was familiar with the installed model. After a mistake like that, I can't refuse this relocation."

"Is this what you want? To leave Shanghai? To leave me?"

Zihao rolls his socks back up and drops them into his suitcase, then zips it shut. The sound is cutting and final. "Whatever we have, Jane, it's not working. It's not for lack of trying. You wanted a divorce, didn't you?" A tired smile crosses his face. "It's been tough for you. Being married to a man you barely know, who only seems to sink lower in your regard the more you learn about him. I'm sorry I couldn't offer you more."

"That's not true," Jane sputters. *I think you're the best person I've ever known.*

"There's the thirty-day cool-down period anyway. I'll go to Shenzhen, and when I'm back, we'll finalize the divorce. This is the last thing that I will do for you." She knows what he's not saying. He won't tell anyone what she's done, but the price is his departure. She won't even get the chance to convince him to stay. "Please don't fight me on this. If roles were reversed, I'd respect your decision. Now let's go to bed. It was a long day for you, wasn't it?"

They get in on their respective sides. Jane turns toward the window, staring out into the darkness. The regret hits her all at once, like a head-on collision. Something in her chest shatters, and she is weeping. The tears are silent at first, but then she can't help but give a snotty sniff to clear her nose.

Arms come around her. Her back is drawn against a warm chest. "Shh," Zihao murmurs. "Don't cry." Despite it all, he holds her. He's still holding her when she falls asleep.

The next day, he's gone.

Jane knows if she remains at home, she'll flip a table and break a bunch of glassware. So she focuses on what she can control. She has a score to settle. She puts on her most badass leather jacket and knee-high boots, and gets on the next bus to AP Plaza. On the ride there, she tries calling Lulu. It goes right to voice mail. She texts Rina. Any luck?

A friend saw Harv at the bank. Lulu wasn't with him.

They aren't on their honeymoon, then. Jane clenches her phone. Lulu's probably under lock and key, and she's done nothing to deserve it.

This anger invigorates her as she clomps up the stairs to Michelangelo's storefront. She screeches to a stop when she sees it. There's no queue in front, no security guard. Even with the blacked-out windows, she knows that inside, the shelves are bare.

No matter. She'll get her attention. "Michelangelo!" she hollers, banging on the window.

"Shut up! You're scaring away customers!" someone yells from downstairs after a few minutes. But Jane ignores them and keeps banging away.

Twenty minutes later, as she's fuming and nursing her raw palm, she hears footsteps on the stairs behind her.

"Someone said you were looking for me." She swivels around. Michelangelo's not dressed in her customary attire, worn to impress her well-to-do guests. Instead, she's got on a chunky sweater and jeans.

Jane leaps up. "About time, Michel—"

"Don't call me that anymore. I've rebranded."

"What am I supposed to call you then?"

"My real name." She pauses. "Mu Chensi."

So this is the identity Michelangelo has held close to her chest all these years, finally given, and Jane didn't even ask for it.

"You've quit the business."

"Yes."

"So you thought because you did the most work, that you would keep all the money for yourself? Pay off your fine and plan a nice little retirement?"

This makes Michelangelo's thin eyebrows come together. "How would I have done that?"

"Drop the act," Jane hisses, temper flaring. "The safe was empty."

"That's because we moved the money." Michelangelo sniffs

haughtily. "I'm insulted you would think that of me. You've been a loyal customer, Jane, but I've also considered you a friend."

"Lulu?" The mention of her friend is like being doused in ice. "Lulu never came anywhere close to the money. She was busy *getting married*."

"Lulu had another plan, one where the money didn't leave in the safe." Michelangelo looks offended she even has to explain any of this. "That's why I made all those counterfeit party favors."

Jane blinks rapidly. Nowhere, in all of their run-throughs of the plan, did this come up. "What counterfeit party favors? Lulu had you do this? When?" Why would Lulu change the plan?

"She was working on a backup plan, just like she told you. When Rina discovered the security issue, and Lulu got a tip from Harv that Peng Ayi was suspicious, we decided to activate it. Lulu was nervous. She wasn't confident Mei's internet café would escape Peng Ayi's investigation. And it would've been a shame to let my hard work go to waste. I manufactured a hundred of those Louis Vuittons. In fact, I kept one as a souvenir." Michelangelo swipes to a photo on her phone. The backpack resembles the ones guests received as they left the venue, with its bright red, leather exterior and festive gold drawstring, except for one difference.

"The checked pattern," Jane breathes, remembering some guests had been miffed when they were given LV-patterned ones instead after security. But the checked bags were fake.

"I built in a hidden compartment for the money. This is the only time I didn't make an exact replica so we could tell which ones were real and which ones were fake."

Everything begins to click into place. All those guests, grumbling as they handed their favors over to the security guards. The giant boxes the favors disappeared into.

When Lulu shut herself in the bathroom, she must have transferred the red envelopes into the checked Louis Vuittons before distributing them. According to Michelangelo, the plan was that once the guests who had received fakes were through security, they were given the real bags, and the fake ones with the money were whisked away.

"You could've told us you were going to do this!" Jane exclaims, thrown by how all these things could've been happening while she didn't have a clue.

"I was going to come up with some reason Rina didn't need to accompany me to the parking lot, but lucky for me, that delightfully handsome best man showed up. I didn't tell either of you, simply because Lulu asked me not to."

The hurt returns, almost overshadowing Jane's incredulity. There are still some things that aren't adding up. "How did you manage to fill a hundred fake bags with red envelopes? That would've taken forever. And how did you direct the security?"

"All I know is after I put the empty safe in Mei's car, I had to take care of the cash. Lulu already helped me fill two trash bags with the envelopes in her changing room. I dropped them off in a bathroom stall and slapped an out-of-service sign on the door. Then, thank goodness, it was time for me to leave. Lulu was supposed to handle the rest. I've been waiting for my payout, too. If you didn't come looking for me, I'd have come for you."

"But I don't know where it is. And I have no way of contacting Lulu."

Michelangelo folds her arms. "Aren't you the best of friends? She must have left you a clue."

Maybe Lulu decided to keep the money for herself. Jane wouldn't fault her for it.

"Friends or not, you better get me my money. I'm opening my own store. I have my eye on a sweet little shop in Jinshan."

"Jinshan? That's so far from here." It's a downgrade. Why would Michelangelo want to leave the bustle and glitz of the city to cater to a lower-class customer?

"It's time for me to move on. Once, all I wanted was to be the best in my field. Now that I am, I'm ready for a new challenge. Perhaps it's time for you, too. I'll give you my new Weibo ID."

After Michelangelo leaves, Jane lingers in the mall, still grappling with what Lulu has done. The guts required to come up with a totally separate, secret plan. A plan she never trusted Rina and Jane with.

How unheard Lulu must have felt, for her not to bring Jane and Rina in. They should've been there, cheering her on. Instead, they were too wrapped up in their own lives. While her friend was daring herself to do bigger things, Jane has been obsessing over insecurities and tendencies she should've outgrown. She always thought she was strong, but has that same unwillingness to budge stunted her?

Move on, Michelangelo had counseled her. Perhaps that's the only thing left to do.

49

1 week after the wedding

RINA

"RINA."

Rina brushes her hair from her face and looks up at where her mom hovers. She has spent the past few days sleeping and mourning the future that's slipped from her grasp. She keeps opening the calendar invitation for her upcoming assessment meeting with the fertilization clinic, knowing she should cancel but never mustering the energy to go through the motions.

Lulu's absence from the apartment became too much, so Rina threw clothes in a suitcase and got on the next train to her parents' house in Suzhou. She has to move out soon anyway, since she can't afford her rent with no income and no roommate.

Rina pushes off the pile of blankets and reaches for her phone. There are missed calls from Jane and texts from Mei. Mei's using her summer break to road trip through Zhejiang, and every day she gets a new message about breaking speed limits or how much she misses driving with her "special plate." Rina helped her talk Xiaoyi and Xiaoyifu into lending her their car, as long as Mei sent them daily updates on where she was.

"You can't protect her forever," she'd told Xiaoyi, who'd initially opposed the idea. "Let her live her life, and she'll trust you more as a result. Besides, her room is starting to smell."

Below the texts are rejections from the last three companies she applied to since quitting her job, reminding Rina that no matter how skilled she is, being a woman of her age will always disqualify her.

"Rina," her mom repeats as she plucks the phone out of her hands. "You've barely eaten since you arrived." Until now, her parents have mostly left her alone, but her mom's concern is starting to show.

"Sorry. I'll get dressed." In the bathroom, she peers at the pillow creases on her face. It's like she's aged ten years. Maybe the exhaustion of always working, always worrying, has finally caught up with her. Or maybe she was always too busy to notice the changes.

In the living room, her mom and dad are side by side on the couch, their postures formal.

"Baobei," her dad says. "Sit. We want to talk to you."

Rina sits on the chair across from them, and her mom urges a plate of peeled and quartered grapefruit toward her. "Eat," she says.

Rina takes one of the smallest pieces and puts it in her mouth. The juice is startlingly sweet.

Her parents trade glances, as if neither of them wants to speak first. Then her mom begins. "Your Ba and I are proud of what you've become. You straddle two worlds, and you move through both with a fluidity that many people hope to achieve. When you insisted on moving back to China, of course we were happy to have you close. But we know you've never seen Shanghai as your true home, and it's your worry for me that keeps you here."

The same argument, then. She has talking points for this. "I've grown to love Shanghai. And it's worth it if it means I can be here if anything happens to you again."

"No parents want to be the reason their child is so afraid. You forget I had a life before I had you, Rina, and I am perfectly capable of taking care of myself."

Her mom regards her, and Rina sees the woman who gave birth to her, who moved her life from China to America without knowing the language and made sure Rina didn't fall behind as she transferred from one school to the other. The woman who taught Rina to build a life that is her own. During her childhood, her mom was always honest. She told Rina how much she missed China, how you always have ties to the place where you were raised. In America, Miranda didn't understand how insurance, credit reports, or school enrollment worked. But she'd figured it out and poured all her energy into providing Rina a comfortable life, always encouraging that anything she wanted to do, she could.

"Rina," her dad says. "Your mom and I are dying watching you like this."

At that, she can no longer look her parents in the face.

"You can come home anytime you like," her mom says. She rises and rolls Rina's suitcase toward her. "But do the things *you* want to do, Rina. You've found ways to be happy here, but I know you wonder about the life you walked away from. Even if you planned your life thinking Shanghai would be forever, it's okay for things to change."

"Our beautiful daughter," her dad says quietly. "Wherever you go, we won't be far."

Rina lifts her head. A tear trickles down her cheek. "It might be a while before I figure things out."

Her mom helps her up. "You have time. But you won't find answers by sleeping all day."

She buys a train ticket to Shanghai leaving that night.

Jane calls her as she's packing. Unlike the past few times, Rina picks up.

"Why haven't you been answering?" Jane asks immediately. She sounds stuffy, like she's sick. "I need to talk to you."

"I'm at my parents'. What is it?"

"I can't go into too much detail over the phone. Have you had any luck getting in touch with Lulu?"

"No. But maybe it's because she doesn't want to talk to us. Maybe marriage suits her."

Jane scoffs. "We might've fucked things up, but there's no way that's true."

Rina has had ample time the past week to think this through. "I'm returning to Shanghai tonight. Let's talk then."

"I'll pick you up at the train station. Can…can I stay with you tonight?" Jane's voice quavers, and Rina stops packing.

"What happened?"

"Zihao left a week ago for Shenzhen. He wants a divorce." There's a long pause, like Jane might be holding back tears. "It's been cold the last few nights. It feels wasteful to turn on the heat for one person."

Rina's never felt worse about being right. "I'll be there soon. We can get a bottle of wine."

Later that night, when Jane picks Rina up from the train station, something about her is different. It's a few moments before Rina realizes she's not wearing makeup. "Are you okay?" she asks.

Jane scratches at the steering wheel. "Not really. But I don't want to talk about it."

"Okay. Whenever you're ready, then."

She thinks she hears Jane sniffle as she starts the car. "I say we demand to see Lulu," Jane declares as they drive away from the station. "Make a big scene until they have no choice but to let us in."

On the train ride, Rina's resolve hardened. Despite everything, she knows Lulu. They both do. This is not the life she wanted. "No. We need to think long-term. We're not just getting her outside for a ten-minute meeting. We want to get her *out*. Forever."

"By the way," Jane says, "Michelangelo doesn't have the money. I don't know where it is. Only Lulu does."

Rina's disbelief grows as Jane fills her in. Once Lulu enacted her backup plan, Mei became only a decoy, meant to focus the police's attention on the car and the abandoned safe, while the money went elsewhere.

In the end, Lulu was the mastermind behind it all. Her quiet, soft-spoken friend, the one she always assumed couldn't handle the world alone.

"Where is it then?" Rina asks.

"I have no clue, but if you still want to freeze your eggs, we're going to need to contact Lulu somehow."

But it's about more than that. "Money or not, we fix this," Rina says. They can't leave their friendship broken, crumbled on the floor of the Sun Island banquet hall. She and Jane have to take responsibility for destroying her trust in them. They owe Lulu an apology.

"We were such shitty friends, it's a wonder she put up with us for so long." Jane grips the steering wheel. "I'm canceling the surgery for now. I've been battling myself for so long, I thought it would fix everything about me. I think… I think I have to talk to someone first. A professional."

Her expression is raw. Rina wishes she could absorb some of that pain, but this is Jane's journey, not hers. The only thing she can do is offer support. "Whatever you decide, I'll be beside you."

When they're back in the apartment, Jane almost trips as she moves Rina's suitcase in. "Tā mā de!"

Rina flicks on the light, remembering the black boxes still occupying half the living room. One is slightly ajar from when she opened it, satin peeking through.

"Ugh, it's Lulu's wedding dresses. Let's burn them. Maybe if we do a special dance, we can cast a curse over the Zhus." Jane gathers the floof of the giant wedding dress in her arms and begins violently tugging it out.

"You'll rip—" Rina goes to stop her, then sees what the fabric has revealed.

Rows of small red backpacks, neatly organized beneath the dress.

Jane's eyes widen. She drops the dress and removes the lid from a second box, then the glamorous qípáo and stained banquet dress wrapped in plastic. Underneath are more bags with the red checked pattern. She inserts her hand in one, and there's a ripping sound. Red envelopes spill to the floor. Jane grabs one, extracting a thick stack of hundred-yuan bills.

They look at each other, shocked, then fall into a frenzy, tearing through the other boxes, rooting around the bags until red envelopes blanket the floor.

Jane rolls around on them, cash clutched in her fists. "I can't fucking believe this!"

"Me neither," Rina murmurs, awed at what Lulu has managed. A plan starts to form in her head. If Lulu could find a way to steal from her own wedding, they certainly can find a way to steal her from the Zhus. Rina won't let Lulu pull away from them so easily.

A good friend is hard to lose. Isn't that what Vic said?

50
2 weeks after the wedding

LULU

IN THE TWO miserable weeks since the wedding, Lulu has been as obedient as possible, following Peng Ayi to the temple, arranging dinners, pouring Peng Ayi's friends tea. It's reminiscent of her job at Scarlet Beauty, except she isn't being paid. Peng Ayi returned Lulu's phone after a few days, but she knows that everything on it is being tracked. She's only called her dad, who said her brother and his wife moved out. After his embarrassing display at the wedding, even Lulu's mom told him to leave or get a job, an unintended consequence of Lulu's scheme. During her visit home before the wedding, she'd purposely let it slip that she wanted the money all for herself so her brother would show up and redirect Peng Ayi's ire from Rina and Jane to Lulu. She hopes her brother uses this change to better himself.

"I did your laundry," her dad said as she was about to hang up, a quaver in his voice. "Lulu, why didn't you bring any of those clothes with you?"

He found the pig. "Ba," Lulu said, gripping her phone tight. "It's going to rain next week. I hope you fix the roof."

Lulu had been concerned the investigation would go longer, but the license plate Mei stole belonged to a high-ranking government official who didn't want to be associated with such an extravagant event, which put an instant end to it. Zhu Shushu raged for a week afterward, sometimes directing his anger at Harv just for being in the room. Those nights, Lulu held Harv's hand until he fell asleep. He hasn't asked her about the missing money again, but sometimes she catches him watching her, a slight frown on his face.

She hopes Rina and Jane discovered the money. That they got what they wanted. Their absence gnaws at her, like a mosquito bite that won't stop itching.

Today is Peng Ayi's weekly tea with her friends in the VIP room of Wanling Tea House. It's the only time she lets Lulu out of her sight. The first week, she brought Lulu with her, which was received poorly. Clearly, everyone wanted to talk about the wedding but couldn't with her there. Now, Peng Ayi leaves her at home with strict instructions for Ling to accompany her if she tries to go out.

Lulu helps Ling bake almond cookies and brings them to Harv. He's been huddled in his home office, even though the Zhus have halted their development plans while they wait for the wedding scandal to die down.

Harv shuts his laptop when he sees her. "Those smell good."

She sets down the tray. "What are you working on?" They've settled into a rhythm that almost feels like friendship.

Harv walks to the door and shuts it before turning to her and resting his back against it. "I'm leaving, Lulu."

"Leaving?" she asks, as she lifts one of the bowls from the tray to place on his desk. "To where?"

"I've been pulling my own funds together these past two weeks and getting my visa approved. Vic said he'd house me while I figure out my next steps."

"Vic? But he's in America…" Her voice trails off. "You're leaving China?"

"You know better than anyone that I can't take this anymore." Harv gestures vaguely around the room. "I've tried my best to be a good son. If there's anything our wedding has shown me, it's that Ba cares more about appearances than he ever will about me. It's about time I stopped depending on my parents and create something I can call my own."

Lulu struggles to wrap her thoughts around what's happening. She's proud of Harv. Choosing to forsake his family must not have been an easy decision. But there's also panic. "What about me?"

"You can do whatever you want. Our certification never got finalized." It's supposed to be this weekend. Lulu's been counting the days with trepidation. "I would take you with me, but I know neither of us would be happy with that."

Lulu feels hollowed out. Everyone gets to leave but her. "But—"

"Xiaojie?" Ling pops her head in, distressed. "The doorman says they won't leave until they talk to you."

"Who?"

Lulu looks over at Harv, who seems unperturbed. "Show us," he says.

They follow Ling to the screen displaying the entrance to the lobby. Two women stand shoulder to shoulder, arms folded. Just the image makes Lulu want to burst into tears.

"I'll say this one more time," one of them says, leaning close to the camera. It's impossible to mistake Jane. "Let the mistress of the house down now."

"We want her now!" Rina yells. "And tell her to bring her passport."

Ling bites her lip. "Should I call security?"

Harv stops her. "I'll handle this, Ling. Why don't you go water the plants?"

"I'll tell them to leave," Lulu says quickly. "Don't tell Peng Ayi—"

But Harv gently lays a hand on her arm, guiding her out of Ling's earshot. "Go with them. Before Ma gets back."

For a moment, she can only stare at him, unable to process what he's saying.

"What are you waiting for? Get your things!"

That spurs her into action, but as she grabs her documents, she keeps waiting for the illusion to collapse. For this to all be a dream.

Harv quietly accompanies her downstairs.

When Jane sees him, she widens her stance. "Don't you dare try to stop us. I'll have you know I was kicked out of my uni pub because I fight dirty."

Harv shakes his head. "I'm sending her off." Before they reach her, he pulls Lulu aside. There's a peace in his expression that wasn't there before. "Thank you for everything. You stuck by me, even though I shouldn't have asked you to, and I can't tell you how much that means to me." He kisses her lightly on the forehead.

"Harv." Lulu catches his hand and repeats the words her dad said to her. "Be happy."

He approaches Jane and Rina and says something to them before he disappears into the elevator.

"I was not expecting that," Jane says once they're all in the car, Lulu in the back seat.

"What did he say?"

Rina blinks. "That he forgives us. Jane, get us out of here before he changes his mind."

Jane peels away from the curb, probably something she learned from Mei. Once they're safely on the highway, she screeches, "Lulu, you crafty bitch! They need to make a documentary of all that dodgy shit you pulled off at the wedding. Fucking brilliant!"

The world feels vivid and new. It's been so long since she's been outside without Peng Ayi's supervision. "H-how did you know when to come?"

"We've been staking out this place, watching Peng Ayi's movements." Rina bites her lip. "Actually, I'm pretty sure Harv saw us a few days ago. He must've known we were coming."

"I told you we should've worn disguises," Jane mutters.

Rina turns around to Lulu. "We wronged you. We should have given you the space to call the shots, but instead, we tore you down." She hands Lulu a card. "I know we agreed as a crew that we wouldn't deposit the wedding money yet, so Jane and I pooled our own money into an account for you. Take it."

Lulu shoves the card back. Money always has a way of disrupting her life. It made her family intolerable and sank its teeth into her friendships. "No, I don't want it."

"Don't be bashful, Lulu," Jane says. "I sold half my bag collection for this, and I can't exactly buy it back."

"Then give it to my dad. Make sure he gets a doctor for his back." If she wants a fresh beginning, it feels unlucky to fund it with the money that almost got her locked away forever.

"At least take this." Rina brandishes a boarding pass, and Lulu flashes back to the wedding, that ticket burning a hole in her bag. The sense of loss when she realized she'd never get to use it. "We got you a one-way ticket to Bangkok. It boards in three hours. Also, I packed your favorite clothes, the ones Peng Ayi's people didn't even bother taking. I might've included too many sweaters." Rina tips a heavy duffel bag into Lulu's lap.

"You know Thailand is tropical, right?" Jane asks.

"She might get cold!"

Lulu breaks in. "This is too sudden—"

"Lulu." Jane pins her down in the rearview. "You've spent your whole life living by other people's rules. Your parents, the Zhus, me and Rina. We're the ones who keep holding you back."

On the way to the airport, Lulu fills Rina and Jane in on her scheme with Harv, reveling in the awe-filled silence that follows. Rina breaks it, asking countless questions about how *exactly* she did it while Jane repeats "I can't fucking believe it." It takes her mind off of what awaits. When they finally arrive at Pudong, both Jane and Rina shift to face her. "So," Jane says. "Are you getting out?"

Lulu gazes at the throngs of people entering and exiting the airport. It was fun to daydream about this moment, but now that it is in front of her, the fear bubbles up. Of leaving everything she knows behind. "Come with me?"

They park and find a dinky tea shop near the security line. It's a step down from Hotpot Palace, but it's the best they can do.

"Did you hear that Hotpot Palace stopped doing specials? I think they realized nobody wants that avant-garde stuff," Rina says.

"We haven't been back in so long. I miss their lamb. The thinness is unmatched," Jane says wistfully.

"We'll go again..." Rina stops, and a look of incredible sadness comes over her. "Honestly, I don't know if I could go without Lulu."

"It wouldn't be the same," Jane agrees.

It's only recently that Lulu put a name to the ache that eats away at her whenever she thinks of the way they parted at her wedding. It was grief. Grief over how the heist had exposed the cracks running through their friendship. She'd wanted them to take the money and get on with their lives, especially now that their relationship had proved to be only a shadow of what she'd thought it was.

Yet they are here, apologizing. Handing her a way out. "I don't regret not telling you about the plan. You were so insistent we didn't need it, I knew you would just try to talk me out of it. And... I wanted to prove I could do it on my own."

"You are capable of anything." Rina touches her hand. "We never should've made you believe otherwise."

"I still don't get it," Jane says. "How did you manage to shove all that money into the bags before people started leaving? How did you get the security to cooperate?"

"I had help from Jiang Hui and my Scarlet Beauty coworkers." Together, they'd been a group of ten. During the toasts, a few of them brought the counterfeit bags to the bathroom to start stuffing in the envelopes until Jiang Hui and Lulu could join them. The others, the tallest and broadest of the bunch, used Lulu's brother's outburst as an opportunity to blend in with the security team so they could direct the bag swaps once the wedding ended.

"Ten of them? You weren't worried they'd run off with the cash?"

"Jiang Hui would've reported them." Jiang Hui had also slipped her the syrup that helped her throw up, giving her a reason to run to the bathroom and vacate the entire hallway. From there, Lulu had directed everyone. Some of her Scarlet Beauty coworkers to hand out counterfeits to the guests, the others stationed at the security checkpoint, ready to take them back and swap them for the real ones as guests made their way through. Jiang Hui to collect her dresses and get them into the boxes of counterfeit bags. "Also, I promised them my split."

"Your entire split?" Jane's incredulous.

"I needed to if I wanted them all onboard." She'd heard her mother's scolding in her head when she offered up the money, but she pushed past it. Her happiest moments in life had come long before Harv's wealth touched her. She knows, without a doubt, she will be fine without it.

"What about Harv?"

"He's joining Vic in the States." Lulu automatically glances Rina's way and sees anguish flicker across her face.

"He changed his number, but I still looked for him. I even visited his bun lady." Rina's voice catches. "He paid for my next order of buns in advance, even after what I did to him."

"You'll see him again," Jane says confidently. "Fate isn't going to keep the two of you apart. Who knows? Things change with time. Old pains fade."

"What about you?" Lulu asks Jane.

"I have my first meeting with a therapist next week. I don't think she's ready for all the shit I'm about to unload on her."

Jane offers her a wry smile. "It's ironic, isn't it? We're all Leftovers again. With nobody except each other."

"Except Lulu's leaving." Rina's chin trembles slightly.

The familiar sensation of guilt entraps Lulu into its arms. It would be so easy to stay. But she can't keep doing things just because everyone else wants her to, and she knows that despite Rina's and Jane's earnestness, their friendship needs time and distance to heal. All three of them have been so caught up in their individual lives that they haven't taken the time to think about how they've changed.

Jane rocks the table. "I bought that ticket, but I still can't believe it."

"I don't know when I'll be able to come back," Lulu says. "I don't know when I'll see you again."

Rina's managed to regain her composure. "Remember all those books you liked to read? This is your adventure, Lulu. You can go anywhere, do anything. We won't be physically in one place, but Jane and I will be cheering you on, wherever you are."

Jane nods, teary-eyed. "And one day, we'll get back together, and you'll have to tell us everything we've missed, so that we'll feel like we were with you the whole time."

Warmth spreads through Lulu, and she's not sure if it's from the scalding sip of tea or from their words.

When it's an hour out from Lulu's flight, Rina and Jane escort her to security. They talk her into accepting some cash, so she can at least get a hotel room when she lands. People glare at them as they cluster near the entrance, but Lulu is reluctant to join the line.

"I hope we stay friends." Jane looks insecure. "We said some pretty shit things to each other, and now we won't even be in the same place."

"I don't think we should make promises. But I know I'm going to try my best." Rina opens her arms wide. "Come here."

They all hug, and Lulu absorbs every detail of this moment.

The fragrance of Rina's hair, the pout of Jane's lips. She whispers "I love you" so softly it's almost lost. The bittersweetness lingers in her mouth as she boards her plane and watches Shanghai fall away from her window. At last, this is goodbye.

epilogue
5 months after the wedding

JANE

"LADY, THAT IS an awful combination. Don't buy it." The clueless woman is currently trying on a green midi skirt with a burgundy cross-body bag, and Jane cannot abide such poor choices. "Give me that." Jane snatches the bag, then calls out to Michelangelo, who's stocking a shelf toward the back of the store. "Do you still have those camel-colored bucket bags with the navy detailing?" She still calls her Michelangelo in private, a little nod to their shared past.

"In the cabinet. There should be a few left."

She finds the bucket bag and marches back over to the woman. "Here," she says, thrusting it into her hand. "Try this instead."

The woman turns up her nose. "This isn't my style."

Jane shrugs. "Sure, but look how well it complements the dress. You've got such a nice figure. That cross-body will clash with it. This bucket bag is a similar size but more fashionable."

When she returns from helping another customer, she notices the woman considering her reflection in a mirror. "I'll take the bag too."

After the postwork rush, Michelangelo saunters over to Jane. "Putting you on sales duty is the best choice I ever made."

"Please. I hate talking to people." Jane leans against the counter, taking in their tiny Jinshan store with satisfaction. At first, Michelangelo balked at having a second person with so little space, but Jane talked her into it by offering to pay half the rent in exchange for commission on every bag she sells.

Jane couldn't have chosen a better business partner than a former con woman. Michelangelo knows her way around all the licenses and commerce regulations, and she always gets material for cheap. They have plenty of heist money left over to put toward new designs and marketing. Sensing Jane's loneliness, Michelangelo even invited her to tea with her nieces. It was clear how much the two women worshiped their aunt, and Jane had spent a lovely afternoon scrolling through Guo Pei's designs with them, the laughter and conversation lifting her mood tremendously.

"I'm going to go through our inventory and figure out which products need an extra push," she tells Michelangelo.

Michelangelo's eyebrows go up. "I can't believe I'm saying this, but you are overworking yourself."

"I'm making us money. Who are you to tell me to stop?"

"Forgive me for being concerned about your health." Michelangelo walks off into their storage room, waving her hand at Jane over her head. "Work yourself to death then, see if I care."

Jane goes into their tiny office and sits in the cross-back chair that always gives her back pain. She analyzes her reflection in the mirror hanging directly across from her. There are new lines on her forehead and some sunspots near her nose. She's aging, but who isn't?

Sometimes, she still wonders if she should've gotten the surgery. But with her brain and hands occupied, she worries about it less. Her mom's voice in her ear has faded away. She gained all of this without, and in spite of, her parents.

Acknowledge your feelings, but remember they're subjective. Her therapist loves saying that. Jane rolls her eyes.

She's busy thinking of ways to sell beaded clutches when a knock sounds against her open door. Probably Michelangelo hounding her again about going home. "I'll be done in a minute."

"You got a job." The male voice makes her raise her head. The pen falls from her hand.

Zihao stands there in a suit, a suitcase at his side. He looks exhausted.

Jane's throat goes dry. "You're back."

The month he was supposed to be in Shenzhen turned into several more. Plenty of times she's woken up in the middle of the night, thinking she heard the door. Or teared up when she saw instant noodles.

They have not spoken in months. Every time she picks up her phone, fear strikes, and she puts it down again. They never filed their divorce claim with the Civil Administration Department, and she's been afraid that if she tries to talk to him, she'll only remind him to.

"I missed you," she whispers. She knows the desires of all the customers who come through her store, but Zihao is remote and unreadable as he takes her in.

"I was afraid I wouldn't be able to recognize you."

It's a simple phrase, and it cuts her to the core. He has still not forgiven her. But he's here, rumpled from the train, and she finds some hope in that.

"How did you know I was here?"

"Your WeChat."

"Oh. Right." Over the past month, Jane has turned her We-Chat into a promotional space for the business, posting photos of her designs, but she's surprised Zihao has followed any of it. His profile doesn't even have a picture, and he barely uses his phone for anything besides calls and email. But he forgot to disable their location sharing, and sometimes Jane observes his little dot in Shenzhen, wondering what he's up to. If he's with someone else.

"I quit my job. I've done all they wanted me to do. I can leave now with my name intact."

Guilt and worry rush back in. She did this to him. Everything she did to get the money put him on that train to Shenzhen. "If you need a break from work, you should take it. I... I can support you." This can be her first step in winning back his trust. She can only hope he accepts.

"Getting a job won't be an issue." Zihao steps away from his suitcase and toward her. "What I wanted to know is if I should be looking in Shanghai."

Jane rises from her desk. Her heart flutters against her rib cage.

"Yes," she says, pushing all of her desperation for him into that word. "Come back. Don't leave me again."

The stony expression falls from his face, and the shy smile she missed appears like the sun from clouds. "I can't wait to be home."

Jane closes up the store while he wanders around, examining everything with curiosity. Jane will have to tell Michelangelo those designs she promised will be delayed.

On the street outside the store, Zihao raises his hand to call a cab, but Jane stops him. "Let's walk a bit."

"You hate walking."

"It's too expensive to take a car from here into the city. The bus station isn't that far."

He gazes down at her, surprised, and she takes the opportunity to press her lips to his.

When she pulls away, it's clear his brain is still catching up. "Don't just stand there," she says. "It's going to take us a while. You can spend that time telling me how much you missed me."

And he does.

5 months after the wedding

RINA

As Rina emerges from the plane into SFO, she basks in the sounds of English. The words carry a layer of dust, but as she drags her suitcase through the airport, that hibernating part of her brain awakens. Slowly, comprehension brushes away the cobwebs until she finds herself eavesdropping on conversations with eagerness. Although she was here a few months ago for her fertility tests, her trip had been rushed so she could make it back in time to attend Jane and Michelangelo's grand opening.

This time it's permanent.

When the plane lifted off, she gripped the armrests of her chair, unable to believe she bought a one-way ticket. Even now, outside the arrivals gate, her hands itch to look for the next flight back to China, just to assure herself there is one. Instead, she tries to open Didi before realizing that here, she needs to use Uber or Lyft.

Her original plan was to stay in San Francisco only a month to kick-start the egg freezing cycle, but when she reconnected with former colleagues to help Zihao with his job search, one of them assumed she was the one looking and forwarded her résumé to someone in the States. It was a start-up that specialized in advocating for better workplace benefits for women.

Jane and Lulu urged her to take it. "Talk to your parents about it," Jane said. "I'm sure they'd agree."

Her mom pared an apple as Rina explained about the job, the opportunity to help other women balance career and family. "I—I want this," she finally said, growing surer as she voiced it. "But I'm so afraid of putting an ocean between us again."

Her mom threw the long ribbon of peel away before cutting a perfect slice and offering it to Rina. A slight smile graced her face. "Then visit often."

On the flight over, alongside the anxiety, there was anticipation, too.

What will it be like to return to the city where she once thought she'd live forever? Does she even remember how to talk to Americans? Will she stick out, a transplant who's spent far too long in the trenches of the nine-nine-six?

She shivers in the Bay Area breeze as she thinks about the pure possibility of this moment. Her new job is putting her up in an apartment for a few months until she can find a place. There is no way she can predict how long she'll stay in America or what will happen to her here, but for now, she is home. Lulu would say that the not knowing is the beauty of it all.

Her phone dings at her Lyft driver's approach. As she searches for her car, she spots a man with ruffled black hair, wearing a T-shirt despite the chill. His bared arms are covered with tattoos, and her eye catches on the same one that stole her attention so long ago. Lotuses, beautiful and pure. Persisting through the mud. It's like remembering a story told long ago.

Her Lyft pulls up in front of her. A woman with bright pink lipstick and a scowl pokes her head out. "Rina?"

Vic is still standing there. As far as she knows, he never came back to Shanghai after the wedding, and she doesn't know when, if ever, she will run into him again like this.

In that moment, two paths appear before her. One where she gets into her Lyft and avoids a one-star rating but agonizes over this decision for months, maybe years. And another that takes her to him.

"Give me a second," she says to her driver, the woman's irritable voice disappearing as she covers the distance between her and Vic.

"Hey. Remember me?"

He turns, and she feels a rush of relief that he looks exactly the same, his eyes still carrying that irreverent spark. This time, there's a little surprise mixed in.

She waits for that light to dim, for him to spin away and get into the sleek black car and drive off for good.

But a slow grin spreads across his face. "How could I forget you?"

She bites her lip. "I'm here for a while. We should catch up. If…if you want." Harv has forgiven the Leftovers for what they did, but she's not sure Vic has. Still, she at least needs to tell him the other truth she kept from him. That her feelings for him were—*are*—real. She is a different person now, and he might be too, but it would be a shame not to give themselves a try.

He tilts his head toward the dark interior of his car. "How about now?"

Her phone buzzes with an alert. Her driver has given up.

She returns his smile. There is so much she needs to say, but right now, all she can do is revel in the second chance fate has thrown her way.

6 months after the wedding

LULU

Lulu doesn't know where her phone is. In fact, she can't remember the last time she used it. Was it two days ago, when she scrolled through pictures of Harv in front of the Golden Gate Bridge, holding a sourdough loaf in one hand and making a peace sign with the other? Unexpectedly, they've kept in touch, and it appears the States are treating him well.

She needs her phone because tonight, she has her monthly call scheduled with Rina and Jane. The prospect puts an extra spring in her step as she walks on the sandy sidewalk leading back to her small apartment. Some shopkeepers wave, and the auntie who sells hats near her apartment greets her merrily. "Waddee ja Lulu!"

When Lulu first arrived, she was terrified. The little Thai she knew was useless. Nobody understood her, and all she wanted was to go home. But she thought of that picture, of her dad and her teacher's dreams for her, and stuck with it. She got a job at a coffee shop so she could practice more, and now she can even have conversations with people about the fishing conditions or silly tourists who book snorkeling tours without knowing how to swim. She probably could've safely returned to Shanghai months ago, but she hasn't had her fill of this place yet. Once she's completely memorized each alley and explored all the islands, perhaps she will start thinking about what happens next.

She finds her phone in the middle of a book she was reading, acting as a temporary bookmark.

After she transferred her contacts, she got rid of her old phone, deciding this was the perfect time to take a break from social media too. The silence was new, compared to the stream of demands she used to get from her mom, her brother, and Peng Ayi. Once in a while, she chats with her dad. Her mom refuses to speak with her, believing Lulu abandoned the family to destitution, even though the money from the gold pig is more than enough for a few years. Besides, her brother now has a job.

She hopes that one day her mom will understand Lulu is not an asset. That there is a future for them as simply mother and daughter.

There are a bunch of unread messages from both Jane and Rina. A picture of Rina and Vic at the fertility clinic. Since they ran into each other a month ago, they've been inseparable. Lulu's glad Rina has him. From what she's read, hormone injections can be difficult without a support system. Lulu was fully prepared to get up in the middle of the night to stay on the phone with her.

Vic keeps making jokes about impregnating me now so I can save the money and take him out to dinner instead.

Yeah, right. You're so in love, it's disgusting.

You're one to say anything!

Lulu can almost hear them bickering, and she's hit with another wave of longing for her friends. Even though she's made a life for herself here, Lulu misses Jane's bluntness and Rina's thoughtful questions, the depth of understanding that is a product of so many years of friendship. Although the wedding brought out their imperfections like blood to the surface of a wound, she has felt the hurt repairing itself until it is only a small scab on their shared history.

Her phone rings with a group call request. She checks the time. They're an hour early.

"I know you're probably busy meditating or taking romantic solo walks on the beach while the sun's setting," Jane says immediately when Lulu answers. Zihao sets down a plate of strawberries for her and waves hi before disappearing again. "But Rina and I had to tell you live. Rina, you ready?"

"Ready." Rina is propped up against her pillows, looking more relaxed than Lulu has ever seen her. She must be settling nicely into her new job. "One. Two. Three!"

At once, the two of them flash pieces of paper. Lulu's eyes catch on the massive letters.

PVG—> BKK.

SFO—> BKK.

Pudong and San Francisco International Airport to Suvarnabhumi Airport.

Lulu's gasp bounces off the walls of her room.

"We're coming, bitch!" Jane screeches.

Rina is more collected, but her eyes are bright. "I can't wait to see you."

It's almost too much excitement after months of solace and tranquility. They spend the rest of the call talking about places they'll go, like Lulu's favorite roti stand or Koh Adang for snorkeling. After they hang up, they continue to send emojis of planes and champagne.

Her friends are coming.

Lulu buys a paper cup of fried bananas off a street vendor before walking to the beach, a book under her arm. She buries her bare feet in the white sand and watches the long-tail boats come in. She adores this feeling of having all the time in the world to do with what she wishes. It may not be forever, but for now, it's perfect.

She closes her eyes, taking in the smell of salt, the sound of gulls' wings flapping as they swoop among the waves. She sends a quiet *thank you* to her former teacher. It's uncreative of her to steal someone else's dream, but she thinks that Wu Laoshi wouldn't have minded *this* theft.

After all, it has set her free.

★ ★ ★ ★ ★

acknowledgments

This book wouldn't be in your hands if not for all the other people who worked on it. My editor, Melanie Fried, whose keen eye and clear vision guided this story and my women to where they needed to be. My incredible agent, Mike Whatnall, who never stopped believing in me. It's been a long, emotional journey, but we made it! Kristina Moore, for getting this book into the right hands. Leah Morse, for navigating me through what it means to be a debut author. I have Elita Sidiropoulou and Alexandra Niit to thank for the lovely cover. All the folks in the marketing, publicity, sales, production, and subrights departments who worked so hard to support this book—thank you.

To my critique partner, June: you saw the very first (pretty awful) version of this book, but you loved it anyway. Thank you for reading everything I write, your insightful feedback, and those daily word sprints. Kristy and Acree, I'm so glad that two incredible writers also happen to be my friends.

Will, you gave me the idea that sparked this novel. Thanks for always being down to brainstorm silly ideas. Jason, you kept asking about my writing and took it seriously, even when publication was a dream that felt as far away as the stars. Alina, I can always count on you to read my stuff and leave a string of ragey Google comments that make me laugh. Daniel, you are the light of my life. Albert and Leslie, thanks for taking my author photos before I was sure I would even need them. Will Charin, thanks for the Thailand insights. If not for you, Lulu would be headed somewhere else with far more visa issues. Lily, for reading and answering my questions about China. Megan, for being my #1 groupie. All the friends who shared in my joy and didn't get sick of me telling them about my book: Winky, Yiming, Angela, Alison, Cynthia, Kristin, Rainbow, Nina.

Mom and Dad, you have always told me that home is waiting for me, even if I fail, and that has given me the strength to try for impossible things. Karen, for shouting about me to everyone you know. 谢谢我在中国的亲人们: 大姨, 二姨, 大姨夫, 二姨夫, 陈煦, 金湛, 你们让中国成为我的第二个家。

discussion questions

1. Who was your favorite character in the novel? Who did you identify with most?

2. The three friends come from such different backgrounds and want such different things from life. Why do you think their friendship still works? How are your own friendships similar or different from theirs?

3. Discuss the ways Jane and Zihao's marriage changes over the course of the novel. Do you expect their marriage will last?

4. A successful career is important to Rina, but she often faces sexism at work. Do you think she had any choice but to quit in the end? How does this dynamic often play out in the real world too?

5. Do you think Lulu made the right choice to go through with the wedding and marry Harv? Why or why not?

6. Discuss the ways that societal expectations impact each character in the novel, not only Jane, Lulu, and Rina, but Harv, Zihao, Mei, and even Lulu's mom. How are these expectations different or similar for the men versus the women? How do the characters give in to or defy these expectations?

7. Discuss the mother-daughter relationships in the novel. How do they shape Jane's, Lulu's, and Rina's approaches to life and their goals? How does Michelangelo act as a sort of surrogate mother for some of the women in the novel?

8. What do you think Jane's, Lulu's, and Rina's lives will be like after the novel? Will they be able to achieve their goals? Or will their goals perhaps change? How have your own life goals, big or small, changed over the course of your life?